SERIES COLLIDE

SERIES COLLIDE

VOLUME 1: LIGHT

KRISTINE KATHRYN RUSCH
AND DEAN WESLEY SMITH

PUBLISHING

Series Collide: Volume 1
Copyright © 2025 by Kristine Kathryn Rusch and Dean Wesley Smith
Published by WMG Publishing
Cover and layout copyright © 2025 by WMG Publishing
Cover design by WMG Publishing
Cover art copyright © grandfailure/Depositphotos

ISBN-13 (ebook): 978-1-56146-505-7
ISBN-13 (trade paperback): 978-1-56146-401-2
ISBN-13 (hardcover): 978-1-56146-424-1

Contents

INTRODUCTION: LIGHT
KRISTINE KATHRYN RUSCH

It turns out that during the course of our long careers, Dean Wesley Smith and I have written at least twenty original series *each*. Yep, we're writing series projects and have done so for a very long time.

Not every series we write in has a short fiction component. Not every short fiction series we write in has a novel component. We let the stories take us where they may.

Heck, these five books—which we call *Series Collide*—are part of a series. Yep, for five years now, we've done "colliding" anthologies for Kickstarter's Make 100, a promotional project that they do every January.

It's an accidental series. We loved putting the first few together, and once we had three, well, then we had to continue. Each book contain twenty stories—ten from me and ten from Dean. To make 100, we needed five books.

So I guess we're doing a series inside of a series.

(Yes, my head hurts too.)

We separate the stories by author. All of Dean's stories get to hang out together, as do all of mine. In these volumes, we've also named which series the individual story comes from. You can look up those stories on our online store, wmgbooks.com or you can find them from your favorite ebook retailer.

The first book in *Series Collide* is one we call "light." The stories are...well, not happy stories per se, but not disturbing stories either. The stories in this volume are funny (in some cases) and romantic (in some cases) and light mysteries (in yet more cases).

These stories range from fantasy to science fiction to contemporary fiction. They include interesting characters, like a guy named Poker Boy as well as cats and dead (but active) protagonists.

We hope that these stories will inspire you to track down the other stories or novels in the series. Oh, and to pick up the next book in *this* series, good old *Series Collide*.

—Kristine Kathryn Rusch

DEAN WESLEY SMITH
SECTION

CUTTING DOWN FRED
A BUCKEY THE SPACE PIRATE STORY
DEAN WESLEY SMITH

ONE

I tried to make love under Fred for the first time on a warm October evening two years ago.

It was right in the middle of Big John's annual Halloween bash, the very same party that keeps three square city blocks of the city up all night.

My current girlfriend, Annie, was in one of her moods, none of which I ever figured out. So when I suggested, after six very fast and hot dances, that we go somewhere cool, take off some costumes and really get hot, she laughed and said she would love to.

But she wanted to go somewhere new. She said she was tired of my apartment and "those old squeaky bed springs." She wanted to be daring. "Really live," was the way I think she put it.

So we ended up under Fred.

We left the party with a wave at Big John and headed downtown. I was wearing my Buckey The Space Pirate costume, with the white tights, white cape, lace shirt, saber, and plumed white hat. Most people thought I looked like one of the Three Musketeers, but what the hell did they know about space pirates, anyway?

Annie had on her Queen of the Alien Warlords' costume made up of black tights, high black boots, and lots of chains over a very open-necked blouse. On her head she wore this three-foot tall jeweled headdress that gave the entire costume a feeling of power. The only problem was that she kept forgetting to duck when going through doors.

I didn't exactly know what Annie had in mind when she said "daring," but I figured Russell Park might fit. And it was close by. I didn't feel like walking too far dressed as Buckey, especially in this part of the city.

Russell Park was the second oldest park in the city. I'd been there a few times, mostly passing through. It was one of those places where old people sat around on the benches and watched the young mothers ignore their children. It measured a half a block wide, a block long, and was filled with benches, small patches of grass, and big old oak trees. But it didn't smell much like a park because there just wasn't enough green to hold back the smells of the city.

We ended up under one of the biggest trees in the park, tucked off in one corner, near a hedge and a wooden bench that looked like no one had sat on it since the First World War. There I hoped we would have the least chance of getting seen, yet give Annie the thrill she needed.

To say Annie was thrilled would have been putting it

lightly. She liked the idea of making love out in the open. In the two months we'd gone out she said we'd never done anything this much "fun."

"My dear Queen Annie," I said, taking my plumed hat off and bowing deeply at the waist while sweeping the hat along the grass. "Will this place of repose suit a lady of your stature?" She always loved it when I went formal on her.

"You have done well, faithful servant," she said, smiling. Then she reached up, took off her headdress, and sat it against the base of the tree. Then the chains came over her head, then the blouse. She was working on taking off the tights before I had enough common sense to start getting undressed too.

She was totally nude and lying on the grass by the time I had gotten my boots and saber off. So instead of finishing undressing, I went to work, kissing that soft skin, starting at her right ear and working my way down. I was doing my best to not miss a spot on that beautiful body, when this deep voice came out of nowhere.

"There was a young lady from Hunt
whose body could take a small punt.
Her mother said, 'Annie,
It matches your fanny,
Which never was that of a runt.'"

I thought my heart was going to explode right out of my chest.

I expected to look up and see a policeman standing there with a big nightstick, slapping it into his palm as he smiled down at us. We were going to end up in jail. I just knew it. Mom would never understand.

So from between her legs I glanced quickly around. No one. At least in sight.

"What did you mean by that?" Annie said, pushing me away and sitting up. "That seemed like a pretty crude thing to say, especially when you were doing what you were doing. And just what the hell is a punt?"

"I didn't—"

"It's a flat-bottomed boat that is propelled by thrusts from a pole," the voice said.

Annie glanced quickly around, then stood up and stared down at me, hands on her hips. "I don't think I like you anymore," she said and pulled on her black tights.

"But I didn't say anything," I pleaded.

"Then who did," she asked. "And you know, if you were any bigger than a pencil, you wouldn't think I was so large."

"A pencil?" I said. "But—"

She pulled her blouse quickly on, grabbed the chains and headdress and stormed off with me still there on the grass trying to get my boots back on. "But— But— But—" I said over and over as she disappeared through an opening in the hedge.

"There was a young fellow of Buckingham
Wrote a treatise on girls and on fucking them.
A learned Parsee
Taught him Gamahuchee,
So he added a chapter on sucking them."

4

"Who's there?" I quickly turned around, but couldn't see anyone. The deep baritone voice sounded like it had come from right beside me. "Come out, damn you!"

I pulled on my boots and saber and checked behind the trunk of the old tree, then in the hedges, and then in the branches of the tree itself. No one. In fact, the entire little park looked completely deserted.

"Aren't you even curious," the voice asked. Again it sounded as if it was coming from right beside my head. I spun around, then checked my shirt for hidden microphones someone might have slipped in at the party. Nothing.

"All right," I said. "I give up. What's the joke?"

"Oh, no joke," the voice said. "But I wonder if you are curious as to what Gamahuchee means. Most people would be."

"Who's talking?" I shouted at the dimly lit park. This was getting damned annoying. It was going to take me a week to calm Annie down, if she would even talk to me again.

"I'll tell you who I am if you first ask me what Gamahuchee means."

"Oh, for hell's sake," I checked once more in the limbs of the tree, in the hedge, and around the trunk. Just one old oak tree. No one anywhere near.

Finally, I gave up and sat down. "All right, what the hell does Gamahuchee mean?"

"No one is really sure," the voice said.

"Great," I said. "You—"

"But it is thought to have a Japanese derivation, and in

the context of the limerick, it refers to oragenitalism. Or, in more current terminology, oral sex.".

"I could have figured out as much," I said. "If I really gave a shit. Now would you please tell me who the hell you are? And where you are so you can laugh and I can kill you?"

"I am the tree you now repose under. I refer to myself as Fred. I am sure you would not like to hear the story of how I came to acquire that name, even though it *is* quite interesting."

"You're right," I said, looking up into the thick green leaves of the tree. "I wouldn't. And I don't buy this for a minute. Where's the speaker hidden?"

"I am really the tree," the voice said, sadly. "Why don't you believe me? Dressed as you are, I had hoped you at least would believe me."

"Well I don't!" I shouted up into the tree. "And there's not a damned thing wrong with how I'm dressed." I felt immediately stupid for shouting. Somewhere, someone was laughing their fool head off and I was playing along. I stood and headed for the entrance to the park. A joke was a joke. But Buckey The Space Pirate had let this one go too far.

TWO

By the next afternoon, no one had come up to me and laughed at how much they had got me. And Annie didn't show one sign of talking to me no matter how much I pounded on her door. The only way she was going to ever speak to me again was if I proved to her that it wasn't me who had accused her of being able to do strange things with boats.

If I uncovered whoever the joker was, I could prove to her it wasn't me. So that evening I found myself back down at the park under the old tree.

"You look much more normal for these times dressed as you are today," the voice said as I walked up. I had on a tee shirt and Levi's. "Would you like to hear another limerick?"

"Whoever you are," I said as calmly as I could. "Please show yourself."

"I am showing myself. I'm shading you from the sun. What more do you want? Don't you like my limericks? I have one I made up for a young couple back thirty, maybe forty years ago. I was much smaller then and they were one of the first who used my shelter for the purpose that you were using it for yesterday. I feel it is one of my best limericks. And by the way, my name is Fred."

"Fred. Sure. You told me." I moved slowly around the tree trying to humor the voice while spotting exactly where the speaker was hidden. "You know you could have at least waited until we finished. And I'm not buying this talking tree line. I know someone's behind all this and when I find out who, I— I—"

"Do what you like," the voice said. "I won't be around much longer for you to believe or not believe."

"Sure." I searched through some high grass near a sprinkler head. "You're just going to pull up roots and walk away. Right?"

"Hardly," Fred said.

"All right then," I said and went back to searching the

trunk, feeling for any loose bark. "Why don't you tell me, for starters, how you can talk. Some witch cast a spell over you or something?"

"I suppose it could be called magic," Fred said. "But I prefer to think of it as the miracle of life. Actually us trees are much more intelligent than you humans think and have very long memories."

"Sure. Sure. All from the miracle of life." I said, as sarcastically as I could make my voice sound. "So how'd that get you a voice?"

"I don't actually know. I don't actually have vocal cords as you do, but I can project my thoughts to make humans hear the thoughts as a voice. You see, ninety-seven years ago, a sailor visited a brothel here in this fine city. The man used a prophylactic. It was disposed of in the alley outside of the brothel and a very young girl found it a short time later. She took an acorn from my mother, put it in the sperm and planted the entire thing here. The young girl watered me carefully for the first two years until she died, ran over by a wagon right in front of me. Poor child. Of course, there was nothing I could have done."

I had kept looking the entire time he had been talking and still hadn't found one hint of any speaker, microphone, or wiring. The voice seemed to come from everywhere around the tree and inside my head at the same time. "You don't really expect me to believe that?" I said.

"You asked," Fred said. "Would you like to hear another limerick? I know all of the good old ones."

"Not just yet." I had come to the realization that this stunt was so well done that I was going to get nowhere unless I played along. Eventually whoever was behind it would slip up. "Say, why don't you tell me how you came to do limericks?"

"If you stood in one place for almost a hundred years, you'd do limericks, too."

With that I granted he had a point. I studied the tree for a foothold. The speaker was probably hidden in the limbs somewhere and I was going to have to climb up there to find it. Best thing to do was keep humoring the voice while being quiet while climbing the tree. "What's this about you not having much longer?"

"Tomorrow, to be exact," Fred said. "That's why I decided to talk to you. Do you realize that I have only talked to seven people in one hundred years? I look back and find that fact most amazing."

"What's going to happen?" I picked my way carefully up the bark like a rock climber going up a sheer face. Finally I got my arms around the lowest limb and pulled myself up.

"See the stakes in the grass?" Fred said. "The ones with the orange ribbons on them?"

I looked back down through the branches. "Sure." They were scattered across this corner of the park. I hadn't noticed them last night with Annie.

"I overheard workmen talking about widening the road. I'm scheduled for the chain saws tomorrow."

"You're kidding?" I finished checking out the limb I was on and climbed higher where I could see the stakes better. They did show a pattern that looked like the street was going to be wider right through the big tree.

"I am afraid I am not kidding," Fred said, his voice

almost too faint for me to hear. Then he got suddenly louder. "But, that is life. Or death. And please do be careful. I've had fifteen children and three adults fall out of my limbs. It is always so painful an occurrence. Actually, the first person who fell out of my limbs was killed by a dinosaur. It was a very sad experience since his wife was standing nearby in the park at the time and never really understood what happened."

"A what?"

"A dinosaur. Actually a Pterosaur angry that he was there. You know that Pterosaurs were large flying reptiles that..."

"Now you have gone too far. First you expect me to believe you are a talking tree and then you expect me to believe that you have been around since the dinosaurs. There were no men during that time. That much I remember from grade school. And you said you were not even a hundred years old."

"You are quite right," Fred said. "But we oak trees have family memories that go back, for lack of a better way of putting it, to our roots, which incidentally, were in the early Cretaceous period in this part of the world."

"Fine," I said, glancing down at the ground below, wondering when the funny farm wagon was going to come and take me away for talking to myself in a tree.

"I can tell you do not believe me."

"No shit," I said. "I am still looking for the microphone so I can get this joke over."

"Please hold onto a limb and I will take you back. Do you have a favorite dinosaur you would like to see?"

"Yeah, sure," I said and started down. "And next you will be telling me I can ride a Triceratops if I want."

Fred laughed softly. "Not hardly, but I can certainly show you why you wouldn't want to ride one."

THREE

Around me the air suddenly shimmered and the branches of the oak seemed to move and sway, as if there was a slight earthquake shaking the roots. I grabbed tight around a limb and held on as I was suddenly hit by a wave of hot and very humid air that smelled of swamp and fresh greenery.

Below me there was a crashing of brush and again the tree seemed to shake. Through the shaking leaves I could see that the city was gone. There was nothing except trees and brush. And below me was the ugliest, most scarred-up Triceratops I could ever imagine.

"Hold on," the voice of Fred inside my head said as the dinosaur bumped into the tree and then started using it to scratch itself. I thought I was on a ride at a carnival.

The dinosaur bumped the tree and I bounced among the limbs. Then the Triceratops backed off, looked at the tree and hit it again.

As I held on for dear life I heard Fred's voice in my head. "See why you wouldn't want to ride one?"

Somehow, as the dinosaur took aim once more on the base of the tree I managed to scream, "Get me out of here!"

And I was back in the tree in the park.

A tree that wasn't moving.

I looked slowly around to make sure that I was where I seemed to be, then carefully pulled my fingers out of the grooves they had dug into the bark.

"Pretty amazing beasts, weren't they?"

I took a deep shuddering breath and let it out. "How did you do that?"

"How do you walk around and drink water without roots? It is just a part of what we are. We can move our conscious minds back and forth through our ancestors and through time. I guess it makes up for not being able to move in real time. You didn't actually leave the park, but I took your mind back with mine. Fun, huh? Now, would you like to hear another limerick now? I have one about a dinosaur."

"No. Thanks." I gave one more quick look to make sure the city was where it should be and there was no Triceratops lurking behind the hedge, then climbed down. Once I was back on the ground I walked quickly around the tree, than sat down.

"You seem upset," Fred said.

"That ride you gave me was really something. I am not saying that I believe you, but can you take me to any time at all?"

"Sure," Fred said. "And to almost any place as long as the oak at the location is, as we say, in my family tree."

I groaned.

"Sorry," Fred said. "But," his voice suddenly sounding sad, "I am afraid that today will be the last day for you to experience any other time, so we should make the best of it."

I climbed back to my feet and walked along the line of

stakes in the grass. They did start at the corner and go inside the edge of the tree. "Just for the sake of argument," I said, "is there something I can do for you? I doubt that I could stop the street from being widened, but—"

"Oh, my dear man," Fred said quickly. "It is so kind of you to ask. I was hoping you would. I have studied the problem at some length and I feel the only solution would be to repeat the process from which I came."

"What?" I asked. I had lost whatever Fred was talking about halfway through.

"In other words," Fred said, "get a rubber, ejaculate into it, put one of my seeds in the resulting solution, and plant it. Very simple, really."

"No way! You must think I was born yesterday?" Now at least I was starting to see the joke. I didn't know how they had pulled off the voice and the dinosaur schtick, but someone was having a great laugh on this one and I wasn't going to play along anymore.

"I'm afraid I do not know when you were born," Fred said. "But I got here by exactly the method I told you. I have watched it happening. I have studied the event many times and I fear it may be my only chance of survival."

"Sure." I made one more quick check of the tree, then studied the stakes. I had to admit it was sure one elaborate gag. And it looked like the only way I was going to get to the prankster was go along and get it over with. Then I could prove to Annie that I didn't say anything and get back on her "good" side.

"All right," I said. "I'll bring back the part of the deal you need from me. Where will I find a seed from you?"

"I will drop an acorn that is ready to sprout," Fred said. "And thank you."

"No problem," I said.

I made one more quick check around the area of Fred to make sure no one was hiding in the bushes laughing their fool heads off, then headed for Annie's house in hopes of her giving me a helping hand. She still wouldn't talk to me or even let me explain what I was trying to do. Not that I really blamed her. So I went back to my place and did it myself. I was back at the tree in an hour.

I checked quickly around to make sure no one was watching, then held the rubber up. "Here you go."

An acorn hit the grass right at my feet. I picked it up, looked at it, then stuck it inside the rubber. "Got any place special you think I should plant it?" I asked, checking the area of the branches it fell from to make sure there was no one sitting up there.

"Anywhere that will be safe," Fred said.

"I'll be back tomorrow morning early." As I headed for the park gate, I heard Fred start into a limerick about a girl from Troy.

FOUR

I took my "package" to mom's house in the suburbs and planted it off to one side in her back yard. She didn't care. As far as she was concerned, I was always doing strange things. And she hadn't even seen me in my Buckey The Space Pirate costume.

I staked out where I planted the seed. I told mom it was a special seed for an exotic tree and needed really special care. She liked that.

I made it back to the park by ten the next morning, but I was way too late. The old tree was in a hundred pieces piled in neat stacks. I watched while the workmen used chain saws on what was left, but I couldn't take it for very long. Even though I knew the entire thing had just been a joke, I couldn't shake the feeling of pain and sadness coming from that wood.

I never did get back with Annie. She wouldn't have anything to do with me. And no one ever came forward and laughed at me about jacking off into a rubber and then planting it. If it was a practical joke, or a hidden camera stunt, I never found out about it. Seems to me that I would have, too. I don't understand why someone would go to all that trouble without pulling the final "gotcha?"

Since I never uncovered the joke, every time I visited Mom I found myself checking on the spot where I had planted the tree. Nothing. Over the winter I pretty much forgot about it.

It wasn't until the following May, while I was mowing Mom's lawn, that I almost ran over the little oak tree. I spent an entire hour cleaning the weeds and grass away from it, then putting up a solid, two-foot-high wire fence around it. It felt kind of funny to know that my sperm had worked as fertilizer for a tree.

I checked back on the little tree all through that summer and fall, telling myself I was crazy each time I did, but yet doing it anyhow. It became one of those little obsessions a person has that they can't explain. I sure in hell made no attempt to tell anyone. Mom loved it. Said she'd never had so much help on the yard.

It wasn't until the following May that something finally happened. I was carefully mowing around the now almost four-foot-tall baby oak tree when I heard this high, child-like voice. At first I thought it was something going wrong with the mower, but after I turned the engine off, I heard:

> *"A bather whose clothing was strewed*
> *By waves that left her quite nude,*
> *Saw a man come along*
> *And unless I am wrong*
> *You expect this line to be crude."*

I sat down hard on the grass. I couldn't believe it. I was either going completely crazy, or it had worked. I had actually planted a tree with my sperm that grew and could talk. No way. That was just too stupid. Just like before, I figured it was either a joke or I had imagined it.

"You know," the little voice said from what seemed like the direction of the little tree. "I have this strange desire to do things to a woman dressed in a costume."

I stretched out on the grass with my face real close to the small trunk of the tree.

"Fred?"

"Hi, Dad," the little tree said. "You want to hear a limerick? Or maybe go see a dinosaur?"

CAT IN LOVE
A PAKHET JONES STORY
DEAN WESLEY SMITH

ONE

I rescue cats all the time. Sort of goes with the job of being a superhero in the world of cats. But until today, I had never had a cat rescue me.

My name is Pakhet Jones. I'm over a hundred and fifty years old and stand just over six feet tall, with golden skin on every inch of my body and a head so bald, it shocks people.

Thomas, the tuxedo cat that had moved in with me after his companion died, had spent the morning in his normal spot, curled up on the back of the tan cloth couch in the Las Vegas sun that was pouring through the main window of my condo in the Ogden. My windows were floor to ceiling and faced south and east, overlooking from ten stories in the air a large part of the Las Vegas valley and the entire Strip.

I had spent the morning doing real world business stuff. I owned numbers of corporations and had the top floor of a downtown office building with employees and everything. My business was basically investment and I had lost track of how many condos, apartment complexes, retail centers, and buildings I owned not only here in Las Vegas, but all over the country.

I had people to keep track of all that and run my many corporations. The top two were superheroes in business management and in accounting. Yes, both areas had super-heroes and I figured it was just easier to hire them. But regularly I had to spend time making sure the people were doing what they were supposed to be doing. I wouldn't be a good boss and owner if I didn't.

So after a hard morning of going over books and reports, I was about to head for what I considered my real office, Cabana #7 at the Beach at Mandalay Bay Resort and Casino. I loved just being there in the sun, soaking in the heat and letting the world just pass me by. I was a superhero in the cat world, after all.

I had just changed into my white bikini and sheer silk cover-up that made my skin glow even more, when I heard a rumbling growl from my living room that seemed to shake the floor.

No way could Thomas have made that noise. I actually had no idea what could make that noise, to be honest, but the sound was so primal it made me shiver and get goose bumps all over my skin.

I stepped out of my bedroom and onto the hardwood golden floors of my living room to come face-to-face with a massive golden African lion not more than ten paces away.

He was bigger than my cloth couch and I could stretch

out on that thing, all six-feet plus of me. The lion's eyes were huge and golden, almost the same color as his shiny coat. He looked very well-tended, so he hadn't come out of the wild.

He roared again and I flat froze.

The sound seemed to fill every pore of my body with an instant desire to flee.

Now I am the god of cats, and can turn into certain types of large jungle cats myself, a superpower I seldom use in Las Vegas. But in my 10th floor condo in downtown Las Vegas, an over-sized African lion is not something you expect as a living room extra.

Besides, he seemed angry.

Real angry.

One of my superpowers is my ability to communicate mentally with cats, so I took a deep breath and said, "Can I help you?"

No.

The big cat's thoughts were clearly angry.

Never a good thing.

Thomas was crouched on the back of the couch, hair on end, frozen, more than likely as disgusted as I was at my first question.

"Can I ask how you got here?"

No.

"Where were you before you arrived here?"

The big cat only roared again and I could smell the rot from its breath. His last meal must have been some time ago. He was clearly getting angrier and I had not one clue what to do.

Or who would do this to me.

19

Or why for that matter. Someone must have teleported this big cat into my living room.

It clearly wasn't a test. I had stopped being tested on my superpowers by my boss fifty years ago. So nothing like that.

And I had no memory of making another superhero or god angry in the last twenty or more years.

So not that.

I glanced over at Thomas and directed my next question at him. "Did you have anything to do with this?"

Thomas didn't bother to respond, but instead just crouched there wide-eyed, staring at the big cat.

Then I heard his thought. *Is that you?*

"Is that who?" I asked.

No response from my cat.

So I turned back to the big guy. "Do you plan on attempting to use me or Thomas there as a meal?"

I knew I could jump Thomas and I away from the big cat if he attacked, now that the shock of having a cat that size in my living room was wearing off.

No.

"So you are here to get my help?"

No.

At that point the big lion looked at Thomas, who seemed to relax and just sit up straight.

The lion was no longer angry, so that must have been fake bluster. Now he seemed almost bashful, looking down at the floor, then back up at Thomas.

"You came for Thomas?" I asked, doing my best to grasp what was happening.

If he will have me.

The big lion stretched out on the floor, feet out in front of it, facing Thomas, and put his head down on his massive paws.

I just stood there, mouth open, not having a clue what to think yet again.

TWO

Silence filled my living room as the big lion stared with baby-eyes at my house cat like a lovesick girl on a first date with her teen idol. Not even the sounds of Vegas made it in through my windows to break this scene.

The big lion and Thomas clearly knew each other, so more than likely these were not their original forms. Thomas was a decent-sized house cat, but compared to the massive lion, he wasn't even a snack before dinner.

"So how about you both revert to your original forms," I said out loud, "so we can all get this settled."

The two cats seemed to stare at each for the longest moment, then a beautiful naked woman with long golden hair was stretched out on my living floor and a naked man who looked more like he had been the model for a thousand Greek statues sat on the back of my couch.

"You are as beautiful as I remember," the Greek man said in ancient Latin as he stood and stepped down off the couch.

The naked woman sort of flowed to her feet as I stood there with my mouth open. This woman made me look short, but had the same golden skin and the most fantastic head of long golden hair I could ever imagine flowing around her.

It was easy for me to imagine getting lost in that hair and that perfect body. Either of them, to be honest.

But the two of them had zero interest in me and my sheer cover-up top.

The two of them stopped slightly apart and just stared into each other's eyes. I have to admit, I was admiring the fantastic beauty of both of them in every detail as they stood there. The gods of my world tended to not be much more than average-looking people. These two looked like the gods imagined in the old myths of just about every culture.

Perfect skin, every feature perfectly proportioned, faces of classic beauty.

They were clearly ancient gods who had just found each other for some reason in my condo's living room.

Right at that moment I realized that I could handle cats, even massive African lions just fine, but I knew nothing at all about ancient gods. And clearly these two went back a very long ways and for some reason had been posing as cats.

I needed some help. Real fast.

"Laverne," I whispered, sort of in the direction of the ceiling.

Laverne was Lady Luck herself, the god in charge of all gods. And she had been around for far, far more thousands of years than I could imagine. She would know what to do with these two.

I had only met Laverne one other time, but she made it clear I could contact her if I needed real help. This seemed to be the moment.

The two beautiful gods, or cats, or whatever they were still just stood there naked in my living room, staring at each other while I stared at them.

At that moment Laverne appeared. She was dressed in a gray power business suit with her long dark hair pulled back tight off her face, giving her long, stern look. And I could tell instantly she was not happy with the two naked figures.

They just stared at each other as Laverne turned to me. "Did you give them permission to come out?"

The ice in the question could have cooled a couple of pitchers of margaritas.

"I told them to return to their normal forms so we could solve what was going on," I said. "I was dealing with a lion and a housecat mooning over each other in my living room. If they had tried to mate I was going to lose furniture."

"And you do not know who they are?"

"I do not," I said.

Laverne nodded and the ice around her questions seemed to melt, thankfully.

She patted my arm as an assurance and turned to the couple, still naked, still just staring into each other's eyes.

She snapped her fingers and they were both dressed, the woman in a long flowing gown and the guy in a long white robe. Both wore sandals.

I felt slightly disappointed.

"Pyramus, Thisbe, you two done yet?" Laverne asked, a little disgust in her voice.

I took a step back. Holy shit!

Pyramus and Thisbe were a myth from Babylon that Shakespeare used for Romeo and Juliet. Actually, he used another author's book to get the story, but that author got the story from the myth.

Now they were standing in my living room.

And then I remembered even more of the myth. It had been a lion in a cave that started the entire thing, letting Pyramus think Thisbe had been eaten, so he killed himself and so on and so on.

That explained the big lion part of this puzzle.

Pyramus and Thisbe turned as one toward Laverne. He had dark, almost black eyes, she had golden eyes that matched her long golden hair. Standing side-by-side, they truly were the perfect-looking couple. And they sure seemed to be in love.

"Have we not been punished enough?" Thisbe asked, her voice low and silky.

"How long has it been?" Laverne asked.

Neither responded.

"Six years is all," Laverne said. "You have ten more to go."

Pyramus started to speak, but Laverne held up her hand, stopping his words in his throat.

"How many times have you two killed each other?"

Both of them looked at the hardwood floor.

"Over the centuries, more times than any of us can count, that's how many," Laverne said, not hiding the disgust in her voice.

Both said nothing.

I actually felt bad for them a little. Clearly their love spats had gone to epic proportions over the centuries.

"So you will serve your full sentence," Laverne said.

"Stay away from each other. I do not want to hear of the two of you being near each other for ten more years. When you are released, if you can find a way to live together, or apart, that will be up to you. But you must live. If you kill each other again or yourselves again, your sentence will double each time."

Now I had no idea how in the heck that worked. I sort of figured if a person or superhero or god was dead, that was the end of things. This must be something different for just them. More than likely something about love eternal and just thinking about it I decided I really didn't want to know.

They both stood staring down at the hardwood floor of my living room like two school children caught kissing in the closet.

"We will break this cycle, I promise you," Laverne said to both of them, her voice softening some.

With that Laverne waved her hand and there was once again a massive golden African lion in my living room and Thomas, my companion cat, was sitting on the floor in front of us.

Then the lion was gone and Thomas flicked his tail and turned around and left the room.

"Thanks, Pak," Laverne said, shaking her head and turning to face me. "You need any explanation?"

I laughed. "Thanks, I think I'm good. Just headed for the pool."

"Sounds tempting," Laverne said. "But can't today."

"You know where I'm at," I said. "Always welcome."

"Thanks," Laverne said. "And as far as those two, they

are harmless to everyone but themselves. Just don't invite them to take their real forms and you should be fine."

With that she vanished, leaving me alone in my own condo, dressed for the pool. And that was exactly where I was headed. It was going to take some time and a lot of sun to get the real image of Thomas out of my head.

And even more time to get the image of his true love out as well.

Two ancient gods could sure get a girl's heart racing, of that there was no doubt.

SHE LOST A PERIOD
A SKY TATE STORY
DEAN WESLEY SMITH

ONE

I love a juicy, bare fact. Bare meaning the fact couldn't be refuted and was just right out there in the open, like the idea that sex happened regularly in Las Vegas. Not a great deal of dispute there.

And juicy meaning something about the fact that gets someone who is observing laughing or hiding a grin behind a palm.

A really perfect fact is one that embarrasses someone for the right reasons, like that person is slime and needs to be embarrassed. That's when facts get really fun and really juicy.

Now, my name is Sky Tate and I'm a superhero in the world of private detectives. Been one for a couple hundred years, almost before there was such a thing. I'm a woman in the field, not something that unusual these days, but I like to play against type at times by wearing a long gray trench coat and a gray Fedora.

My long beak of a Roman nose also gets me a little disguise at times, when I need it. Sometimes I do, sometimes I don't.

I got the standard superhero powers of being able to teleport from one location to another, and I also stopped aging right around the age of 28, which thankfully was my best-looking age.

I can also read a person's mind with a simple touch, which comes in real handy more times than not.

It was right at one in the afternoon and I was parked in my favorite booth, my second office as I liked to call it, in Rocky's Tavern down off of Sahara a few blocks from the Strip.

Rocky's was owned by Rocky, thus the original name to the joint. He's a superhero in the bartending world, but I honestly had no idea what he did besides sit behind the bar and read a newspaper and let me meet clients. The bar was tucked in a corner of an older strip mall and there wasn't even much of a sign above the door. It smelled a lot like an old neighborhood bar from the days when smoking was still allowed in a bar. I had a hunch that smoke smell was baked into the wood on the walls and the yellowed plastic beer signs.

Rocky's had its regulars, usually after work or late into the night. I tended to be the only customer during the day most days.

I had my computer set up on the tabletop and was just finishing off some chicken fried rice and pot stickers from

Lenny's four doors up. I had gotten me and Rocky both lunch, something I did a few times a week for letting me sit in his place and not drink anything but a diet soda.

I had really hoped to finish checking some quarterly reports from a few real estate investments I had around town and then I planned to go back to my condo and catch a nap. But from the bright light of the front door to Rocky's opening, I had a hunch I wasn't going to get all that done. Especially the nap.

Just call it a hunch. Detectives have hunches.

Rocky looked up from behind the bar and took one look at the new person, shook his head, and went back to reading.

It took me a moment after the door closed and the bright light cleared to see the woman standing there blinking as her eyes fought to adjust to what must seem like total blackness. Coming in from a bright Las Vegas day into a dark corner bar is just impossible to do with any kind of grace. Better to just freeze and wait for your eyes to adjust, which she was doing, giving me enough time to really study her.

She was maybe thirty, with a very prim and proper white blouse and business skirt, business blue, of course. Her brown hair was pulled back tight and tucked into some sort of bun on the top and back of her head. She had what looked to be reading glasses tucked in her hair and I doubted she remembered they were even there.

I had to admit one thing, though. Even in the dark, she had a nice figure stacked on great legs under those prim clothes.

She seemed to be about my height at five-ten, and she

had one of those classic beauty faces that she clearly didn't know she had and didn't know what to do with even if she realized she was beautiful.

Just as Rocky knew this one wasn't one of his afternoon drinkers, I knew this one was looking for me.

"To your right," I said. "Your eyes will adjust in a minute."

She turned to her right and moved slowly and carefully, her nose clearly picking up the old baked-in cigarette smoke by the distaste painting her face.

As she got closer, doing an admirable job of not bumping into any of the half-dozen tables Rocky had scattered around the place, she said, "I'm looking for private detective Sky Tate."

"You found her," I said.

I stood and went toward her and took her elbow to guide her to my booth.

By touching her, I instantly knew why she was looking for me.

Her name was Sheila Mair and she was just transforming into a superhero. She didn't know that yet since none of us know about the superhero world until we slowly become one and get training.

No, she was worried that she had stopped menstruating, which we all do when we become a superhero. But she had never had sex with a man or a woman for that matter and had no idea how she might be pregnant. And was too embarrassed to go to a doctor just yet.

So she wanted me to find out if she had been drugged

and raped or something along those lines before she went to a doctor.

In all my years as a detective, I had never been hired to figure out why a woman's period was late. Nope, not once. I'm betting that's not even in the detective manual, which I am sure exists somewhere.

This woman had been born and raised in Las Vegas, had gone through grad school and had worked in the real world for six years and still she had no real idea about sex. She hadn't even had a close relationship with another person. I didn't think that was possible.

Oh, my.

But the area she was going to be a superhero in was even more amazing. She had a burning interest in food and beverage and service, even got a master's in those areas, something I didn't know was possible. And she was headed toward being a superhero in the world of beverage service. Bartenders and cocktail workers.

A woman who knew next to nothing about relationships or sex as a superhero beverage server in Las Vegas.

Oh, my, oh, my.

"Thank you," she said, making sure she was sitting prim and proper in the booth across from me.

I gathered up the remains of my lunch and asked, "Would you like a water or orange juice or soda?"

Again she wrinkled her nose, something I was starting to enjoy the look of, actually, in a Samantha Stevens kind of cute way.

"Rocky gets top sanitary ratings without a blemish every

inspection," I said, answering the thought I knew she was having.

"Damned straight!" Rocky said from the other side of the room.

That sort of startled her so she said, "A diet soda, please."

Rocky stood and headed down the bar to bring me and her a diet as I put my lunch remains on the bar and went back to sit across from her.

She leaned forward toward me when I sat down.

She whispered. "Can we talk privately in here?"

"We certainly can," I said. "And trust me, we have a lot to talk about and you have a lot of people to meet. You have far more problems than just missing your period."

She jerked back like I had shot her.

"Detective," I said. "I know things."

"Budding sup, huh?" Rocky asked, putting the two glasses on the wooden table on napkins.

"Afraid so," I said. "In your area, actually."

"They have an aura about them," he said, shaking his head. "Good luck. Let me know when you want me to call Bradley."

And with that he turned away, leaving poor Sheila shocked and confused and clearly worried she had walked into a madhouse.

Bradley was the god of bars and beverage service, a brash, take-no-prisoners kind of guy. Sheila wasn't quite up to meeting her new boss just yet.

From the looks of her, maybe not for a few weeks or a few months.

If this wasn't such a real problem, I'd be laughing my ass off right now.

TWO

I t was time for me to do the twenty questions on poor Sheila so she would think she had found a real detective for the moment.

"Okay, have you been to a doctor for your problem?"

I knew she had not, but I needed to run through the questions at least.

She shook her head and I let that go as enough for now.

"So you think you might be pregnant?" I asked.

"I can't be," she said, a slight touch of panic in her voice.

"Can't be or don't want to be?" I asked, again knowing the answer.

"Can't be," she said. "I've never had sex with a man that I know of. So that's why I need your help, to find out if I was drugged and raped."

I reached across the table so I could touch her hand. This poor woman was scared out of her mind. Something about sex just petrified her.

"Never been interested in a man or a woman?"

There had been a couple women she had been attracted to back in high school. That popped into her mind and then vanished. Something had shut off that sexual part of her and there had been nothing since. And my mind reading just wasn't good enough to get at the problem, let alone know what to do to deal with it.

"Not really," she said, shaking her head slowly.

I patted her hand and sat back. "You came to me for help. That correct?"

She nodded.

"So I'm going to need some help, and that means I'm going to need to start introducing you to a brand new world."

"What kind of world?" she asked.

"An amazing one," I said. "But you are going to be shocked and I promise I will explain everything."

She looked very worried. "Maybe I should just go to a doctor."

"Oh trust me," I said. "A regular medical doctor will not be able to figure out what is happening to you. But I can tell you without a doubt, you were not raped. You are very, very healthy, more than most normal people. And you will never have a period again."

"You can know that?" she asked, giving me a very wide-eyed look that I liked more than the frown wrinkled Bewitched look.

I nodded. "I know that for a fact."

I stood and picked up my computer and put it away in its carry bag.

She was looking puzzled.

"I need you to come with me."

"Can I ask where?" she asked, standing and smoothing down her prim and proper skirt.

"We need to go to some friend's condo in the Ogden," I said. "Get you some help."

I turned and said loudly, "Rocky, I'm taking Sheila to Marble and Sims, see if they can help?"

"Nice meeting you Sheila," Rocky said, waving from behind the bar. "It's going to be fun working with you. Trust what Sky tells you and you'll be fine."

Sheila had that puzzled frown on her face when she turned to ask me what Rocky meant.

At that moment I jumped her to Marble's and Sim's condo.

She looked around, started to say something, then really looked around, then bless her, she passed out and I caught her and put her on the couch.

Better I suppose than just having her stand and scream. I figured it could have gone either way.

THREE

I got Sheila comfortable, then looked up at the ceiling and said loudly, "Marble! Sims! Could use some help."

A moment later two of the most beautiful women I had ever had the pleasure to know appeared beside me. Both were slightly taller than me, both as perfectly proportioned as a woman's body got, and both wore jeans and silk blouses and tennis shoes.

Sim's long blonde hair was combed out straight and perfect as she always wore it. Today Marble had colored her hair a light green to match her nails and her light green blouse.

Both Marble and Sims were ghost agents. Both had formally been superheroes, but both had been killed and kept over as ghosts to help people. Basically they crawled inside of people's minds and helped where they could. They both seemed to love it. A full day of that would drive me nuts.

"Sorry to barge into your place like this," I said. "Needed some help to figure out the next step with this one."

I pointed to Sheila on the couch.

"So who is the cutie?" Marble asked, moving over and studying Sheila.

"She looks really uptight," Sims said.

"She's going to be a superhero and knows nothing about any of this world," I said. "In fact she passed out when I jumped us here from Rocky's."

"Oh, the poor thing," Sims said and Marble nodded.

"She came to me to figure out why her period stopped," I said.

"Detectives do that now?" Marble asked.

"I guess we do," I said, shaking my head as they both laughed.

"Why would she come to you?" Sims asked.

"She thought she was pregnant, even though she has never had sex with a man or a woman in her entire life. Or at least that is all I can get out of her mind."

"Oh, wow," Marble said, staring down at Sheila. "Something really horrid happened to this sweet thing."

"And to make it worse, she's going to be a superhero in the world of beverage service."

Marble and Sims both just stared at me. Both their mouths were open.

"I can see why you came here," Marble said. "You wouldn't want to turn her over to Bradley for training until she had at least this problem cleared out."

"Exactly my thinking," I said.

"I'll go in," Marble said to Sims. "There might be abuse back there in her past and no point in your needing to deal with that."

Sims nodded. I knew that Sims back a few hundred years ago had been badly abused before she became a superhero and now a ghost agent.

Marble, without hesitation, moved over and sort of sunk into Sheila, swallowed up completely by the sleeping future superhero.

"You know I've seen you two do that dozens of times," I said, "and I'm still not used to it."

"Just not a natural thing to see," Sims said.

With that we both just stood in silence staring down at Sheila, waiting for Marble to emerge.

I had to admit, seeing Sheila so relaxed, she was even more beautiful than I had first thought.

It took almost a full five minutes before Marble stood and came away from the sleeping Sheila.

Sheila motioned that we should go into the kitchen area and Sims went ahead and got Marble a glass of water. I had to get my own, since Sim's couldn't pick up a real glass for me.

"That bad, huh?" I asked as we three sat at the glass-topping dining room table. The view over downtown Vegas and the Strip beyond was amazing here. And the afternoon light felt wonderful. I needed to get out of Rocky's a little more during the day.

Marble sipped the water, then sort of shrugged.

"Nothing bad at all," she said. "In fact, nothing at all. Period. That's what took me so long."

"Nothing?" I asked. I had no idea how that could be.

"Nothing," Marble said. "Sheila just never had that part of her brain turned on, in a manner of speaking. On an intellectual level, she understands sex, can use it to her advantage, can stay away from it if she needs to. She just flat has no interest."

"And nothing caused that disconnect?" Sims asked.

"No event in her past, nothing," Marble said. "She tried a few affairs with other girls and it did nothing for her. At one point in college she even took some sexual awareness classes, tried a lot of innovative sex toys and everything. Nothing. And never had any interest in marriage, relationships, or children. They just never cross her mind."

I just shook my head. "I can't imagine existing without sex in my life."

"We've noticed," Sims said, smiling, and I think I actually blushed, remembering a few of those wonderful nights in that monster bed of theirs. The things two ghosts can do to a person is beyond sinful.

"So," I said, smiling back at Sims, then turning to Marble. "She doesn't need help fixing any kind of sexual problem?"

"Nope. She's just fine the way she is and actually this might help her in her new line of work. Without that sexual drive sometimes clouding her vision, she should be able to out think just damn near anyone in an alcohol environment."

"So what do we do now?" I asked. I honestly was at a loss.

Marble glanced over at Sheila still asleep on the couch. "How about I go back in, plant a few suggestions that she be more accepting of the superhero world. Then we spend a few hours with her this afternoon showing her a few ropes before turning her back over to Rocky and Bradley."

"Ease the transition some," I said. "Wish someone would have been around to help me with that as well."

"Yeah, me too," Sims said. "And if we do that she will know she has friends to turn to for help when she needs it."

"I like it," I said.

Marble took another drink of water and then went back over and sunk into Sheila once again.

This time she was gone for less than a minute before she came out and came back over to us. "I gave her the power to see me and Sims," Marble said.

Sims laughed. "A new trick we just learned. See how it works."

I nodded. I remembered clearly the first few times I had worked with them, I hadn't been able to see them. I had to have Laverne change my brain in some way to be able to finally see them and all their beauty.

At that moment Sheila yawned, looked around and sat up like a Lazy Boy Rocker had blown a fuse under her.

"Over here," I said, standing and indicating the table. "I'll get you a glass of water. Come on over and join us."

Sheila stood, smoothed down her skirt and looked around, moving slowly toward the table.

"What a view," she said. "A beautiful place."

"It is their place," I said. "I just crashed it by bringing you here. Marble and Sims, meet Sheila."

"Thank you for the use of your beautiful place," Sheila said, extending her hand to Marble as she sat down.

Marble smiled. "You have a lot of things to learn about this new world, so might as well start now."

Marble reached for Sheila's hand and their hands passed right through each other.

Sheila jerked back, staring at her hand.

"No, you are not dead," I said, putting the glass of water in front of her. "But they are. They are what is called ghost agents. We all work together trying to help people."

"We?" she said, looking up at Marble and then at Sims.

"Yes, we," I said. "Every area of life is watched over in some way by superheroes and gods. I work in the area of detectives."

"When I was a superhero," Sims said, "before I was killed and recruited as a ghost agent, I worked in banking."

"I was a superhero in the world of real estate," Marble said.

Sheils looked at all three of us and I was impressed that the help Marble had given her was keeping Sheila calm.

"Superheroes?" she asked. "Does that mean we all have powers?"

I nodded.

"So you could read my mind when you touched my elbow," Sheila said, looking at me.

"I could," I said, surprised she figured that out so quickly. "A good skill for a detective to have."

"And you just transported me here?" Sheila asked.

"You might have that ability in a little time," I said.

"And Rocky said I was a budding sup, meaning superhero. He could see it?"

Again I nodded. "Wow, you don't miss much." I had a hunch in the world she was going into, that was going to be a critical trait.

"And I'm going to work with Rocky?"

"In the same area, it appears," I said. "Superhero in the beverage service area. Best I can tell."

Marble nodded agreement.

And with that, Sheila actually perked up and smiled like a kid who had just gotten her favorite toy under a Christmas tree.

I glanced at Marble who was just sitting there with an amused grin. Sims was looking a little shocked, actually.

I was feeling a little shocked as well, to be honest. Back a few hundred years before when I first learned about the world of superheroes, I had denied it for a couple of years at least. And Sheila knows more already than I knew in my first twenty years.

So for the next hour the four of us sat and talked and laughed and filled Sheila in on things like why her period had stopped and how she would never age again. And the differences between superheroes and gods. And who Laverne, Lady Luck was who ran everything.

Finally, after an hour Sheila asked, "Would you three escort me to talk with Rocky and meet Bradley?"

41

"We would love to," I said as we all stood.

A moment later we were all standing in Rocky's back room, just in case he had customers.

"Didn't expect to see you back so soon," Rocky said, smiling at Sheila. "These four get you all filled in?"

"They are wonderful," Sheila said.

"Just know you can come to me or any of them at any point," Rocky said, being surprisingly nice, a side of him I had seldom seen under that gruff exterior and stained apron.

He got us all seated around one of his tables and diet sodas in hand before he said to Sheila, "Ready to meet Bradley?"

Sheila nodded and Rocky glanced at the ceiling and said, "Bradley, can you join me for a moment?"

Bradley appeared next to the table. He was a short guy I had only met a few times before. He had on a silk suit and a silk blue tie and his hair was combed back off his head. He was a handsome man, just not my type and way too short.

Sheila stood instantly, then rushed Bradley and hugged him.

Now the entire table looked shocked.

Both Sheila and Bradley were holding each other at arm's length and laughing and smiling like two old friends.

"I was wondering when you were going to make the final turn," he said. "Just didn't know what I could say."

She laughed. "I found some great help. And I understand why you couldn't say anything. You didn't dare."

"Okay, okay, you're killing us here," I said.

Bradley put his arm around Sheila, not in a sexual way,

but more like a big brother way as they turned to face the table-full of shocked faces.

"Sheila has been my office manager and right hand for the past four years. I knew she would turn when she got to the right age. I've just been waiting and training her on the business side."

I just shook my head. I had ignored all her job-related stuff when I read her mind, staying focused on the other problems. And clearly Marble hadn't noticed it either, since she was looking for trouble areas, not happy places.

Bradley pulled up a chair to the table next to where Sheila was sitting and then said to Rocky, "Think you could spare a couple real drinks in celebration?"

Rocky appeared behind the bar and a moment later was back with a scotch on the rocks for Bradley and a Tequila Sunrise for Sheila. I'd have to ask him later how he knew that's what they wanted to drink, but it clearly was.

They toasted each other and then Bradley turned to the four of us. "Okay, I want to hear every juicy detail about what happened today."

And detail by juicy detail, we all told him, with Sheila starting by telling how she had hired me to find out why her period had stopped.

"I didn't know detectives did that," Bradley said, smiling.

"We do now," I said, trying to keep a straight face. "It's going on my business card."

And that got a toast from everyone around the table.

WHISTLE FOR HELP
A MARBLE GRANT STORY
DEAN WESLEY SMITH

ONE

T he guy let out a wolf whistle that seemed to echo off into the distance and I looked around to see who the jerk was and who he was whistling at.

He stood against a stone wall near the pool area of the Golden Nugget Hotel and Casino in downtown Las Vegas. On the other side of a glass wall near him were dozens of men and women in bathing suits enjoying the late fall warm day.

The jerk looked to be about thirty, had what looked like a very stiff drink in his hand, and a smile on his face.

He was handsome in an odd sort of way, with dark brown hair and wide shoulders. Clearly he had some money and enough confidence to fill a pool no one in their right mind would swim in.

He radiated smug and security.

I hated men like that.

Confidence was one thing, smug and self-righteousness was another. Rudeness pretty well topped the list of disgusting things I hated. This guy had a trifecta going on.

Sims, my partner and lover, was walking beside me along the carpeted hallway. She looked around as well, frowning.

The whistle was that loud and disgusting.

We did make one attractive pair of women, I had to admit, considering we were both over a hundred years old and dead. Both of us were trim and had long hair. My hair tended to shade between dark blue and purple depending on my mood the night before. Sims had stunningly beautiful blonde hair I loved running my fingers through.

And she was a natural. I knew that fact up close and personal.

Today we had on our normal work clothes of jeans, tennis shoes, and silk blouses. Mine was blue today, hers was orange and did wonderful things to her blue eyes.

So if we were alive, the guy might have been spouting his rudeness at us. It happened when I was alive more than I wanted to admit, especially back about sixty years ago when women were more property or objects than equals. But this guy couldn't see us since we were Ghost Agents, so he had to have been going after some other woman or man.

And a drunk who would act like that in the middle of the afternoon often meant there were other problems brewing for him or his victim in the very near future.

But there didn't seem to be anyone else but us in the hallway that would elicit that kind of crap from a pig.

There were three older couples in the hallway, all pulling suitcases. And an older bellman.

We were the only two women within his sight.

Sims realized the same thing and said softly, "Think that jerk can see us?"

"Let's go find out," I said.

We both turned around and headed back toward the guy. He just stood there, smiling, clearly expecting us to just walk past.

But when we stopped in front of him and turned to face him direct on, I thought he was going to pass out.

"Pretty damn rude, don't you think?" Sims asked him.

"You heard me?" the guy said, his voice weak.

"They heard that out on the Strip," I said.

"That's not possible," he said, all the confidence in his body draining out and vanishing like mist. He seemed to almost shrivel in on himself.

"Why isn't that possible?" I asked.

I had a hunch I knew the answer, but I had to hear him say it.

"Because I'm dead," he said. "No one can see me."

"Well, shit," Sims said. "And you think being dead excuses that kind of rudeness?"

The guy opened his mouth like a fish gasping for air and no words came out. He just shook his head.

In all my life I had never seen such panic in one poor guy's eyes.

"So how'd you die?" I asked. "Pinched the wrong woman's ass and she beat your weak ass to a pulp?"

"Wife's boyfriend," he said, his voice rasping.

I thought for a moment he might start to cry.

"How long ago and where?" Sims asked. "Not saying I believe a jerk like you, but tell me anyway."

I loved how Sims wasn't letting up on the guy. After that show of rudeness, ghost or not, I didn't much feel like giving him a break either.

"Suite on the 14ᵗʰ floor," the guy said. "About a year ago now, I think. I've lost track of time. I've never been able to have anyone talk to me or even see me until now. Not even sure if I'm still sane and making you two up."

Sims looked at me with a questioning look as the guy slumped to the ground in front of us and stared at the floor.

Sims sat on one side of him and I sat on the other. Even if he had been a jerk, it was time for us to see if we could help the guy.

"What's your name?" I asked.

"John Cahlan," he said. "From Seattle."

"So you said your wife's boyfriend killed you?" Sims asked.

He nodded. "Poisoned to make it look like a heart attack. I listened to her and him talk about it after I was dead. I even tried to hit them I was so angry, but my hands went through them and I felt their true thoughts about me."

"You were a jerk, right?" Sims asked.

The guy shook his head. "They thought I was a loser, a weak person who never took any chances." His voice got very soft. "They were right."

"That why you were acting like a macho ass?" I asked. "Pretending to be something you are not?"

He nodded.

47

Then he looked at me, tears in his eyes. "Are you dead as well?"

"We both are," I said. "And now it's our job to find out why you didn't move on to the next world when you died."

"I would appreciate that," he said, taking a shuddering breath.

Sims patted his leg and he jumped.

More than likely that was the first physical contact he had felt in a year. Something had gone horribly wrong with John Cahlan.

Sims and I needed to find out exactly what.

TWO

Without standing up from beside the John Cahlan, I called out to Jewel.

Jewel appeared standing in front of us and suddenly looked very puzzled.

Jewel was the ghost agent who had trained both me and Sims when we died early this year. She actually looked a great deal like us. Same body shape, same look in age, and she wore jeans, tennis shoes, and a cotton blouse that looked light and comfortable.

"Meet John Cahlan," I said to Jewel, indicating the guy between me and Sims staring down at the ground. "John, this is Jewel. Another Ghost Agent."

Before John could even look up, Jewel said, "He's a ghost?"

"Been here for a year," Sims said. "Alone."

Beside me John just nodded, looking up at Jewel.

"Not possible," she said. "I'll be right back."

With that she vanished.

"I am gathering that it is not normal for a person to be a ghost," John said, "without other ghosts knowing about it. Right?"

"Seems that way," I said.

It seemed to me from Jewel's reaction that something had gone very wrong. My gut sense is that John here had been meant to catch a ride on a tunnel of light and something happened. He didn't seem to be the ghost agent type, but I had only met a few ghost agents, so I honestly didn't know.

"What did you do for a living, John?"

He laughed in a sort of self-deprecating way. "After my behavior you would never believe me if I told you."

"Try us," Sims said.

"I was a psychologist," he said. "Working with women and their issues."

"And you didn't see your wife and her boyfriend coming?" Sims asked.

He shook his head. "Too busy with my practice to pay any attention at all to what I was doing to my marriage. Textbook, huh?"

"So did you learn anything more about women over the last year?" Sims asked.

"How could I?" he asked, turning to look at Sims.

"You can climb into live people and read their thoughts," I said.

"I avoided doing that at all costs," he said, almost shuddering.

"And you never left this hotel?" I asked.

"I didn't know I could," he said. "I thought ghosts had to stay near where they died."

I coughed to hide my laugh.

"How in the hell did you live in a crowded hotel for a year without touching people?" Sims asked.

"Stayed in an empty room during busy times," he said, "and if someone came into the room I walked through the wall to another room. I ate in the restaurants either right before they opened or right after they closed. I didn't know ghosts had to drink and eat and all that sort of thing."

"Wow," I said.

Sims just nodded and the three of us sat there against the wall as live humans went past.

I felt very sorry for John now. His boorish behavior earlier was explained away as far as I was concerned. He was literally going slowly insane.

In his spot, I think I would have stayed mostly drunk, a different form of insanity.

At that moment Jewel and another woman appeared in front of us.

The woman with Jewel had short red hair, large glasses, and wore a heavy raincoat and jeans. She was clearly not from Las Vegas.

"Oh, my, John," she said, reaching down and offering him her hand.

He took it and she helped him to his feet.

Sims and I stood as well.

"My name is Jennifer," she said, smiling at him. "We didn't expect you until next year. We thought you had survived the poison attack by your wife and boyfriend."

He shook his head, clearly puzzled.

"You have been here this entire time?" she asked. "No training?"

"Training for what?" he asked.

"I'll explain it all," she said.

At that moment Jennifer turned to Jewel. "Thank you. My team in Seattle will get John up to speed."

Jewel nodded and with that Jennifer and John vanished.

Jewel just shook her head. "They did that sort of thing with me and Tommy as well. We didn't meet another ghost agent for a full day after we died and then he left us on our own to get down here."

"Having trouble imagining being left alone for a full year," Sims said.

I just shuddered.

"How did you even see him?" Jewel asked.

"He was an ass," Sims said.

Jewel looked puzzled and I laughed. "We'll tell you the entire sordid story over lunch in the buffet. Call Tommy, he won't believe this one since you two have been in this hotel a lot over the last year."

"You are right, he won't," Jewel said, laughing.

THREE

S ix months later, as Sims and I were eating lunch in a small café down off of Fremont Street, John appeared.

He was carrying a large bouquet of flowers and two huge boxes of chocolates.

He was smiling and had lost the haunted and lost look in his eyes.

His hair was styled, his suit gray silk without a tie, and his shoes expensive.

Unlike the day we met him, this John was completely put together.

"I come to say thank you," he said, bowing and handing us each a box of chocolates almost as large as the small table we were sitting at. "For saving me and my sanity in the nick of time."

"Not whistling at women anymore?" Sims asked, smiling.

"You were my first and my last," John said, smiling back.

I melted at the smile and I have a hunch Sims was feeling the same way.

With that we stacked the chocolates and flowers on an empty table and invited him to lunch.

It turned out he was a very nice, very smart guy. And funny.

Really funny.

And hot.

Fan-yourself-with-a-menu hot.

Both Sims and I agreed later that night while lying in bed and working on one of the boxes of chocolates that if he promised to not whistle, he might be a fun one to invite home one night.

"I got a hunch that if we did that," I said, "I would be the one whistling in pure ecstasy."

"Pretty sure it would be both of us," she said, laughing.

And just the thought of that led to the chocolate being dumped on the floor and the sheets messed up. And there might have been whistling, but I was far, far too busy to notice.

THE CASE OF THE DOG-BIT ARM

A PILGRIM HUGH INCIDENT

DEAN WESLEY SMITH

ONE

Pilgrim Hugh seemed to thrive on strange phone calls. He got a lot of them from all over the Portland area, asking for his help with one thing or another. Almost always the calls came from police departments stuck on an odd problem of some fashion or another.

The call that came in on this fine, warm September morning was no different. Just flat strange, plain and simple. And yet interesting enough that he took the call.

The day was one of those perfect days that often happened in Oregon in the fall. Cool morning, warm afternoon, no real humidity. In September the kids were back in school and the world to Pilgrim just seemed to be at peace with itself as people went about their lives and jobs.

Except that Pilgrim was in a very foul mood. Carrie, his best friend and assistant, was leaving him next week to go back to school and the very idea of that just depressed the hell out of him, even on a perfect day.

He had on his normal jeans and a blue t-shirt that said simply, "Don't Ask."

So far no one had. And that suited him just fine.

He was peddling slowly on a stationary bike while looking out over the city. He felt at thirty-two that he needed to start doing something to keep in shape. His doctor said he was in great shape and at the perfect weight, but Pilgrim still felt like he needed to do something. He called it his "Portland Rich Guilt."

Pilgrim was so rich, he really didn't need to work at any job. His grandmother on his mother's side had left him more money than he knew what to do with just two months after his one and only divorce. At that point he had been out of law school for three years and pretty much hated working corporate law. His stint in corporate law lasted almost exactly the same amount of time as his marriage. Two years.

He had been good at corporate law and really bad at marriage. And had hated them both.

Somehow, after the money had arrived and he drank and traveled for a year, he had managed to start a law firm and hire great lawyers who liked working in law a lot more than he did. And then he had gone back to school and gotten his private investigator's license because it sounded like fun.

After a short time he sort of combined the law firm and the private investigation firm into what was now one of the largest and most powerful law firms in the state.

Hugh and Associates now occupied five floors of a downtown high-rise that Pilgrim also owned. His office and the entire private investigation section filled the top floor. The four floors below were the legal part of the firm. He had started out rich from his grandmother's money and now was even richer by hiring the right people and taking the right cases and buying the right buildings.

Carrie, Pilgrim's assistant, limo driver, and best friend since grade school, would be heading off to law school this fall for her third and final year before joining the legal side of his firm. He secretly hoped she would come back and remain on the investigation side of the business. They were a great team and he was going to miss her while she was down south in Eugene at school.

But he knew she was never coming back to be his assistant. Unlike him, she discovered she had a passion for the law and loved it.

And that thought of her not returning to be his assistant had him depressed. They would stay friends, sure. But he had loved all the time she had worked with him.

When the morning's strange call came in from the Tigard police chief, Pilgrim listened to the story while working at a Diet Coke and exercising on his stationary bike and looking out over the city and the Willamette River, trying to let the beautiful fall day brighten his darkening mood.

Everyone in this city rode bikes. Riding a stationary bike sort of made him feel a little more like the rest of the population. Carrie thought he was just fooling himself and had warned him a few times that to get any benefit from being on the bike, he actually had to peddle it faster and sweat a little.

He saw little point in that. Especially today.

From what the Chief of Police of Tigard told him in the call, it seemed they had a body.

A dead body.

Sort of.

Actually, they only had a male arm and a right hand that a dog had brought back to the dog's home in a neighborhood of Tigard. The Chief wanted Pilgrim to come and see if he could make any sense of it and try to help them figure out where the rest of the body was located.

It seemed the dog was being of little help.

Pilgrim told the chief they would be there in thirty minutes, then climbed off the bike, took a damp towel to his face even though he hadn't been sweating at all, and headed out of his office door.

Carrie was as tall as his six feet and today wore tight white short-shorts and a green t-shirt from the University of Oregon. As normal with Carrie, her outfit left little to the imagination.

She could walk down a sidewalk and cause car wrecks from both men and women staring at her.

Beside her stood Donna Marks, the assistant Carrie was training to take her spot this year. And, as Carrie reminded him, to take her spot permanently since after graduation Carrie was coming back and working with Ben two floors down in the corporate legal department of the firm.

Donna was shorter than Carrie, maybe five-six, and today she wore jeans and a blue blouse tucked-in. She had short brown hair and wide brown eyes that made her seem far more innocent than Pilgrim figured she was. She was thirty and divorced and had a smile that could light up a room when she used it.

Carrie loved her and said he would as well given time.

He would see about that. At the moment he didn't want anyone but Carrie.

"Did you get all that?" he asked as the three of them headed for the door to the office suite. He had always told Carrie to listen in to all his phone calls on cases. The practice just saved him time in explaining things to her and she often heard things he missed.

"We did, boss," she said. "The Case of the Dog-Bite Arm sounds like it's going to be interesting."

Pilgrim just moaned and shook his head.

Carrie always named all their cases like they were old detective books. Pilgrim liked that habit, he had to admit, even though he always made snide comments about it.

He glanced around at Donna as they reached the elevator. "So what's your take on this?"

Donna had a small notebook in her hand on top of a small tablet. She also had a pen stuck behind her ear being held there by her hair.

"I think this is a case of one hand not knowing what the other is doing."

She actually said that directly to Pilgrim without looking away and without breaking into a smile.

Pilgrim laughed and shook his head, then looked at Carrie who was smiling. "You found one like you?"

"She's better," Carrie said as they got into the elevator.

"I am," Donna said, smiling at Pilgrim. "I'm faster on computers, been trained in high-speed driving and car chases, and I am an expert marksman on ten different categories of guns."

"Are you going to decide to go to law school on me?" Pilgrim asked as the elevator doors closed. He had known all that about Donna before Carrie decided to bring her on board. But it was nice to see her stand up like that for herself with humor. On some of the things they did, she was going to need it.

Just putting up with him every day she was going to need a really good sense of humor and patience.

"Already been to law school," she said, smiling. "Dropped out before the last finals of my third year because I hated the idea of being a lawyer."

Now that hadn't been on her resume, so he turned and faced her. "So now you decide to come to work for a law firm?"

"I want to work as a private investigator and you're the best in the business."

He turned and smiled at Carrie. "I'm starting to like her."

"Good thing, Boss," Carrie said. "Because I'm not coming back. Remember?"

"Something I'm trying not to think about," he said, his mood suddenly foul again.

TWO

D onna was driving and pulled the limo up to the curb in front of a brown house in a quiet neighborhood in Tigard, Oregon, a suburb of Portland about five miles to the south of the downtown area. The area was built on rolling hills covered in large pine trees.

Three Tigard police cars blocked the street in both directions and one had had to move to let them through.

Carrie sat in the back with him, but they hadn't talked much on the way out, thanks to his mood.

The stretch limo served as their office and had more high-tech computer gear and surveillance equipment than Pilgrim could remember. A bunch of it Carrie had had installed over the years. And she knew how to run it all. He was good on computers, but not as good as she was. He hoped Donna was as good as she said, otherwise, this beast of a vehicle was just going to be a very expensive limo and nothing more.

The Tigard Chief of Police came down the sidewalk from a 1960s style ranch house to greet them. The house looked well-kept and had a fence around the backyard, more than likely to keep the dog in.

Chief Danny, as Pilgrim liked to call him, had red hair, far too many freckles on his face, and brown eyes that seemed to see everything. He was at least fifty, but looked younger unless you actually got close.

He extended his hand to Pilgrim and shook the firm, calloused hand. "Thanks for coming."

The Chief nodded to Carrie, who then introduced Donna as Pilgrim's new assistant and he nodded to her as well before turning back to the house to explain the situation.

Around them the wonderful day was starting to warm up just slightly, but in the shade of the large trees it felt perfect to Pilgrim. The neighborhood was an older one, the trees all grown, the sidewalks cracked with tree roots. The Portland area was full of perfect family neighborhoods just like this one. Sometimes he wondered why he didn't live out like this instead of in a penthouse condo in the Pearl District downtown.

"Dog came from that direction," the Chief said, pointing up the street. "The dog dropped the arm on the back porch. You want to see it?"

"Pictures would be enough," Pilgrim said.

The Chief nodded to Carrie and said, "I'll have someone send them along in a moment."

"Thanks," Carrie said.

"So you have men searching the park at the top of the hill?" Pilgrim asked.

"We've already been all over it and up and down every alley around here. Nothing."

"Fingerprints?"

"Nothing on file local," the chief said. "We're searching larger data bases now."

"Send those fingerprints along as well, would you?" Pilgrim asked and the Chief nodded.

"Any identifying marks on the hand or arm?" Carrie asked.

"Besides a dog's teeth marks, nothing," the chief said. "No ring or ring mark, no tattoos, no scars, nothing."

"How was the arm removed from the body?" Pilgrim was starting to get an idea of what they were dealing with here, but he still needed more information.

"The bone and skin looked like it was cut cleanly right below the shoulder with a very sharp blade."

"Before or after death," Carrie asked a fraction of a second before Pilgrim could.

Donna just stood taking notes.

"The guy was dead when the arm was cut off," the Chief said. "And at one point the hand and arm had been cleaned and put on ice."

Pilgrim nodded. He knew exactly where the arm had come from and why. He was surprised no one on the force had clued to it as well.

"Give us five minutes. But do send those pictures and fingerprints as soon as possible."

Carrie handed him a card with the e-mail address on it as Pilgrim turned back to the limo and crawled in. This was going to be an interesting case for Donna to start on.

A great test.

He took a can of Diet Coke from the fridge and then sat in his normal chair near the back of the limo's large passenger area. He flipped a switch hidden under his seat. Two computer screens appeared out of the side and a desk with a keyboard swung up out of the floor and clicked into place in front of him.

Carrie crawled in behind Pilgrim, grabbed a bottle of water, and took her normal spot up behind the driver's seat. She punched a hidden button and a computer console and two large screens wrapped out around her, making her look like she was suddenly in more of a command chair than a limo seat near a wet bar.

Her fingers instantly went to work on the keyboard.

Pilgrim looked at his screens and didn't bother. Carrie or Donna would find the information far faster than he would. So he just left the computer screens in front of him sit idle.

"You going to miss this?" he asked Carrie as Donna climbed in and pulled the door closed.

Donna sat facing the wet bar in the middle of the limo and in a moment was also surrounded by keyboards and screens as well.

"A little," Carrie said. "Not so much the private investigation cases, but I'll miss being around you all the time."

"A very nice thing to say."

THREE

Carrie turned to Donna who was typing faster than Pilgrim had ever seen anyone type before. "So, you know where the arm came from?"

Pilgrim knew generally where the arm had come from, but not how the dog got it. He liked how Carrie was using this to test Donna as well.

"Oh, sure," Donna said as her fingers flew over the keyboard. "Just trying to get the address now."

A moment later Donna hit one last key, studied the screen for a moment, then smiled. "Three houses up the street on the same side of the street as the dog's home."

Carrie actually seemed slightly surprised. "And how did you get that information?"

Donna shrugged and looked at Pilgrim. He was doing his best to keep a straight face.

"Easy," Donna said. "The arm was clearly from a medical school here in the area. More than likely a student took it home for study, so I did a search cross-referencing this neighborhood with all the medical students at all the universities in the entire Willamette Valley and southern Washington and included the teaching hospitals in the area."

Donna twisted a screen around so that both Carrie and Pilgrim could see the picture of a young woman with black hair smiling for her student I.D.

"Peta Edwards," Donna said. "Part Native American, part German. Perfect grades. She lives here with her parents to save money."

"Shall we go tell the poor girl about her missing homework?" Pilgrim asked, punching the button that retracted all the computer equipment around him.

Donna and Carrie both did the same and then Donna went out into the wonderful, fall afternoon air first.

Pilgrim followed carrying his Diet Coke can and motioned for Chief Danny to follow them up the sidewalk as Carrie got out and locked the limo.

As they walked, Donna explained to the chief where the arm had come from.

"And you figured all that out in two minutes in that limo of yours?" the Chief asked, clearly surprised and happy he didn't have a murder on his hands.

"Actually," Pilgrim said, "Donna got the address of the

student. And I'll bet you'll find an empty medical school cooler on the back porch. More than likely the poor student doesn't even know the arm is gone yet."

The Chief laughed as the four of them turned up the sidewalk toward the front of another 1960s ranch-style home nestled in among the trees. This one had no fence around the backyard.

"Chief," Donna said, "I kind of feel bad for this poor girl. You're more than likely going to have to write her instructor an official note."

Pilgrim moaned softly and looked at Carrie, who was smiling from ear-to-ear.

But Chief Danny didn't see the next thing coming at all and Donna was keeping a perfectly straight and serious face. Pilgrim was going to have to remember his new assistant could do that, or he would walk into a few of these traps as well.

"Why's that?" the Chief asked, stumbling and falling into Donna's punch line.

"Because no one's going to believe her when she says the dog ate her homework."

Chief Danny just shook his head as he looked at Donna who was still holding a perfect poker face.

Then he turned back to Pilgrim. "Where did you find this one?"

Pilgrim pointed to Carrie, trying to look innocent. "She found her."

And then as the chief turned away to knock on the door, trying to contain his laughter, Pilgrim mouthed to Carrie.

"Thank you."

THE 13TH FLOOR PROBLEM
A POKER BOY STORY
DEAN WESLEY SMITH

ONE

As a professional poker player, I don't have any superstitions. Not a one. I don't believe that if I won a tournament with one sock inside out, that I needed to always wear one sock inside out for good luck. I know for a fact that Lady Luck, actually named Laverne, paid no attention at all to how my socks were worn, or if I threw salt over my shoulder, or if I walked under a ladder.

She was just too busy. Now don't take me wrong, I wouldn't want to cross her, but she just wasn't the type to pay attention to the small stuff.

In life and in poker, I have had my fair share of good luck and bad luck, even though as Poker Boy, I know Lady Luck likes me, and my team. In fact, one of her four daughters, Terri, the Queen of Clubs, has just joined my team of superheroes.

My team works to save the world when it needs saving and it is often Lady Luck who gives us the assignments.

As it happened, just luck or coincidence or whatever, most of my team was having lunch in my office when we learned about what we came to call "The 13th Floor Problem."

My office, actually it's my team's office, but everyone calls it my office, floats about five hundred feet above the top floor of MGM Grand Hotel and Casino. It has windows on all four sides, floor-to-ceiling, with a view that was worth more than I wanted to ever imagine.

How it stayed in position was beyond me, even though Stan said I was the one who put it there and kept it there. As far as I was concerned, it stayed in place by some sort of magic I didn't understand. There were a lot of things in the world of gods and superheroes that I didn't understand and how my office worked was one of those things.

The office was, of course, invisible, and, as Stan said, out of phase with the real world so that if a plane hit it, the plane would pass right through. I'm sure if that happened, it would give everyone in the office a heart attack. The last thing I wanted was a plane passing through me.

But the office did have a wonderful view of the Strip and the airport and the entire city around it. Patty Ledgerwood (aka Front Desk Girl and my girlfriend and sidekick) and I often came up here at night and sat together and watched the stars and the planes landing and the cars on the Strip and all the bright lights spread out below us. As I said, a view worth more than I can imagine.

I had decorated the office so it looked like an exact

replica of the 1960s diner booth the team used to meet in. The Diner, as the place is called, is in the downtown Vegas area on a side street a block from the Horseshoe Casino and Hotel.

Just as in the Diner downtown, this booth had slick, red seats on three sides. I had added wooden chairs that could be pulled up to the end of the booth and a couple tall, tree-like plants behind the booth to give the place a little less cold feel.

The booth filled most of the room and could seat eight in a pinch.

There were only three ways to get up to the office. I had put a door leading to Patti's apartment and another door leading to the Diner in downtown Vegas. You step through and you were instantly in the other place. Otherwise you had to teleport.

I could teleport, but besides Stan, the God of Poker and my boss, I was the only one on the team who could. Everyone else either hitched a ride here with me or Stan or used the door from the Diner.

I was told it was rare that a lowly superhero like me could teleport. Or step between instants of time. But I had learned how to do both. I figured if I could learn it, so could other superheroes, like my girlfriend, Patty. She was a super-hero working in the hotel hospitality area of the Gods.

She was willing to learn, so we had worked on it a few times, so far without luck. But we had time and one of Patty's superhero traits was extreme patience. She had to have that to put up with me at times. I was a professional poker player, after all.

It had become a habit for the team to have lunch

together in my office around the big booth at one in the afternoon. We all liked the view and the companionship. Sometimes being a superhero could get lonely, at least that's what others told me. As a poker player, I always had people around me. It was part of the job.

And I was lucky enough to be tangled up with Patty.

Screamer and his wife, Terri, were sitting at the table working on burgers and vanilla shakes that Madge from the Diner had brought up. Having the great food and milkshakes from the Diner in downtown Vegas just a step through a door away was a great benefit.

Screamer had been a member of the team since we started. He was a superhero working with the police and could, with a touch, connect minds and be inside another person's mind. He got his nickname Screamer from making hardened criminals scream in fear from the images he put in their heads.

Terri was Lady Luck's daughter and a superhero in the beverage side of things. She and Screamer had been separated for a number of years while he got his newly acquired brain-reading powers under control. Now that they had worked out a way to be together, they never seemed to be apart.

Patty worked at the MGM Grand front desk and was on lunch break, so she still had on her front desk outfit and her long, brown hair pulled back tight. She nibbled at a salad while I worked at a cheeseburger with a huge basket of fries. I had switched away from my standard vanilla milkshake today for a cherry Diet Coke. Patty was mixing my fries with her salad, taking a bite of lettuce, then a fry.

Stan, the God of Poker, and my boss, also had a cheeseburger. He had on his standard tan slacks, tan shirt, and tan vest. He was the most nondescript man I had ever met. You could almost look right at him and not notice him. That made him downright scary on a poker table.

I had just taken a huge bite of my cheeseburger when Laverne, Lady Luck herself, appeared, pulled up a chair, sat at the booth, and grabbed one of my fries. Between her and Patty, I was going to be lucky to get any of them.

Laverne wore her normal gray silk business pants suit and had her hair pulled back tight, giving her face a stark beauty and sternness. She just radiated power and toughness.

And not once being around her did I fail to get nervous. Having Lady Luck herself just come to have lunch with you was a stunning thing I would never get over.

"Hey, Mom," Terri said, working at her hamburger and leaning against Screamer.

I managed to get most of the ketchup off my chin and nodded to her. Stan just kept working on his cheeseburger.

Madge appeared out of the door from the diner and smiled at Laverne. "Anything I can get for you?"

Madge was the waitress and the owner of the Diner downtown. She was also a superhero in the food and beverage industry and seemed to have been around the world of the gods for a very long time. She was fairly short and clearly overweight and she always wore a dress far, far too tight and too short for someone her size. She had a gruff way about her, but was always willing to help out the team where she could. She knew everyone, which had helped a few times on different assignments we had tackled.

Laverne shook her head. "Thanks, Madge, but we have a problem we need to get started on."

I swallowed the last of the bite of my cheeseburger I had been chewing on and pushed the rest away. When Laverne came looking for us like this, it meant eating was going to take a back seat very quickly.

Besides, my stomach was already twisting from my sense of looming danger, so putting more food down there wasn't a good idea at the moment.

"What's happening?" Stan asked, then took another bite of his cheeseburger.

"All the thirteenth floors are vanishing," Laverne said, as if she said a statement like that every day.

Then she took another fry.

"No building or hotel in this city has a thirteenth floor," Terri said, looking puzzled.

"Floor Twelve B or the Fourteenth Floor, whatever they are called," Laverne said, shrugging. "They are all vanishing. They will still be there, so no building is going to fall down, but the floors will become totally invisible by midnight."

"The Magician is back," Madge said, shaking her head and sighing in a way I had never heard before.

"Maybe," Laverne said, taking one more fry. She gave me that serious stare that scared me down to my very toes. "And if The Magician is behind this in any way, we need to stop him. And quickly."

At that, she vanished with one of my French fries in her hand.

The stunned silence around the office matched how I felt.

I just wish I had a clue what was happening.

And how she seemed to know something that was going to happen in two days.

And who the hell The Magician was.

TWO

E veryone had stopped eating.

Terri was just shaking her head, her long black hair going back and forth around her face.

Madge was frowning, never a good sign when a waitress used to attempting to smile was frowning.

Stan looked angry and Patty looked confused, just as I was feeling.

"Time for milkshakes," Madge said.

At that moment every bit of food on the table vanished and Madge turned and stepped through the door back to the Diner.

The group had a habit of ordering milkshakes when we were working on a problem. Usually only big problems. So Madge thought this problem big enough for milkshakes and had cleared the table.

Again not a good sign.

I stared at the place on the booth where my French fries had been and kind of wished I had the power to bring them back. And then I wondered where they had gone, and then finally decided I didn't want to know any of those details. Not at the moment, anyway.

I glanced around at my team, then decided that none of

them were going to speak, so it was up to me to be my normal clueless self and ask dumb questions. Sometimes my dumb questions got to the heart of the problem facing us, sometimes they just made me look silly for asking.

I wanted to start with how someone knew what was going to happen two days in the future, but decided on something more basic. "So someone want to give me the background on The Magician?"

"Right now he goes by Nick Scipio," Stan said without looking up. "He's been around for longer than anyone knows for certain. The protector and father, basically, of modern magic. Over the centuries he's taken many names when free, from Dedi in Egypt to Robert-Houdin."

"Is he a god?" Patty asked.

"He's an elf," Stan said.

I moaned. We had dealt a number of times with the elves and trolls and their fights. Because I had caught the one person causing elves and trolls to always battle, I was honored in their hidden casino here in Vegas, but I seldom went there. Just often enough to not insult them by never going there.

"You said something about him being free?" Screamer asked, and Terri nodded beside him, her black hair moving around her face.

"He is sort of locked up in a time cell," Stan said, "between moments of time, that should make it impossible for him to escape. But he often does. It's been a good fifty years since his last escape, at least that I heard about."

"So why make all the 13th floors disappear?" I asked.

"You could ask him yourself," Madge said, appearing from the doorway of the Diner carrying six milkshakes.

Behind her strolled a tall, thin man with black hair covering the tips of his pointed ears. He wore a white frilly shirt like he was on the way to a wedding and a long, black cape. In one hand he carried a cane, but clearly didn't need it.

"I figured Madge would know where you all met," he said, his voice low and soothing in an odd way.

He looked around at the view, clearly impressed, then he stopped in front of the booth and bowed slightly. "The Magician, at your service. And I want to be very clear that I will have nothing to do with the building floors disappearing in just under two days. But I must admit, it's a nice bit. I kind of wish I had thought of it."

He pulled up a chair and sat on it, facing all of us.

"Vanilla as always," Madge asked, placing the milkshake in front of him and then continuing on with the rest of ours.

"A wonderful memory," The Magician said. "Now a glass of fine whiskey and a cigar and I would be as happy as can be."

"Drink your milkshake, Nick," Madge said, shaking her head and moving off to one side behind the booth. She never sat with us, but often took part in the meetings and it was clear she had no desire to miss this one.

"Good seeing you again, Stan," The Magician said, as he stirred his milkshake and sipped it.

I stared at Stan, then back at Nick Scipio, The Magician. Clearly they had history. And I was just about to ask what that history was when Lady Luck appeared and scooted into the booth beside her daughter.

"Nick," she said, nodding.

The Magician bowed slightly. "I am honored, as always."

"Cut the crap," Laverne said, "and explain to me what's happening and how you know about it."

When Lady Luck gets blunt, things really have to be going wrong. This just looked worse and worse by the moment.

THREE

T he magician didn't let Lady Luck's brashness even seem to phase him. He took a sip of his milkshake, nodded a thank-you in Madge's direction, and then turned to face Lady Luck. From my position beside Patty across from Teri and her mother, I could see Nick's dark eyes. And I watched them closely as he spoke, seeing if I could get a read on him and if he was lying.

"In my little confines," The Magician said, "which are very comfortable, I might add, I have sometimes been able to see out ahead in time. Not far, and often not that accurately, since the future is always in flux by events of the present. But I did see that in two days all the 13th floors of every building in Las Vegas will become invisible. For some reason, all authorities will, at the time, know this will happen and will have all the floors from twelve-up completely evacuated. It will cause a very large event that will be difficult at best to explain away, except as a magician's illusion gone horribly wrong."

"I know all that," Laverne said, waving her hand in dismissal. "So who could actually pull off this kind of illusion?"

"Besides me?" The Magician asked. "No one. Which is why I don't think this is an illusion."

"Magic?" Stan asked as Lady Luck frowned.

Silence fell over the booth. And I had no idea why so many of them were upset. We were sitting in a booth in an invisible office five hundred feet above the MGM Grand Hotel and Casino. If that wasn't magic, what were we talking about?

"So who could pull off this level of magic?" Lady Luck finally asked. "And why would anyone break the ban?"

I wanted to scream WHAT BAN? But instead I just sat watching The Magician. From what I could tell, he had been telling the truth and seemed as worried as the rest of the people around the table.

I'm sure I looked worried as well, but not for the same reason. I was worried because I had no idea what they were talking about.

"I don't know the answer to that," The Magician said. "But I will be glad to help find out. If this actually happens, it will give all magicians a bad name and magicians in general will take the blame since it will be the only way to explain away such an event."

"Thanks," Lady Luck said, nodding. "You up for talking to your people?"

He took another long sip of the vanilla milkshake, then nodded. "Let's go."

"The rest of you keep working on this," Laverne said.

And she and The Magician vanished.

I sat there in the silence they left behind, so confused I didn't even have a question to ask. So Patty got the ball rolling.

"What did he do?"

Stan shook his head. "Not much, actually. Just pissed off the wrong god at the wrong time with a stupid trick. He and Laverne actually like each other, so she put him in a comfortable cell to keep him out of the way for a few centuries. He comes out, or as he likes to call it, "escapes" when he wants or needs to."

"So," I said, taking a deep breath, "someone want to explain to me the difference in magic and what is holding this office in the air?"

Screamer and Teri both laughed and Stan just shook his head. Patty just patted my leg, which meant my question was really stupid.

"Real magic," Teri said, "not the illusions that magicians do, is powered from the dark side. It does not come from any one person or skill, but by tapping into the pool of dark energy that rests just under the surface of everything."

Stan nodded and looked at me. "Your power to teleport, step between moments of time, and keep this place in the air comes from you, the depth of your ability to help others. It is a power of your mind and who you are. Just as studying another person and knowing how they are going to act in a hand of cards is a trained skill."

"Okay," was all I could manage to say. I sure didn't feel like I had a powerful mind. Far from it at the moment, in fact.

"That's why some of us can see slightly into the future as well," Stan said. "Like you watch a person and can predict a play or know his cards, others can watch life and know what might be possible in the future. A skill."

Well, that sort of explained that question at least, so I nodded.

He looked squarely at me and then went on, his tone and voice very, very clear. "All our powers are powers of light and come out of who we are and our own skills and talents. Nothing we do is actually magic."

I decided to just keep pushing my ignorance out there for everyone to see. "So this stunt of making entire floors invisible comes from a magic that is banned?"

Stan and Terri both nodded.

Stan said, "Actual magic has been banned for centuries, but some people try it anyway at times."

"And what happens to them?" Patty asked.

"The dark magic consumes them," Screamer said, his voice sounding disgusted. "And they became part of the dark pool of power. Not something I would ever want to experience. Think of the worst images of hell and multiply that by one hundred."

With that the silence just settled over the room again. Outside the windows, the sun was shining, planes were landing at the airport, and the world kept going, unaware that entire slices of buildings were about to vanish.

I took a sip of my milkshake and let the coolness calm me

a little. I just couldn't get one word out of my head and I finally just blurted it out. "Why?"

"Why do they get consumed?" Screamer asked, looking at me as if I had lost my mind completely.

"No," I said, shaking my head. "Why make floors invisible? If this really is someone using magic and risking his or her life to do so, why do this stunt? It seems very petty, has no obvious return for the stunt, and flat makes no sense."

And yet again the silence filled my office around the booth.

I was right.

I knew it. And their lack of an answer confirmed that for me.

No one who knew how to do dark magic and the repercussions from the use of dark magic would ever do something this stupid and out in the open.

And for no gain that I could see.

Suddenly I had yet another idea.

"What happens if this isn't real dark magic? What happens if it is a superhero having some issues with power control?"

Stan looked at me with a look that I couldn't read, but that wasn't unusual for me with Stan. He was the God of Poker, after all.

"Are you suggesting," Screamer asked, leaning forward, "that what is about to happen to all the 13th floors might be nothing more than an accident about to happen?"

"Possible," I said. "So what kind of superhero needs to learn to make things vanish in their training?"

Teri started to say something, then shut her mouth and shook her head.

Screamer just shook his head.

Stan and Patty both said nothing.

Finally, from behind the booth Madge said, "Cleaners. And some food superheroes as well."

"Like you made our lunch remains vanish," I said, glancing back at her.

She nodded.

"Are there Gods of Cleaners and Superheroes of cleaning?" I asked, then knew the answer. Of course there were. I had watched a person come into a room and it seemed to just get clean, as if by some sort of magic, which was more-than-likely a special power. I always admired people who could do that type of cleaning, since every time I tried to clean something, it looked worse instead of better.

"Damn," Stan said softly. Then he said, "Everyone's with me."

"Except me," Madge said. "I'll have milkshakes ready for you when you get back."

Stan nodded and then a moment later all five of us were standing in a huge warehouse that smelled of ammonia and other cleaning solutions.

FOUR

The building around us was so large I couldn't see any wall in any direction. Nothing but aisles between huge stacks of cases of what looked like varied cleaning solutions and supplies.

The roof had to be ten stories overhead, the lights dim, the floor smooth concrete, and the temperature worse than air conditioning set too low. The stack closest to me had to go up four or five stories into the air, pallet on top of pallet. How they stayed stacked like that was anyone's guess, or how anyone did the stacking was another skill I really didn't want to watch anytime soon.

A moment after we arrived, the Magician and Lady Luck arrived as well.

She turned to me. "You think this might be a new superhero having issues with powers?"

I nodded. "An idea that makes sense. Other than to do as an illusion, this future event makes no sense otherwise."

The Magician nodded. "Now I see why these people hang around with you."

"Thanks," I said, "but why are we standing here in this warehouse?"

"What, you don't like my office or something?" a voice blurted behind me.

I spun around to face a short, stout, matronly woman wearing a light blue cleaning uniform. On the cloth sewn-on name badge it read "Hygieia" and under that it said in small letters "Call me Jean."

Laverne stepped up in front of me to face the new woman before I could say anything about her "office."

"Jean, thanks for meeting with us," Laverne said, her voice very stern, so much so that I shuddered slightly. "Every

13th floor of every building in Las Vegas is going to vanish in just under two days."

"Good," Jean said, shrugging. "We won't have to clean them."

"We think it's one of your people who is going to cause the problem," Laverne said.

She frowned at Laverne, started to say something, then stopped and really looked around at all of us. "Stan, Poker Boy, Patty Ledgerwood, Screamer, your daughter, and The Magician. You have the A-Team on this, so it must be serious."

"It is," Laverne said. "Very serious. We can't let this happen. Are you training someone in the Las Vegas area?"

"Always training someone it seems," Jean said.

Beside her a very, very short man appeared wearing a hood over his head and only allowing just part of his face to show. I had no idea who he was or what his job was.

"You are training one called Dee, my sister," the short man said, his voice very deep.

"Oh, yeah, her," Jean said, nodding. "She's a strange talent, very powerful, only been on the job a few months, but seems to learn quickly."

"She has many fears," the short man said. Then he vanished.

At that point I had about fifty questions I wanted to ask, but as I had learned years before, when dealing with Gods, it was better to just keep silent and let them go on and then have someone explain later what happened.

"I'm not sure how Dee having fears could cause this," Jean said, looking puzzled.

"Maybe she's afraid of the number thirteen," I said, instantly breaking my rule about keeping my mouth shut.

Silence.

And in a huge warehouse with the ceiling towering four stories over my head, that silence seemed awful loud as everyone stared at me.

Finally Jean said, "I will bring Dee."

I instantly felt sorry for the poor girl. If I had been brought into a group like this, I would have more than likely fainted during my first years of being a superhero.

"Hold on," I said before the God of Cleaning could jump away. "I'm afraid, as a new superhero, she won't be able to answer any questions with a crowd like this. This group still intimidates me at times and I've been at this for a decade or so."

Jean nodded. "What would you suggest, Poker Boy?"

"Patty and I could go talk with her alone and the rest of you can keep track of how the conversation goes."

Jean glanced at Laverne who nodded.

"She is working on the third floor of the Golden Nugget. Tall, skinny, very young and very smart."

"Blind camera spot end of the hall," Stan said, "against the wall across from the elevators."

I nodded and jumped with Patty to that spot.

FIVE

F aint music played in the hallway and it smelled like the carpets had just been vacuumed. Down the plush hallway to our right was a maid's cart, so we headed in that direction.

As we neared the cart a tall woman with red hair appeared wearing a maid's uniform and carrying an armload of towels. She smiled at us, then dropped the towels into her cart. She was very young and hadn't yet seemed to grow into her body or her face.

It was clearly Dee. Under the sleeves of her shirt I could see signs of tattoos and another tattoo peaked out of her high collar.

As she started to turn back to go into the room I said, "Dee, we need to talk with you."

She stopped, suddenly looking puzzled. Her bright green eyes got very round.

"I am Poker Boy, this is Patty Ledgerwood."

Patty extended her hand. "Great to meet you," Patty said, giving the young superhero her best calming power.

Dee shook Patty's hand and seemed to relax a little. I didn't add in my calming power just yet, but I had a hunch I was going to need it.

"Your boss, Jean, says great things about you," I said.

Suddenly Dee looked panicked again. I remember early on in my superhero starting months, I thought no one knew I was secretly a superhero, so I was always shocked when another person knew that. Like me, she was going to be surprised as she learned just how many superheroes and gods there really were.

At the end of the hallway, the elevator dinged and the door started to open. So I slipped us out of time and into an instant between moments of time so that we wouldn't be disturbed. Since we were in a hallway and couldn't hear any traffic noise outside, nothing seemed to change, so Dee didn't notice.

"How do you know Jean?" Dee asked, looking first at Patty, who was still smiling and then back at me.

"We know many of the different gods," Patty said. "I work in the hospitality area and Poker Boy here works in the poker area, just as you work in the cleaning area. We are all at the same level, just under different departments."

Dee nodded and relaxed again. This girl really, really was the nervous type, of that there was no doubt.

I decided since Jean and Laverne and Stan were watching, to just jump to the problem. "Dee, are you scheduled in two days to clean Floor 14 here?"

Panic flipped across Dee's face and I sent calming waves at her, just as Patty was doing, trying to help her stay under control. I could feel my calming and trust-me power boosted a little as well, more than likely from Stan.

Dee calmed down and then nodded. "It's the 13th floor and I'm deathly afraid of it. I don't know what to do."

"We can help," Patty said, smiling as both of us kept aiming our combined calming powers at the young superhero. We were hitting Dee with so much calming juice, we could have put a horse to sleep smiling.

"But it's part of my job to clean that floor," Dee said, looking like she was about to burst into tears.

Suddenly I had another idea.

"We can help with that if you let us," I said. "We can help you never fear anything with the number 13 again."

"You could do that?" Dee asked. "And Jean wouldn't mind?"

"If it's going to help you do your job," Patty said, "I'm sure she wouldn't mind at all."

Dee stared at me, then at Patty for a moment. I could feel Stan boosting my "trust-me" power I was pouring at Dee.

Finally Dee nodded.

"Stan, bring Screamer," I said into the air.

A moment later Stan and Screamer appeared.

Dee jumped. "Are you gods?"

"He is," Screamer said, smiling at Dee as he pointed at Stan. "Great to meet you, Dee."

Screamer extended his hand and the moment he touched Dee, she froze.

Patty and I kept our calming powers aimed at Dee and turned up to full power.

"Need help to clean this out, Stan," Screamer said.

Stan nodded and touched Screamer's shoulder. I knew at that moment in time they were both inside Dee's mind, working to clear out her fears of the number thirteen without really hurting her or changing her in any way and leaving no trace they had been in there.

After a moment Stan nodded and dropped his hand from Screamer's shoulder. Then Screamer let go of Dee's hand.

"So what can you do to help me?" Dee asked, staring at Screamer and then at Stan.

"Do you still fear the number thirteen?" I asked.

She frowned for a moment, then shook her head. "No, I don't. Wow, you guys are good."

"We'll let you get back to work now," Patty said, touching Dee's arm one more time to really leave a calming and pleasant feel with the young superhero.

"Thanks," Dee said, smiling. "I hope to see you again."

As I dropped the time shield and jumped all of us back to my office in the air over the MGM Grand Hotel, all I kept thinking about was that I had no doubt we were going to see more of that young superhero in the future. I had a hunch she might just be helping the team down the road at times.

I guess that was my way of seeing into the future a little.

Madge was waiting for us with freshly made milkshakes. Laverne and The Magician and Terri appeared a moment after we did.

"Jean thanks you all," Laverne said. "As do I."

"I thank you as well," The Magician said, bowing slightly. "Your quick thinking and action has saved illusionists everywhere from a very difficult black eye."

Smiling, I slid into the booth and Patty slid in beside me as Terri gave Screamer a big kiss and then joined us.

It had seemed like hours ago that my French fries had disappeared from the table, but actually, this time, we had saved the city in just under a half hour.

"Madge," I asked, smiling at her as she placed the last milkshake on the table, "is there any chance you could make those French fries reappear?"

"Make that two orders," Lady Luck said, sliding into the booth beside her daughter.

"Three, if you don't mind," The Magician said, pulling up a chair.

Madge laughed and turned for the door to the Diner. "I had a hunch you would want some after lunch got shortened, so four orders of fries are cooking right now."

"Seeing the future again, Miss Madge?" The Magician asked, winking.

She smiled at him and winked back. "Depends if you have enough magic up that sleeve of yours to handle a future me."

"Have I ever failed you, Miss Madge?"

Madge laughed like a young girl and disappeared through the door.

All Patty and I and Screamer and Terri could do was just stare open-mouthed at The Magician as he sipped on his milkshake, smiling.

Lady Luck just shook her head as I tried desperately to clear the image out of my mind of a tall, skinny elf and an overweight waitress together.

I have a hunch it's burned there forever.

THE CASE OF THE DEAD LADY BLUES

A PILGRIM HUGH INCIDENT

DEAN WESLEY SMITH

ONE

Pilgrim Hugh stared at the body of the woman even though he had no desire to stare or look or even glance. Blue was just not an attractive color on a redhead, and this woman had clearly been very attractive in her pink-skinned time.

Dead was not attractive either. And she was most certainly dead, stretched out in the middle of the polished oak floor.

Her skin was deep blue, clashing with her long red hair. Her white slinky dress also seemed a pale blue from the shade of her skin showing through. The dress left little to the imagination, allowing Pilgrim to see clearly more than she likely wanted him to see in her own death.

Chances are she no longer cared, however.

The apartment where she lay had been scrubbed clean.

The oak hardwood floors had been polished, the off-white walls all wiped down to a gloss, and not a stick of furniture or window blinds or anything else but a blue body remained.

And the temperature was set at a comfortable seventy degrees on the thermostat on the wall. Outside, the July day was a hot one for Portland, Oregon, one of those ninety-plus days the weather people liked to proclaim as dangerous. Just walking from his limo to the apartment building had forced him to break out into a sweat under his dress shirt, jeans, and tennis shoes.

The room around him had more of an antiseptic hospital smell than a crime scene, but Pilgrim was pretty convinced he was standing in a crime scene. He had seen his share over the years helping police with varied investigations.

This might be someone really sick who did this.

As a private detective who helped the police on cases, he was usually called to a crime scene long after a body was removed, however. This time he was the one calling the police to a body. Actually, his assistant Donna Marks was doing the calling just outside the door.

He had ended up a private eye through a series of strange events. First, three years of law school and a failed first marriage while working for a corporate law firm had convinced him he wasn't a normal lawyer.

Or a decent standard husband either.

Then his grandmother had died and left him more money than he could imagine, which sent him on a year of traveling and drinking, which also eventually got boring.

So he went back to school to become a private detective, but soon learned, after he hung out his shingle, that being a private eye wasn't what the books described. It was all computer work and long boring hours of nothingness trying to watch someone.

At that point, he had finally figured out that he bored easily and needed some excitement and challenges in his life. So with some of his grandmother's money, he set up Hugh and Associates, a combination law firm and private investigative firm. Then he had hired a couple great associates who took all the boring cases and made the firm lots of money and they hired even more associates that he had no desire to meet who also made him lots and lots of money.

And he bought apartments around the town that also made him money, so his grandmother's fortune had gotten bigger even with his best efforts to spend it all.

He had then offered his investigative state-of-the-art services for free to all the surrounding police forces. After a few years, he had solved a bunch of cases and was now called regularly. Interesting stuff.

Seldom boring.

For the first two years of being a private eye, his best friend from school, Carrie, had been his assistant, but she had fallen in love with the law side of the firm, gone back to law school, and now worked on the floor below his office doing law stuff that seemed boring to him, but that she seemed to thrive on.

Before she left, Carrie had trained Donna Marks to be his special assistant. At times he had to admit, Donna was better at her job being his assistant than Carrie had been.

At the moment, he could hear Donna's voice in the

hallway outside the apartment. From the sounds of it, the Portland Police would be here shortly.

He looked at the apartment key in his hand. Nothing unusual about it at all. It had come to his office by Priority Mail with a simple typed note that read: Go here at noon for the most puzzling crime of your career.

Then the address of the apartment, no signature.

Had the person who murdered this woman sent the note?

Or had the woman even been murdered?

No clues in the note at all, just the reference to crime and all printed out on standard white paper. He had all of it in his limo to give to the police.

This was puzzling. The note was right about that much.

He took a slow walk around the small studio apartment, looking for any clues or anything that seemed odd besides the fact that everything was scrubbed to an inch of its paint job. Even the small bathroom shone like a bad commercial.

Whoever had cleaned this place had done a great job of it.

He went back to the dead woman and just stared at her.

The blue woman in the white dress lay in the middle of the hardwood floor, her feet together and aimed toward the door into the hallway. Her hands were grasped over her stomach, as if resting. Her eyes were closed.

He moved closer and bent down carefully to not touch anything.

She had on makeup, but not too much. There was just enough to accent her face, even with the shade of blue of her skin. Her bright red hair was combed back and arranged around her face on the floor. She almost seemed to be smiling.

The blue skin color was clearly covering every inch of visible skin and from the blue tint coming through the sheer white dress, all of her body.

She had no obvious signs of trauma, but he sure wasn't going to move her to look for any. However, he did carefully, using one knuckle, touch her skin on the side of her arm.

Room temperature. And she had no smell at all.

None.

He had been in rooms after murder victims were taken away and the smell of death always remained.

No smell of life or death with this woman.

He stood and stepped back toward the apartment door as Donna came in. She was wearing white shorts that fit like a glove, a brown tank top, and tennis shoes. She had short brown hair and wide brown eyes and when smiling, she could light up a room.

She was divorced, thirty, and an expert on computers, high-speed driving, and weapons. So far he had only needed her for the computers, thankfully.

"You would think blue lady there would smell," Donna said. "And I don't see any blood anywhere."

"More than likely it would have been blue," Pilgrim said.

"Are we going down that blue road?" she asked.

"Not until the men in blue get here," he said.

She moaned and turned for the hallway. "I'm calling a blue moratorium on bad jokes until we get this solved."

"Deal," he said.

Over her shoulder she said, "I'm going back to the limo

to do some research on how skin can become that shade and exactly who this woman used to be."

"The police will want the letter," he said.

"Already have it in a bag," she said without looking back.

He shook his head and went back to staring at the redhead with the blue skin resting peacefully on the floor.

The letter writer had been correct. It was a crime for someone so beautiful and young to be dead, no matter how it happened.

TWO

Pilgrim Hugh heard the police before he saw them as they thundered up the stairs and then along the hallway toward the apartment door. This apartment was on the second floor and since there was a park across the street, the only things that could look in the windows were the birds in the far trees.

Since Donna had told the police there was a body, more than likely the first to arrive would be the closest patrol officers to secure the scene. The detectives would follow in their own sweet time.

"Sir," a policeman said, "please turn around."

Pilgrim did as he was told, arms away from his body. Then he smiled.

"Officer Daniels," he said. "Great seeing you again."

Daniels had been the officer on scene on a number of Pilgrim's strange cases over the years. He looked like the perfect image of a college quarterback, with strong shoulders, dark hair, a jutting chin, and a wide smile. He and Carrie had flirted a great deal at times, but as far as Pilgrim knew, nothing had come of it.

"Mr. Hugh," Daniels said, smiling and stepping forward and shaking Pilgrim's hand.

"Wow, a blue woman," the other officer said from beside Daniels.

"Yeah, real blue," Daniels said, looking past Pilgrim at the body. "And she was a looker before she got the dye job."

"Dye job?" Pilgrim asked. "Something I'm missing these days in the newest trend."

"Don't get me started," the other officer said, moving back into the hallway to stand beside the door.

"Some kids have moved past tattoos into full-body dye jobs," Daniels said, shaking his head. "The green ones are just flat disgusting and some of the dyes glow in the dark. Damn creepy if you ask me."

"You're kidding?" Pilgrim had no idea how he had missed this recent fad. He really needed to get out of that office at the top of the building a little more. It didn't help that his apartment was the penthouse above his office.

Daniels just shook his head. "Wish I was."

Pilgrim handed Daniels the key to the apartment. "This was sent to me with a note. Donna has the note and the envelope in the limo outside when the detectives want it. That's where I'll be waiting as well."

"Carrie not with you today?" Daniels asked.

"Working back at the firm," Hugh said. "But if you haven't met Donna yet, you'll love her."

"Looking forward to it," Daniels said, smiling.

Pilgrim took one last look at the blue woman and headed out.

Puzzling, yes.

Crime, maybe.

Solution, nothing yet.

THREE

"The blue woman used to be the renter of record on the apartment," Donna said as Pilgrim Hugh climbed into the limo.

This stretch limo was far more than just a nice ride around town. It had state of the art computer stations that folded down into hidden compartments and many other features.

The cool air in the limo felt good after the short walk from the front of the apartment building through the hot July afternoon. Donna handed him a bottle of cold water from the fridge near her station in the center of the limo compartment and then went back to her screens.

Pilgrim took a drink as he got into his seat and punched a button so that his computer station would come up and wrap around him.

"Incoming," Donna said.

She had sent him the image of the redheaded woman. The photo was a glamour shot with her standing with a white dress in a snowstorm of something white. Even with the images slightly blurred from the art work, it was clearly the blue woman.

"Her name is Deirdre Blue," Donna said. "But it seems she went by the first name of Deep and I am not kidding about the last name. Both parents dead, no siblings."

"Deep Blue?" he asked, staring at his screen.

"Deep Blue," Donna said. "And I'm sticking to the moratorium on the jokes."

"Think that name might be a reason she ended up the way she did?" he asked.

Donna laughed. "Wouldn't bet against it."

Pilgrim had his computer screens up and Donna was giving him all the data she had found about Deep Blue. She had worked at a downtown clothing store until a month ago, and also as a professional clothing model. She had been twenty-six and single, and had a degree in design and business. Not a dumb woman by any means and clearly successful in a hard field.

"So what happened a month ago at her job?" he asked.

Donna shook her head. "I hacked into the store employment records to save time and it only shows that she quit with standard notice. No reason given."

Pilgrim ignored the hacked part and nodded. Clearly Deep had no criminal record, had worked as a model at times and at the clothing store and had lived in a small studio apartment. It all seemed so standard.

He dug deeper into the records for the apartment and found that she had given notice at the first of the month and moved out, paying for a professional cleaning service to clean everything and give all her furnishings to charities. The apartment was still paid for until the end of the month.

"What the hell was this woman planning?" Donna

asked, staring at her screen. "Quit her job, gave up her apartment, and then dyed herself blue to match her name."

"I'm not sure she did that to herself," Pilgrim said. "And I want to figure out who would kill her and then take her back to her own apartment, one that she had already moved out of. And then why write us to find her?"

Donna looked over at him. "It's the writing us that is the key to all this."

"You're right," he said. "Who and why?" That was the part that made no sense to him at all.

"The package came priority mail," Donna said. "At least a full day, maybe two. She would have had a pretty ripe odor after two days on that floor."

Pilgrim knew exactly what Donna was thinking.

"Any cameras around this building on the street or the alley behind the building near the garbage bins?"

Donna's fingers were flying over the keys of her computer. After a moment, images of traffic cams started appearing on his screen.

"I figured the person who staged her would make sure we got the mail first," Donna said, "then stage her right ahead of us getting there, so I'm checking traffic cams from an hour or so ago going backward in time."

"Doing that would show a respect for Deep," he said. "Not that she was killed."

Donna glanced at him and nodded, then turned back to her screens.

"I got another idea as well," he said. "How much you want to bet this person is still watching in some fashion?"

"No bet in a blue moon," Donna said.

He shook his head.

"Sorry," she said. "Slipped out."

"Can you scan that building around the apartment for any stray signals. I didn't see any hidden cams in that apartment, but doesn't mean they aren't there."

As Donna's fingers sort of danced a happy dance on her computer keyboard, he started through the videos. It didn't take him long since Donna had narrowed the choices down so much. A mortuary van had turned onto the street where the three-story apartment building was situated just thirty minutes before they got here.

Stanton Mortuary.

Deep Blue had been embalmed and the marks covered. No wonder her skin felt room temperature.

He suddenly knew that even though the body didn't smell, he was getting a distinct odor of fish in all this.

He quickly hacked into the Stanton Mortuary files to find the records of a Deep Blue who died five days ago from a massive brain tumor. She had spent most of the last month in hospice care. Her service had been yesterday.

As he looked quickly through the photos of family and friends, he ran across one photo of five girls in college. And with one look at the photo, he knew exactly what had happened.

"Got it," Donna said. "Camera signal from the apartment to a nearby source."

He pointed to the hidden computer area that Carrie used when with them. "Check her computer and I think you'll find the signal."

Donna looked really puzzled, but did as he suggested

and ten seconds later Donna nodded. "The signal is being transferred from here. But how, these systems are guarded better than any system I have ever seen. I know, I set up most of the walls."

"Break into the signal and tell Carrie we solved it."

"Of course," Donna said, smiling.

He glanced at the clock on his computer screen. "Tell her it only took twenty-one minutes. Tell her to send in the mortuary van again to pick up Deep. And ask her how her dates with Officer Daniels have gone."

Donna just frowned at the date part, but did as she was told.

Pilgrim clicked off his computer and let it retract back into its hiding spot, then sat back with his cold bottle of water and waited.

It took exactly fifty seconds for a knock to come to the side door of the limo.

"Get the chief a cold bottle of water," he said to Donna, who opened the door for the chief to climb in and then handed him a bottle of water from the fridge.

"Man, that was fast," Chief Craig said as he sat across from Pilgrim with a sigh. The chief was a thin man, who seemed to dominate every room he was in with his combination stern look and smile. He had worked up through the ranks and was a popular chief, both with his officers and with the city government, a hard trick to pull off.

"How did Carrie get you to allow this stunt?" Pilgrim asked as Donna let her computer screens vanish back into their home so she could turn and join the conversation.

"It wasn't Carrie," the chief said. "Carrie just helped. I

was friends of the family with the Blues and before they died, I promised them I would watch over Deep."

"But then she got the inoperable brain tumor," Pilgrim said.

The chief nodded, clearly sad. "She had heard so much about you from Carrie at their girls' nights out, that she wanted to use her death to test you, for the fun of it. Sort of a last request."

"You tried to talk her out of it, I presume," Donna said.

"We all did," the chief said, laughing. "Deep was really strong-willed when she wanted to be, even right down to the end."

"And beyond, it seems," Pilgrim said. "But I have a hunch there was more to this than just a last wish."

The chief laughed and then nodded. "Deep had a lot of money from insurance after her parents died. She wanted it to go to good causes, but couldn't decide which cause to give it to or how to divide it up."

"You're kidding me," Donna said. "Us solving this will result in some charities getting money and others not so much."

The chief nodded. "All the charities get some," the chief said, "including a few police funds, but with you solving it in twenty-one minutes, the large share goes to a fund to help the fisheries on the Columbia."

Pilgrim was just shaking his head. Only his best friend Carrie could have come up with such a strange test. But he had to admit, it had kept him entertained for a bit.

"We were going to pull the plug at one hour," the chief said.

"Did Carrie say it would never take us that long," Donna asked.

"Actually," the chief said, "she wasn't sure."

"How much money is the top charity getting?" Pilgrim asked.

"Quarter of a million."

"And how many charities were standing to gain from this?"

"Five total."

Pilgrim smiled. "I'll toss in enough so that all the charities get the same quarter million, as long as it all comes in under Deep Blue's name."

"I'm sure Carrie can make that happen," Chief Craig said. "And thanks."

"Thank you for honoring the tragic death of a young woman by following her wishes," Pilgrim said, "even as strange as they were."

The chief nodded. "I just wish you two had taken another ten minutes."

Pilgrim laughed.

"Why?" Donna asked.

"I had thirty-one minutes in the office pool."

"Who had twenty-one minutes?" Donna asked.

"Let me guess," Pilgrim said. "Daniels."

"Got it in one," the chief said, laughing. He handed Donna back his empty water bottle.

"Thanks again for the donations. Very kind of you. Now I got to go make sure Deep gets back to where she needs to go to be cremated."

The chief started to climb out into the warm air. Then

he turned back and said, "Thanks also for keeping the blue jokes under control. The Blue family were really nice people and Deep was a wonderful woman. All gone far too soon."

He left and closed the door.

Donna took a long drink of cold water, then asked, "Back to the office, Boss?"

"Let's go get some lunch first and let Carrie wonder for a while how we reacted to all this," Pilgrim said, smiling. "Your choice."

She nodded and climbed out to move up to the driver's seat. He had a hunch he knew exactly where they would be eating. The Blue Diamond Grill. It was close and had great sandwiches.

He was right about that, but surprised when Donna ordered the Blue Plate Special and they actually had one. Who knew?

THE LADY OF WHISPERING VALLEY

A BUCKEY THE SPACE PIRATE STORY

DEAN WESLEY SMITH

ONE

"Why is it that I don't see you in your space pirate costume anymore?" Fred asked, his voice filling the air around me but seeming to come from no one location.

I tried to ignore him and focus on my textbook for advanced economics for a final I had coming in a week.

Fred was my talking oak tree friend. I had planted him in my mother's backyard a number of years back as an acorn. He now stood almost twenty feet tall. I spent a lot of time studying in a lawn chair under his shade in the summer, considering I was in my last year of college to get a degree in business with a combined major in horticulture. Having a talking oak tree for a best friend could get a person interested in growing trees and other plants.

I knew it was kind of sad that a talking oak tree, who had a fondness for limericks, was my best friend, but it was true.

Pathetic, but true.

Fred could not only talk, but like all oak trees, he could travel through time to where other oak trees were in the past. And if I was holding onto him, he could take me along as well, a trick that had come in fantastically helpful for a couple history classes I had been taking.

Six months earlier, he had taken me into the past and introduced me to a wonderful woman my age named Mary that he talked to as well. She lived in 1871 outside of Boise, Idaho.

We had fallen for each other instantly, as Fred knew we would.

Mary was my age of twenty-five and had been widowed three years earlier. She lived alone in a cabin surrounded by oak trees. She had wonderful brown hair that mostly she kept pulled back and large brown eyes. I was five-ten and she was five-five and we made the perfect couple, or at least Fred told us we did. I tended to agree with him on that point.

I spent a lot of time in her cabin with her. She was the love of my life, even though as far as I was concerned, she had been dead for almost a hundred and fifty years.

We were working on that problem, or we both wanted to, but mostly we just didn't talk about it. Living a few miles apart or a city apart might have been something we could fix, but living over a hundred and forty years apart seemed to be far too much.

So we just enjoyed the time we had together, thanks to Fred, and ignored the big problem.

Besides meeting and falling in love with Mary, what was nice about Fred being able to take me there was that he could bring me back to within seconds of when I left, even though I had spent a week or more with Mary. That kept me from missing too many things in this time.

And he could return me after a week in my time to within an hour of the last time I left Mary.

"Well?" Fred asked, not letting go of his question even though I ignored him the first time. "Why don't you dress like a pirate anymore?"

I closed the book and sighed. "Honestly, I dressed in my Buckey the Space Pirate costume to go to science fiction conventions to meet girls."

I had to admit, it was a good costume. Tights tucked into tall black boots, a long coat with brass buttons, a wide belt with a sword hanging from it at a suggestive angle, and a wide-brimmed hat with a big feather.

Girls loved it.

"I have gotten a little old for that now," I said to Fred, "and besides, if you have forgotten, I have a girlfriend now."

"Oh, yes, I do remember our first meeting with you in your costume," Fred said. "Something about a punt and a runt and..."

"Don't even go there," I said, remembering that date I had with a wonderful woman with a body that would never end. She and I ended up down in the park under Fred, before he was cut down and before I saved him by planting him in my mother's backyard.

Fred had decided, right at the wrong moment, as my

date and I had a meeting of the bodies, to spout some limerick about the size of a certain part of her body.

She had thought it me insulting her and had never talked to me again.

Considering what Fred had said about her body part in that limerick, I didn't blame her in the slightest.

"As I said," trying to get him from talking about that night, "I have a girlfriend now."

"Well," Fred said, "not actually now in the literal sense of the word, but I understand your meaning."

"Thank you," I said. "I sure wish Mary could spend time here with me. It would make things so much easier."

"She can," Fred said.

With that, I damn near fell off my lawn chair.

TWO

After I regained my balance, I looked up into the leaves of the little oak tree. "Why didn't you tell us?"

"Neither of you asked," Fred said. "You seemed very comfortable in the situation in Mary's cabin."

"How?" I asked. "How can she come here?"

"The same way you return to her time," Fred said. "If she was here she would need to stay over oak roots or under oak limbs to remain. Same rules you follow in the past."

"Would you mind bringing her here?"

I thought I could hear him laugh slightly. Fred often laughed at me. After standing around and thinking for hundreds of thousands of years, it seemed oak trees had a superiority complex.

A moment later Mary was standing with her hand against the young oak tree, looking around.

I again damn near tipped over my lawn chair again as I rushed to stand up and hug her.

"Do not move too far," Fred said. "My young roots have not expanded out to even a respectable length yet."

Mary felt wonderful in my arms.

She had on her riding jeans and a light blouse and a wide-brimmed hat. More than likely Fred had suggested she prepare for a warm summer day.

After I kissed her, she looked around, smiling. "So this is where the young Fred of your time resides."

"This and in every other oak tree on the planet," Fred said, sounding a little indignant. He did that a lot.

Mary laughed and kept staring at her surroundings.

I glanced around at my mother's backyard, seeing it for the first time in a while. The yard had a chain-link fence around it and a small shed to hold the lawnmower to one side, but otherwise it was just a patch of mowed grass with a small and snide oak tree growing to one side.

And Mom's house looked like any other house along the street from the back, with a small covered back porch and a couple chairs on it.

I just hoped Mom didn't take this moment to look out the window. If she did, I was going to have some explaining to do.

I pointed out to Mary what few landmarks there were in the backyard and then said to Fred, "Could you jump us downtown near where you and I met? The street there is lined with oak and Mary can get an idea of what the modern world is really like."

"That is a splendid idea," Fred said.

A moment later Mary and I were standing under a massive old oak in a large park in the center of the city.

Traffic sped past on the two-lane road that bordered the park and some thirty- and forty-story buildings towered nearby.

She took my hand and grasped it tightly. I couldn't even begin to imagine what she was feeling.

"Oh, my," Mary said, staring first at the cars and then at the tall modern buildings, "the future is a wonder-filled place."

"That it is," I said.

After a moment, she turned to face me, a look of worry in her eyes. "What do you see in a simple woman from the past like me?"

For some reason I had my wits about me at that moment. "I would love you no matter what time you came from. But do you love me because I live in this madhouse of a time?"

"Of course," she said, kissing me. Her smile when she pulled away could light up a room.

And I think I was smiling just as large and wide.

Suddenly, being born almost a hundred and fifty years apart from the woman you loved didn't seem like such an insurmountable problem.

THREE

After walking along the park for a ways, staying under the large oaks, I finally turned to Mary. "I love you. If you are willing, I would much like to start talking about how we solve this living situation we find ourselves in."

"Why Mr. Buckey Pirate sir," she said, smiling at me. "Are you asking me to live in sin with you?"

"I am, my fair lady," I said, bowing slightly and pretending to tip my hat. "And a wonderful sin it will be."

"Then how can I refuse such a sordid offer," she said, smiling, "if we can figure out how to work out this confusion of two worlds."

"I may have a few suggestions on the living aspects," Fred said, his voice almost echoing under the large oaks. "Not in the matter of the sin aspect. However, if needed, I have watched many thousands of human couples in copulation over the centuries and I am sure that..."

"Fred," I said, holding up my hand. "Thank you."

Mary was blushing and laughing.

"Could we go to Mary's cabin and the three of us have a discussion?" I asked.

Mary nodded. "Yes, please."

A moment later we were standing inside Mary's wonderful log cabin tucked into a stand of oaks in 1871 in a narrow valley outside of Boise, Idaho. The valley was called *Whispering Valley* for a reason I had not yet asked Mary about.

I really loved this place with its wonderful river-stone

fireplace and large overstuffed furniture, including a couch that could lull anyone into a nap.

And Mary had a featherbed in her bedroom like nothing I could have ever imagined sleeping on. Why modern mattresses had gone to firm and hard was beyond me. Mary's featherbed just almost wrapped around me and cradled me to sleep.

Of course, having Mary beside me didn't hurt that feeling of contentment.

When we arrived, the large main room of the cabin smelled of fresh bread and light wood smoke, a combined smell that I knew I could never get tired of.

Mary made us both a cup of tea from the hot water she had left on the wood-burning stove before she left to visit me. I actually, in her time, had only left her about three hours before. But in my time I had attended a few classes, spent a night in my apartment studying, and taken one test.

We sat at her kitchen table, facing each other. I told her what I had done over the last day since I had left earlier this morning.

She nodded and said, "I can now, after this short excursion into your time, finally start to visualize some of what you talk about. I hope to learn much more about your time."

"I hope you can live there with me as well, as I live here with you," I said. "Fred, is that possible?"

"Very much so," Fred said, his deep voice filling the kitchen and living area as it always did.

"I worry," Mary said. "Are we not to become a burden

on you with our constant requests to move back and forth through time?"

I nodded. I worried the same thing.

Fred chuckled. "I have lived for hundreds of thousands of years. My species, which will include me, will live for a hundred thousand years into the future. I will far outlive you both and will treasure our short time together and write limericks about you both for many to enjoy into the future."

I laughed. "So that means you won't mind?"

"It will find it no bother at all," Fred said.

Mary looked at me and smiled. Then she said to Fred, "If I haven't said this lately, I would like to say this again. Thank you for introducing me to this fine man."

"You are more than welcome," Fred said.

I could almost imagine Fred bowing to Mary. If an oak tree outside of a Disney cartoon could bow.

"So what is your suggestion?" I asked Fred.

"You must learn to think as a person unstuck in time," Fred said. "I know humans have no sense of time and very little memory. So this thinking will be a strain, but I can help."

Mary frowned. She had no idea what he was talking about either.

"Would you try that idea again with a few fewer insults to humanity and a few more concrete ideas?" I asked.

"Create your home here, in this valley, to live in at any point in time," Fred said.

Suddenly I realized what Fred was driving at in his usual Fred fashion.

"Do you own this home?" I asked Mary.

She nodded. "And the one hundred and eighty acres around it as well going up the valley and on both sides of the valley. My husband's father homesteaded it and passed it on to his son and I got the land and the home when he died."

I could see in Mary's eyes that she was starting to understand as well.

"You will need to plant a lot of oak trees all over this land in the coming years," I said to her.

She smiled. "That will be my pleasure."

"And mine as well," Fred said.

"And I need to do some research on how to pass this land down in trust," I said. "So that I will inherit it at the age of 25."

"That sounds like a very logical solution," Fred said.

I could hear in Fred's voice the sound of almost pity at the poor stupid humans. And it dawned on me why.

"Of course, in my time," I said, "Mary has already set up the trust and the land is about to transfer to my name. Is that correct?"

Fred chuckled. A condescending chuckle, but I'll take it.

"Can we see what we will work so hard in this time to accomplish in a future time?" Mary asked.

"Of course," Fred said.

A moment later we were standing near the remains of her old cabin, long since crumbled to a pile of rotted logs. I could see the stones of the fireplace to one side. Weeds covered the remains.

"Now that makes me sad," Mary said.

"We can build brand new," I said.

She nodded and turned to look around.

A forest of tall, strong oak seemed to spread over the landscape and down a shallow hill and around a stream.

As far as they could see under the canopy of oak, the land remained clear and empty.

"You left forty acres unplanted down on the lower side to sell off to get money to build a dream home here," Fred said.

"Wow," Mary said, looking around. "I planted all of these? This is wonderfully beautiful."

"You both will plant these," Fred said, his voice echoing again in the shady, cool area of the old oaks.

"How will I be able to move beyond the roots of leaves of an already planted tree?" I asked.

"Look to your right about ten steps," Fred said.

We followed his instructions, but all we could see were acorns littering the ground.

I picked one up. "Is this what you are talking about?"

"It is," Fred said. "You hold in your hand the essence of the beginning of life of my species."

I couldn't believe what I was thinking.

"Are you telling me that if I carry around an acorn in Mary's time, and she carries around one in my time, we can go anywhere?"

"Of course you can," Fred said. "As long as you do not remove the acorn from your person outside of the influence of an oak tree's branches or roots. If you do, you will just return to your own time where you left."

I glanced at Mary, who was looking shocked as well.

"Why didn't you tell us?" I asked.

"You did not ask," Fred said. "It is one of the great failings of all humanity, actually, to not ask the right question at the right time. I have watched the results of that for far longer than I care to remember."

"But you can remember thousands of couples copulating," Mary asked, smiling at me.

"That is a very different matter," Fred said. "And fodder for many a limerick, I might add."

"I can only imagine," I said.

"No need to imagine," Fred said. "I would be glad to share as many limericks as you would like to hear about the copulation patterns of your species. For example:

> *"There was a young woman from Spain,*
> *"Whose body seemed quite plain,..."*

"Fred," I said, interrupting him, "I promise to listen to your limericks but right now I think Mary and I need to get busy making sure this wonderful place comes to pass. We have a lot of work and planning to do."

"I agree," Fred said.

"And we need to get on with this planning to live in the sin offer I have been made," Mary said, smiling at me.

I pretended to tip my hat. "That my lady, will be no work at all. Only pleasure."

She kissed me and I kissed her back.

We stood there under the large oaks in the beautiful valley, holding and kissing each other until Fred said simply...

> *There was a young lady named Grace,*

Who loved to be held in embrace.
She hugged and she tugged
But no lover remained
For her lips were on the side of her face.

I'm fairly certain Mary laughed first, even though we both knew that laughing at the oak tree's limericks did nothing but encourage him.

WHY DELAY? JUST RUB
A BRYANT STREET STORY

DEAN WESLEY SMITH

J ack had finally, after a year of promising and far, far too much gentle nagging and reminders from Connie, his wife, agreed to clean out the garage.

The June day was dark and overcast, threatening rain. Not a day he wanted to be on the golf course anyway. And June sports sucked on television.

Really sucked unless you loved baseball.

So cleaning out the ten years of accumulation and dirt and dust in the large two-car garage finally hit the top of the priority list just because there was nothing better to do.

Nothing.

Absolutely nothing.

And it would buy him some husband points in the great game of marriage.

Jack thought of himself as an average man in the scheme of things. He didn't much mind that. He had started his own accounting firm that now had two offices and five accountants working for him. So he was a successful average guy.

He kept himself in moderate shape for forty years old, with only a small gut and a slight balding spot on the top of his head. He mostly kept himself in shape by walking on nice days from his office to lunch and then on the golf course on weekends. Plus Connie was a sensible cook so he didn't overeat.

Jack actually never did much of anything in excess. Excess was just not his style.

He didn't smoke and drank very little and then only socially and on weekends.

And had been married to Connie since college and had never even thought of straying with another woman.

He had the best woman in the world as a partner, why would he?

They had two kids in college now, both staying in their respective schools during the summer to work part-time jobs instead of coming home. Both had promised they would be home for the 4th of July, which had always been a big deal for Jack. He liked the patriotism and the fireworks, although he wouldn't allow his kids to ever have any fireworks. Just too dangerous.

Connie, his wife, still looked stunning at forty. She was thin, with short brown hair and a wide smile that people liked. She was the funny one of the two of them. The one with the sense of humor; the one that people liked to talk to.

She could charm a group of people in minutes.

She went to the gym every day during the week and owned her own clothing store in the local mall that was doing very well. She had been talking with him about opening a second store and he could see no reason why not.

To Jack, Connie was the dream girl of his life, always had been, always would be. He had no idea why she stayed with him, but she seemed to like their quiet life and routine.

Sometimes he worried about that. Worried about her being with him. But only sometimes.

Again, he never did anything to excess, including worry.

When he had finally agreed to clean out the garage, Connie was excited. She had bought extra trashcans for the job and a lot of extra big black trash bags as well. Plus a number of spray cleaners and a box of rags usually used when painting.

Jack was fairly certain that the garage wasn't that dirty or had that much trash in it. But he never complained when Connie over-prepared for anything. It was one of the many things he loved about her.

He opened both doors to the wide driveway. They had a large four-bedroom, three-bath home in a nice subdivision not too far from downtown. He drove a blue SUV and Connie drove a green minivan. Both cars were sitting in their normal parking spaces on the driveway. Neither of their cars had seen the inside of the garage in five years.

Maybe it was past time to do this chore.

The neighborhood looked quiet for a summer Saturday afternoon and the sky had darkened. The air had a calm, muggy feel about it and if he had been a betting man, which he was not, he would bet the predicted rain wasn't far off.

Connie had put on a long white apron over her slacks and white blouse and had slipped on an old pair of running shoes. She pointed to an area beside the garage. "We'll stack the trash there and I'll have it picked up next week."

"A good idea," he said, looking at the piles of stuff for the first time in years with actual natural light on the subject. Where had they gotten all this crap?

More than likely much of it was from the kids.

"We put the stuff still good enough to donate here when we get a spot big enough," Connie said, pointing to a spot near one garage door on her car's side. "I'll have someone come to pick it up next week as well."

"Perfect," he said.

She handed him a pair of work gloves and then pulled on a pair herself.

"This is going to be fun," she said.

That he was convinced would not happen, but it would get done. And that would free up a bunch of time on nice weekends for golf.

They both started on the same pile, mostly pulling items that they both knew were trash and bagging it. And he had been right, most of the trash was from the kids. Leftover parts of their lives that now he and Connie were just bagging and tossing to the curb.

Interesting how that happened with children.

And then, when he and Connie were gone, the kids would come in and toss their lives to the curb. The cycle of things.

After a while, he and Connie had a spot cleared enough to start stacking some items that looked like they could be good enough to donate to a local charity. If it ended up being enough, it would be a nice tax deduction.

If nothing else, he was always the accountant.

Two old kids' bikes started that pile. Then a box of dishes from their first apartment. Opening that box had made them both laugh. The dishes had the worst flower patterns on them that he had ever seen. He had hated those dishes and thought they had vanished a decade ago.

Well, now they would be gone.

Then he found a half-molded old cardboard box and opened it.

Inside was a stack of old pans, some strange metal figures, and an old metal lamp. It looked like it was copper, dented and tarnished, and had the shape of a lamp from India.

"Where did this come from?" he asked, pulling out the lamp and holding it up. It seemed empty and there wasn't a wick in the spout end.

Connie shook her head and came over closer to look. "Not a clue," she said. "More than likely something one of the kids found and brought home for some reason. Maybe as a prop in one of their plays."

He nodded. That made sense. Both his kids had done plays all the way through high school. Costumes and props were always coming home with them.

He was about to toss the beat-up old lamp on the charity pile when some printing on one side caught his eye.

He rubbed off the dirt to see what it said and damned if smoke didn't come from the top of the old lamp, everything froze around him, and a tall guy with some sort of turban on his head appeared out of the smoke. The guy wore big, baggy pants and had on no shirt.

And wow, did he have some muscles.

"Wow, nifty prop," Jack said. "Connie, take a look at this."

When he glanced over, she was frozen in place, a hand reaching for something in the pile, her face smudged with some dirt.

Jack glanced back at the tall guy with his arms crossed like a Mr. Clean commercial standing in his garage.

The guy looked real.

How bad of a cliché was this?

"Connie, nice joke!" Jack said, turning back to her.

She hadn't moved. No one, even in good shape, could hold the position she was in for more than a few seconds.

"Who are you?" Jack asked the big, impossible man standing in his Saturday cleanup project.

The man pointed at the lamp still in Jack's hand.

Jack glanced down at the lamp. On the side the words read, "Rub me once for the Genie to appear, rub me twice to get a wish."

Jack quickly set the lamp down and went over to Connie. She was still in the same position.

He moved her arm in closer to her body. He could move her just fine, so he went into the kitchen, got a chair and brought it out and worked her around until she was sitting down.

The guy was still standing in the garage, his arms crossed over his bare chest.

Jack went back inside and tried to call the police, but all the lines were dead. Nothing at all was working.

Everything was frozen.

He went back out to the guy and just stared at the hunk of man.

He flat didn't believe the guy was a genie, but he was going to play along with the gag until someone started laughing.

"Can you talk to me, answer questions?"

The man did not move. He just kept staring straight ahead like there was something real important on the garage wall.

Connie kept sitting on the chair. She hadn't moved at all.

Jack went out to look up and down the street and that was when he saw a few raindrops just hanging in the air.

Time had really stopped around this guy.

Oh, shit!

How was this possible?

Genies in lamps didn't exist in American suburbia. They existed in old fairytales and kids' books.

Jack reached up and touched one drop of water with a finger. It didn't move.

And nothing was supporting it.

"Shit! Shit! Shit!"

Jack seldom swore, even on the golf course, but he figured this time if any was appropriate.

He moved back around the big man with the cloth on his head and carefully picked up the lamp.

Nothing had changed.

And there was no writing on the other side or on the bottom of the old thing.

He set the lamp down carefully on the concrete garage

floor and went back into the house to get a glass of water and try to think.

Of course, the water wouldn't come out of the tap and he couldn't get the fridge open.

He was going to have to rub that stupid lamp to get this to end.

But none of this could be happening. Magic wasn't real. This had to be an illusion of some sort.

But if it was real, what should he wish for? He had seen enough bad movies and bad cartoons to know that wishes from genies never turned out as well as hoped.

He sat down at the kitchen table and looked around the house. What would he wish for? He had a beautiful wife he loved, a great home, enough money.

And if he said he wished for nothing, that might be how he ended up.

So he had to be careful. If this was real, which it seemed to be, he needed to ask for something innocent.

But what?

What did he really want?

He could ask for a better golf game, but he wouldn't feel right about that because the fun of golf was in the chase, not just suddenly, magically being better.

He flat couldn't think of anything.

He stood and went back out into the large garage.

Connie was still sitting in the position he had left her. She looked even more beautiful than before, even with the smudge on her cheek.

He had no idea why she stayed with him.

And then he realized that question had been bothering

him for a long, long time. They had a comfortable relationship, based on family and familiarity and habit.

Was he nothing more than a habit to her?

He finally had the chance to know.

He picked up the lamp, then carefully thought through his question and rubbed the lamp solidly.

The genie's large dark eyes focused on Jack.

"Your wish?"

"I do not understand why Connie, my wife, has stayed with me for all these years. I would like to know if she has ever had an affair with another man or woman while we have been married?"

"No," the genie said. "She has not."

Then the genie laughed, a sound that Jack was certain might break a few windows if it got louder.

As smoke started to come from the lamp and swirl around the genie, the big man shook his head. "You two really need to get a life. And that's coming from a guy who lives in an old lamp."

"Why?" Jack asked.

The genie shook his head. "She asked the exact same thing about you."

"She did?"

The genie laughed again. "She doesn't understand why you have stayed with her all these years either. Try talking more, would you?"

Then he was gone.

And so was the memory of the genie being there.

Outside the garage door, the rain was just starting to fall.

"What am I doing sitting down?" Connie asked, looking around.

Jack had no idea. He just tossed the lamp into the charity pile and went to her.

"I ever tell you how beautiful you are?" he said as she sat there, looking very stunned.

She laughed and stood. "Nice try, mister. How did I get sitting there on one of our good kitchen chairs?"

"Don't ask me why you are lounging around," he said. "I've been sorting through junk."

He kissed her and turned back to the shrinking pile. It would be nice to get his car back in here again. He had to admit that.

And besides, on a rainy summer afternoon, what better thing was there to do than spend the day with the love of his life, no matter what he was doing.

A big, booming voice inside Jack's head said, *"Now that's better."*

Then Jack thought he heard a laugh, but it was actually only thunder in the distance.

WILL YOU STILL LOVE ME IN FIVE MINUTES?
A MARBLE GRANT STORY

DEAN WESLEY SMITH

W hen you are a ghost and hopping from one person's head to another, you really see and hear some weird stuff. My partner, lover, and best friend, Sims, and I roam all over Las Vegas being voyeurs of people's deepest thoughts and emotions.

It is our job as ghost agents.

We do it to help people and find bad people. Sometimes it is hard to tell the difference at first pass. Every person I have ever dipped inside as a ghost agent has bad thoughts, usually buried deep, but would never ever act on them.

And at times we run into someone who does bad things just as a matter of course, so to them, everything they do is normal. And that's really hard to spot at a quick glance as well.

But the psychopaths are the worst. They lie so much and so regularly, that when you dip into their thinking, to them what they are saying is the truth. And they completely believe it.

Combine that with narcissism and there is just no way of telling what is happening in that person's head because a truth to them just changes without even realizing they are changing it. Thankfully, those people are few and far between.

But they do end up in Las Vegas. The town seems to attract them.

To my understanding of how it works, two narcissistic psychopaths could really never work together. Sort of against both of their pathologies since both must be in charge.

But one fine warm Monday afternoon, as Sims and I were walking the brightly colored Wynn casino, we ran into two.

Together.

And about to be married.

How we even spotted the two out of the crowd was their auras. Both were dark and close to their bodies. Not black magic kind of dark, just lack of colors.

On both of them.

That means they had little emotions and didn't care about anything outside of themselves, thus why the auras had sucked in tight to their bodies.

Sims and I were both in our working clothes as we called it. Since no one but superheroes and other ghosts could see us, we dressed comfortably in running shoes, jeans, and silk blouses. Today my hair color was an off blue, almost turquoise, while Sims' hair was her normal long blond that she kept pulled back while we worked.

The two narcissistic psychopaths we noticed with the weird auras were clearly being treated by the casino as high rollers. Both were dressed in silk, expensive shoes, and jewelry and watches that looked like they could buy a dozen houses.

They were what a newspaper would call "beautiful people," although I didn't find either one of them attractive.

He was walking with her on his arm like she was a trophy wife and she was walking as if she had caught the best fish in the husband pond. And she had a diamond ring on her finger that was so large, if it fell off it would put a dent in the carpet.

They had the images down perfectly.

A hotel employee walked behind them a decent distance, clearly to see to their needs like a dog owner picking up his dog's poop.

"So you want to see what that's all about?" I asked Sims as they strode past us.

"Oh, heavens yes," Sims said. "I get the woman first, then we can trade."

We ran quickly down the hall and sank into them. The moment I got inside the guy's mind, I was shocked, but not really surprised.

He was dead broke.

In fact, worse than broke. He had borrowed money from a loan shark in Chicago to get to Vegas in order to meet a rich woman and marry her. He believed it was his god-given right to be rich and the woman named Stephanie on his arm would be his way to do it.

At some point, when the sex got dull, he planned on

killing her and taking all her money. But he would figure that out later. Right now the sex and her money was worth putting up with her for a time, even though he really didn't like her that much. She didn't pay him enough attention and was too focused on herself.

He needed to make sure that she never discovered the ring was a theater prop. If she did, he figured he would just claim that he had been taken. Maybe get some sympathy sex in the process.

I backed out of the guy and walked behind them until Sims left the woman.

"Well?" I asked as we walked along behind them.

"She's dead broke," Sims said. "Borrowed money to get the outfit she's wearing and needs to keep up the sham that she has money until they get married later today."

I just broke out laughing and Sims looked at me for a moment, then started to smile.

"Don't tell me he's broke as well?"

I nodded. "Pulling the same scam on her. He's even in nasty debt with some loan sharks in Chicago and the ring is a theater prop. Rolex is fake."

"Jewelry is all costume," Jewel said. "And she can't even afford them."

Sims and I both broke into choking laughter. Two narcissistic psychopaths trying to scam each other.

It didn't get any better than this.

Finally I managed to take a deep breath and ask Sims, "Does she like him?"

"Not really," Sims said.

"Let me guess," I said. "She's staying with him for the

sex and the money and plans to kill him when the sex gets dull."

"Exactly," Sims said, shaking her head and laughing.

"So we need to figure out how to make sure these two don't kill each other once they learn the truth."

Sims nodded and I looked up and said, "Jewel, a little advice."

A moment later Jewel appeared next to us in the high-ceilinged hallway of the Wynn shops where our two broke pretenders were window shopping.

Jewel was the ghost agent who had trained us and before she had been killed, she was an actual doctor.

"We got two narcissistic psychopaths together," I said to Jewel as Sims pointed the two out.

"Oh, my, those auras are something, aren't they?" Jewel said. "Not a thought for another person."

"Exactly," Sims said.

"But our problem is that both are dead broke and pretending to be super rich to marry the other one for the money."

"They are getting married here in the casino's chapel in one hour," Sims said.

"Oh, how funny," Jewel said, shaking her head.

"So we know we can't change the nature of their pathologies," Sims said. "So any suggestion on how to keep them from killing each other when they discover the truth?"

Jewel just smiled. "Let's make them love each other. I am assuming right now they don't."

"They don't," I said, and then I started laughing. The idea was just perfect. It would cause two narcissists to actually care about someone else to make themselves happy.

"So let's go make them fall completely in love with the other person when they say their I dos," Jewel said. "I'll go in with you both in each one to make sure we get it planted so deeply it will never wear off."

Sims looked at Jewel and then me. "Are we creating a monster? Two narcissistic psychopaths in love and working as a team? These types are bad enough when working alone."

"Oh, real good point," Jewel said. "Let's make them love each other completely and never want anything to happen to the other, but they think the other is dumb as a rock and only their own ideas are worth anything."

Once again I was laughing. Doing that would make sure that they never worked together on anything, but stayed together fighting and loving for the rest of their lives. That would consume all of their attention.

Perfect.

With the three of us working inside Stephanie's head, we planted all the new controls solidly deep down. Just like she would always be a narcissistic psychopath, she would always love her husband and think every idea he had was stupid.

We finished up with him just as they got to the wedding chapel. We then stood in the back, watching.

The hotel had made the chapel look beautiful and the manager told them that the hotel was treating them to a five-course meal right afterwards.

Even though the ceremony was in a really top-scale hotel and in a beautiful room, it felt quick and sort of cheap. But the change to the two getting married was startling. The moment they said "I do" the look in their eyes shifted toward the other one.

And the kiss went on so long, the poor hotel manager turned red.

"They thought the sex was good before," Sims said, smiling. "Add love into it and it will get better."

The next day Sims and I went back to see how they were doing and found them holding hands across a cloth tablecloth in one of the hotel restaurants.

I went into Stephanie while Sims ducked into her husband.

Stephanie was surprised at how much she had fallen for her now husband, how much she loved him, and she was worried about how she was going to tell him she had been lying to him about having money.

She loved him so much she was worried he was going to hate her.

I planted a deep suggestion that no matter what he said, she would still love him forever, just to back up what we had done yesterday.

Then I left and Sims appeared just a moment later from the guy. I told her what Stephanie was worried about and what I had done and Sims said the husband was feeling the same way. And he was worried about how they were going to pay for the hotel room since all the expenses were on his card and he had gotten notice this morning that it was being shut off.

"Let's go back into both of them and plant the need to tell the other person their secret right here at lunch?"

"Great idea," Sims said, laughing. "And then we can watch how they figure out together how to get out of the mess they are in here without actually working together."

So I went back inside Stephanie and planted the suggestion and then got out and stood back as Sims did the same for the husband.

Fifteen minutes later they both knew the other person was dead broke and they couldn't even pay for the hotel and this lunch.

So Stephanie had an idea and husband told her it was stupid and he had an idea and she told him it was stupid.

And they were both not happy.

So in disgust, he just signed the lunch check to their room, offered his hand, and said simply, "Big bed."

She took his hand. "Is that all men think about is sex?"

"Yes," he said, smiling as she stood.

"That's a really stupid idea considering the problems we have," she said.

"I know," he said, smiling as they walked off, arm-in-arm and clearly in love.

I looked at Sims who was watching them wide-eyed. Then she turned to me.

"Did we end up creating a monster after all?"

"Maybe," I said, nodding. "But whatever they come up with, it will be stupid we can be assured of that."

Sims laughed. "And will involve sex."

"More than likely," I said, taking Sims' arm and turning her toward the hallway. "And ain't nothing stupid about that at all."

KRISTINE KATHRYN RUSCH SECTION

KNOWING JACK
A ROZ & JACK STORY
KRISTINE GRAYSON

Roz tugged the darkroom door shut and locked it, slipping the key into the pocket of her long black skirt. The stench dissipated a little, although the studio smelled strongly of chemicals, a scent that never entirely vanished.

She leaned against the door and listened, hearing nothing. Good solid oak blocked the smells and the sound. Fortunately, no one had entered the studio while she had been in the dark room. She wasn't quite ready to handle customers.

The studio was large, given the size of Lattville. The town had decided to rename itself just recently. Most of its signs still read Lateville, so named because many of the miners who had arrived here before the war thought they had missed all the gold.

They hadn't. The actual name of the town should have been Earlyville, since most of those miners were long gone by the time gold had actually been discovered. Lattville grew, thanks to the discovery and the fact that it was a stop on the main stagecoach route that covered Northern California.

Even so, despite Lattville's size, a fair number of people had found their way into this studio. Portraits of the latest governor hung on the wall, alongside one of California's senators, and the former presidential candidate John C. Fremont.

More portraits cluttered the floor behind the main desk, where visitors signed in and paid their bills. A brocade divan sat at one end of the room, a conventional sofa and rocking chair grouping at the other.

The studio was utterly silent and hot. The windows didn't open, making the place oppressive. She made her way through the clutter to the business desk, stopping to look at the family portrait prominently displayed on the wall behind her.

The portrait had been taken outside and the girls had lined up in age order, getting their pretty white dresses stained with grass. Roz ran her fingers across the white painted date, unable to believe that the portrait was ten years old. The vivid expressions on the faces made it seem newer somehow.

Roz glanced at the full-length mirror nearby. The studio provided it so that clients could check their appearance before getting a portrait taken. She almost didn't recognize herself. Age had changed her face, making it narrower, lining it. The carefree look she'd had as a girl was gone now.

Too many years of struggle. Too much hardship.

She tucked a loose strand of brown hair behind her ear. The white blouse already showed the wear of the day and the black skirt had flakes of dirt or dust or something on it. She brushed at the skirt and then straightened, putting a hand behind her back. She hated corsets. They always left her short of breath.

But today she had to look presentable.

At that moment, the studio door opened. She turned.

The men standing in the doorway had clearly not come for a portrait. The tall man had piercing blue eyes and a strength to his face. His boots were muddy and left a trail on the runner just inside the door. The second man was shorter, older, and balding. He looked both official and apologetic.

"Mrs. Driscoll?" he asked, then stepped forward, hands out. "I almost didn't recognize you, my dear. What has it been? Eight years?"

Roz had no idea. She didn't recognize him at all. "At least that."

He took her hands and smiled at her. "How is your husband?"

"He's been busy of late."

The balding man nodded. Behind him, the tall man cleared his throat.

"I'm afraid this isn't a social call, m'dear," the balding man said. "I'm looking for your father."

Roz was prepared for this. She squeezed the balding man's hands. "I'm minding the store today."

"I can see that, but—"

"Let me, sheriff," the tall man said. "This is a matter of some urgency. Where is Mr. Cooper?"

"Dealing with family matters," Roz said. "Can I help you?"

"This isn't a job for a woman," the tall man said.

Roz gave him a small smile. "I've been around photography and portraiture for most of my life. I'm a skilled photographer. If you came here for a portrait, then I can help you."

The sheriff let go of her hands. Color fused his round cheeks. "This really isn't a job for a woman, ma'am. We don't want a portrait of us. We need something else photographed."

"Oh?" She let her voice grow cold. "I've photographed dozens of people. I've even photographed corpses, felons, and miners."

"I never took Peter Driscoll to be a man who would allow his wife to do such things." The sheriff was frowning, as if he wanted to take her husband to task.

"He can't prevent something he doesn't know about," Roz said, and was pleased to see that both men were shocked.

"When will your father return?" the tall man asked.

"I don't know," she said. "Not today, certainly."

"We need a photographer this afternoon," the tall man said.

"Harold," the sheriff said. "Perhaps we can skip it this one time."

Harold. Could she be so lucky? There was only one Harold who insisted on photographs. Roz had never met Harold Adams, but she had heard of him. She hadn't realized that Harold Adams himself would be the security on that coach. If she had known, she would have had more faith in her plan.

Roz threaded her fingers together, pressing them so hard that her knuckles were turning white.

"You've never worked with Wells Fargo before, have you? We need a photographer. A real one." Harold nodded to her. "I'm sorry to have bothered you, ma'am."

"Please," she said. "Let me do the work."

Harold shook his head. "No matter what your husband thinks, this job is not appropriate for a woman."

The sheriff gave her an apologetic—if confused—glance and started out. She took a step after them.

"If you need photographs today," she said, her voice shaking, "I'm all you have."

Harold stopped just outside the door, blocking the light. He glared at the sheriff, who shrugged.

"This is true, then?" Harold asked.

"Look around," the sheriff said. "Did you see another portrait studio?"

"Surely someone else takes photographs here."

"Nope." The sheriff looked apologetic. "But I don't think it matters. They can photograph him in Sacramento—"

"We've waited before," Harold said. "The photograph never gets taken, or they take a photograph of a corpse wearing a white cloth over his face to respect the dead. That does not satisfy my boss."

The sheriff sighed. "You'd think your boss would be satisfied that we caught the bastard."

Harold glanced at Roz, apparently trying to see if the language had offended her. "Ma'am, we have in Lattville's little jail, the man who tried to rob the Wells Fargo stage-coach this morning."

Roz's cheeks flushed. She willed the reaction to vanish. She hoped the men would think that she was nervous, not that she already knew about the robbery. Of course, the entire town probably knew about the robbery by now.

"We need him photographed," Harold was saying. "The Wells Fargo Bank in San Francisco keeps photographs of all the robbers who have been foiled trying to rob Wells Fargo trains and stagecoaches. It's quite a collection, and it is to the point that if we miss even one of these bandits, we—those of us who work security for the company—could get fired."

Roz was breathing shallowly.

"It should be enough that we caught the son of a bitch." The sheriff shook his head slightly as if he thought this was all foolishness. Then he realized what he said and in front of whom, and tipped an imaginary hat to her. "No offense meant, ma'am."

"None taken," she said, even though she was even more uncomfortable than she'd been when they walked in. She had to show them she was up to this task.

"Are you still willing to take the job, ma'am?" the tall man asked. "Wells Fargo pays handsomely for its portraits."

She made herself swallow, a difficult task against her dry throat. "Then by all means," she said, trying to sound nonchalant. "Let's go."

E ven though the jail was three blocks away, it took her nearly a half hour to arrive. She had to load the photographer's wagon, its canvas side emblazoned with *M.C. Cooper and Family, Photographers*. The equipment was heavier than what she was used to, and there wasn't a lot of room in the wagon. It was filled with boxes and had obviously not been used for photography for a long time.

The entire town would probably think she was crazy to take the wagon three blocks, but she needed it.

The mule wasn't used to her, and tried to kick her as she hooked it up to the wagon. She managed, somehow, leaving her skirt muddy and her white blouse heavy with sweat. Damned corset cut into her ribs and she would have given anything for a deep, sweet breath of air.

Then she had to make the drive, which was harder than she had expected. Twice in three blocks, she nearly got stuck in the mud. No one in his right mind would try to rob a stagecoach with the roads as foul as these. Anything carrying weight would get stuck and, the stagecoach driver, knowing that, would probably have extra security or take additional precautions of some sort.

Harold Adams was waiting outside the jail for her when she arrived. He offered to take her equipment in for her, but she stopped him.

"I'd like to see what I'll be photographing first," she said.

"All right." He held open the door for her and she stepped inside.

The main room was small and crowded. The low ceiling made it seem even smaller and the pot-bellied stove in the far corner took up much of the room. A rickety desk stood nearby along with two chairs.

The sheriff sat on one of them, holding a ring of keys. In place of the wall directly behind him were rows of iron bars. It took her eyes a moment to adjust to the dim interior before she saw a slight door framed in the metal.

Sweat ran down her spine, pooling at the bottom of her corset, making it stick to her.

"Nervous, Mrs. Driscoll?" Harold asked. "I thought you'd said you'd done this before."

"Not here," she said. "I'm only visiting Lattville. The jails I've been in have all been larger."

Harold frowned, but said nothing. The sheriff stood. "Where's your equipment?"

"Outside," she said. "I want to see what I'm photographing first."

"Your father will have my hide," he said as he unlocked the main door.

"He just might," she said following the sheriff into the small hallway that opened onto the two tiny cells, "but by then, the deed'll be done."

The first cell was empty. In the second, a man sat on the cot, his handcuffed hands hanging between his knees. Roz's breath caught.

"Ma'am?" the sheriff asked.

"Does he have to be trussed up like that inside his cell?"

"He's a dangerous criminal, ma'am. Wanted in five states. Thought we should take some precautions."

She nodded. She had known that about the prisoner. In

fact, she knew more about him than the men beside her did. Her gaze met his and a familiar flash of longing shot through her. Despite the mud streaking his too-thin face, the mats in his long brown hair, and the anger that flashed through his dark brown eyes, her husband was still the handsomest man she had ever seen.

"You want me to photograph him in here?" she asked.

"Where else would you do it?" the sheriff asked.

"Well, you see," she said, "we have a problem. There're no windows back here and the light is faint. We will not get a good photograph in these conditions."

Harold stood in the iron doorway. "What do you suggest?"

"We could put a half dozen lanterns in the cell and hope for the best."

"This jail's made of wood," Harold said. "That would be highly impractical."

She turned toward him. He shrugged.

"One kick," he said, "and the prisoner might start a fire and escape in the confusion."

Fires were useful in wooden jails. Roz knew that from experience. She tried not to smile at the memory. It was important that she stay in character.

"You're the one who wanted the photograph," she said. "How have you done this in the past?"

He sighed. "Usually we have a window or a better light source. Or a brick jail."

The sheriff glared at Harold.

"So what do you suggest?" she asked.

"You go set up on the sidewalk. We'll bring him outside for just one moment."

She nodded, then looked at Jack who hadn't moved off the cot. His face was red with fury.

"You say he robbed a stagecoach?" she asked.

"I say he attempted to." Harold sounded satisfied.

"But he's wanted in—what? four states?"

"Five," the sheriff said.

"We finally caught him," Harold said.

"You've been waiting for him?" Her voice rose ever so slightly.

Harold nodded. "We knew he'd slip up once. We just didn't expect the slip-up to be literal."

"Literal?" she asked.

"He fell as he tried to unhook the strongbox."

She couldn't resist. She looked at the cell. Jack's nostrils were flaring, his hands clenched with the effort he made to keep silent.

"Honestly, ma'am, I don't think we'd've caught him otherwise. He snuck up on us quiet as a cat and had the guards knocked down and the box nearly off before we even knew what happened."

"My arrest had nothing to do with you people," Jack said. Roz willed him to keep silent. "I'd've been long gone if the coach hadn't got stuck at that moment, and threw me off balance."

"See?" Harold said. "He even admits it."

"Well, do you expect him to do otherwise?" Roz asked. "You caught him red-handed."

She directed that last toward Jack, with just enough of

an I-told-you-so in her voice so that he—and he alone—could catch it.

He looked away.

"Let's get this done before the light fades outside." Harold was showing his familiarity with photography. Having him here had been a stroke of luck. He'd overseen the photographing of nearly a dozen criminals for the San Francisco bank since the war ended.

"All right." She swished her way toward the iron doors, praying that Jack would help her work this scam. He was angry enough at her that he might not participate. They had fought about this robbery and he had done it against her advice.

It had taken all her strength to plan his rescue. She'd started before he'd even gotten caught. In fact, she had told him that was what she would do.

The fact that she had been right made him furious. She could tell. But fury or no, he had to cooperate with her or he might get sent away. They certainly had enough evidence against him this time.

"*She's* going to take my photograph?" Jack asked, and Roz had to use all her acting skills not to sigh with relief. "This is even stupider than it sounded when you first mentioned it."

"You don't get an opinion," the sheriff said.

Roz stepped through the iron doors, nodded at Harold, and paused when she reached the main door. "You think the sidewalk just out front will work or should I set up in the street? I'm muddy enough that it doesn't matter."

Harold walked to the door with her and peered at the

sky. The thin winter sun was halfway down the horizon. He had been right; the light would be gone soon. Her struggle with the mule had taken longer than she thought.

"Guess we'd better use the street."

She nodded and walked to the wagon. She climbed in, grabbed her pistols out of one of the boxes she had put in there that morning, and slipped them into the pockets of her skirt. One of them clanged against the key.

She had forgotten about it. She certainly didn't need it any longer. She fished it out of her pocket and tossed it outside the wagon, hearing the key plunk into the mud.

Now watch the sheriff try to get old man Cooper and his two pruney daughters out of that dark room. Someone would have to knock the door down—once they realized the three of them were inside.

It had been Roz's second stroke of luck that the oldest daughter had come home for the first time in years—and an even greater stroke of luck that the real Mrs. Driscoll was a shrew. The moment she'd seen Roz's gun, she'd started screaming at her father about this backwater town and how she'd hated it and that this was precisely why she had stayed away for so long and never brought her children here. Her father had merely looked at Roz as if wishing she would shoot him then and there.

From the back, Roz unloaded the oldest camera she had found and set it on its tripod in the middle of the street. If her luck continued, she might be able to keep some of the photographic equipment. She hadn't lied about her abilities there. She was a very good photographer, when she got the chance to practice her trade.

As she was adjusting the curtain on the back of the camera, she watched the lens as Harold brought Jack out of the jail. The sheriff followed, carrying a shotgun, but with the muzzle pointed toward the street.

Harold hadn't put Jack in leg irons—maybe the sheriff didn't have any—but Harold did have a Colt pointed at the center of Jack's back.

"Make it fast, Mrs. Driscoll," he said.

"All right." She stood and walked over to them. "Let me position you so that the camera doesn't see you at all."

Harold nodded, clearly having been through this before. She moved him so that his body was as far from Jack's as possible. Harold kept the gun trained on Jack. She pulled Harold a little to the left.

"Hmm," she said. "Maybe this'll work after all."

Then she reached into her pocket and removed both pistols, shoving one against Harold's chin and pointing the other at the sheriff.

They both looked stunned.

"Try something," she said to them, "and Harold won't have a face."

"Tell them to drop the guns, Roz," Jack said.

"I was getting to that," she said, annoyed.

"Roz?" the sheriff asked. "I thought you were Abby Driscoll."

"Your mistake," Roz said, pushing the gun even harder against Harold's chin. "And do drop your weapons. You know how unstable we women are."

Harold dropped his gun. Out of the corner of her eye, Roz saw it fall. Jack crouched, grabbing for it, at the very moment the sheriff fired. The mule brayed nervously, but didn't move. The bullet missed Jack—the third great stroke of luck.

She didn't want to think about it. She'd lose her nerve.

"Now, what did you go and do that for?" Roz cocked the hammer on the gun under Harold's chin. Sweat dripped off his face. "I'm so sorry, Harold, but your friend the sheriff here wants you dead."

"Put the rifle down," Harold said.

Jack was holding Harold's gun in his handcuffed hands. He pointed it at the sheriff.

"Rifle down," Jack said. "I'm not a delicate flower like my wife. I will shoot you."

Lies. Jack had never hurt anyone. He stole, scammed, and charmed, but he never killed.

"And if you kill my husband," Roz said, "this delicate flower will blow Harold's brains all over main street."

The sheriff's rifle clattered onto the wooden sidewalk.

"Now what?" Jack asked softly.

"The wagon, darling," Roz said.

"It's attached to a mule," he said.

"So am I," she said, not looking at him. "Sometimes the arrangement works."

He cursed and sloshed toward the wagon.

"I don't suppose you have keys to his handcuffs," she said to Harold.

"No."

"Well, then," she said, "I'll simply have to shoot them off later."

"Roz!" Jack sounded angry.

She grabbed Harold by the front of his shirt and pulled him toward the wagon. When she reached the wagon, she braced one hand against it.

Jack was sitting on the wagon, reins in one hand and the gun, still pointed at the sheriff, in the other. He was twisted awkwardly because his hands were still bound together at the wrists. "Roz, hurry."

She wasn't about to hurry. If she did this wrong, they were as good as dead.

"I will shoot you, Harold," she said, "but I don't want to today."

With that, she shoved him backwards at the same time she hooked one foot behind his knee and pulled his leg out from under him. The mud, which had given her and Jack trouble all day, finally worked in her favor. Harold landed with a splash.

Roz swung herself onto the board and clucked at the mule—

—who didn't move.

"Told you," Jack said. "There's got to be some good horses nearby."

The sheriff was reaching for his rifle and Roz shot the wall above his head.

The second gunshot scared the mule and it leapt forward with surprising speed. The wagon, balanced better with Jack up front and the camera gone, managed to move with the mule. If they didn't get stuck, they would be home free.

"We don't need the damn wagon," Jack said.

Roz was peering behind them, ready to shoot anyone that followed. "We need to get something out of this godforsaken town."

"They'll find us fast with this thing."

"No, they won't," she said. "I have a plan."

People were pouring into the main street, which was disappearing behind them. Harold was standing and calling for his horse.

"You always have a plan," Jack said.

She couldn't tell if he was making fun of her or not. "If I hadn't had one today, you'd still be in that damn jail. I'm the one that saw that photo gallery in the stupid bank and I'm the one who figured out how to use it. It was easier than I thought. I thought I was going to have to pretend to be a traveling photographer, but thanks to the damn daughter—"

"Roz," Jack said. "I'm grateful."

No one was following them, yet, but the road was getting treacherous. Roz glanced over at him, saw the fondness on his face which was getting even muddier thanks to the gobs of goo being kicked up by the mule.

"Really?" she asked.

"Really," he said. "But we do need to dump the wagon."

She sighed. "I want the equipment."

"Photography equipment is too bulky. I tell you that in every town. It'll mark us—"

"I know," she said. "At the next crossroads, we jump."

"What?" he asked. "That's your plan? Jumping off a moving wagon?"

She nodded, debating whether or not she should tell him

about the fresh horses and buckboard she had actually paid for with the last of their money and had hidden that morning before she had come to rescue him.

Then she decided against telling him. He'd have to trust her.

"I don't like your plan," he said.

"You didn't like my plan yesterday either, so you didn't listen and look where it got us."

He was silent for a moment. Then he said, "I owe you, Roz."

"I know." She leaned over and kissed him. He tasted good.

"Roz," he said against her. "I'm driving."

The crossroads was just ahead. She recognized it. She looked behind them. Still no one. But Harold and that sheriff would be coming soon.

"Ready?" she asked.

"I always am," he said.

"Good," she said, "because we're getting off here."

She shoved him toward the edge of the wagon. He dropped the reins and she didn't pick them up. The mule was doing fine on his own—he didn't need to be whipped in the butt for encouragement.

"Jump!" she said to Jack.

He did, and she followed. The mud was harder than it looked, knocking what little wind she had right out of her.

Jack, as usual, seemed just fine.

"Damn corset," she said when she could.

"I'll help you out of it," he said, reaching for her blouse.

"Not here," she said. "There's a stream just down this road. We clean up there, and then get out of here."

"Think they'll come this way?"

"Not for a while," she said. "They've got a photographer to free and a photographer's wagon to follow. Besides, we're not heading that way. We're going east."

"East?" He peered at her.

She gave him her best smile, even though she was muddy and tired and out of breath. "I want my photography studio, and to do that, Jack, you gotta go where the people are."

"Who ever heard of migrating east?" he asked, but she could tell he wasn't averse to the idea like he would have been just the day before.

She brought her hands up and thoroughly kissed his dear, muddy face. When she was through, she said, "We've been doing things your way long enough."

"And it's worked out fine," he said.

"If you think fine is broke and homeless."

"But a photography studio," he said. "Who would go to a female photographer?"

"Harold Adams."

"You just proved my point." Jack raised his hands slightly, and stared at the handcuffs. He sighed. "I don't want to go straight."

"Who said anything about going straight?" she said and got to her feet. "Now let's get out of here."

"You'll have to tell me the plan," he said as he stood.

"Why?" she asked. "It always works out better if you don't know."

"I'm not that bad," he said.

"That's a matter of opinion, Jack," she said as she led him down the road toward their fresh horses and new wagon. In the distance, she could hear the mule braying. She smiled at hers, happy to have him back.

They'd go straight. But she wouldn't tell him that yet. One thing at a time.

After all, planning ahead was the key to knowing Jack.

THE ONE THAT GOT AWAY
A SEAVY COUNTY STORY

KRISTINE KATHRYN RUSCH

It happened at the Thursday night blackjack tournament, and we were miffed. Not because it happened, but because of *when* it happened. And to get to that will take a bit of explaining, both about the tournament and about us.

There are about ten of us, and we call ourselves the Tuesday/Thursday regulars because we never miss a tournament. The local Native American casino—the Spirit Winds —held an open tournament every Tuesday and Thursday. Anyone could play if he put up twenty bucks, and if he won, he got a share of the pot. The pot consisted of the buy-in fees and the buy-back fees, plus another hundred added by the casino. The casino made no money on the tournament. The game was a freebie designed to get people into the casino—and it got me there twice a week.

Me, and nine others. There were more regulars than us, of course, but we were the ones who never skipped a week. I was a pretty good player—I'd made a living counting cards in the mid-seventies—and I'd swear that Tigo Jones had professional card-playing experience as well. Five more of the regulars played basic strategy, and the rest, well, they relied upon luck or God or their moods to supply their strategy. It worked for them every once in a while.

In blackjack, you learn to honor luck.

The good players just try to minimize it. They try to rely on skill. But luck can win out, in the end, if you're not careful.

On most nights, pot's only worth about two hundred to the winner, a hundred to second place, and fifty to third, with four dinner comps to sop the folks who made it to the final round. What that means is that there's good money in this for me and Tigo because we place every four tournaments we play. A few regulars are losing money each time they play, and about five—those basic strategy guys—are giving their gambling fund an occasional shot in the arm.

It's all in good fun, and we've become a family of sorts—the kind of family that barflies make or old ladies make when they work on church social after church social. We look after each other, and we gossip about each other, and we tolerate each other, whether we like each other or not.

We also know who's crazy and who isn't, and, except for Joey, the kid who is pissing his inheritance away twenty dollars at a time, no one who shows up for the blackjack tournaments at Spirit Winds is crazy.

Or, at least, that's what we hope.

T hat night, I noticed a few strange things before I even made it to Spirit Winds. For one thing, the ocean was so black it was impossible to see. Now, the ocean is never black. It reflects light—and even if the sky is completely dark, the ocean isn't because it's reflecting the light of nearby homes. In fact, I like the ocean on cloudy nights because it has a luminescence all its own, a glow that makes it look alive from within.

The second strange thing was that there was no wind. None. Zero, zip, zilch. We usually have a breeze in Seavy Village and often have more than that. The ocean again. It is a major part of our lives.

And the final strange thing was the power outage that swept through the neighborhoods like anxious fingers pinching out candles. I didn't know about that until later— the casino has backup generators—and if I had known, well, it would have made no difference.

I would have been at the tournament anyway.

I have nothing better to do.

You see, I call myself retired, but really what I am is hiding out. I'm good enough to play in big tournaments, but when Spirit Winds holds its semi-annual $10,000 tournament, I'm conveniently out of town. That way, I don't have to fill out a 1099, and I don't have to show three pieces of I.D., and all the correct tax information. Because I don't have three valid pieces of I.D., and I haven't filed taxes since 1978, the year I fled Nevada with the wrong kind of folks at my heels. I moved too fast to get any fake I.D., and so I lived off cash for far too long. By the time I had settled down, I didn't know anybody in that business anymore. The government had closed the loopholes making fake I.D.s simple for anyone with half a brain, and I really didn't want to put fingers out to the criminal element, since it was the criminal element I'd been running from.

I confessed to a local banker with hippie sympathies, let him think I had been underground since my college activist days, and had him set me up a checking account. It's amazing what a man can do with a checking account—the lies he can tell to get him a real life in a small town.

But it couldn't get me a driver's license, nor could it get me a credit card. I still use cash much of the time, and a lot of that cash comes from my safety deposit box in the aforementioned bank. The gambling at the small casino is just incidental. I figure I'm old enough now that no one would recognize me and my problem is so out of date that the folks who were looking for me are either dead or in prison. But I have learned to be cautious by nature. I don't rub anyone the wrong way.

And I never, ever call attention to myself.

The tournament was big that night, bigger than it had ever been. Later I learned the reason: the power outage. The casino was packed on a Thursday because much of Seavy Village had lost their lights, their heat, and their cable. I had been in the casino since mid-afternoon. I'd been on a roll at one of the regular tables, parlaying my lucky hundred-dollar chip into six thousand. Normally that puts you in tax declaration territory, but I would get five hundred on one table, then pocket it, and move to the next. I was hot that afternoon, and it felt good.

Lucky streaks are important. Knowing how to maximize them is even more important, and that's what I was doing. Perfecting the old skills.

When I reached six grand, my brain shut off, and I decided to replenish it with food. I had a solitary dinner at the buffet, and then wandered to the tournament tables.

There were a lot of unfamiliar faces around the table, and I was burdened with a small fortune in chips, stuck in my pockets and my fanny pack. I couldn't take anything to the car because I didn't have one, and I also didn't have time to walk home. I'd been in that situation before, and I'd learned not to be too friendly. The last time I'd told one of the regulars about my run and a pit boss overheard. I had to spend a good fifteen minutes making a show of losing the money at various tables.

Normally the pit bosses don't tell on me. They tolerate me and Tigo and the other local professionals. It's the out-of-towners they kick out of the casino. Oregonians and their dislike of "foreigners." Gotta love 'em.

That night, though, I wasn't taking any chances. I leaned against one of the slot machines and smoked a cigarette, adding to the thick, slightly bluish air already growing around the tables. The casino is new and modern—no tokens for slots, only cash and cards—with high ceilings, good traffic flow. The place feels more like a spa than a casino, especially the casinos of my heyday. I still miss the chink-chink of tokens as they clink out of the machines. I'm not sure I'll ever get used to those electronic beeps. But not even the modern recycling system was taking care of the cigarette smoke. In a blue-collar town like Seavy Village, card players get nervous when more than $50 is on the line.

That night, forty players had signed up for the tournament, and the pot tipped a grand for the first time since the casino opened.

I'll leave out the detailed descriptions of the rounds, although I can recite all of it, every card, every bet, from the first round, the semi-final round, and the buy-back round. I know by what percentage Tigo beat the odds when he doubled down on eighteen and got a three. I know the exact moment luck abandoned Cherise, and it wasn't when she drew a twenty to the dealer's twenty-one. I even know that I made a small mistake on the twenty-ninth hand, and if the cards hadn't gone my way, I would have been out— deservedly so—and it would have peeved me to no end.

I rarely make mistakes.

I can't afford it.

No. I won't say much about the game except that tempers flared early, even among the regulars, because of the amount of money on the table. And people left angry when they were eliminated because everyone could taste their share of the pot.

When it came to the final hand, only the players and the regulars were left.

Tigo and I were on the table, of course, along with the idiot Joey whose luck was running better than usual, and

Smoky Butler who was a dealer at another casino on the other side of the coast range. The rest of the players weren't regulars. Two were bad betters and even worse strategists who managed to get the right cards at the right time, and the other one was a black-haired woman who'd caught all of our attention.

She looked like she should be in Monte Carlo, not Seavy Village, Oregon. She wore a black cocktail dress cut in a modified v that revealed more cleavage than I had seen in years. Her hair was pulled into a chignon and over it she wore a cloche hat complete with small veil. Her lips were dark red, and she smoked a cigarette through a cigarette holder.

And she wasn't lucky.

She was good.

Almost as good as me.

The cards were running hot and cold that night, and our pal Joey's luck ran out first. He was off the table in five hands. Then we lost the first of the two bad betters. The second was holding in, but not worth our time. He was out by the eleventh hand.

The rest of us, though. The rest of us had a game.

For our buy-in, the casino gives us $500 in tournament chips (which you can't carry to the real tables) per game. The winner, of course, is the person with the most chips after fifteen hands.

By end of the eleventh hand, I had fifteen hundred eighty-five dollars in phony chips.

Tigo had fifteen hundred seventy-five.

Smoky Butler had fifteen hundred and fifty.

And the woman, well, she had two thousand even.

For the first time since I'd left Nevada, I was in a black-jack game where everyone knew how to play. That meant they knew how to draw cards, they knew how to bet, and they knew strategy.

I damned near licked my lips and rubbed my hands together in glee. Instead, I crouched over my chips as if I were protecting them from prying eyes.

We all put out our bets.

The lady put out a hundred.

Smoky put out a hundred and fifty.

Tigo a hundred and twenty-five.

And me, a hundred and fifteen.

Then Rosco, the dealer, began the hand. I was first base (a revolving position), and he gave me an ace of clubs.

Followed by an ace of diamonds for Tigo, an ace of spades for Smoky, and an ace of hearts for the lady.

"They should be playing poker," someone said from behind me.

Rosco gave himself a three of hearts. Then he reached toward the shoe for my next card.

At that moment, the lights went out. The place was pitch black except for several small red dots made by the tips of a hundred cigarettes. I fell across my cards and chips, and Rosco yelled, "Freeze!" to the tournament players. The pit bosses were yelling and the dealers were shouting orders, and some old lady near the slots was wailing at the top of her lungs.

All the time, I kept thinking that this shouldn't be happening. It couldn't be happening. The casino had generators. They should have kicked in. (At the time, I didn't know they'd already kicked in, which meant that they shouldn't have gone off—at least, not all at once.)

Then the lights came back up, or I thought they did, until I realized that the overhead lights in the casino were white, not green. Everyone looked as if they were peering at each other through a fish tank. Even the mystery lady looked green. She was holding her cigarette holder over her chips, and glaring at us all angrily, as if we had caused the problem.

The pit bosses were looking mighty scared. I don't know how much money they had to protect, in chips mostly because the cash disappeared into slots beneath the tables, but I knew it was a lot. And there were more civilians in the casino than pit bosses. Security guards had stationed themselves near the casino banks, and other employees had fanned themselves around the room.

I had never seen anything like it, but it made sense. The casino had to have a drill policy for all types of emergencies.

The place was hot and smoky and everything was green. I kept my hands over my chips and scanned for the source of the light.

As I did, a wind came up. First it licked my hair—or what's left of it—and then it cleared the smoke. At first, I thought the air recycling system had turned back on. Then I realized something greater was happening here.

The source of the green lights were small dervishes the size of my coffee saucers at home. They looked like the alien spaceship out of *E.T.*, only shrunk down into toy specials for McDonalds' Happy Meals. Except they worked. Their top was a dark cone, and their base was a rotating series of lights, all various shades of green.

And there must have been thousands of them in that small space. Maybe even millions of them.

They hovered over various tables, avoided the slot machines, and disappeared into the back. The poker room was filled with them. I could see them from my vantage points, lined up like tiny aircraft carriers facing a city, the poker players backing against the wall, hands up.

Five crafts found their places over our table, and a sixth placed itself above the dealer. The woman pulled a small pistol from her handbag, and a pit boss immediately grabbed it from her—firearms are illegal on Indian land. He pointed it, wobbling for a moment, at one of the little crafts, then Rosco said,

"If you shoot one and it explodes and we get that green goo all over us and we die, you're going to regret that."

"He'll regret it more if the bullet hits one of us," Smoky said.

"It could ricochet," Tigo added.

The pit boss let the weapon fall to his side. The woman glared at him.

"I wouldn't have missed," she said, as if she blamed him for taking away her opportunity.

The little crafts were above us, whirling and creating the breeze. Rosco had his hand on the money slot. So, it seemed, did every other dealer in the place. We all stared at the things.

"What are they?" Tigo whispered.

I took the question as rhetorical, and apparently everyone else did too because no one answered him.

One of the pit bosses was on the phone, talking with the 911 dispatch. He was whispering loudly, so loudly he may as well have been shouting: "No, really, I'm not kidding. Please…"

Aside from the whirs, the soft mumbles of scared patrons, and the wailing woman, the casino was eerily quiet. No electronic beeps and buzzes, no blaring music, no tinkling chords of winning slots. The silence unnerved me more than anything.

"What do they want?" Tigo whispered.

"Ask them," Smoky snapped.

"I feel like I'm in a James Bond movie," the woman said, and that started a ripple of panic through the pit bosses. They apparently hadn't thought of the things as high tech theft devices.

"If you were in a James Bond movie, my dear," I said, "you'd have better lighting." No one looked good in that ugly green. Not even the most beautiful woman in the place.

Then, as if on cue, green lights flared out of the bottom of the tiny crafts. I backed away from the table, chips forgotten. So did everyone else. Rosco let go of his hold on the money slot, and one of the pit bosses screamed at him but— I noted—did not make a move toward the money, the table or any of the lights.

The lights hit the table and I expected to see big burning holes appear. I was ready to run for cover—all of this going through my mind in the half second it took, mind you— when I realized what was going on.

The cards rose off the surface, whirling and twirling as if they were in a tornado. For a moment, the entire casino was filled with swirling cards. It looked like an elaborate fan dance, or as if green sea gulls were swarming the beach or like an electronic kaleidoscope performance designed especially for us.

Then one by one the cards slid into the crafts through a slot in the sides. They made a slight ca-thunk! as they entered. Then the green tractor lights—what else could they be called?—went out, and the little green ships whirled away.

The doormen and the folks in the parking lot at the time all say the little ships sped out the doors and into a larger ship that had been hovering over the ocean. A number of green slots opened on it, letting the little ships through, and then they disappeared into the night.

The ocean, which had been dark, regained its luminescence, and slowly the lights flickered on all over town.

At least, that's what the outdoor folks said.

Inside, it was chaos. People started shouting and screaming, and that wailing woman continued. A few people stampeded toward the door, and one relatively fit young man got trampled just enough to later attempt a suit against the casino.

Then the lights came back on. The slot machines groaned as they started up, then beeped through their start-up protocol. The slot players, the video poker players, and the keno players all continued with their games except for a few sensible folks who decided to call it a night and left.

I have no idea what happened inside the poker room, but at the tournament table, we counted our chips. The pit bosses put the game on hold as they made sure the money was fine.

It soon became clear the only thing missing from the casino were the cards.

All of them.

Including the decks stored in the back rooms, and the discards waiting to be trucked off the place, and even the little souvenir cards in the gift shop.

Gone.

All gone.

The pit boss who had called 911 was off the phone, saying the police were going to arrive soon, but I suspected it would take them some time. If, as people were saying, things were a mess all over town, it would take the police a while to get anywhere.

"We still have money on the table," Smoky said.

"And a game to finish," Tigo said.

"How do you propose we do that with no cards?" Rosco asked.

"We know what was dealt," the woman said

"But we don't know the order in the rest of the shoe," I said.

"We're going to shuffle a new shoe and start over," Rosco said, "just as soon as we get cards."

"We need the other three players," Tigo said. I glanced around me. Joe was standing behind me as he usually did after he got knocked out of a tournament, but the others were nowhere to be seen.

"We're going to have to put this game on hold until the cops arrive anyway," the pit boss said.

"Until we get cards," Rosco added.

"Besides, everyone'll have to report what they saw," Smoky said.

At that point, the woman and I both stood up. "I think my luck has just run out," the woman said.

"Mine, too," I said.

We left the table and headed toward the door.

"Hey!" Tigo said behind us. "We can't replay the game without you guys!"

"I think the game is forfeit," the woman said.

"Yeah, have the casino put the pot in for next week," I said, knowing they never would.

Then she and I walked through the casino, side by side. The conversations were strangely muted, only a few people discussing what they saw. As we stepped outside, we ran into chaos, cars cramming the parking lot, attendants staring at the sky, a warm bath of light all over the town.

A familiar bath of light.

I had missed it more than I realized.

I turned to her. "There's a nice coffee place about a block from here. Care for a walk?"

"I'd love it," she said.

And we had a nice cup of coffee, and a nice evening, and a nice night, and an even better morning. I never learned her name and she never learned mine, but we both knew that we had left the casino for the exact same reason.

We didn't need to see the police.

Or the media.

Or anyone else, for that matter.

"What do you think they wanted with the cards?" she asked long around midnight.

"I don't know," I said. "Maybe they use bigger shoes than we do."

And a little later, I said, "That, by far, has to be the strangest thing I ever saw in a casino."

"Really?" she responded. "I've seen stranger."

But she never elaborated and I didn't ask her to.

Some stories are better kept close to the vest.

You see, that isn't the strangest thing I'd ever seen in a casino either.

But it's the only one I'll admit to.

And I only do that because I'm a regular and it's a shared group experience. A bit of local legend—the one game that never finished, the pot that got away.

Well away. The casino had to shut down both the poker and blackjack tables for two days while it ordered cards from all over the country. During that time, regulars gave interviews on every show from *CNN* to *Inside Edition*. Except for me.

I laid low for a while even after my lady left. Laid low and watched the skies.

And wondered—

What would have happened on the thirteenth hand if we had all blackjacked on the twelfth?

What would have happened then?

Un-Familiar
A Winston & Ruby Story
KRISTINE KATHRYN RUSCH

First major storm of the year. A typical November winter storm that had hit, for some reason, in mid-October. The newscasters on the Portland television stations were blathering about how unusual it all was, and then comparing it to the Columbus Day Storm of 1962, which was what they always did whenever storms looked bigger than average.

Winston ignored the coverage as best he could, although he kept it running on the tiny ancient television he had put on a high shelf fifteen years before. He hunched over his work table in the back of his small store, and continued making potions. Over the last several years, his little business had grown—not here in Seavy Village, but on the web. On the advice of one of his colleagues, he had moved his mail-order business online, and thanks to great customer reviews, he could have had more work than he could possibly do.

Most internet entrepreneurs simply hired help, but

Winston couldn't do that. He had small magicks, yes, but he had *magic*, and that was rare enough. It would have taken him years to train the right person to master the potions and tiny spells that he had created—and that was if he wanted to teach someone else, which he decidedly did not.

He didn't want an apprentice. He had *been* an apprentice (all of the magical had), and he knew that the best way to train someone was 24/7, supervising every little thing.

Winston liked his time alone. He saw people daily—or at least, weekly—in his store, and that was more than enough for him. Occasionally he had coffee with friends, and even more occasionally, he went to someone's home for dinner.

Those occasions were always dicey, though, since he had to bring his familiar, Ruby. And, as he liked to say, she was 10% familiar and 90% cat, which meant that she was never the most gracious creature. Plus, she hated it whenever someone interfered with her routine.

At the thought of her, Winston raised his head. He hadn't heard her complain about anything in the past five minutes. She had been sustaining a running commentary about the weather news, primarily reminding the newscasters (who could, of course, not hear her), that *Columbus Day was in* October, *you idiots, so therefore storms like this in* October *weren't unusual or unprecedented.*

She'd been saying a version of that for days now from her usual perch on the bench near the unopened cans of Fancy Feast that he kept in the back of the store, as if her own brain had been stuck in repeat.

Winston had learned over the years that she got stuck like that whenever something disturbed her greatly. He had found her in a storm, shortly after his beloved familiar Buster died, and while Ruby claimed that storms didn't bother her, she still cuddled a little too close whenever the sustained winds gusted higher than 20 miles per hour.

So the fact that she wasn't here, near him, struck Winston as odd.

And that thought, sudden as it was, shook him.

His heart started to pound hard, like it always did whenever she wasn't following her usual patterns. She'd been kidnapped early in their relationship, and he never forgot that feeling of sheer terror he'd had while she was gone. Whenever she varied her routine, his mind always found that memory, and rubbed it, like a particularly jagged rock he was trying to file down.

Ruby wasn't the only one who got stuck when she panicked.

He made himself take a deep breath. The potion he was working on wasn't one he could abandon in the middle without dire consequences, so he made himself finish the last two steps. Then he bottled the potion, cleaned out the container, and got off his chair.

He hoped—like he always did when he had to choose between finishing a potion and doing something truly important like finding Ruby—that the extra 90 seconds hadn't cost him something—some*one*—dear.

The bell over the door of his shop rang, and he hurried through the beaded curtains to the front, almost before he could stop himself. If someone had taken her outside—

But no one had. Instead, a woman with a small light-gray dog cradled in her arms peered at the glittering

Halloween jewelry that a local designer had convinced Winston to carry for the month of October. The woman turned ever so slightly, and he had a horrid moment where he couldn't stifle the rude thought that had risen in his mind:

She reminded him of Cruella De Vil.

He'd always hated that particular Disney character. Pencil-thin, wearing a coat made of Dalmatian fur, and carrying a long cigarette holder in her manicured hand, her hair black and white, and her make-up cherry red.

He had imprinted on her early, deciding that anyone who murdered dogs for clothes wasn't just a villain, but a super villain.

He'd never really seen a woman like that ever in his life, and hoped he never would. This woman didn't quite look like Cruella De Vil but there was something about her...

Granted, this woman was too thin—almost brittle—and she had dramatically salt-and-pepper hair, but she was dressed in Northwest casual instead of Disney Supervillain. Her skinny jeans did make her legs look like pencils, but she had on the kind of all-weather boots perfect for this kind of stormy weather instead of black heels. She wore a red cable-knit sweater, and no make-up at all.

If it wasn't for the trapped expression on the dog's face, Winston might have thought the woman was completely harmless.

Ruby sat on the checkout counter, staring at the dog. At first, Winston thought she was terrified of it. Ruby wasn't terrified of much, but occasionally dogs upset her more than she wanted to admit.

Although no dog this small should have ever bothered her. As she had once said to him about another dog of equal size, *Terrified? Oh, please. I could eat him for lunch.*

The dog, which seemed like some kind of toy poodle-Chihuahua mix, had its large eyes cast downward. Except for that trapped look it had given Winston when he showed up, the dog seemed like a true toy. It hadn't moved much at all, not even as a gigantic gust of wind violently shook the glass window recessed into the front of the shop.

Ruby was pure black and tiny. She sat so completely still that she looked like a statue. The woman wasn't giving her the time of day, which most people with pets did, but the dog seemed aware that Ruby was there.

Or maybe Winston was just projecting.

The woman turned toward Winston, tilting her head up ever so that she could look down her slightly upturned nose at him.

He had been wrong initially: she had the large eyes, high cheekbones, and wide mouth of a 1960s Disney villain.

"I thought this was a magic shop," she said snidely. "Clearly, I was wrong."

She stalked toward the door, brushing against the shelves, threatening to dislodge some of the jewelry.

"Stop her," Ruby whispered.

"What?" the woman asked, and turned. She had heard that sotto voce whisper of Ruby's, which almost no one except Winston could hear.

Dammit. The woman had real magic.

"Um." Winston wasn't sure if Ruby wanted him to stop the woman from messing up the shop or if Ruby wanted him to stop the woman from leaving. "What kind of magic are you looking for?"

The woman gave him half a smile, then shook her head. She lifted the poor little dog, who was now trembling like a Chihuahua, and peered into its face. It leaned back as if it couldn't stand looking at her.

"What do you think, Rufus?" she asked. "Do you think we should give this amateur the time of day?"

The dog gave Winston another trapped look, as if it was too downtrodden to even ask for help.

"Well, never mind," she said, tucking the dog under her arm. "You *are* useless, aren't you? I have no idea why I ended up with a *toy* instead of a dog, but there you are."

"Stop her," Ruby hissed, softer this time.

Rain, blown by a strong gust of wind, pelted the window hard. Both the woman and the dog jumped. Ruby remained perfectly still.

Winston finally realized what was going on with his cat. She *was* terrified—of the woman, not of the dog.

"What are you looking for?" he asked the woman in his most friendly tone.

"Competence," she snapped, and reached for the door.

"*Stop* her." Ruby's voice almost sounded like it was inside Winston's head. Maybe it was. He had no idea if she could do that—if any familiar could do that—but if anyone could, it would be his Ruby.

He waved his fingers ever so slightly behind the counter, sealing the door closed. He had a magic spell covering the entire front of the building, mostly so that it would hold up during winds like the ones predicted for this afternoon.

He had reinforced the spell after Ruby's kidnapping so that he could trap anyone he wanted inside the store. Not for very long, because his magic was small, but long enough to call his friend on the Seavy Village police force, Scott Park.

The woman looked at Winston a little sideways, almost as if she knew that he had trapped her inside the building. Almost as if she had felt the spell slip past her and trigger his magical lock on the door.

He'd had help with this spell. Powerful help, from his old mentor, so the spell would hold anyone, no matter how formidable. Just not for very long.

"I didn't realize you needed business that badly," the woman said, with a half-smile on her face.

At that moment, the dog bit the flesh underneath her arm so hard that Winston heard the crunch.

The woman yelped, and dropped him. The dog scrambled toward the back of the counter, his claws scraping against the wood floor.

Ruby jumped down beside him, and herded him into the back of the shop, nose in his butt as if he were a misbehaving kitten.

The woman cursed, grabbed the soft flesh under her arm, and glared at Winston.

"Well, don't just stand there," she said. "Get him. Get my dog."

Winston almost listened to her. She was using some kind of compel spell—something that showed a massive amount of disrespect. Wizards didn't spell other wizards— unless the wizards using the spell were on the dark side of the magical coin or unless the wizards were dealing with someone so inferior that they were the equivalent of the unmagical.

It was his turn to raise his head. "Why don't you call your dog?" he asked quietly. "He *is* a dog, right? They're taught to obey commands. Unless they were not treated properly."

"Who are you to question how I handle my dog?" she snapped. "Get out of my way."

Instead, Winston blocked her. "You're not allowed in the back of my shop."

She waved a hand, and he felt the magic arrive just before it shoved him. He managed to keep his feet planted.

He had small magicks, but he had learned to defend against great magicks. It had been part of his training, the tests, the things that determined his gift was tinier than most.

"This is *my* shop," he said. "I will shut down your magic in here if you do not treat me and mine with the proper respect."

Something banged in the back, then banged again. He recognized the sound. The back door. Somehow, someone had opened it, and now the wind was repeatedly slamming it against the wall.

"What *is* that?" she asked.

"I'll see," he said. He started for the beaded curtain, and then stopped. "It's warded back here. You come back here, and I can't promise you'll be able to ever perform magic again."

She raised her chin. "You clearly don't have the magic for that."

"You're right," he said. "I don't. But many of my clients do."

She stared at him. She clearly couldn't tell if he was bluffing or not. Maybe her magic didn't work that way. Or maybe she didn't have much magic either.

"You stay out here. You don't touch anything," Winston said. "I'll be right back."

Then he slipped through the beaded curtain, hoping to hell that she would listen to him. His skin actually tingled, as if he could feel her gaze on him. The air was alive with the potential of magic.

He hadn't been lying to her, at least not completely. He had a small ward on the door to the back, so no customer would wander into his workshop accidentally. If a non-magical someone touched any of the potions or some of the spelled ingredients, they could get hurt, or worse.

He didn't like to think about it, so he protected against it.

He stepped into the ward curtain, feeling it like he usually did not. That told him the magic potential in the air was as strong as he had feared.

But that prickly feeling eased as he made it through the ward curtain. Instead, a very real wind hit him, along with droplets of rain. The floor was wet in front of the door, and everything he kept near there was scattered.

He peered out the door, stomach clenched, looking for Ruby, looking for the tiny dog—Rufus, the woman had called him—and he didn't see them. If Ruby had gotten outside, she would be huddled next to the building.

Although she had shoved a dog into the back room,

which had surprised Winston. Maybe she would surprise him again.

"Psst," a familiar sultry voice said ever so softly.

He looked down. Ruby was pressed against the wall underneath his work table. He had hung a curtain there so that she could sleep behind it and feel protected on her particularly vulnerable days.

She almost never used it.

In fact, she wasn't using it now. She was standing in front of it, and the curtain was vibrating.

The vibration wasn't caused by the wind. The curtain vibrated in the same way that the little dog had trembled when he was in the woman's arms.

"Tell her he ran away," Ruby said.

"Rube," Winston said. "I can't—"

"*Tell her*," Ruby said. "Or I'll accompany him into the storm myself."

Big threat from a tiny cat. Winston was going to call her on her bluff—she would never go outside voluntarily, not in a storm like this—and then he saw her eyes.

They glowed yellow, like they often did in this light. And they did so when she was terrified, but standing her ground.

"You're going to tell me what's going on," he said.

"Not now," Ruby said. "Just get rid of her."

Winston took a deep breath. He had a familiar to keep his spells fresh and his mind from wandering. She kept his magic strong. On the day he met her, she had reminded him that she had a small magic of her own. The protection for his magic came from hers.

Which meant he trusted her every time he made a potion, every time he cast a spell.

He had to trust her right now.

He took a deep breath and faced that warded curtain. He thinned it just enough that the wind from the open door could swirl into the store itself.

Then he pulled the beaded curtain back, and let the distress he was already feeling show on his face.

The woman was standing near the counter.

"I can't find him back here," Winston said.

"You fool!" The woman pushed toward him. "You let Rufus get out."

Winston shook his head. "The door was open when I got back there. I have no idea how. My cat can't open doors."

He wasn't sure if that was true. He had a hunch Ruby could do anything she put her mind to. And that door had gotten open somehow. He had seen her investigating the pull lever on that door more than once.

He had even cautioned her away from it.

The woman glared at him, then started into the back. Winston held up a hand, stopping her.

"You can't come back here," he said.

"The hell I can't," she said, and pushed past him.

This time, he let her. He knew what it was like to lose a familiar, a friend, a pet. It didn't matter how gruff the person was, their attachment to their companion was probably intense.

He stayed to one side of the woman, though, so that she couldn't move past him and into the workspace proper. He didn't want her anywhere near Ruby. In fact, he didn't glance at Ruby once, not wanting to give her away.

He hoped she had vanished behind her curtain.

"Rufus?" the woman said, her voice harsh. "Rufus, you little son of a bitch, where the hell are you?"

She sounded furious. Her face was red.

Winston swallowed hard, thinking she was a little too angry, hoping that the anger was coming from fear, and nothing else.

She went to the door, put her hand on the edge and peered into the storm. The wind plastered her hair backwards. She leaned out, shouting, but Winston couldn't hear her over the howl of the storm.

He wanted to look at Ruby, but didn't. He wanted to know if the dog had emerged.

Usually it was hard for a familiar to resist their person's voice.

The woman stepped back inside, water dripping off her face, and soaking the front of her sweater.

"Little bastard," she said tightly. "This is the fifth time this month he's tried to run away, and I'm of half a mind to let him this time."

"Is he—?" Winston stopped the question. He had been about to ask if the dog was her familiar, because he had never heard anyone talk about a familiar like this. Everyone he knew—every wizard he knew—spoke of their familiar with great respect, and not a little awe. He wasn't sure now if the dog was anything else to her.

"Is he what?" she asked. "An ungrateful little vicious little creature? Yes, he is."

She ran a hand under her arm, then looked at her palm.

"I could've sworn he broke the skin," she said more to herself than Winston.

Winston swallowed. He couldn't keep the question back.

"*Is* he your familiar?"

She raised her head, her eyes meeting Winston's. "Why else would I have a dog? You think I *like* having a creature like that, shadowing me everywhere, unable to use the toilet and take care of his own bathroom needs, requiring day-to-day care like a *child*?"

Winston stiffened. "If he's outside right now, he could die out there."

"Let him," she said, and wiped her hand on her jeans. "I'm done with him."

"But he's your familiar," Winston said, confused.

"He's the third over the past four years," she said, "and by far the worst of all of them. I hope to hell something *does* happen to him, because if it does, I get another one."

A chill ran through Winston, and it wasn't because of the wind, still swirling in the back room.

"Get out of my store," he said.

"I need help finding that stupid animal," she said.

"I'm not helping you," Winston said. "I've never heard of anyone talking about a familiar like that. You're cruel."

She shook her head. "You're one of my colleagues. You need to help me. A magical being is loose on your city streets."

It sounded so dramatic. And so silly.

"I don't have to help you," Winston said. "I owe you nothing."

"You lost my dog," she said.

She didn't even call the dog a familiar. She leaned toward Winston, apparently trying to intimidate him.

Normally she would have. She was taller, thinner, and probably had more magic than he ever would.

But he was angry now. He couldn't believe how she talked about a creature that helped her, about her life companion, a small being she had been trusted with.

"I want you out of here," Winston said evenly. "I don't need someone like you contaminating my space."

Her lips thinned. She looked at him with great contempt. "What'll you do when I leave? Sage the place?"

Probably a demon cleanse would be safer, he thought, but knew better than to say.

"Just get out," he said. "Or I'll call the police."

Her pencil-thin eyebrows rose. "The police? How very pedestrian of you."

She started back to the front of the store, but he waved his hand toward the back. "Your dog went out that way," Winston lied.

Her eyes narrowed. "You're going to force me to find that creature, aren't you? It won't do any good. He's probably dead already."

"Get. Out." Winston didn't move. He wanted to have the kind of spells his mentor did, the kind that made him seem bigger or stronger or meaner. He needed more than his outrage to get rid of this woman.

She half-smiled, as if he were the most pitiful thing she had ever seen.

Then she swept past him through the back door, and into the pouring rain.

He slammed the door shut, warded it, spelled it, and then hexed it against her in particular.

He went to the front, to make sure no one else had walked in while he was confronting her. Then he made sure that she hadn't come back in either. He waved his hands, revealing any shades she might have left behind or little power traps.

She hadn't done any of that. In fact, the remnants of her magic was gray.

No one's magic, remnant or not, should look gray. That was odd, all by itself.

He took a deep breath, then went into the back. He grabbed a potion bottle with an atomizer—an actual cleanse spell in a jar, one of his bestselling products. People wanted it to clean houses or other buildings where murders had occurred and the taint of the past remained, where horrid individuals had lived or some kind of terrible event was planned.

He had never expected to use it in one of his own treasured places. But he did, and slowly the tension in his body eased.

When he was done, he realized that Ruby had come out from beneath his work table. She sat as still as she had before, and for a moment, he worried that she had been placed under some kind of spell.

After all, her behavior hadn't been normal at all. He had never seen her do anything like this.

"Thank you, Big Boy," she said, and at that moment, he realized she was all right.

"You want to tell me what's going on?" he asked.

"You think a dog would mind eating cat food?" she asked.

Dogs ate cat *poop*. Winston suspected a dog would be happy with cat food. But he didn't say either thing. Instead, he let his surprise at her generosity show.

"You're going to share your Fancy Feast?" he asked.

"Well, when you put it that way..." She licked at her shoulder as if it annoyed her. "Let's buy him some food."

"Let's give him the tuna feast," Winston said. "It's what we have. Besides, I don't want to leave yet. It's windy, and she could still be lurking outside."

Ruby's ears went straight back. "Good point."

Then she looked behind herself at the still-trembling curtain.

"He needs water, too," she said, "although I'm loathe to give it to him, since he'll have to go outside after that."

Winston hadn't even thought of that aspect of having a dog around. He hoped that the woman still wasn't lurking.

"You want to tell me now what's going on?" he asked.

"It should be obvious." Ruby stood, stretched, and then looked under the curtain. "C'mon, Dog. Get out here and meet my guy."

The dog peered around the curtain. He had poodle curls along with the narrow face and big features of a Chihuahua.

He looked like a mix, but a cute one—or he would have, if he hadn't looked like he might collapse from sheer terror.

Winston had been wrong about his color, too. The dog wasn't light-gray. His fur was dirty and his curls were matted. Winston suspected that underneath the grime, the dog was white or maybe a light brown.

Winston grabbed a plastic bowl from the pile Ruby had made him buy for her. He filled it with water from the utility sink near his work space.

"Hi," Winston said, as he set the water down. The dog skitted backwards as if Winston had raised a fist. Winston's heart clenched. What made a dog do that?

But his heart had clenched because he knew. The dog had skitted away because he *expected* a fist.

So, Winston decided to handle this formally. "I'm Winston. I'm Ruby's wizard. And you're...?"

"His name is Rufus," Ruby said as if Winston was hard of hearing. "He doesn't talk."

"I thought all familiars talk," Winston said.

"They do," she said.

"He's not a familiar?"

"Oh, he is," she said. "He just doesn't talk."

Then she went over to the dog and head-butted him the way that cats did when they were being affectionate with each other.

The dog's eyes got wider. If he could have backed up farther, he clearly would have.

"Oh, for God's sake," Ruby said. "I was trying to comfort you. Get out here and drink something. And I can see your ribs, so you need to eat. Let Winston look at you. He doesn't have a mean bone in his entire body."

The dog gave her a frightened, startled look, then tensed even more.

Winston was about to put the food and water down, and then leave, so that Ruby could handle the dog, when the dog took a tentative step forward. He was shaking so badly that it looked like he might topple off his tiny little legs.

Winston wasn't sure if that was hunger, or if it was terror. Maybe it was both.

The dog stepped into the better light on the floor outside of the work table. Winston managed to catch an involuntary gasp before it became loud enough for Ruby and the dog to hear.

Ruby had been right: that dog's ribs were visible. All of his bones were. And in addition to being filthy, he was missing patches of fur. He had scarred flesh along his sides and his back legs.

His front half appeared normal enough. The rest was probably hidden whenever the woman placed the dog beneath her arm.

The dog clearly saw the horror that Winston couldn't hide in his face.

Winston spoke softly.

"Here you go," he said, setting the water down. "I'll open a can of food in a minute."

"His name is Rufus," Ruby said.

The dog looked at her sadly, then gazed at the water as if it was a delicacy.

"He can tell me his name when he's ready," Winston

said. Somehow "Rufus" just didn't seem like the right name for this little fellow.

Ruby's eyes narrowed, but she didn't contradict Winston, even though she might have disagreed with him.

He couldn't tell, and he could usually tell what her mood was exactly.

She had moved to one side, and she was sitting perfectly still again. She clearly didn't want to startle the little dog.

"Go ahead," Winston said as softly as he had before. "That water's all for you. Feel free to drink as much of it as you need. When it's gone, I'll give you more."

The dog buried his face in the water, and lapped it loudly. Ruby slowly closed her eyes as if the sound annoyed her.

Or maybe she was appalled at the clear thirst the dog showed.

Winston was.

He stood slowly, not wanting to terrify the dog. Then Winston moved to his workbench and opened a can of Fancy Feast tuna. He dumped it onto one of Ruby's plates. He hesitated for a moment, then smiled just a little to himself. He opened a second can for his beloved cat. She wasn't supposed to have too much food in the middle of the day, because it sometimes made her complain about being stuffed, but he would make an exception today.

She had been spectacular so far.

He gave her the food first, to show the dog that Winston meant no harm as he approached.

The dog watched him with big wary eyes.

Winston set the food beside the dog and eased backwards.

Ruby was delicately eating, taking small bites, even though tuna was her absolute favorite. The dog looked at her, then looked at Winston, waiting.

"Go ahead," Winston said, his heart breaking again. "The entire plate is for you."

The dog watched warily. Winston had the sense the dog couldn't bring himself to eat in front of Winston.

"I'm going to go out front for a moment," Winston said. "I need to pick up that jewelry. The back door here is locked and spelled and hexed against that woman. You're safe here."

Ruby raised her head, and looked at him in surprise. She had a glob of tuna on her chin.

"Eat, Dog," she said. "This is the best stuff in the world."

Then she put her head down and continued to chow.

Winston stepped out front. As he did, he repaired the ward that he had thinned so that the woman could go into the back.

Her magical presence was completely gone, but the front still looked unsettled. She had moved a number of things and, it looked like she had stolen one of his potion bottles. Of course, it would be one of the colored glass antique bottles.

The Halloween jewelry was scattered. He picked it up, and returned it to the display shelf, noting that some of it was missing as well.

She had shoplifted from him.

He smiled.

It was a mistake he could use.

He walked to the counter. His three-year-old Mac stood near the wall, humming like it always did. He had two newer computers—one a laptop which he kept mostly at home, and another up-to-date desktop in the back.

He kept his records backed up on all three, but only this one had easy access to the security cameras that Scott Park insisted Winston place around the store.

Winston logged on, put in his password, and then accessed the footage. Before he did, though, he made sure that the footage was backed up on the network.

No matter how much he used computers, he was still klutzy with them, screwing things up because technology was not, and never had been, intuitive for him.

Then he reversed the footage to the moment the woman walked in the store. He saw her squeeze the dog tightly, and tried not to look at the poor dog's desperate face.

The wind rattled the windows outside, making Winston jump. He looked out, saw that the rain was now falling so hard he couldn't see across the street.

He hoped the woman had not found shelter. He hoped she was drowning.

His own vehemence startled him. He usually wasn't that man, but the dog's face, the scars, the mats...

He made himself focus on the footage again, watching her free left hand. He expected to see magic—the bottle floating into her purse, the jewelry finding its own way into her pockets—but he didn't.

Her hand swept the bottle into her open purse before Winston had even appeared. She palmed the jewelry while he was talking to her.

When he went into the back, she turned around and grabbed some of the ready-made small spells that he sold as samples of his wares.

That surprised him. Spells were personal; she couldn't study them and figure out his recipes—and he wasn't sure why she would want to.

He had assumed from the start that she had more magic than he did. He was never wrong about such things.

But that graying of her magic meant something had gone wrong. He had no idea what that something would have been.

And then he raised his head and looked at the beaded curtain.

He's the third over the past four years, she had said, *and by far the worst of all of them.*

Familiars kept magic from curdling.

Familiars, not the wizards, controlled the purity of the magic.

Familiars made sure the wizards were effective, not the other way around.

Winston resisted the urge to run into the back and ask the dog what, if anything, he had done. But that dog was so traumatized that startling him wouldn't help.

Then Winston looked back at the footage, hating the way his thought had suddenly gone. The dog ran into the back, and distracted Winston. It hadn't been a ploy, had it, so she could steal more?

He considered that thought for a moment. He could, he supposed, use some kind of spell on the dog, see if the dog had larceny in his little heart. Winston had a few of those spells in his arsenal, even though they were a little sophisticated for him. He had thought it was useful to learn them, considering he was running a retail store.

The dog wouldn't know he was casting the spell—if the dog were a regular dog. But the dog was a familiar. He would probably feel the magic.

And it just seemed wrong to even do this. Because that dog had been tortured. He was clearly terrified. He had bit his wizard and escaped, and Ruby had helped him.

Winston trusted Ruby. She always laughed at his larceny spells. She would say, *Hey, Big Boy, just ask me. I'll tell you who's good and who's not.*

And she would. All he had to do was ask her now. He only used the spells when she was asleep in the back, and sometimes not even then, learning to trust his own instincts.

Right now, his instincts told him that the little dog had escaped, and the woman, rather than being upset about losing her companion, had taken the opportunity to steal some minor spells from Winston.

He hated her anew.

She had probably tortured that tiny creature to get him to make her magic work again. The dog had stopped her, but stopping her was killing him. Or rather, she had been.

Winston's hands were shaking as he picked up the phone beside the counter. He had Scott Park's cell phone on speed-dial.

Park picked up the phone quickly. "Winston? Everything okay?"

"No," Winston said. "I had a shoplifter, and I think we might be able to catch her."

"I'm not so sure," Park said. "Half the force is unavailable right now. Storm-related emergencies. You caught me between mine."

Winston looked at the window. The rain had stopped, but the horizon was blurry. More rain was coming, and soon.

"Well," Winston said, "if there's an emergency, there's an emergency. Just let me know."

"No worries," Park said, and hung up.

Winston took a deep breath, then opened the drawer beneath the counter and removed a brand new thumb drive. He'd done this with shoplifters before, and the police always wanted the footage. But they wanted to—in Park's words— "harvest it" themselves, to that they could make the case that no one had tampered with it.

Winston was relieved she hadn't used her magic. He could make a legitimate case against her in the real world.

The door to the shop rattled, and he realized that Park was standing outside. His red hair was plastered against his head. He wore a blue rain slicker over his uniform, and black rain pants tucked into heavy boots.

He lifted his hands in a what-the-heck? gesture.

At that moment, Winston realized he had never unlocked the front door after the woman left.

He reversed the spells, and unlocked the actual physical lock manually. He had used a lot of magic already today, and it seemed to come easier than usual.

Maybe that was a stress response. Emergencies, even small ones, sometimes made the magical reserve a little more plentiful.

Park shook the door one more time and it opened. He frowned. He knew about Ruby, knew about real magic, so he didn't seem too concerned about the door unlocking itself.

He squished his way inside, and grimaced. "Wow. It smells like tuna in here. Is that why the door was locked?"

"No," Winston said. "Long story."

He waved Park over, and started to show him the footage as Ruby bounded out of the back. She leapt on the counter so hard that she slid and nearly slipped off the other side.

Park smiled. Winston didn't. Ruby was clearly upset.

"You didn't tell us he was coming," she said to Winston. "Now, he's hiding again. *What were you thinking?*"

Park looked at Winston. "Who is hiding?"

Winston held up one finger and then dealt with Ruby.

"I'm sorry," he said. "I wasn't thinking. I found some evidence she was shoplifting, so I asked Scott here to get her arrested."

Ruby gave Winston a disgusted look. "This is *not* a problem humans can resolve."

"I don't want this woman back in the store," Winston said, "and, honestly, I don't want her to get her dog back."

"Dog?" Park asked.

"In a minute, Scott, I'm sorry," Winston said without looking at him. He continued to look at Ruby, whose tail was twitching with agitation. "I am doing what I can here, Ruby."

"I have this under control," she said. "*I* do. There is nothing that humans can do."

"I know," Winston said. "Not on the familiar part. But she did break some laws—"

"Not even on the familiar part." Ruby was crouched now, her tail switching back and forth. She was furious. "*I* have this."

Winston was about to argue with her again, when he stopped. "What do you mean?"

"*You* don't govern familiars," she snapped. "We govern ourselves. Rufus has asked to be removed. I'm helping with that. He's here for a reason."

Winston frowned. He had no idea how familiars governed themselves. It didn't surprise him that they had some kind of mechanism. He had quizzed Ruby about it the day she arrived, by asking if his previous familiar, Buster, had sent her.

What do you think we have, a referral service? She had countered that long-ago day.

For a moment, Winston had believed her. And then she had mentioned Buster as if she had known him. Winston had called her on it, and she had said, *We all know each other. Familiar doesn't come from your magic practices. It comes from ours. Buster had a feeling you and I'd work out.*

And they had.

The mysterious magic of familiars.

"I don't want her to get another familiar," Winston said. "I want her punished."

Ruby's tail stopped moving. She rose from her crouch, then looked at Park. "What happens when someone gets caught shoplifting?"

"It depends on how often she did it, and what she stole," Park said.

"She's been stealing her way across Oregon to get here," Ruby said. "I can help you."

"It would be nice if someone helped me," Park said. "Because I have no idea what's going on."

Winston put a hand on Park's arm. The rain slicker was soaked-through despite its waterproof material.

"One more question before I answer you," Winston said. He looked at Ruby. "Ruby, how can you make sure she never gets any more familiars?"

"Maybe. We have a referral service," Ruby said.

"You said when I met you—"

"I never said that." Ruby raised one paw, licked it, then set it back down. "And besides, Rufus refused to support her magic. He's been leaching it away, every time she tried a spell. He just—well, he finally let us know he was in trouble. He wanted her stopped. I think he did that, don't you?"

Then Ruby jumped off the counter and walked into the back, tail high. Somehow she managed to get that tail through the beaded curtain without touching any of it.

She had never looked more beautiful to Winston. Or strong.

"What was that?" Park asked.

"A really long story," Winston said.

He sighed, and finished reversing the video. Then, as the woman came in, he narrated the events.

It took more than thirty minutes, between the visuals, Park's questions, Winston's answers, and Park's desire to see the dog. No emergencies happened, and the storm seemed to be abating.

After Winston had finished with the initial footage, he paused ever so briefly so that Park could contact the department. Ruby had come out twice, first with the woman's real name, and then with a memorized (sort of) list of stores. Ruby got the information garbled, but Park said it was good enough to catch the woman.

He called it all in, and then settled back for the rest of the question-and-answer session.

Finally, he ended with, "Can I see the dog?"

Winston shook his head. "The dog's pretty skittish. I think he will probably need a lot of time to recover. You have enough to go on here, without the animal cruelty charge, right?"

"Oh, yeah," Park said. "I'd just—he looks so terrified. I love dogs. I'd like to help however I can. Maybe if I just get some food for you—"

"Oooo, Officer." Ruby spoke from the floor. Winston hadn't even noticed her coming in. "Please get food. I hate sharing mine."

She jumped on the counter much more slowly and gracefully than she had the first time.

She walked over to Park and rubbed on his wet arm.

Park looked at Winston. For the second time that day, Winston saw panic on someone else's face.

"What's this for?" Park asked Winston. "What did I do?"

"It's what you're going to do," Ruby said.

"The food?" Park asked. "That's the least I can do."

"No," Ruby said. "You're going to come with me."

She jumped down and headed toward the back. Park didn't move. Instead he frowned at Winston.

"What's this about?" Park asked.

Winston shrugged.

"I don't have all day," Ruby said.

Park stood, adjusted the rain slicker, and followed her. Winston followed them both.

The little dog sat on the work bench beside Ruby's stash of food. The dog didn't look composed, although his face was cleaner. Either he had dipped it in the water dish or Ruby had bathed his front. Which would have been a heck of a sacrifice for her, considering what she said about the way dogs smelled.

The dog was shaking visibly.

"Hey, pup," Park said, extending his hand, and bending over so that he didn't dominate. "I'm Scott."

The dog's eyes were huge. The shaking was so bad that a pen on the bench beside him started to roll.

Winston wanted to step forward and catch it, but he didn't. He didn't want to upset the dog.

Park looked over his shoulder at Winston. "*She* did this?" he asked.

Winston nodded.

Park cursed softly, then turned back toward the dog. Park's hand had remained out the entire time.

"I'm going to make sure she never hurts anyone again," Park said quietly. "I'll make sure you're safe."

The dog stopped trembling. His gaze was locked on

Park's. Then, slowly, as if it took all of the dog's strength, he leaned forward and sniffed Park's fingers.

Park remained motionless. So did Winston. Ruby threaded herself around Park's legs, as if she approved.

Then, the dog licked Park's fingers.

Park smiled. "May I pet you?" he asked.

"Carefully. I'm pretty bruised," the dog said. His voice was deep, as if he were the size of a German Shepherd.

It took all of Winston's self-control not to move when the dog spoke.

Park eased his hand over the dog's tiny head, letting the dog do all the moving so that Park didn't touch anything that was still sore.

"We need to get a vet to check you out," Park said.

"Yeah, I was afraid of that," the dog said.

"You're not microchipped, are you?" Park asked.

"You have to care about someone to do that," the dog said.

"Familiars don't need it," Winston said. "They're—"

"He's not a familiar," Ruby said from the floor.

Winston felt the usual irritation at Ruby's literal mindedness. "She said he was a familiar."

"Yes," Ruby said. "He *was.*"

"He talks," Winston said.

"He's right here," the dog said. "I am *no longer* a familiar."

Now, Winston was confused. "You still talk."

"To some," the dog said.

"Okay," Winston said. "But regular dogs don't speak like humans."

"I am not a regular dog." The dog let Park scratch behind his ears. Park, to his credit, hadn't done anything to indicate he was listening to the conversation or that it disturbed him.

"Clearly," Winston said, "but—"

"I am not a regular dog, and I am no longer a familiar. I am un-familiar," the dog said.

"And before you get into some kind of weird Who's-on-First thing," Ruby said, citing one of her favorite comedy routines (she said it proved the human method of communication was lacking), "that is what we call former familiars who have retired."

"Does that mean you're going to be a regular dog?" Winston asked.

The dog stiffened, and Park stopped scratching.

"Did I hit something?" he asked.

"No," the dog said. "Your friend, kind as he is, called me regular."

"I'm sure he didn't mean it," Park said.

"He's not willing to go back into the fray," Ruby said. "We'll have to find him a safe place to live."

"That shouldn't be hard," Park said.

The dog looked at him. Then the dog raised his right paw in a classic doggy handshake pose.

"I'm Percival," the dog said. "Rufus was never my name. It was what *she* called me. I cannot abide that name."

Park took the dog's paw gently. "Pleased to meet you, Percival."

"Would you have room in your abode for one very small unobtrusive dog?" Percival asked.

"No," Park said, and Winston's breath caught.

How could Park turn down that offer? Would it set poor Percival back?

But Percival hadn't withdrawn his paw, and Park still hadn't moved.

"I don't want an unobtrusive dog," Park said. "I want you."

Percival's tail thumped. Then his head fell forward, and he nearly collapsed.

Park picked him up. "We have to get him to the vet."

Percival lifted his head over Park's arm. "I'm all right," Percival said. "Just exhausted."

And relieved, Winston thought. His gaze met Ruby's. Her whiskers were forward, her eyes bright. She looked very pleased with herself.

She broke eye contact with Winston first, and then jumped onto the bench where Percival had been a moment before.

"We have to get one thing straight, *un*-familiar," she said to him. "You're a dog."

He looked at her over Park's arm.

"I shall never bathe you again." She stood, shook her right hind foot as if she were shaking dirt off it, and then walked to her still full plate. She had her back to the room, her ears tilted toward them all so she wouldn't miss a word that was said.

Park smiled at Winston. Winston smiled back.

Percival sighed and closed his eyes.

Winston nodded at the dog in Park's arms and mouthed, *You okay with this?*

Park nodded.

"I'm just fine," he said softly. "I think we'll both be just fine."

The Strangeness Of The Day

A Charming Universe Story

Kristine Kathryn Rusch & Kristine Grayson

J ust once, she thought, just once, she would like a little magic in her life. She believed magic was possible, on days when the sun shone through the clouds, on afternoons when rainbows dotted the countryside, on mornings when the light was so sharp it looked as if everything had been freshly made.

Not on a day like this. On a day like this, all she wanted was someone to come home to, a man to cook her meals and rub her feet, and laugh at the sheer strangeness of the day.

That was what she was thinking about as she exited the elevator into the bowels of the parking structure below her office building. The concrete structure smelled like gas fumes, and the lighting, even in the middle of the day, was a gray fluorescent that made her think of rain.

She rounded a corner, her heels clicking on the concrete, and saw a man sitting on the back of a 1974 Lincoln, holding a cigarette lighter in one hand, and a snake in the other.

The snake was alive, and twisting.

She swallowed, uncertain whether or not to keep walking. The man was gorgeous: long black hair, brown eyes, smooth skin the color of toffee. He wore a shimmery gray silk suit that accented his broad shoulders and long legs, and on his feet he wore cowboy boots trimmed with real silver.

Nora pulled her purse tight against her side. She would walk around the car and continue toward hers as if she saw nothing wrong.

"Who'zat?" A nasal male voice demanded.

"Probably someone on the way to her car." The responding voice was deep and smooth, soft and in control. Even without clear eyesight, Nora knew who spoke second.

A tiny man stood on the bumper of the Lincoln. The first man had slid across the hood to make room for the small guy. The little guy was perfectly proportioned, square with a pugnacious face, a nose that obviously had been broken several times, and powerful arms. He wore dark blue jeans and a T-shirt with a pack of cigarettes rolled up in the sleeve.

"It'd be nice to have a woman," the tiny man said.

His companion smiled. The snake wrapped itself around his wrist. "Things are a bit different now," he said. "You can't just have any woman."

As he said that last, his gaze met Nora's. His brown eyes sparkled as if they shared a joke.

She wasn't in the mood to share anything, no matter how gorgeous he was. She had a video deposition to take, a lunch to grab on the run, and a court appearance at two. She didn't have time for any of this.

"Excuse me," she said, and tried to hurry past them. The little man scurried along the bumper until he could extend his small arm in front of her.

"Who are you?" he asked in his annoying nasal voice.

She had had enough of their strangeness. She rose to her full five feet four inches (in heels) and said, "Nora Barr. I'm a lawyer." She added that last so that they wouldn't screw with her.

The tall man raised his eyebrows and looked at the little man. The little man shrugged. "Told you we needed a woman," he said.

S o that was how she found herself back in her office, the two men seated across from her, looking at her degrees and framed prints cluttering the fake wood paneling on the wall. She had sent her assistant Charlene to do the video deposition, rationalizing that Charlene needed the experience, knowing that she would regret this action should that particular case go to trial. But she really didn't want to leave Charlene alone with these two—Nora wasn't sure she wanted to be alone with them either—but she felt compelled to listen to their case.

The little man sat like an overgrown child in her green metal office chair. His stubby legs extended over the seat, and didn't even pretend to try for the ground. Like a little boy, he put his hands on the armrests as if he were trying to hold himself in place. He watched her every move, and she wasn't sure she liked that.

The other man slid into the remaining chair as if it were built for him. He had pushed the chair back so that he could extend his long legs. His booted feet still hit the metal edge of her desk, rattling it. The snake had disappeared, probably hiding in his suit, and he had also hidden the cigarette lighter.

"All right," she said, leaning forward and folding her hands together in what she hoped was a business-like position. "What can I do for you?"

"Can you have someone tested for a witch?" the little man asked.

"That never worked," the other man growled.

"Exactly," the little man said.

Nora glanced at her watch. "I have to be in court in less than ninety minutes."

"Right," the gorgeous man said. "I—"

"If she can't have her tested for a witch, perhaps tarred and feathered—?"

"Wrong century."

"Hung from a tree until she's dead?"

"Wrong century."

"Boiled in oil?"

"You know no one did that."

Nora slapped her hands on her desk and stood. "I do appreciate the comedy routine, but I also bill by the hour, and so far you gentlemen have taken up nearly fifteen minutes of your free session. So unless there's a realistic way I can help you—"

"I'm sorry." The good-looking man stood too. "I get so preoccupied I forget that the rest of the world doesn't work the way I do." He extended his hand. "I'm Blackstone."

"The Blackstone?" she asked with just a trace of sarcasm in her voice.

"Well, actually, yes, but not the one you're thinking of. He, in fact, was the imposter, but that's a long story which ended rather nastily for all concerned. He—"

"Blackstone," she said, sinking down to her desk. This would be a long interview. "Is that a first or last name?"

"It's a surname," he said, sitting too. "My given name is Aethelstan."

"Aethelstan?" Whatever she had expected, it wasn't that.

He shrugged prettily. "It was in style once."

"A long, long time ago," the little man added.

"And you are?" she asked him.

"Let's just call me Panza," the little man said. "Sancho Panza."

She shook her head. "If you want me to do something for you in a court of law, I'll need your legal name."

The little guy shrugged. "It's not me you're helping," he said. "It's Blackstone."

She sighed. Why did she feel as if she had been taken, and she hadn't known what for? "All right, Mr. Blackstone," she said, "what can I help you with?"

"You charge what?" he asked. The question sounded rude. As he spoke, the snake stuck its head out of his shirt and looked at her as if it, too, expected an answer.

"Two hundred dollars an hour, plus a—" she almost quoted her regular rate, then decided to double it because these two were proving to be so much trouble—"plus a thousand dollar retainer."

"A thousand dollar—?" the little man said, strangling on the last word. "In my day, you could run a country on a thousand dollars."

"In your day, there was no such thing as dollars," Blackstone muttered.

"As I told you in the parking garage, the first hour of the consultation is free." She glanced at her watch. "However, you're rapidly running out of time."

"What do you prefer?" Blackstone asked. "A check or cash?"

"Or gold?" the little man added. She would be damned if she would think of him as Sancho Panza.

"A check is fine," she said. No sense taking currency. With these two, it could just as easily be forged, and then where would she be? The worst thing a check could do was bounce.

Blackstone put a hand inside his suit coat and brought out a checkbook. A pen appeared in his other hand. She hadn't seen him take it from anywhere. He poised it over the paper. "To you or the law firm?"

She was still nonplussed by the appearance of the pen. "Um," she said, wishing she could gather herself more quickly in this man's presence. "The law firm."

He wrote the check, signed it with a flourish, then handed it to her. She glanced at it, noting his name in bold and only a post office box for an address. It was time, she thought, to get serious.

She pulled out a legal pad and took her pen out of its

holder. "Let's get your exact address and phone, starting with you, Mr. Blackstone, and then going with your friend here."

"You don't need me," the little man said. "I already told you."

"Then I'll have to ask you to leave," she said.

"I don't mind him staying," Blackstone said, leaning back as he said so.

"I do," she said.

Blackstone raised an eyebrow. The little man scowled. "You got books in the waiting area?"

"Law books," Nora said.

"Good enough," he said, and let himself out.

The room felt three times larger without him. She wasn't certain how a person that tiny could fill such a big space.

"Mr. Blackstone," she said, not missing a beat, "street address and phone number?"

He gave her both with an ease that made her uncomfortable. She wasn't sure why it did; most people could recite their addresses in their sleep. But everything about him seemed strange.

"So," she said again. "How can I help you?"

To her surprise, a flush covered his cheeks. He threaded his hands together, glanced nervously at the door, and then said, "A—dear friend of mine—has been in a—coma—for—some time. Her—guardian—won't let me near her, and although I've fought for that right for—some time—I haven't made any progress."

"And you want me to—what? Contact the guardian?"

"Isn't there anything legal you can do?" he asked.

"Depends," she said. "What's your exact relationship?"

His flush grew deeper. She sighed inwardly. Girlfriend. Right. But then, she had a rule about getting involved with clients anyway.

"She's—ah—someone special to me."

God, she hated clients like this. They wanted her to fix whatever it was, but they weren't forthcoming right from the start. Her favorite second-year law professor had warned them all about this, but she had thought he was exaggerating until she hung out her shingle and began to interact with the great unwashed.

"Special." She let her tone go dry. "As in fiancée? Lover?"

"No," he said. "But she will be."

She closed her eyes. Will be. He had hopes, but the woman probably didn't. Which meant he was a stalker. Why were all the gorgeous ones also crazy? She opened her eyes. He was watching her, looking puzzled.

"Look, Mr. Blackstone," she said. "I can't help you in any legal way unless the woman in question is in some way a relative. I'm sorry, but that's just the law. You'll have to accept the situation for what it is and move on."

She pushed his check back toward him.

"You can't help me?" he asked, sounding a bit astounded.

She shook her head. "Not me, not any lawyer. You have no rights with someone who is just a friend. The guardian has legal control."

The snake stuck its head out farther and hissed softly. Its long forked tongue curled as it did so. He shushed it, and pushed it back inside his coat.

"This is becoming untenable," he said.

"I'm sorry." Her heart had started pounding hard. He had made her nervous from the beginning, but she had thought his strangeness harmless. Now she wasn't sure.

He took the check, stood, and held out his hand. "Sorry to take all of your time," he said.

"The first hour's free," she said lightly. But it had cost her a good deposition.

"Nonetheless," he said. "I appreciate your candor." And then he slipped out the door and out, she hoped, of her life. Still, as a precaution, she made notes of the entire strange meeting. Her secretary had been complaining about the dullness of the routine lately; she would get a kick out of this.

Nora didn't think of Blackstone again. She had chalked up the interview to one of those weird experiences that attorneys sometimes had, and she had moved on. So, two weeks later, as she was leaving the courthouse after a particularly successful trial, she was surprised to receive a call from her secretary, saying that Blackstone had requested her presence immediately at an address that put him squarely in the center of the Westside suburbs. Nora protested: she had told him she wouldn't be his attorney, but her secretary insisted.

"I think he's in some kind of trouble," she said.

It took Nora ten minutes on the freeway to get to the neighborhood Blackstone had indicated. As she got closer, she watched a cloud of inky black smoke loom over that section of town. Fire equipment and ambulances screamed by her, slowing her trip. Each time she pulled to the side of the road, she cursed slightly, and she wondered what she was getting herself into.

The exit was jammed with milling people, emergency vehicles and baffled onlookers. The inky black smoke was rising from an area two blocks over. It looked serious.

A roadblock greeted her halfway down the street. A cop she didn't recognize rapped on her window. As she rolled it down, she said, "I'm Mr. Blackstone's attorney. He just called me."

The cop waved her through.

As she drove past the roadblock, she felt as if she had entered a nightmare. Burning bits of wood littered the road, and she had to constantly swerve around them. Several homes were on fire, their residents outside, holding hoses on them or weeping. A couple of cars parked alongside the street had large holes through their roofs and sides, as if someone—or something—had punched through the metal. The air was filled with ash, and the smell of smoke was so overpowering, she continually sneezed.

The address her secretary had given her was right in the middle of the devastation. Police cars blocked the entire road. She couldn't drive any farther. She really didn't want to get out, but she felt she had no choice.

She sighed, grabbed her tennis shoes from their spot beneath the passenger seat, and removed her lucky Ferragamos. She shoved her nylon covered feet into the tennies, and got out of the car.

It was worse outside. The stench permeated everything.

Bits of charred wood and flame floated down with the ash. The sky was so dark, it seemed as if a severe storm were about to break overhead. Her eyes watered. People were sobbing, police band radios were crackling voices and static, and firemen were yelling directions at each other. She stepped over hoses and blackened debris, not quite sure where she was going, but knowing she'd recognize it when she saw it.

And she did. The five policemen were standing around Blackstone. He was on a green lawn, untouched by flames, its flowers an obscene reminder of what the neighborhood had been just hours before. A woman was sprawled on the driveway face down; her position was unnatural, the turn of her head, the clawed tension in her fingers all confirmed what Nora feared.

The woman was dead.

A shiver ran through Nora despite the dry heat from nearby flames. She didn't do criminal work. She was a civil attorney; this was way out of her league.

She rounded a 1970s brown and orange VW microbus, and headed toward the police. No one tried to stop her. The microbus rocked slightly, and as she looked up, she could have sworn she saw Sancho Panza or whoever the hell he was moving behind the window. Then, when she blinked, he was gone.

She swallowed against the smoke-ravaged dryness of her throat. She had to stay focused. She had to somehow get through these next few moments and then get out of here.

Blackstone's face softened when he saw her. It had been hard lines and angles before. Now it was gentle, rounded, as if someone had changed the lighting or he had become a different person somehow. She felt the transition as much as saw it, and remembered suddenly, uncomfortably, the transition people said Ted Bundy's face went through when he was angry.

She was in much too deep. At least she knew it.

She stopped beside one of the police officers, a middle-aged man whose soft stomach edged over his belt. His face was soot-streaked, and his eyes were red.

"I'm Mr. Blackstone's attorney," Nora said in her best don't-screw-with-me-voice. "What's going on here?"

"Nora," Blackstone said, his voice warm. "Get my partner. We're going to need your help."

"What's going on?" she asked again.

The cop looked around as if what she saw explained everything. "Your client destroyed this neighborhood." Then he nodded at the dead woman. "We're not sure what happened there. All we know is that folks placed her as alive not fifteen minutes ago."

"What are you charging him with?"

"What aren't we charging him with? Carrying incendiary devices. Arson. Murder and attempted murder, I would say."

"Nora," Blackstone said again. "Get Sancho. We need to secure the glass case and we don't have much time."

"You shouldn't be talking," Nora said. "Listen, I'll meet you at the jail. And if possible, I'll have a criminal defense attorney there as well. We'll get you out—"

"I'm not worried about me," he said. "Get Sancho—"

"You coming with us, lady?" the police officer asked.

"Where are you taking him?"

"Downtown," the officer said. "This one goes right to the jail. We're not taking no chances."

"Nora—"

She pointed a finger at Blackstone. He flinched visibly. "I don't want to hear another word from you. You will not speak again until you are in the presence of an attorney. Is that clear?"

He nodded. She had no idea if they had already Mirandized him, but she wasn't taking any chances.

The cops led him away. He looked over his shoulder once and mouthed, "Remember." She wouldn't forget. Even though she wanted to.

She brushed a strand of hair out of her face. The smoke was making her woozy. She didn't want to think about what he had done to destroy this neighborhood. She didn't want to think about that feeling she had gotten earlier, when she had first met with him, when she felt that he was a stalker. She wondered how much she had seen at that moment, and how much she had missed.

Well, it wouldn't be her problem for long. She would turn it over to someone else, and that would be it. Except that he wanted her to do something, something with a glass case.

She passed the VW microbus and as she did, the passenger window rolled down a crack. A tiny face pressed against it. "I'm going to your office," a voice whispered.

Sancho. She suppressed a sigh and didn't even nod as she passed him. The last thing she wanted was for the cops to investigate the microbus. Who knew what they would find inside? She couldn't believe they hadn't cordoned it off already as part of the crime scene.

She climbed over hoses, and returned to her own car. It was covered in a film of ash. As she settled into the driver's side, she turned on the wipers. The ash smeared all over the glass.

He had destroyed a neighborhood and maybe killed a woman. Was this because Nora hadn't helped him? Or was something else going on here, something she didn't entirely understand?

She started the car, and executed a series of small Y-turns in the tiny space, careful not to run over any hoses. The situation looked grim. Houses were still burning. She wondered how many would be gone by nightfall.

If she had to lay a bet, she would bet on all of them.

She was shaking as she drove back to her office. Shaking and slightly woozy from the smoke. Her nylons were ripped and she didn't know how she had done that, and her best suit was covered in soot and ash. She smelled like charred wood, and she doubted that smell would ever come off.

Traffic was horrible—backed up for miles as people gawked at the smoke, and pulled over for the occasional ambulance. When she got herself together enough to speak, she called her secretary and had a conference call with Max Raichelson, the best defense attorney in the city, maybe in the entire state. She and Max had been close in law school—

she had even hoped he would ask her out—but nothing had come of it. After graduation, they had gone their own ways.

He agreed to meet Blackstone ("You're kidding, right?" Max asked) at the police station.

The problem was no longer hers. Except she didn't tell Max about Sancho. And she didn't want to think about him either. She wanted simply to get on with her life as if nothing happened. She knew that would be impossible, but in the spirit of pretense, she flicked on the radio to get her mind on something else.

Instantly a shrill female voice, filtered through a phone line, grated on her nerves. She was about to flip away, when a professional radio voice broke in and clearly hung up on the caller.

"Crackpots," the announcer said. "We have a situation and all we get are crank calls."

"Several dozen of them, though, Dave," said a professional female voice. "Don't you think we should pay attention to them?"

"No," Dave said. "To recap, there's been an incident—"

He started to describe the neighborhood she had just left, adding nothing to what she already knew. Fortunately he didn't have Blackstone's name and he didn't seem to know about the dead woman. At that moment, the radio was reporting that no one had died.

"—another caller from the neighborhood," the woman announcer was saying. "And this one we both happen to know. It's Rick Ayers, our morning news announcer. Rick?"

"Stefanie." Rick's voice crackled over the phone lines and through Nora's radio. She had turned off the main highway, but traffic was still backed up. It was dark as night around her. The smoke had settled over the valley. "Even though Dave thinks the other callers are cranks, they aren't."

"Come on, Rick. Two people fighting with fire? It gets out of control? A big wild fireball battle like something out of Tolkien? We're supposed to believe that?"

Now they really had her attention. Nora glanced at the radio as if she could gauge its truthfulness just by looking at it. She was still shaking.

"'Fraid so," Rick said. "I was across the street. I got the kids out and down the block as fast as possible. There were two people involved—a man and a woman. The man had been coming out of the woman's garage. He had a glass case in front of him, and it appeared to be full. That's what got my attention. He wasn't carrying the glass case. It was floating in front of him."

"And what were you drinking this afternoon?" Dave asked. It didn't sound like banter.

"I wasn't. He put it in an orange and brown VW microbus when the woman comes out of her house and lobs a ball of fire at him. He deflects it, and it lands on a neighbor's house. That's when I got the kids and sent them down the block, knocking on doors. I think we got the place evacuated by the time the fire fight started in earnest."

"You mean to tell me...?"

Nora pulled into the underground parking lot beneath her building and momentarily lost the signal. Instead of regaining it, she shut off the radio, not really wanting to think about what she had just learned.

She had wished for magic. She simply didn't like the form it was taking.

She pulled into her normal parking space, opened her door, and heard a clang. She frowned, wondering if she had hit the car next to her.

Only it wasn't a car. It was a brown and orange VW microbus.

Sancho or whatever the hell his name was crawled from under her door. "Man am I going to have a headache," he said, one hand cradling the side of his face.

"What's going on?" she asked again.

"You don't want to know."

"I'm supposed to know," she said. "I'm supposed to help you."

"Let's go to your office," Sancho said.

She sighed and grabbed her briefcase. She decided she was enough of a mess to forgo the heels. Indeed, when she got to her floor and exited, wandering down the hall, Sancho behind her, her secretary squealed.

"Are you all right, Ms. Barr?"

"Fine," she said. "Although I could use a couple of bottles of water, pronto. I don't think I've ever been this thirsty."

Then she showed the little man into her office, and closed the door. He headed toward the chair he had used before. She didn't know how he had managed to stay soot-free from all the smoke and fire, nor how the microbus had gotten to the garage ahead of her.

"I won't do anything for you," she said, crossing around

to her desk and placing her briefcase on it, "until I know your real name."

He placed a birth certificate, a social security card, a passport, and a driver's license on her blotter. They all showed his name to be Sancho Panza, and the driver's license and passport photos confirmed that the name belonged to him.

She shoved them back at him, more angrily than she would have liked. "I don't deal in fake ID," she said.

"Neither do I," he said.

She glanced at it again. The driver's license had the supposedly unduplicatable holographic sticker just under the photo. The passport was old with several stamps already inside. If it had passed customs, it was good enough for her.

"I still don't believe it," she said.

"You don't have to." He settled in his chair. "Just help us."

"I already got a defense attorney for Blackstone."

"Fine," Panza said, as if he didn't care. "The most important thing is the glass case."

"Yes," Nora said. She took a recorder out of her briefcase, then closed the case, and set it on the floor. "I understand that he levitated it out of someone's garage."

"How he got it isn't your concern," Panza said. "Helping him with it is."

"I don't deal in stolen property," she said.

"It's not stolen," Panza said. There was a knock on her door. "Come in," Nora said. Her secretary brought in four cold bottles of water.

"Need a glass?" her secretary asked.

Nora shook her head. "Thanks."

Her secretary left. Nora offered one bottle to Panza, but he declined.

"I really don't want to be involved," she said.

"You're already involved. You identified yourself as Blackstone's attorney. People will come to you."

It was a weak argument, as arguments went. She opened a bottle of water, and took a long, long drink from it. The coolness felt good against her parched throat. The smoke and heat had dehydrated her.

"Why did Blackstone destroy that neighborhood?"

"He didn't," Panza said.

"Someone did," she said.

"Don't worry about it," Panza said.

"I have to worry about it." She ran a hand over her face, felt the soot flake off. "People make jokes about lawyers having no ethics, but that's not true. I can't help him and stay true to myself if I know he destroyed that neighborhood."

Panza clenched a fist, hit the arm of the chair, and then shook his head. "What if I told you everything will be fixed?"

She laughed, and felt its bitterness. "That can't be fixed. Not in the way I would want."

"And that is?"

"To make it seem as if today never happened. But people don't forget. Even if everything were made better, people would remember and—"

"Say no more." Panza stood in the chair. She was constantly amazed at how small he was. "We can do that."

"Sure," she said. "And pigs fly."

"Not without help," he said, and he seemed perfectly serious. "Now. Assist us."

He wouldn't go away. And no matter how ethical she got, the images wouldn't go away. She might as well see what they wanted. "Tell me what you need," she said.

"I need you to store our microbus," he said.

"You can do that."

He shook his head. "We can't know where it is. Only you can know. You'll store it for us, and then when we come and get it, everything will be safe."

"It doesn't sound legal."

"It is. All you have to do is find a garage, rent it, and keep the microbus there. We might not come for it for years."

"Years?" Nora asked.

"Years." He reached into the breast pocket of his shirt and removed an envelope. The envelope was four times the size of the pocket. "This should cover rent for the next twenty years, plus your fees and time, based on the estimate you gave Blackstone when you first met. If it takes us longer to get the microbus, we will send more money."

She took the envelope. It was too thin to be holding cash. Instead she found a very ornate check for a very lot of money. It was issued by Quixotic, Inc. and signed by Sancho Panza. "I'll have to verify the funds," she said.

"Of course."

She took the envelope, stood, and walked to the front office. There she had her secretary call and verify the check. It was good.

She came back in, tapping the envelope against her hand.

The little man was still standing in the chair. He was watching her. She closed the door and leaned on it.

"Here's what I'm willing to do," she said. "I will take your money, and put it in a special account. I will have the rental for the garage removed from that account, and my monthly fee. I will keep the keys here, but I will not inspect the microbus. I will not touch the microbus after I take it to the garage, and I will not relinquish the keys to anyone but you or Mr. Blackstone—ever. Is that clear?"

"Will the account bear interest?" Panza asked.

"Yes," she said.

"And who gets the interest?"

"Probably the person who owns the garage, when you don't come back in twenty years," she said.

The little man smiled. "I like you," he said. "If Blackstone's heart weren't imprisoned, I bet he would too."

After Panza left, she dictated the necessary instructions to her secretary. Then she went home, showered, changed into jeans and a sweatshirt and drank another gallon of water. Her eyes were still red. The smoke cloud remained over the city. Even though she had cleared her own lungs, the smell of smoke went everywhere with her. She shut off the radio because she couldn't stand the constant jabber about the "Battle of the Wizards" as one of the stations had dubbed the day's events.

She found a brand-new garage complex on the edge of

town, and signed a year's lease with an option for renewal. Then she drove back, got the microbus, and took it to the garage. It drove like a VW Bug—an old VW Bug—that was about to explode. Something weighed the back down, and made corners difficult. But she didn't look. She didn't want to.

She parked the microbus in the garage, pulled down the door, and locked it with a brand-new lock that required a combination and a key. Then she took a cab back to her office.

It was getting dark, and she could no longer see the smoke.

As she was walking in the door, her phone rang. Her secretary was long gone. The main room was dark. She stumbled against a chair as she reached for the desk, and managed a shaky hello, just as she realized she should have let the service get the call.

"Nora?"

It took her a moment to recognize the voice. "Max? How did it go with Blackstone?"

"Buy me a drink," Max said. "No. Buy me fifteen drinks, and pour me into a cab. I really don't want to go home."

That bad. It was that bad. And she had already helped him. She had already implicated herself by taking care of the microbus.

"All right," she said. "Where?"

"Grady's."

Grady's. It had been the law school's watering hole. She hadn't been there since she graduated. At least she was dressed for it. She grabbed her purse and took her car down to campus.

It wasn't hard to find Max. He was the only man over thirty in the place. Even if he wasn't, the silk suit in a bar filled with jeans, T-shirts, and tattoos would have been a dead giveaway.

He sat in a booth in the back, and looked as if he had already had a few drinks. She slid in across from him, and a tired smile crossed his lined face. She had liked Max more than she cared to admit. He had made quite a name for himself. They had always exchanged pleasantries when they passed in the courthouse, but they hadn't had time for much else.

She had missed him. She hadn't realized how much.

A waitress with studs in her eyebrows, cheeks, and nose made her way to the table. Nora ordered a beer, and found that she had to choose a microbrewery instead. Finally Max ordered for her—and paid for it.

When she protested, he grinned. "You got me the case."

"You asked me to buy," she said.

"I've just made more money for doing nothing than I've ever made for doing something," he said.

She frowned.

"I cashed one very large check on the way back from the jail this afternoon," he said, "and I verified the funds before I did. It's good. I'm supposed to give some to you. Finder's fee."

He slid a check across the table. She gasped at the amount. "Max—"

"No," he said. "Don't argue. After what I saw today. Don't argue."

She rubbed her eyes. "What did you see?"

"I saw police forget a crime was committed. I saw a dead body get up and walk. Your friend Blackstone promises me I'll remember all this, but he says no one else will. No one else—except you."

"Tell me," she said.

And so he did.

"The coroner's office is in the basement of the main police station," Max started.

"I know," Nora said.

"Well, I wasn't sure," he said. "You never know what civil attorneys know about the criminal system. I got to the station at the same time the corpse of that woman did, and as I was walking to the elevator, the ambulance had pulled up in front of the double doors." The attendants opened up the ambulance doors, and were starting to remove the body when it sat up.

Everyone jumped and then one of the attendants said, "Well, that happens sometimes."

But what didn't happen was the body unhooking itself from the straps and getting off the gurney. Max was already in the elevator. The woman joined him.

She was like nothing he had ever seen before, long dark hair with a streak of white along the side, a black robe untouched by the smoke, and long curved fingernails, almost like talons. The doors closed as the attendants came running forward. Max huddled in the side of the elevator, planning to get off on any floor.

The doors opened on his floor and he hurried off. The woman hurried behind him. Max veered toward the sergeant in charge. Several police officers tried to restrain the woman. The attendants were running up the stairs, yelling.

Max asked to see his client, and was led into an interview room. Blackstone was leaning against a chair, feet out. He smiled. "You must be the attorney Nora sent," he said. "Sorry to have wasted your time."

"Are they going to let you out?" Max asked.

"You'll see," Blackstone said.

At that moment, the woman somehow burst through the locked door. "Where is she?" the woman shouted.

Blackstone shrugged.

"I know you know," she said.

"Actually, I don't." He seemed very calm. "You'd think after a thousand years this would grow old, Millicent."

"I will not let you have her."

"You won't let anyone experience true love," he said. "But she's somewhere even I can't find her."

The woman crossed the room, and before Max or anyone could stop her, she grabbed Blackstone's head. She held it with one hand and sparks flew all around. She frowned at him, as if she were trying to pull every thought from his head. Then she cursed and shoved him away.

"You won't get away with this," the woman said. "I will find her."

"You have fifteen years, Millicent, and then she's on her own."

"She's too young."

"She's too beautiful. Women leave home well before they turn one thousand. You're just jealous."

The woman narrowed her eyes, and waved an arm and disappeared.

Blackstone stood and took Max's arm. "There's going to be chaos in a moment," he said. "Just follow my lead."

Then a police detective came into the room. "Max!" he said. "What are you doing here?"

"Showing me around," Blackstone said before Max could answer. "I hope you don't mind."

Max was stunned. This was a man who had been under arrest a moment before, and no one seemed to notice. In fact, at that point, Max checked Blackstone's wrists for cuffs and saw none.

And then Blackstone calmly led the two of them out of the precinct and into the parking garage. The ambulance attendants were sitting on the edge of the microbus, looking winded.

"You didn't call for an ambulance did you?" one of them asked Max.

"No," he said.

"I don't get it," the attendant said to his companion. "How did we end up here?"

Then Blackstone led Max to his car, and gave him the check "for his time and services," instructing him to split it with Nora. "I'm sorry you had to see this," he said. "You can't forget because you were in my presence when everything reverted. And Nora can't forget because then—well, then I'd be, as your generation so quaintly puts it, screwed. But we did as she asked and put everything back the way it was."

"What's going on here?" Max asked.

"You don't want to know," Blackstone said.

"But I do," Max said.

"All right," Blackstone said. "But it's not my fault if you fail to believe me."

"Well?" Nora asked. "What was going on?"

"You know," Max said, leaning over his fourth beer. His words were becoming slurred. "When I drove here, there wasn't any smoke. And no one said a word about anything on the radio. It was strange. So I swung over to the neighborhood. It looks fine. No burned houses. No ashes. Just flowers and porches and electric lights."

"Max," she said, worrying that he might lose complete control before he got to the point. "What did he tell you?"

"He said that fairy tales are true. Sort of."

"Great," Nora said leaning back.

"And we got in the middle of Snow White and the Seven Dwarves. Only there was only one dwarf. And she didn't bite into a poison apple. It was a spell. But the glass case was correct—"

"Max." A chill ran down Nora's back. "From the beginning."

"Blackstone is a wizard." Max ran a hand over his face as

if he were trying to hide the words. "Over a thousand years ago he fell in love with a witch's daughter. Only the witch didn't want anyone near her daughter, so she hid the daughter with her assistant, a magical dwarf named—"

"Sancho Panza."

Max looked at her strangely. "Merlin, actually. After the great Merlin of old. But the dwarf was a good friend of Blackstone's, and he managed to get Blackstone and the girl together. What they didn't know was that the witch had put a curse on them so when they kissed, the girl passed out. Merlin knew the girl would die if she didn't get back to the witch to remove the spell, but Blackstone outsmarted the witch. He put the girl in a glass coffin. She would remain as she was, not alive and not dead, until the spell was removed. Merlin knew the witch's spell would wear off after fifteen years if the witch didn't know where the girl was. But before they could hide the coffin, the witch stole it. Over the centuries, Blackstone has stolen it back. But he's never been able to hide it from the witch. She's telepathic. She's always been able to pull the information from him. Until now. As long as he doesn't know where the coffin is, the witch won't either."

"Shit," Nora said.

"You know, don't you?" Max asked.

"I have a hunch," Nora said.

Max held up his hand. "Well don't tell me. I don't want to be any more involved than I already am." He got up and swayed once. "I told you what I know. Now I'm leaving."

"Max, we have to investigate."

He shook his head, then caught the table to hold himself

in place. "It would raise too many questions," he said. "Like, if there is a woman in a glass coffin in your possession, is she dead? And if so, are you an accessory after the fact? And if she isn't, what then? Do we believe she's been alive but asleep for a thousand years? And isn't that Sleeping Beauty? Doesn't the prince get to wake her with a kiss? Where did this going to sleep with a kiss come from? It seems all wrong to me."

He stumbled forward. "I am going home to pretend this was all a drunken fantasy."

"And the money?" Nora asked.

"I'll pretend I defended a mobster and it was so traumatic I forgot all about it." He wandered out, clutching the back of booths for support.

She sat there, trembling. He was right. She had said she wouldn't investigate what was in that microbus. But now, it seemed, she had no choice.

S he had to go to her office first to get the key to the lock she had put on the garage. As she drove, she noted a full moon over the town. The air smelled fresh, with the trace of night flowers. She paused before making the turn-off to her office, then drove down the freeway to the neighborhood.

Streetlights were on the entire way, and the roads were clear of debris and emergency vehicles. As she pulled onto the residential streets, she saw the silhouettes of houses trailing off into the distance. Some had lights on. Many, by this time, had their lights off. Vehicles were parked in the street as if they belonged there.

She pulled over to the curb, parking between the two houses where she thought, but wasn't certain, the microbus had been parked earlier. She got out and wandered to the lawn, recognizing its greenery and its flowers from the afternoon. This was the place. She would bet her practice on it. And yet the neighborhood stood around it. Nothing was destroyed.

A porch light came on at the house behind her. She frowned. That house probably belonged to the radio personality. He had seemed like the nosy type. She slipped back into her car and drove away.

A feeling of disorientation that had nothing to do with the beer swept through her. Maybe when she got back to her office, she wouldn't even find a key. Maybe in the morning, Max would deny having this conversation with her. Maybe none of this had happened.

Maybe.

But it felt as if it had.

She pulled into the parking garage beneath her building and got out of her car. As she walked, she passed a 1974 Lincoln. A little man stood on its fender, and a tall man leaned against its hood. He wore a shimmery gray silk suit that accented his broad shoulders and long legs, and on his feet he wore cowboy boots trimmed with real silver. A snake peeked its head out of his sleeve.

"You know," he said in that rich warm voice of his, "if you get the key and go to the microbus, I'll simply have to follow you. And if I follow you all of this will be for naught."

"Max tells me there's a woman in that glass case."

"And she's alive," Blackstone said. "She's been asleep for a thousand years. If you help us, she'll sleep for fifteen more."

"Why can't your friend get the information out of my brain?"

"Because it's not there," Blackstone said. "Right now, all you have is supposition. She could probe, but her powers won't let her unearth supposition. They'll only unearth fact."

"The fact is I have your microbus. She'll know that."

"You have my microbus," the little man said. "Sancho Panza's microbus."

"And we all know that's not your name," Nora snapped.

"No," the little man said. "You suspect that's not my name. You know that I have all the legal documentation to prove that it is."

She smoothed a hand over her hair, and took a deep breath. "This afternoon," she said. "I saw a destroyed neighborhood and a dead woman. I saw the police lead you away in cuffs."

"Yes," Blackstone said.

"But you're here, and the neighborhood's back the way it was, and Max says the woman's not dead."

Blackstone's smile was small. "We live differently from you, Sancho and I. And we don't really die."

"So you're saying what I saw was real."

"For that moment," he said. "But you asked us to fix it, to put it back. So we did."

"For the record," the little man said. "She was the one who destroyed everything, not us."

"What if she's the one who is in the right?" Nora asked.

"You don't even know what the battle's about," Blackstone said.

Nora crossed her arms. "Enlighten me."

"Love," Blackstone said. "It's about love."

"Seems to me it's about possession," Nora said. "There's a woman who has been asleep for a thousand years because her family and her boyfriend are fighting over her. Seems to me that she has no say in this matter."

The little man put his face in his hands. Blackstone frowned. The snake hissed at her.

"What happens if I raise the coffin lid?" Nora asked. "Will I wake her up?"

Blackstone shook his head. "You'll destroy my spell, but not the death spell. If you open that coffin, she'll die."

"Lovely," Nora said. She started for the elevators. Midway there, she stopped. "If all of this happens in fifteen years, why did you pay me for twenty?"

Blackstone hadn't moved. The snake had wrapped itself around his arm. The little man had disappeared along the side of the Lincoln. "I didn't pay you," Blackstone said.

"Why did your friend, then?"

Blackstone raised his beautiful silver eyes to hers. "The world has changed," he said. "She's been sleeping for a thousand years. It'll take her time to adjust, time to find herself again. She'll need to make decisions, need to make choices, and she can't make good choices when she first wakes up. Five years may not be enough. You might get a renewal after that."

"You expect me to babysit?" Nora asked.

"I expect nothing," he said. "But my friend here expects you to find competent help for any problem that might arise during your service to him. If that's too much to ask, tell us now. We'll find someone else."

Nora pushed a strand of hair off her face. The hair still smelled faintly of smoke. "The battle between you and this woman, this witch, is over?"

"It will be," he said, "if she can't find what she's looking for."

"And she won't find it," Nora said, "as long as I help your friend."

"You could say that." Blackstone lifted an edge of his sleeve. The snake crawled inside.

"That's giving me a lot of control over something that's important to you," Nora said.

"Yes." Blackstone stood. He seemed taller than he had before.

"Why?" she asked. "Why me?"

"Because," he said. "You believe just enough to take a chance."

"Believe," she muttered. Could he hear thoughts too? Had he known what she had been thinking the day she met him? She shook her head. She couldn't believe that. It was one thing too many. "What happens to you?"

But her words echoed in the empty garage. Blackstone, the snake, the little man, and the Lincoln were gone. She rested a hand on a rusted Beamer, more to hold herself up than anything else.

"I guess that answers my question," she said. She stared at the elevator, and thought about the key on the wall in her office. The key with the combination taped to it.

She could look now and satisfy her curiosity. Or she could do what she was supposed to do, and let things alone. She believed that a neighborhood burned down. She knew the neighborhood was fine now. She had seen it. Just like she had seen it burn this afternoon.

And that was the secret: she could no longer trust her senses. What if she went inside that VW microbus and found a glass coffin? And what if a woman were inside? And what if she opened it and ruined the spell? She wouldn't know how to find Blackstone or his little friend Sancho. She wouldn't know how to make everything better again.

Her own car keys were digging into the skin of her right hand. She started back to her car. She wasn't going to go. And it wasn't because of true love. Or fear that she might ruin a spell.

She had been given a strange gift these last two weeks. Someone had shown her that magic could exist. What if she went to that microbus and there was no glass coffin inside? There was no woman? Would she have to question everything she had seen? Would she want to?

When she reached her car, she got inside, and picked up the phone. Before she even knew what she was doing, she asked directory assistance to dial Max's home number. The phone rang six times. She was about to hang up when Max answered.

"Max?" she asked.

"You looked," he said.

And in that response she felt a deep and profound relief. She hadn't imagined any of this. Or if she had, Max was suffering the same delusion.

"No," she said. "But I'd realized we had skipped dinner. You want to go?"

"Now?" he asked.

"Yes," she said.

"Is this...a date?"

There was enough hesitation in his voice to make her hesitate too. But dating Max was something she had wanted to do since college. And she had never taken the initiative before. "Yes," she said.

He laughed. "Who'd've thought—after a day like this— well, maybe wishes do come true."

"Max?" she said.

"Sorry," he said. "Muttering. I'd love dinner. I think I'm a little more sober than I was before."

"I'll pick you up," she said. "In ten minutes."

She hung up before he could say no. And then she realized he wouldn't. Two shy people, finally getting their wish. She wondered if that was part of Blackstone's payment, and then decided she wouldn't think about Blackstone any more.

She leaned her head against the steering wheel and giggled. She was the one who wanted a little magic in her life, just once. And she had gotten more than a little. She had gotten too much.

Be careful what you wish for, her grandmother used to say.

Well, Nora's wish that day two weeks before had been a two-fold wish. She turned the key in the ignition. Max wasn't going to cook, and he probably wasn't going to rub her feet unless things moved faster than she expected. But he would certainly discuss the strangeness of the day with her, and that would be enough.

For now.

THE CHARMING WAY
A CHARMING UNIVERSE STORY
KRISTINE GRAYSON

BOOK FAIR.

The very words of the sign filled Mellie with loathing. Book Fair indeed. More like Book Unfair.

Every time someone wrote something down, they got it wrong. She'd learned that in her exceptionally long life.

Not that she was old—not by any stretch. In fact, by the standards of her people, she was in early middle age. She'd been in early middle age, it seemed, for most of her adult life. Of course that wasn't true. She'd only been in early middle age for her life in the public eye—two very different things.

And now she was paying for it.

She stood with her hands on her hips (which hadn't expanded [much] since she was a beautiful young girl, who caught the eye of every man) and looked at the pavilion, with the banner strung across its multitude of doors.

The Largest Book Fair in the World! the banner proclaimed in bright red letters. The largest book fair with

240

the largest number of publishers, writers, readers and moguls—movie and gaming and every other type the entertainment industry had come up with.

It probably should be called *Mogul Fair* (Mogul Unfair?). But they weren't pitching Moguls (although someone probably should; it was her experience that anyone with a shred of power [present company included] should be pitched across a room [or down a staircase] every now and then); they were pitching books.

This season's books, next season's books, books for every race, creed, and constituency, large books, small books and the all-important evergreen books which were not, as she once believed, books about evergreens, but books that never went out of style, like *Little Women* or anything by Jane Austen or, dammit, that villain Hans Christian Andersen.

Not that he started it all. He didn't. It was those Grimm brothers, two better named individuals she had never met.

It didn't matter that Mellie had set them straight. By then, their "tales" were already on the market, poisoning the well, so to speak. (Or the apple. Those boys did love their poisons. It would have been so much better for all concerned if they had turned their attention to crime fiction. They could have invented the entire category. But noooo. They had to focus on what they called "fairies" as misnamed as their little "tales.") She made herself breathe. Even alone with her own thoughts, she couldn't help going on a bit of a rant about those creepy little men.

She made herself turn away from the pavilion and walk to the back of her minivan. With the push of a button, the hatchback unlocked (now *that* was magic) and she pulled the thing open.

Fifty signs and placards leaned haphazardly against each other. Last time, she'd only needed twenty. She hoped she would use all fifty this time.

She glanced at her watch. One hour until the Book Unfair opened.

Half an hour until her group showed up.

Mellie turned her attention to the pavilion again. Impossible to tell where she'd get the most media exposure. Certainly not at those doors, with the handicapped ramp blocking access along one side.

Once someone else arrived to help her hand out the placards, she could leave for a few minutes and reconnoiter.

She wanted the maximum amount of airtime for the minimum amount of exposure. She'd learned long ago that if you gave the media too much time in the beginning, they'd distort everything you said.

Better to parcel out information bit by bit.

The Book Unfair was only her first salvo.

But, she knew, it would be the most important.

He parked his silver Mercedes at the far end of the massive parking lot. He did it not so that he wouldn't be recognized—he wouldn't anyway—but because he'd learned long ago that if he parked his Mercedes anywhere near the front, the car would either end up with door dings, key scratches, or would go missing.

He reached into the glove box and removed his prized purple bookseller's badge. He had worked two years to acquire that thing. Not that he minded. It still amazed him that no one at the palace had thought of opening a bookstore on the grounds.

He could still hear his father's initial objection: *We are not shopkeepers!* he'd said in that tone that meant shopkeepers were lower than scullery maids. In fact, shopkeepers had become his father's favorite epithet in the past few decades, scullery maid being both politically and familially incorrect.

It took some convincing—the resident scholars had to prove to his father's satisfaction that true shopkeepers made a living at what they did, and in no way would a bookstore on the palace grounds provide anyone's living—but the bookstore finally happened.

With it came a myriad of book catalogues and discounts and advanced reading copies and a little bit of bookish swag.

He'd been in heaven. Particularly when he realized he could attend every single book fair in the Greater World and get free books.

Not that he couldn't pay for his own books—he could, as well as books for each person in the entire kingdom (which he did last year, to much complaint: it seemed everyone thought they would be tested on the contents of said gift book. Not everyone loved reading as much as he did, more's the pity).

Books had been his retreat since boyhood. He loved hiding in imaginary worlds. Back then, books were harder to come by, often hidden in monasteries (and going to those had caused some consternation for his parents until they realized he was reading, not practicing for his future profession). Once the printing press caught on, he bought his own books—he now devoted the entire winter palace to his collection—but it still wasn't enough.

If he could, he would read every single book ever written —or at least scan them, trying to get a sense of them. Even with the unusually long life granted to people of the Third Kingdom, especially when compared with people in the Greater World (the world that had provided his Mercedes and this quite exciting book fair), he would never achieve it. There were simply too many existing books in too many languages, with too many more being written all the time.

He felt overwhelmed when he thought of all the books he hadn't read, all the books he wanted to read, and all the books he would want to read. Not to mention all the books that he hadn't heard of.

Those dismayed him the most.

Hence, the book fair.

He was told to come early. There was a breakfast for booksellers—coffee and donuts, the website said, free of charge. He loved this idea of free as an enticement. He wondered if he could use it for anything back home.

The morning was clear with the promise of great heat. A smog bank had started to form over the city, and he couldn't see the ocean, although the brochures assured him it was somewhere nearby. The parking lot looked like a city all by itself. It went on for blocks, delineated only by signs that labeled the rows with double letters.

The only other car in this part of the lot wasn't a car at

all but one of those minivans built so that families could take their possessions and their entertainment systems with them.

The attractive black-haired woman unloading a passel of signs from the van looked familiar to him, but he couldn't remember where he had seen her before.

He wasn't about to go ask her either. His divorce had left him feeling very insecure, especially around women. Whenever he saw a pretty woman, the words of his ex-wife rose in his head.

She had screamed them at him in that very last fight, the horrible unforgettable fight when she took the glass slipper —the thing that defined all that was good and pure in their relationship—and heaved it against the wall above his head.

Not so charming now, are you, asshole? Nope, not charming at all.

He had to concede she had a point—although he never would have conceded it to her. Still, those formerly dulcet tones echoed in his brain whenever he looked in the mirror and saw not the square-jawed hero who saved her from a life of poverty, but a balding, paunchy middle-aged man who would never achieve his full potential—not without killing his father, and that was a different story entirely.

Charming squared his shoulders and pinned his precious name badge to his shirt. The name badge did not use his real name. It used his nom de plum—which sounded a lot more romantic than The Name He Used Because His Real Name Was Stupid.

He called himself Dave. Dave Encanto, for those who required last names. His family didn't even have a last name —that's how long they'd been around—and even though he knew Prince was now considered a last name, he couldn't bring himself to use it.

He couldn't bring himself to use any name, really. He still thought of himself as Charming even though he knew his ex was right—he wasn't "charming" any more. Not that he didn't try. It was just that charming used to come easily to him, when he had a head full of black black hair, and an unwrinkled face, and the squarest of square jaws.

Prince Charming was a young man's name, in truth, and then only the name of an arrogant young man. To use that name now would seem like wish fulfillment or a really bad joke. He couldn't go with P.C. because the initials had been usurped, and people would catch the double irony of a prince trying to be p.c. with his own name change.

And as for Prince—that name was overused. In addition to the musician, princes abounded. People named their horses Prince, for heaven's sake, and their dogs, and their surrogate children. In other words, only the nutty named a human being Prince these days, and much as Charming resented his father, he couldn't put either of his parents in the nutty category.

So he told people to call him Dave, which was emphatically not a family name. Too many family names had been co-opted as well—Edward, George, Louis, Philippe, even Harry not just by another prince, but by some potter's kid as well.

Dave, not David, a man who could go anywhere incognito any time he liked. Gone were the days when people would do a double-take, and some would say, *Aren't you...?*

or *You know you look just like that prince—whatshisname?—Charming.*

Now they nodded and looked past him, hoping to see someone more important. Which was why he preferred the Greater World to the Third Kingdom. In the Greater World, they knew he wasn't *the* Prince Charming. To them, *the* Prince Charming was a man in a fairy tale, a creature of unattainable perfection, or—more accurately (he believed)—a cartoon character, an animated hero.

He was none of those things. True, he had a longer than usual life, but that caused longer than usual problems—like waiting for his father, who also had a longer than usual life, to kick the proverbial bucket (which in the Third Kingdom, wasn't as proverbial as you might think).

But as for magical powers, Charming had none. Besides that all-encompassing charm, which Ella had told him in no uncertain terms was gone now. Ella, who got his estates, half of his money, and custody of their two daughters because—true to form—his father wouldn't let him contest the divorce over *girls*.

He sighed and started across the monstrous parking lot. Several other cars were pouring into the first entrance, way up front, near the doors. The parking there, he knew from the e-mails he had gotten, was reserved for booksellers and the disabled—or the differently abled, as he had been bidden to say. The e-mails claimed he would need the close-in parking for the hundreds of pounds of books he would lug back to his car at regular intervals. But he had lugged chain mail and two injured companions over a hundred miles. He figured he could handle a few books.

The attractive woman had pulled out the last sign. He saw the initials—PETA—and felt a surge of disappointment. He'd seen what those animal rights lovers had done to his mother's favorite fur coat the one and only time he had taken her to the Metropolitan Opera in Manhattan. His mother had been horribly traumatized, although not so badly that she didn't implore him to bring the entire cast of the Met to the Third Kingdom at the end of every opera season.

He walked around the woman, and headed toward the pavilion, ready for coffee, donuts, and some insight into this season's bestsellers.

Mellie watched the well-dressed man walk the length of the parking lot. He wore what was known as business casual—a long-sleeved shirt and dark pants (no suit coat, no tie) but he still looked elegant. Some of that was the clothing itself; there was nothing casual about it. It was tailored to fit—and fit it did, over a well-muscled back, broad shoulders, and a nice tight—

She shook her head and looked away. If she really thought about it, she had to acknowledge that men were the source of her troubles. From her know-it-all first husband who had left her a young widow with two extremely young daughters to her beloved second husband who stupidly introduced her as a fait accompli to his own daughter, starting a resentment that continued to this day, men had been the root cause of her dilemmas from the moment she hit the public eye.

Of course, she had handled things badly. She always thought that any publicity was good publicity. Little did she realize that once someone had defined you to the media, then it didn't matter how many charities you gave to or how many advanced degrees you had, you would always be the evil stepmother, the wicked witch, or worse, the aging malignant crone.

At least she had avoided that last category—for now, anyway. She felt it hovering around her, like the flying monkeys from the stupid Hollywood version of the *Wizard of Oz*. The Wicked Witch of the West. Now *that* was a misunderstood woman.

"Mellie?"

She turned. The man behind her was exceptionally attractive. He also left a trail of wet footprints heading west. He was a selkie whose real name she did not (of course) know. He carried his pelt over his right arm and this time he wore human clothing.

He had actually stopped their first protest earlier this year by pulling off his pelt and having nothing suitable on underneath it. (Although she could see why the human storytellers had felt threatened by these creatures from the sea; not only were they preternaturally good-looking, they were also very well endowed.)

"As people show up, will you hand out signs?" she asked. "I need to figure out where we'll stage our protest."

She shoved the last pile of signs at him, not giving him a

chance to say anything, and then she hurried along the parking lot.

Midway there, she realized she was trying to catch that ever-so-elegant man and she slowed her steps.

She had sworn off men decades ago.

She wasn't about to let one distract her now.

The coffee was bitter and only the inedible coconut-covered donuts were left. He should have arrived earlier. Still he poured himself a cup, grabbed one of the few remaining paper plates, and found a maple bar crammed against the back of the donut box. Then he settled into a chair at the back of the room.

The panel was already talking about social media and whether or not it meant the death of the book, a topic that always broke his heart. He understood the importance of stories—he'd been raised on stories. Bards had come to his father's court before Charming could even read. But the best stories were the ones he accessed privately—and a screen never really felt private to him.

Still, he listened politely, getting more and more discouraged, until he finished his maple bar and fled the room.

The doors to the main exhibition hall were locked, with guards standing out front. The guards didn't look that formidable—two fat security guards in uniform, and several bookish types with their arms crossed, trying to look tough.

He sighed and decided to explore. He knew from his convention packet that there were side rooms, meeting rooms, conference rooms, and the all-important media room where the famous people, from the writers to the politicians/actors/musicians who loaned their names to books, gave interviews about whatever seemed important at the time.

The hallways were unbelievably wide so that they could accommodate crowds and wheelchairs, and yet he was the only person in them, except for the occasional publishing house salesman scrambling to put the finishing touches on a booth. From a distance, he caught the scent of cafeteria food, and remembered that they would all be able to buy lunch here if they were so inclined.

He was inclined, especially after that maple bar. There were no restaurants close, and he didn't want to lose his parking space.

The media room wasn't a room; it was an entire wing, with smaller rooms designated as green rooms, and larger rooms with actual mini studios, all set up to record certain kinds of programming. Surprisingly, these rooms were unlocked, but they were filled with young attractive people who all looked important and busy.

He peered in one, only to feel someone against his back.

He turned. The attractive woman from the parking lot stood there. She was tall and thin and exceedingly familiar. Her eyes were filled with intelligence, accented by her very good bone structure. This was a woman who had been a pretty young girl and had become striking in middle age. She would be lovely even into old age, so long as she didn't let that mouth of hers remain twisted like that.

"Charming, right?" she said. "The question is which one?"

He leaned against the door jam, feeling startled. Not just that she had recognized him, but that she knew there was more than one Prince Charming.

Which meant she wasn't a native of the Greater World. She came from one of the Kingdoms. But again, the question was which one.

"My name is Dave," he said as dismissively as he could.

"Yeah, I see that." She grabbed his prized purple badge, looked at it, and then dropped it against his shirt. "Dave Encanto. You're not fooling anyone, 'Dave.' Why are you here? To shut me down?"

He frowned at her. Clearly they'd met but he couldn't remember when and he certainly didn't understand her comment. He didn't have the power to shut down anyone. Not in the Greater World, anyway.

"Listen," he said, "I know everyone has a right to their opinion, but I do think tossing paint on little old ladies going into the opera takes things a bit too far. When I said I would shut you all down, it was only because I was angry, and it was, after all, my mother's fur coat that you ruined—"

"You don't know who I am, do you?" the woman said.

"No-oo," he said. "Just that you're with that animal rights group."

"Clearly we need a new acronym," she said more to herself than to him. Then she sighed. "P. E. T. A. which stands for People for the Ethical Treatment of *Archetypes*, not animals. We had the acronym long before those animal people stole it from us. They were just better at getting press coverage. Like everyone else on the planet, including you, 'Dave.' You know everyone wants to find their Prince Charming. Everyone—women, gay guys. Even real men, they want what Prince Charming has. You don't need a publicist. You just need to bask in your princely charmingness."

He studied her, too stunned to say much. He was always stunned in the face of bitterness, although these days he was beginning to understand it. Bitterness and the feeling that no one else knew exactly what you were going through.

He could have given her his litany—the paunch that wouldn't go away no matter how much he exercised, the increasing irrelevance, the fact that he hadn't seen his girls in nearly a year—but he didn't. Instead, he frowned.

"You're not one of the fairy godmothers," he said. "They were always unbelievably happy for no apparent reason. Disney got that right at least. Bippity Boppity Boo and all that."

She tilted her head at him, obviously intrigued.

"You can't be one of the old crones either, because they do look like the witches in Macbeth—Shakespeare had clearly been to one of the Kingdoms, maybe more than once."

She raised her eyebrows.

"And you're beautiful, more beautiful now than you probably ever were as a girl." He wasn't coming on to her; it just wasn't in his nature. He was stating a fact. "So you're probably one of the stepmothers. I would guess Snow White's. Which means we met at a party, gosh, a century or two ago, when someone decided we should clear up the

Charming mess and the stepmothers gossip and see if we could take care of those Brothers Grimm."

"*I* thought," she said. "It wasn't someone. It was me. I hosted that party."

He nodded, remembering now. It was one of the first large scale events ever held in the Greater World. There had been too many arguments about which kingdom would host, so someone—this woman, maybe?—decided to rent a castle in Germany of all places, that white one with the towers along the Rhine that Disney later used in one of its films—for the three-day catered affair.

Nothing had gotten settled, and in fact, he could point to the entire event as the beginning of the end of his marriage. Ella met the wives of the other Charmings, and they started talking about their marriages, and things got said. The other Charmings apparently treated their wives like princesses. Not that he hadn't. But he also expected her to think for herself, and do something other than spend the King's gold.

He'd said that more than once, and he'd made the mistake of saying it in front of his father, who then harped on it forever. Apparently—at least according to Charming's ex-wife—the other Charmings never said anything bad about their wives.

Charming thought that was just one-upmanship. People —charming or not—said things they regretted. Maybe the other wives just hadn't been as sensitive to slights as Ella had been. Either way, Ella had been dissatisfied with the relationship ever since.

Charming looked at the attractive woman, who

continued to stare at him. She really was beautiful. He remembered noticing that in Germany all those years ago. He had noticed and thought she had gotten a bad rep, considering everything. All she and the other stepmothers wanted was a little respect.

"You never answered me," he said. "Are you Snow White's stepmother?"

"Are you Sleeping Beauty's Prince Charming?" she asked, apparently not willing to show him hers until he showed her his. But in asking the question, he got his answer. She was Snow White's stepmother.

"I married Ella," he said. "The fairy tales still call her CinderElla, which really isn't fair. She never was covered in dirt, not even when I first met her."

"Thin and shapely and beautiful and oh, so, young." That bitterness again. "Why is it that men like you always go for women like her?"

"I was a boy," he said. "And she was a girl, not a woman. We weren't really old enough to commit to anything."

The woman let out a small "huh" of surprise. "So all three Charmings have divorced now."

That news made him grunt with surprise. He hadn't known that. He thought the other Charmings lived in perpetual wedded bliss. Happily ever after and all that.

The woman didn't seem to notice his surprise. She was saying, "Isn't that just the way of things? I suppose you blame the women's movement as well?"

The other Princes Charming had blamed the Greater World's women's movement? Seriously?

He knew where the fault in his marriage was, and it wasn't with some amorphous movement in another world.

"Ella and I weren't compatible from the beginning," he said. "She's very into the social whirl, the dresses, the dancing, and me, well..."

He grabbed his badge. He was going to shake it ruefully. Instead, his fingers closed protectively around it.

"I'm bookish," he said. "Quiet. A bit of—what do they call it here in the Greater World?—a nerd."

"A nerd," the woman repeated, as if she couldn't quite believe what she was hearing.

"And," he said, mostly to cover the blush he could feel warming his cheeks, "I'm certain my father didn't help any. He wanted sons, and he blamed Ella when we didn't have any. There was no explaining genetics to him. X and Y chromosomes are beyond him. He'd been urging me to throw her off after our first daughter was born. But then, he also wanted me to use the old-fashioned King Henry the Eighth method."

"Divorce," the woman said.

"No," Charming said, trying to be circumspect. He was conscious of the fact that the number of people around them was beginning to grow. "Henry's other method of disposing of his wives."

"Oh, my," she said. "He really is the tyrant, isn't he?"

Charming nodded, a bit uncomfortably. He tried not to look at his father's deeds—or misdeeds. Not that they were illegal. Whatever the King did was legal; that was the law of the land. But he didn't have to like it.

"I prefer it here," he said. "In the Greater World."

With books, books and more books being created all the time. Not to mention movies and television and games. He was even beginning to like Twitter novels, even though that panel this morning had shaken him more than he wanted to admit. He didn't want the book to die. He wanted it to live, in its lovely hand-held form, for the rest of his (exceptionally long) life.

"Of course you prefer it here," she said. "The Greater World loves you. You're an ideal. Everyone wants to be you or have you or marry you. You're not considered a bitter, witchy woman past her sell-by date who's jealous of younger women and can't come to terms with her lost potential."

Well, they had the bitterness spot on, he thought, but didn't say. Still, he really didn't care about charming her. She had made up her mind about him on very little evidence—mostly on what other people thought—so he knew better than to try to change her mind.

Although, he couldn't prevent himself from saying, "Aren't you jealous, though? I mean, really?"

Her eyes widened. Had no one spoken to her like this before?

"Look," he said, holding out his hands. "You're the one who made the comment about me marrying a girl who was 'thin, shapely, and oh so young.' That's sounds a little bitter and jealous to me."

"Of course it would to you," she snapped. "I suppose you think I tried to kill Snow White, like the fairy tales say."

"No, I don't," he said. If she had tried, she would have been imprisoned when Snow White married the other Charming. Imprisoned or beheaded.

"People like you believe in the fairy tales. Why shouldn't you? You live one." Her tone got even more strident.

He sighed. He didn't think divorce was part of the fairy tale, but he couldn't get a word in. She hadn't stopped talking.

"People like you don't understand people like me. You have everything in life, and you don't understand people who have to fight for every scrap—"

"You're right," he said flatly.

She stopped, as if she was surprised at his words. Apparently, she didn't expect him to admit anything.

But he wasn't going to say what he really thought. He hated it when conversations veered in this direction. He was in a damned if he did and damned if he didn't situation. If he said he understood, he'd have to prove it, with life experience that she might or might not believe. And if he said he didn't understand, then she'd try to convince him. So he gave her his standard answer.

"I don't understand people who like to fight," he said. "I never have. So have a good book fair, and I'll see you around."

He slipped past her into the hallway, feeling unsettled and somewhat disappointed. He had liked her at first, anyway, and it wasn't often that he found a woman attractive anymore. Most women his age had given up or had snared the right man and weren't interested in meeting anyone new.

Technically, he should marry a younger woman and give his father the heir that his father was clamoring for, but he'd already married a young woman, and that hadn't gotten him anywhere. And besides, he had children. Two lovely, intelligent daughters whom he didn't see enough.

And who was to say that a girl couldn't inherit? If his father died before Charming did, he'd make a decree that his daughters could take over.

It was the least he could do.

The doors to the main exhibition hall were opening as he walked past, and his heart took a small leap. He was still unsettled—he really hadn't expected to find someone from the kingdoms here—but he was getting past that. And considering how big this place was, he probably wouldn't see her again.

Which bothered him a little bit more than he was willing to admit.

Okay, so she had been unfair. She launched into her rant without thinking about who she was talking to.

Not that she could convince a Charming that Archetypes needed protecting. His archetype—handsome, heroic, *perfect*—was desirable.

Hers wasn't.

Still, she leaned against the door to the main media screening room, hoping her heart would stop pounding. She hadn't meant to yell at him. She'd learned over the years that no one responded well to the whole "you don't understand" thing, even if they didn't understand.

But she had years—no, decades—of unfairness trapped inside her, and it wanted to flood out. And she wasn't about to go into therapy. That would just be buying into another version of the stereotype.

It took her a moment to gather herself. She always said things she regretted later. No amount of living or practical experience could change that about her.

And she did regret yelling at him.

Maybe if she saw him later in the weekend, she would apologize.

Maybe.

But first, she had a group of protesters to organize.

This hallway was big enough, and it wasn't roped off. It was perfect. It would give her all the media attention she needed. She might even be able to stage an interruption on one of the panels being held in the studios.

She ran her hands over her hair (still naturally black, except for a Cruella de Vil white streak that she had to color so that she wouldn't look like her properly infamous cousin), and headed back down the hallway.

Time to gather the troops.

She had a book unfair to interrupt—

And she was going to do it with style.

He was beginning to understand the thinking behind parking close. He had already made four heavily laden trips back to the car, and it wasn't even noon yet. The day promised to be one of the hottest of the year so far, and if he didn't get some Gatorade, he might just perish—long life or no long life.

He carefully avoided the van, even though he saw no one around it. During one of his trips, he'd seen a motley gathering of people—some looking a little less human than others. He was pretty convinced he saw Rumpelstiltskin there. The canny old dwarf had convinced most people he could spin straw into gold, but really his major skill was turning nothing into something—which wasn't that far from Charming's skill.

Not that Charming had ever used it.

But he wasn't going to think about PETA. Or anyone from the kingdoms. He had enough reading material in the car to last him the entire trip plus some, and he still hadn't gone through the first aisle in the first exhibition hall.

If he felt overwhelmed by the number of books before, he felt worse now. Booth after booth after booth, representing publisher after publisher after publisher, filled with book after book after book, all of them for this season's list or next season's. No one had back stock, except in the catalogue, although some of the evergreen books did have backers deeper in the pavilion—at least that was what his program said.

His program also gave him listings of panels. He could get into all of them with his lovely purple badge.

He was torn between listening to writers or picking up their wares. He wished he could do both. And in some cases, he could, since some of the panels were being filmed for—well, maybe not for posterity, but for people who hadn't attended at all.

Even with two more days of this, he doubted he would see much of it. Not just the panels, but the books, the related materials, the third and fourth exhibition halls. He was actually despairing of getting through the entire thing, even though another book dealer, seeing his sadness, commiserated.

Don't worry, chum, the other dealer said. *I've been coming for twenty years, and I've never once left the main exhibition area.*

As if that made him feel better.

For the first time in his life, he wished he had magic so that he had could explore every single one of the nooks and crannies. But even he knew that wasn't how magic worked. He'd have to pay some horrible price for that wish, and he wasn't willing to do it.

He'd already paid price enough when he married Ella.

He was just coming back into the hall when he saw her —that woman—Snow White's stepmother. What was her name? He didn't know for sure, which wasn't that unusual. In the kingdoms, names had power, especially to the magical.

And if his memory was right (and he wasn't sure it was), she had some magical powers.

How could anyone with magic be bitter? He wouldn't have been. Of course, he didn't understand how anyone with magic could be a failure either, but a bunch of them were.

More than a bunch really. Most of them.

Still, he found her strangely compelling and just a little sad. He actually understood her rant—a little, anyway. He'd seen the way that his father and others had treated Ella's stepmother, who hadn't been a bad woman. She had just been desperate. Her husband had died, leaving her with a stepdaughter she hadn't known about, a house that wasn't paid for, and two daughters of her own.

Sure she struggled, and yes, she had been verbally abusive to Ella—by Greater World parlance. In the Third Kingdom, she had been kind. She hadn't turned Ella out of the house. She'd fed her, clothed her (if poorly), and had given her a roof over her head, when she'd been within her legal right to abandon her.

As a wedding present to Ella, his father had imprisoned her stepmother, and Ella thought that just punishment. She'd been gleeful about it, which had disturbed Charming then even though he was besotted with her.

Now he was appalled—and a bit suspicious. He had a hunch the fact that the stepsisters got blinded at the reception by a pack of out-of-control birds had more to do with magic of the paid-for variety than the bad luck everyone had attributed it to.

He shuddered. Then he shoved the overstuffed bags in his car and headed back to the pavilion.

Halfway there, he saw one of the woman's PETA companions, who was—unless Charming missed the guess—a flying monkey. Only he had stuffed his wings into a 1960s Sergeant Pepper's coat and put on a hat, a fake ZZ-Top beard and sunglasses. He looked human enough, until you peered and realized that bluish fur covered not only the skin around his eyes and his forehead, but also his hands and forearms.

He carried two signs, and Charming gasped when he saw them:

Book Unfair! Destroy the Lies!

As he got closer, he could smell the scent of fresh Magic Marker. The flying monkey loped ahead of him.

"Excuse me," Charming said. "Are you with PETA?"

He said it the way the animal rights group did—pee-tah —and the monkey's mouth tightened into a little frown.

"I'm with P.E.T.A.," he snapped. "People for the Ethical Treatment—"

"Of Archetypes, I know," Charming said. "What's this about unfair books?"

The monkey stopped. "You read these things?"

"Books?" Charming asked. "Of course. Why else would I be here?"

"You're being brainwashed," the monkey said. "You don't understand the evil being perpetrated by these horrible fairy tales."

"Fairy tales," Charming repeated. He knew that "fairy tales" were how the Greater World absorbed the history of the kingdoms. Some of the tales were wrong, and some were not quite as wrong. They were about as accurate as the dime novels from the old Wild West, just a lot more popular.

"That's right," the monkey said. "They're lies. Damn lies. And they've got to be stopped."

"The fairy tales have to be stopped," Charming repeated because he didn't entirely understand this. "Fairy tales have been around for hundreds of years."

"That's hundreds of years too long," the monkey said. "We've got to put an end to this madness."

"By protesting a book fair?" Charming couldn't keep the incredulousness out of his voice.

"We have to start somewhere," the monkey said, and loped even faster, so that he got ahead of Charming.

Charming watched him go. He was confused. They thought they could—what? Stop the spread of fairy tales? Make fantastic literature go away?

To what end?

He needed to go back to the exhibition hall, but he found himself following the monkey instead.

Mellie ended up with fifty-one protesters, fifty-two if she counted herself.

The problem was that they were the bottom of the barrel. The selkie no one had heard of, a few flying monkeys, Rumpelstiltskin (who liked to be part of any kind of political action), and Bluebeard, of all people. None of the other stepmothers, none of the witches, none of the crones. The magical fish had sent their regrets, claiming they would take part if she held the next protest on the Santa Monica Pier—as if she believed that, which she didn't.

It seemed like every time she tried to rally the troops, the troops scattered to the wind.

Still, she decided to go through this, although she decided to shorten the protest to only a few hours for one day, instead of several hours over the life of the conference. Maybe she could get an interview—or better yet, some face time with some of the publishers and movie moguls. They would understand.

Forty-five of her protestors were already marching

through the hall, shouting *Death to Fairy Tales!* The rest were handing out flyers explaining PETA's position on fairy tales and why they were evil, along with the URL of the website she had started back when she first conceived of the protest idea.

So far, all the TV people had done when the marching started was shut the doors to the studios, so the sound of the protests didn't drown out the panels. Once the flying monkey got back with the two extra signs she'd asked him to draw for her, she'd change the tone of the protest a little. She'd have the entire group yelling *Book Unfair!* which was bound to get someone's attention.

The hallway seemed smaller with fifty bodies in it, even if all fifty were of varying (and often smaller) sizes. She kept peering around the corner, waiting for that damn monkey, and she heaved a sigh of relief when she finally saw him.

Although the relief turned to dread when she saw who was following the monkey. Charming. Looking...angry?

For some reason, she didn't think any of the Charmings got angry.

The monkey stopped when he saw her and handed her one of the signs. He started to go into an explanation of his lack of artistry—he really couldn't do proper calligraphy with Magic Markers—but she didn't care.

Instead, she stepped past him and right in front of Charming.

"You want to ban books?" he said, his voice strained. "Are you kidding me?"

"Not ban them, exactly," she said, hoping she sounded calm. "Just reduce the lies a bit."

"You think fairy tales are lies?" he said.

"Well, you clearly don't because—"

"Oh," he snapped, "don't start that 'people like you' crap again. People like me know that happily ever after is a crock. I'm divorced, remember?"

She bit her lower lip. She really hadn't put that together.

"You know what your problem is?" he said, his voice getting louder. "You don't know how lucky you are."

His arrogance took her breath away. "Lucky?"

"Lucky," he said. "You're beautiful, you're smart, you're successful enough to travel the Greater World, for heaven's sake, and all you care about is what people think of you."

"I do not," she said.

"You do too." He swept an arm toward the protestors. "Are you really an Archetype? Nowadays? Maybe a century ago, when women didn't have as many opportunities. And maybe when you couldn't choose your own identity. But who in this world knows who you are unless you point it out to them? And when you do, they think you're crazy."

"You don't know—"

"I do know!" He was yelling now. "Of course I know. Do you know what some officious little American government prick did when I told him my real name after I passed my driving test? Do you?"

She swallowed. "No."

"He laughed." Charming lowered his voice. "He laughed and said my parents ought to be shot."

She smiled. She couldn't help herself. She could picture that. She, at least, didn't have to go around introducing herself as the Evil Stepmother because that wasn't her real name. Never had been.

"Go ahead," he said, with some heat. "Laugh. But it's not fun. I actually prefer Dave. No one laughs when I say my name is Dave."

"Hey!" A door opened near Mellie. A man peered out. "Can you people pipe down? We're taping in here."

The nearest flying monkey—whose name she always forgot—raised his sign and waved it in the man's face. "This book fair is unfair!" the monkey said. "It's—"

"Yeah, yeah, yeah," the man said. "Someone is always publishing something someone else objects to. Whoopee ding dong do."

Then he slammed the door closed.

Mellie stared at it for a moment. Her heart sank. All this planning, to be dismissed with a single whoopee ding dong do.

The protestors had stopped marching and shouting.

"What do you want us to do, Mellie?" the selkie asked.

She didn't know. She had no idea any more.

So she shrugged. "Take a lunch break."

They set their signs down and bolted out of the hallway. She wondered if she'd ever see them again.

She didn't want to look at Charming. He would be laughing. He would gloat. Or he would be gone already.

But she couldn't help herself.

She looked.

He had an expression of compassion on his face. "It really bothers you what they think, doesn't it?" he said softly.

Her lower lip trembled, and she bit it. Hard. Evil step-mothers weren't supposed to cry. Nor were they supposed to care about the opinion of a Charming.

But here she was, on the verge of tears, in front of a Charming who actually appealed to her.

"Back when I was thin and shapely and beautiful and oh, so young, I didn't care," she said. "But then more thin and shapely and beautiful and oh, so young things showed up and I stopped being important, and I would say something a little sarcastic, and I suddenly got called old and bitter and jealous, and it just went downhill, no matter what I did. Words hurt, Charming. Words hurt."

He nodded. "So you thought you could control the words."

"Isn't that what you do with that golden voice of yours and that marvelously soothing manner? Don't you control the words?"

He gave her a rueful smile. "If I did, don't you think I would have ended up with custody of my daughters?"

Mellie looked at him, really looked at him, for the first time. He was very handsome. Elegant, not quite as trim as he could be, and just a hint of a bald spot that he might not even know about. A few lines around the eyes.

Not as young as he used to be either.

Seasoned.

Like her.

Only no one called him old and bitter and jealous.

But he had called himself a nerd.

"What are you doing here in the Greater World?" she asked.

"Me?" his voice squeaked just a little. "Getting books. I told you. I read a lot."

She picked up his badge. It was purple, not for royalty, like she'd initially thought, but for booksellers. "You got an illegal badge?"

"No," he said. "I sell books back home."

"You're a merchant?" She couldn't quite keep the incredulousness from her tone.

He straightened his shoulders as if by making himself taller he would become more powerful. "It's an honorable profession."

He was being defensive. That surprised her. "I just thought being prince was profession enough."

"Maybe in the Greater World," he said. "Here princes have to give speeches and do good works and have meetings with other princes. Back home, all I do is wait for my father to die."

He flushed a dark red.

"I didn't mean that the way it sounded," he said.

"I know what you mean," she said. "You like it better here."

He nodded.

"Why?"

He waved his badge at her. "People don't have any expectations of Dave the Bookseller. Except one."

"What's that?" she asked, actually curious.

"They expect him to know a lot about books."

A nd as he said that, he suddenly knew how to solve her problem. He held out his hand.

"Come with me," he said.

She frowned at him, then she looked down at his hand as if she expected him to be holding a dagger. "Why?"

"Because you're going about this wrong," he said.

"Going about what wrong?" she asked.

"Getting them to think better of you," he said.

"They need to know that we're not evil. We're just people, doing the best we could with a bad hand—"

"I know," he said. "I know what the perception is, and I know how wrong it is. But you can't change it by telling people they're wrong. That whole 'people like you' thing—"

"I'm sorry I said that," she said. "It's rude."

"So are these placards," he said. "They insult book people."

"They do?" she asked.

"But I know another way to convince them," he said.

"A Charming way?" she asked.

"Exactly," he said, and grabbed her hand. "Come on."

H e dragged her to the exhibition hall. She had only walked past it; she hadn't looked inside. But she did now.

It was bigger than any castle audience hall she had ever seen, and it was crammed full of booths and books and people. More people than she could ever imagine.

One of the security guards looked for her badge, but

somehow Charming got her past him. Something about an assistant. She didn't listen closely. She was too awed by the size of this hall.

She had no idea how many books there were.

"What do you think of vampires?" Charming asked as they hurried down an aisle.

It was such a non sequitur that she actually stopped. "Vampires?" she said.

"Or werewolves," he said. "Or zombies."

She shrugged. "Zombies don't exist," she said.

"Okay, then. Vampires. Werewolves. Creatures of the night. You think they're misunderstood?"

"I think they're scary," she said. "The handful I've met anyway. Predators. Real predators who think of us as prey."

"Yet they're half human, right?"

"Werewolves are," she said. "Technically vampires used to be human, and they have some vestiges—"

"So that's a yes," Charming said. "They care about their reputation too. About the time we started dealing with those Grimm people, they had to deal with someone named Stoker. He let the Great World know about them—"

"So?" she said.

"And the Greater World heard how evil they are," Charming said.

"And you think that's bad?" she asked. She didn't think so. Vampires scared her more than werewolves who were, at least, predictable.

"What I think is irrelevant," Charming said. "But what the Greater World thinks, now that matters."

He swept his arm toward a wall of books.

"Behold," he said.

She looked at what he was pointing at. Book after book after book about vampires. Not about how evil they were or how dangerous. But how sexy they were. There was even a movie magazine dedicated to the rise of the sexy vampire, and movie posters with the vampires looking longingly at young women—not like they were going to eat the women, but like they were in love with them.

"You're kidding, right?" she said.

"No," Charming said. "Vampires are all the rage now. Teenagers dress up like them. Prince Charming is passé. Now they all want to fall in love with Edward."

"Edward?" she asked.

"Long story," he said. "Suffice to say that the vampires used to be as angry about their own image as you are."

"So what did they do?" she asked.

"They started writing."

She blinked at him. Writing? Seriously?

He must have seen her shock, because he said, "You can't defeat the power of the book. But you can make it work for you."

"You think I should write about being an evil stepmother?"

"Why not? It worked for the Wicked Witch of the West." He grabbed a book off the shelf with a green witch on the cover. "She's got her own sympathetic Broadway play now and it's going to be a movie or so I hear, and she has her own soundtrack, not that horrible thing from the *Wizard of Oz*, and—"

"Me?" she said. "Write?"

"If you can't," he said, "I'm sure there are a lot of writers here who'll write the book for you."

"They'd do that?" she asked.

"For the right amount of money," he said.

"You're playing some kind of joke on me, right?'

"No," he said. "Ask anyone."

So she did. She started walking down the hall, asking people about vampires. She got a lot of opinions. Older people thought they were evil, but the younger ones talked about how sexy they were, and some even tried to shove vampire novels in her hands.

After a while, Charming showed up beside her with cloth bags covered in logos. As people shoved books at her, he took them and put them in the bags.

"Study materials," he said to her very softly.

"They give this stuff away?" she asked.

"Only to people they consider influential," he said. "Like me."

"So they know you're a Charming?" she asked.

He waved the badge at her. "I'm a bookseller. We're more important than any prince."

She tilted her head at him. "I really don't understand this place."

"I know," he said. "Why don't you let me show it to you?"

He slung the book bags over his shoulder and tucked her hand in the crook of his arm. Together they walked through the exhibition hall. She saw vampires, vampires, and more vampires, followed by werewolves and even a few zombies as romantic leads, no matter how fictitious they were.

And she saw people talking about books and arguing about them. Occasionally Charming would join them. He didn't seem like a prince. More like a really nice man.

A man who didn't believe in happily ever after.

But then again, neither did she.

Although she did like learning a thing or two.

And he had a lot to teach her about the Greater World. And books. And transforming wicked stepmothers into romantic heroines.

Sexy heroines.

Women who deserved their own princes charming, even if those princes were a little older, a little balder, and a whole lot nerdier than expected.

Standing Up For Grace
An Imperia Encanto Adventure
KRISTINE GRAYSON

ONE

Here, in the Greater World, the kids think that fairy tales are all hearts and flowers and unicorns and pink ponies. Everything has gold glitter and with the wave of a wand, every wish comes true. The Greater World includes LaLa Land, a place that prides itself on making up all these lies.

Until she actually moved here, Imperia Encanto thought LaLa Land—Los Angeles—was this wonderful mecca. But now that she lives here, she's been discovering the truth. Los Angeles isn't a mecca—at least not the mecca she imagined from the books she read back in the Kingdom.

Los Angeles is hot. It's in the desert. It does have some lovely flowering plants, but the sunlight is harsh. And the people have really, really rough edges.

No wonder they want to believe in fairy tales.

Too bad the fairy tales are all lies.

Imperia Encanto wants to tell those kids about all the lies, but her dad won't let her. Her dad is one of the Princes Charming. Out here, they call him Cinderella's Prince Charming, but he calls himself Dave Encanto. That last name thing took a while to get used to, but not as much as the way people think about Imperia's other life, calling it a fairy tale, like that's a good thing.

In a sideways way that fairy tale thing is how Imperia ended up in the principal's office. Imperia is nursing a sore hand, and hoping her dad won't be upset at her when she gets home. Dad doesn't scream or yell. He frowns.

And when a man whose greatest magical ability is charm frowns, you know you've done something bad.

Imperia does not have the ability to charm. Or, at least, she doesn't have much of it. If she had it, she wouldn't have had to punch Skylar Kennedy Campbell to get her to leave Imperia's little sister Grace alone. But Imperia couldn't stop Skylar with talk, so Imperia had to resort to violence.

And Daddy is going to hate that, especially since he thinks Imperia has charm and just refuses to use it.

Everyone in her father's side of the family is supposed to have some charm. That's just the way things work in the Kingdoms.

There are many Kingdoms, and they overlap with the Greater World which, Daddy says, is the real world, although Imperia isn't so sure. Imperia was born in the Kingdom— the Third Kingdom, to be precise—and it always seemed pretty real to her, especially when Mom took her and Grace and dumped them on the castle steps like so much flour.

Your granddad will know what to do with you, Mom said, with that flat look in her eyes. Mom had that flat look for weeks before she dumped the girls. It was like Mom didn't care about anything except this toothy guy she met in a pub. But that was weird, even for Mom. Because Mom did care about stuff. It was just usually stuff that no one else in the family cared about.

Fortunately, Mom didn't say any of this stuff to Grace. Just to Imperia. Because Grace wouldn't've been able to deal with it.

Grace is four years younger than Imperia, but Grace at eight is a lot younger than Imperia ever was at eight. Maybe that's because Imperia had to deal not just with Mom, but with Grandmother as well—not Grandmama Lavinia (she loves Grandmama Lavinia, Mom's stepmom) but Dad's mother, the Queen, who is Very Proper. But it must be said in Grandmother's favor that she did cry when she found out that Daddy was bringing the girls to the Greater World, because Grandmother cannot easily come here. Grandfather hates it here, even though he's never left the Kingdom.

He thinks that Daddy is running away from his responsibilities. Daddy says he has no responsibilities except waiting for Grandfather to die.

Imperia wasn't supposed to hear that conversation— although it wasn't a conversation, it was a fight, and they had it just outside the throne room, which she had been exploring because there was nothing better to do, and besides, one day All This Would Be Hers, or so her grandmother told her in a whisper, as if that excited Grandmother a lot more than it excited anyone else.

The problem with the Kingdom, according to both her grandmothers, is that women get no respect there. In fact, Grandfather wouldn't let Daddy fight the divorce with Mom even though Daddy wanted to, because Grandfather didn't believe in fighting over girls (Imperia wasn't supposed to have heard that either, but she did, and she didn't tell anybody, not even Grace. Especially not Grace. Grace would've cried. Imperia never ever ever cries. Crying is for babies). So Daddy had to do what Grandfather said because, even though there are courts in the Kingdom, Grandfather is the Ultimate Authority, and he can overrule anyone.

Daddy says giving up the girls broke his heart. He said that in the fight Imperia wasn't supposed to hear. Then Daddy said, You make it sound like I shouldn't even love my daughters to Grandfather, and Grandfather said, You can love whomever you want, but you still have to follow the rules, and the rules say that the Kingdom goes to the male heir. And Daddy said, Unless there is no male heir, and after me, there isn't. My daughters deserve to rule. And Grandfather said, That Greater World has corrupted you more than you know.

Which is why Imperia thought the Greater World would be better. She thought it would be hearts and flowers and unicorns and pink ponies and wands with gold glitter. But it isn't.

Some things are better here. There's no Grandfather for one thing, and Daddy's around all the time, and he loves being a Daddy, even if he's scared he's doing it wrong. And the weather isn't bad, it's just different, all that sunshine and no forests and lots and lots of buildings.

Imperia loves Daddy's new house, which isn't a castle at all, but something called a Tudor, and you can walk from one side of it to the other in less than five minutes, and she loves the bookstore that Daddy is building, and she thought she'd love school.

She really thought she'd love school.

But she was wrong.

TWO

School is Warren Excellence Academy of Beverly Hills. Warren Excellence Academy of Beverly Hills is the place to send your children to school, or, at least, that's what its website says. The website doesn't give an address or even list staff, although it does mention the school's founder, Ansible Warren, of the Los Angeles Warrens—an old, old LA family (that goes back more than 100 years, which is younger than Daddy is, but is old for the non-magical, at least that's what Imperia has learned). Ansible Warren believed in Education, and more importantly, apparently, Education Without RiffRaff—at least that's what the spoof website says.

The spoof website also has a tab for tuition, which the real website does not. The spoof website's tuition page says simply, If You Need to Ask About Tuition, You Cannot Afford Excellence.

Which makes Imperia a little uncomfortable. She has learned in the short time she's been visiting the Greater World that royalty here isn't hereditary (although she hears there are a few places in the Greater World where it is), but is based on how much money someone has.

Fortunately, Daddy has lots and lots of money because gold is really valuable here, and the one thing the Kingdom has a lot of is gold. So Imperia is royalty in both places, and she thought that would get her an advantage in school, but she was wrong.

Seems she's missing one other thing that makes for royalty in Southern California. Fame.

Everyone has heard of Prince Charming. No one, it seems, has heard of his oldest daughter Imperia. Apparently, no one has heard of any part of the so-called Cinderella story after the "And They Shall Live Happily Ever After" was recited at her parents' wedding. Apparently, no one here knows that happily ever after doesn't always work for the folk who inspired fairy tales or that her parents were the biggest mismatch of their generation or that her parents finally had no other choice except to get divorced.

Anyway, Imperia couldn't wait to go to Warren Academy, and then she did, and it was awful because on the first day, the very first day, the girls there made Grace cry.

And because Grace has cried every day since, Imperia is in the principal's office, with her hand bandaged, because she had to visit the school nurse before ending up here, and she has discovered that Greater World nurses don't have magic wands, they have antibiotics and bandages and they say things like "It'll take some time to heal" and "You're lucky you didn't break anything" like they can't fix anything at all.

The principal's office has wood paneling and a fireplace even though Imperia's pretty sure that's for show, since they're in Los Angeles (pardon: they're in Beverly Hills. Los Angeles is a different town—a poorer town) and Los Angeles (Beverly Hills) is really hot and Imperia can't imagine ever using the fireplace.

There's a receptionist in this front room, and a beautiful carved door leading to the actual principal's office, and another door—not as beautiful—with a sign on it for the assistant principal. But Imperia will have to deal with the real principal because Daddy's been dealing with the real principal.

Daddy's come in here a couple of times to complain about the way that Grace is being treated, and he's done everything, including threatening to take the girls elsewhere, although no one really knows where elsewhere is. Finally, he talked to a friend of his who has a lot of kids and that friend said that maybe the girls were picking on Grace because they were too scared to pick on Imperia and Imperia should just stop them the next time they picked on Grace.

Imperia and Grace were both raised to fight their own battles, so Imperia standing up for Grace was a pretty revolutionary idea. Or at least, to Daddy it seems revolutionary because he doesn't know about all the things that Imperia does behind the scenes for Grace, how Imperia protects her and makes sure she doesn't hear anything, and makes sure she has a good book to read and a quiet place to be. Imperia always stands up for Grace, but usually not against bullies, because in the Kingdom, no one bullies the Prince's daughters, even if they don't like the Prince.

Here, though, here is different, and no one seems to care who they all are, not that Imperia can tell them, because

STANDING UP FOR GRACE

everyone here thinks fairy tales are make-believe. So Imperia can't say, I'm next in line to the throne, and expect it to mean anything, and she can't threaten them with her grandfather's Ultimate Authority, and her glares don't seem to be working either.

She has no real tricks any more and she tried to tell Daddy that, but he didn't understand. Daddy's a pacifist, and he's probably not going to like the way that Imperia defended Grace—Daddy's going to hate the idea of fists— and Imperia doesn't want the principal to say anything. Imperia's been sitting on the expensive leather chair next to the reception desk, hugging her legs to her chest and resting her face against her knees, wondering how she's going to manipulate this conversation.

After all, Imperia doesn't have charm and she's too young to have magic (Girls don't come into their magic until they're too old to have children), and so she's just going to have to wing it. And time has proven that Imperia isn't good at winging things.

"Miss Encanto," the receptionist says, putting a hand on the little thing that looks like an earbud jutting out of her ear. "Principal Daley will see you now."

Imperia takes a deep breath but through her nose, a trick she learned a long time ago. If she takes it through her nose, no one knows she's trying to calm nerves. Grandmother taught her that and a few other tricks, all designed to show how strong she is even when she's not feeling strong at all.

Then Imperia puts her feet down decisively and stands up straight, raising her chin just like Grandmother taught her to do. It makes her look regal, or so Grandmother says, and right now, Imperia needs regal.

She doesn't have anything else to help her. She can't even rely on clothes to help her (which is Mom's best way of coping) because she has to wear the stupid school uniform, all black and gray with a white shirt that inevitably gets covered with food stains, and a coat over it all that's really hot, especially at moments like this. She also has to wear knee socks and the most uncomfortable black shoes ever invented.

No one looks good in this outfit which, Daddy says, is the point.

But Imperia is trying. She walks to that ornate door, pulls it open, and steps inside.

The principal's office smells of lavender and old wood. Normally, Imperia would like those smells, but this moment isn't normal. She stands with her hands behind her back because she knows better than to sit uninvited. Not that the chairs in here are comfortable. They're wooden chairs with red leather seats, designed as miniature torture chambers (as Daddy said after he sat in one), but they do match the couch off to one side.

Principal Daley sits behind her desk. She's a tiny woman with a pile of black hair. She gets to wear whatever she wants, which is usually something silk and expensive. Even her glasses are expensive. Right now, they're perched on the edge of her nose, a chain hanging from the earpieces on either side of her face. The chain glitters in the overhead light. Principal Daley is reading a piece of paper and doesn't even look up as Imperia stands there.

"Don't hover, child," Principal Daley says, immediately putting Imperia on the defensive.

She's not hovering. She's standing, waiting like she was trained to do. But she forgets: No one in the Greater World knows the finer points of etiquette. (If they knew the finer points of etiquette—and they knew who she was—they would all bow their heads as she passed.)

Imperia moves toward the chair slowly because, after all, Principal Daley didn't tell her to sit, just told her to stop hovering. Imperia's beginning to figure out how elliptically conversation works in the Greater World, and assumes that a command to stop hovering is also a command to sit down.

So she does. Gingerly.

Principal Daley sets her paper down, takes off her glasses, and lets them fall against her chest. "How is your sister?"

I don't know, Imperia wants to say. Your goons dragged me off before I could check.

But she knows better. Daddy said to treat Principal Daley the way Imperia would treat Grandfather because Warren Excellence Academy is Principal Daley's little kingdom. So Imperia knows better than to mouth off.

But she isn't quite sure how to answer the question, so she falls back on the cliché about honesty and the best policy.

"The last time I saw her, she was standing with her hand over her mouth," Imperia says.

"Hmm." Principal Daley's lips twitch. Imperia wonders if she's hiding a smile, then decides that's not possible. Principals and kings don't smile, at least not involuntarily. "I see you took the matter into your own hands."

Imperia doesn't answer that. It's an incriminating—if true—statement that's better left alone.

"Your father has been quite angry with us about the way Grace has been treated," Principal Daley says.

"He's not the only one," Imperia blurts, then bites her lower lip.

"He calls it bullying," Principal Daley says.

"It is bullying," Imperia says. "They're calling her names. She cries every day, and you're not doing anything."

So much for watching her tongue.

"That's why you decided to do something on your own."

Imperia sits tall in the chair, keeps her shoulders back and meets Principal Daley's gaze. Imperia is not going to admit she's wrong, because she's not wrong, no matter what the rules are, no matter what Daddy says about violence. Skylar Kennedy Campbell wasn't listening to reason. Skylar Kennedy Campbell wasn't listening at all.

And besides, nothing can compare to the feeling that Imperia had when Skylar Kennedy Campbell toppled backwards, her nose gushing blood all over her white shirt, and her eyes filling with tears.

"You do realize that Skylar's parents are going to want an apology," Principal Daley says.

"They're not going to get one." Imperia crosses her arms.

"No, I suppose not." Principal Daley sighs. "So I'll give you a choice. You can apologize or I can talk with your father."

"Talk to him," Imperia says. "He's the one who told me

that I should stand up for Grace. Someone has to and it's clear this school is not going to."

Principal Daley's mouth thins, just like Grandmother's when she's trying not to speak her mind. "I can also write you up. In this school you have three warnings before you get expelled. If you get expelled, you will be part of a list sent to other exclusive schools in the area notifying them about problem children."

"Is a write-up a warning?" Imperia asks.

"Yes," Principal Daley says.

"Then give me a damn warning," Imperia says, hearing an echo of her grandfather's voice in her own. "And if swearing gets me another warning so be it. I'm not ashamed of what I've done. I think you people play favorites here, and because my family is unknown and Skylar's isn't, you're favoring her. My father will understand and he and Grace are the only people I care about."

The principal's eyes brighten for just a moment. It's almost a twinkle. Imperia has the distinct impression that she's both amusing and impressing the principal, but the principal can't say anything because she's afraid of Skylar's family.

Which makes Imperia even angrier.

"For the record," Imperia says as she stands up, "I really don't care if you expel me. I thought school would be wonderful here, but it's not. It's all about who you are, not about what you can learn. So expel me. I'd rather be home-schooled anyway. And it would certainly be better for Grace."

"Hmm." Principal Daley says, picking up that paper and

putting the glasses back on her nose. "Would it be better for Grace? After all, if you get expelled, she won't have a protector here."

Imperia straightens. "She'll leave with me."

"Ah, but your sister is getting marvelous grades and behaves beautifully, even when faced with difficult circumstances."

Principal Daley's twinkle suddenly reveals itself as something evil. She isn't admiring Imperia. Principal Daley knows she has Imperia beaten.

"If you get expelled, your sister will remain," Principal Daley says.

Imperia opens her mouth to say, Daddy will take her out of school, and Daddy probably will, but Imperia doesn't know that for sure, and besides, why continue to argue with Principal Daley? The woman is the king here, and kings always win when they fight on their home turf.

Even if Imperia and Grace leave, especially if they leave, Principal Daley will still think she won.

"Am I excused?" Imperia asks.

"You're not excused, child, but you may leave," Principal Daley says.

Imperia stares at her for a moment, but Principal Daley studies the paper in front of her as if Imperia doesn't exist. Which makes Imperia even angrier, just like it's supposed to.

Finally, she turns, leaves, and concentrates very, very hard on not slamming that carved door shut. She doesn't want Principal Daley to know just how mad she really is.

Imperia doesn't want Principal Daley to know that she's won.

. . .

THREE

At least Grace is better. Imperia finds her in the crowded cafeteria, which is more like a restaurant, with potted plants and more damn wood, as if this stupid school was in some snowy mountainous region instead of one of the hottest places Imperia has ever seen.

The cafeteria smells like hamburgers and pizza, but it has a huge salad bar and a low-fat menu that rivals some of the area's most exclusive restaurants. A lot of kids are supposed to eat only from the low-fat menu, and there are employees here who actually enforce parental food decrees.

Imperia is glad she isn't under a parental food decree, but she does think the food in the place could improve. There is no mutton, for example, nor is there any stewed pigeon, both favorites of hers. The game meats are frowned upon—she isn't supposed to admit that she's eaten wild boar, apparently—but bland chicken breast is okay.

She thought the food would be better here in the Greater World too, but she was wrong about that as well.

Fortunately, she and Grace share a lunch period so Imperia's been able to defend Grace. Most of the trouble happens at lunch, although this morning's trouble happened before class even started. Then Imperia spent two hours in the principal's office which, even she has to admit, hadn't gone as well as she would have liked.

After leaving the principal's office, Imperia hurried to the cafeteria only to find Grace sitting calmly at one of the back tables, having a toasted ham-and-cheese sandwich, something she's fallen in love with. Imperia hasn't found anything to love yet on the menu, but she hasn't really looked, as busy as she's been defending Grace.

This lunch period, though, Grace is happily munching away, a closed book beside her. The closed book is odd too (Grace usually reads in crowds) but even odder is that Grace is grinning—at a gaggle of girls who are sitting with her.

Imperia doesn't recognize any of them.

Her stomach clenches and she wonders what these girls have planned for Grace. Especially since Grace is looking particularly relaxed, and when Grace looks relaxed, she also looks pretty. Normally, everyone agrees that Imperia is the family beauty, much as she resents it since her so-called beauty comes from Mom. (In fact, Imperia looks exactly like Mom did at the same age, minus the ashes and the dirt, of course.)

But Grace looks like a blond version of Dad, all square-jawed and blue-eyed. Grandmother says Grace will grow into her looks, but that's not a phrase that anyone likes, especially Grace, who wants to have her looks now.

It's hard to be the duckling in a family of swans, particularly a somewhat chubby duckling with a square jaw and a shy manner. Shy chubby ducklings usually get ignored, which Imperia is beginning to think preferable to this relentless bullying that Grace has endured since they've come to the Warren Excellence Academy.

And Imperia is afraid the bullying is going to start again.

Imperia stalks over to the table, her hands already

clenched into fists. The bruises on her right hand ache as she does this, but she tries to ignore it all.

Grace looks up as Imperia gets closer and smiles as if she's really, really happy. Now Imperia is very worried, because she knows how this stuff works: Get the victim to go along, thinking that she's in the group now, and then say or do something so crushing that it destroys the girl's spirit.

Imperia wants to say she's never done anything like that, but of course she can't. She's the second in line to the throne, for heaven's sake. If someone needed crushing—and a few kids did back at the palace—then Imperia found it best to do the crushing herself.

"Grace," Imperia says with some caution in her voice. All the other girls at the table look up, and Imperia realizes they're Grace's age. The girls who've been picking on Grace are older.

Some of these girls are a bit portly and a few wear somewhat hideous glasses. One girl has a French manicure—or would if she hadn't chewed off the tips and the cuticles—and another girl has braids that are coming loose.

"This is my sister Imperia," Grace says with pride.

The girls murmur and nod and look away. Imperia recognizes their response. They're in awe of her.

That makes Imperia's brain hurt. No one has been in awe of her here in the Greater World. No one at all.

She wants to ask, Is everything okay? but she isn't sure how to do it without embarrassing Grace. So Imperia thinks about another gambit which is How did this happen? but that gambit is as bad as Is everything okay? because if she says it, it'll sound like Grace doesn't deserve friends, and of all the people Imperia has ever known, Grace is the one who deserves friends the most.

But Grace knows her, and Grace gets this smug little smile on her face, like she understands Imperia's struggle.

"They all wanted to meet you," Grace says. "They've never seen anybody deck Skylar before."

Good, Imperia thinks. Great. I'm a hero to eight-year-olds.

"Somebody probably should've decked her a long time ago," Imperia says.

The little girls giggle, then cover their mouths as if laughing at that sentence is forbidden. Maybe it is. Imperia doesn't get all of the rules in this place yet.

"Nobody stands up to Skylar," says one of the little girls. She has glasses so thick that her eyes look like huge on her tiny face. Everything else about her is perfect though, from the knot on her little bowtie to the layered cut of her red hair. "Her Mom is the biggest box office star in the world."

Imperia frowns. "Her mom? I don't know a movie star named Campbell."

"Because that's not her last name, silly," one of the other little girls says. She's a thin thing with a chin so pointed that she looks like one of the drawings in those fairy tale books Daddy doesn't like.

Imperia doesn't want to know who this famous mom is because if she knows, she'll have to hate her, and she doesn't want to hate any movie star for any reason except a bad movie. Movies are still too new and precious to her to risk on a personal problem.

"I don't care who her mom is," Imperia says. "People

should be judged for who they are, not for who their parents are."

All of the little girls stare at her, eyes as huge as the glasses-girl's. The little girls are quiet, and then Imperia realizes that they aren't the only ones. Everyone has gotten quiet. There isn't a single conversation in the room, and almost all of the tables are full.

Not even the adults are talking. One of the cafeteria monitors—the people who keep track of the parental food decree—crosses her arms and leans back as if she's expecting a show.

The hair on the back of Imperia's neck rises, and she knows without anyone telling her that someone is standing behind her.

She turns around slowly.

Four of Skylar's friends stand in a half-circle, sleeves rolled up, hair pulled back. These girls are big, with something Daddy calls gym-muscles, because he says people here in the Greater World don't have weapons practice or know how to ride horses or understand the importance of walking everywhere. Daddy says gym muscles are almost like fake muscles because they don't deliver the way that real muscles (properly worked out) do.

Still, Imperia's heart starts beating really hard, and she knows she's in for it. She wonders if the grown-ups will step in to stop the impending fight. Probably not, if Skylar's Mom is rich and superfamous. The grown-ups will probably wait until the fight gets underway, then take some cell phone pictures to sell to the tabloids (or to Skylar's mom), and then maybe someone will step in.

Imperia knows all about the tabloids. Principal Daley warned her about them before Imperia even had a day of classes, saying that a kid could get expelled for selling pictures to a tabloid. And since Imperia didn't (at that moment) know what a tabloid was, she assured the principal that she wouldn't do anything of the sort.

At the moment, however, tabloids are the least of her worries. Imperia is outnumbered and probably outclassed. And in no way are Grace's little friends going to help her.

So Imperia has to take the offensive.

She summons the part of her that's most like her Grand-father, stands as straight as she can, looks down her nose at Skylar's friends (even though most of them are taller than she is) and says in her most condescending voice, "I see that Skylar couldn't be bothered with defending herself."

"She had to go to the hospital, you freak," says Mikayla Aberdeen. She's the tallest girl, and pretty athletic. She wants to play professional basketball, and the gym teacher says she might have a shot if she continues growing.

She's also the daughter of some super agent, whatever that is, and thinks she's super important herself because of it.

"The hospital?" Imperia says, impressed despite herself.

She punched Skylar hard—she knows that by how bruised her hand is—but she never thought that punch would do more than hurt Skylar's pride. "That little tap sent her to the hospital? Really?"

"You broke her nose," says Rose Browning. Rose is more hanger-on than important, even though one of her two moms is some kind of bigwig lawyer. Rose is too thin— Imperia has caught her puking up her lunch in the bathroom more than once—and Imperia knows she can take her if she has to.

"She's going to have to have plastic surgery," Georgia LaCrosti says. Georgia is the one to watch. She's the one with all the gym muscles and she's Skylar's right-hand girl.

"Well, good," says a voice from behind Imperia. "After all, Barbies should be made of plastic."

Imperia's heart is really pounding now. She turns just enough to see who is behind her. She doesn't know the girl's name, although she recognizes her. She's watched this girl from afar, admiring her courage. Her white shirt is one size too big and she leaves it untucked. She rolls her skirt up so that it's a mini, and her socks down so that they hug her ankles. She has two jackets for her uniform. She's ripped the sleeves off one jacket and she wears it as much as she can. Sometimes the teachers make her wear the other jacket—the one with sleeves—but even that she's managed to customize by ripping the school's logo off the pocket.

"Shut up, Janie, this isn't your fight," Mikayla says.

"It isn't yours either," this new girl, this Janie, says. "I'll bet that Skylar told you to do this, told you do something nasty that'll embarrass the crap out of Empire here, and then put it on YouTube or something."

Imperia doesn't want to correct her over the name, because this Janie seems to be on a roll.

"You're just little Skylar suck-ups," Janie says. "Which is so stupid, since my grandfather can buy and sell her mom if he wants to—wait! He has bought her, like a half dozen times."

Janie put her arm through Imperia's, startling Imperia.

She can't remember the last time anyone who wasn't family touched her.

"C'mon, Empire," Janie says. "Let's have lunch."

And then she leads Imperia toward the burger side of the cafeteria, the area that Skylar's friends usually ignore.

"Thanks," Imperia says. She wants to slide her arm away, but she doesn't want to seem ungrateful. "You didn't have to stand up for me, but I'm glad you did."

Janie grins at her. Imperia's surprised to see that her teeth aren't perfect. They have gaps along the bottom. Her haircut looks hand-done.

"Of course, I had to stand up for you," Janie says. "You punched Skylar. Do you know how long I've wanted to do that?"

Imperia swallows. She knows there's an ebb and flow here she doesn't understand. "You seem like the kind of person who does what she wants."

"Oh, I wish," Janie says. "I'm already in it with my grandfather. Imagine if I showed up on YouTube punching out Skylar Kennedy Campbell. God, the press would love that."

"Um." Imperia winces because she knows she's about to ask a stupid question, but she does anyway. "Am I supposed to know who your grandfather is?"

She also wants to ask why he can buy and sell people. Imperia thought that was illegal in the Greater World—it certainly is in the Third Kingdom (although not in all the Kingdoms)—but she's willing to concede she can be wrong about what's allowed here and what's not.

"My grandfather owns the biggest studio in Hollywood," Janie says. "Or at least, he's the majority shareholder. He used to run it, but now my dad does, not that it matters."

"Why wouldn't it matter?" Imperia asks.

"My dad's on his fifth wife," Janie says, as if that explains it all.

"So?"

"Jeez," Janie says, "You are new, aren't you? My mom was wife number three."

Imperia is still frowning. She knows she should understand this, but she doesn't. After all, her parents are the only divorced people she knows personally. And all of her friends in the Kingdom—well, she doesn't have friends there, but all of the kids her age, the ones she's allowed to play with— those kids come from intact families, as Grandfather loves to point out.

"God," Janie says, clearly recognizing Imperia's silence for the confusion that it is. "Wife number three means there are two families after mine. I'm not even sure Dad knows what my name is, not that it matters. He sends checks every month, which keep Mom in clothes and clubs and me and my brother in this hellhole."

"And your grandfather?" Imperia asks, not sure if she should.

"He knows who I am. He makes it his business to know everything about everyone, and he'd kill me if I show up in the press or on YouTube or cussing on my Facebook page. He has minions to keep track of all of that stuff."

"Sounds like my grandfather," Imperia says, only she

doesn't add that her grandfather doesn't even know what Facebook is.

"Your grandfather has a studio?" Janie asks.

"I wish," Imperia says, not willing to say much more. "Having a studio sounds cool."

Janie grins. "It can be. But mostly, it's just—you know, like his job. But it impresses the masses."

Then she looks over her shoulder at Skylar's friends who are still clustering as if they can't believe that Janie took Imperia away from them.

Imperia's heart starts to pound again. "You don't think they're going to go after my sister again, do you?"

"Naw," Janie says. "Your sister is too easy. You're the challenge. And with that punch, you made sure they're going to go after you."

"Goodie," Imperia says without enthusiasm. "By the way, my name is actually Imperia."

"Imperia Encanto, I know," Janie says. "But I like Empire better. It's a statement."

"I don't need to make a statement," Imperia says.

"That's probably true," Janie says, clapping her on the back and propelling her toward the food. "Your fists were pretty damn eloquent."

"My fists are pretty damn sore," Imperia says.

"Small price to pay for breaking Skylar Campbell's nose," Janie says. "Too bad we didn't get a video of that. That would've been epic."

"I prefer to work in secret," Imperia says.

Janie laughs. "Well, you failed at that part. But who

cares? There's a new Queen in town. Long live Empire Encanto."

A shiver runs through Imperia. Is her royal blood that obvious? Or is Janie just making some kind of joke?

This time, Imperia doesn't ask. Instead, she steps up to the counter, orders a cheeseburger, and hopes the conversation goes a whole new way.

FOUR

Not only did the conversation go a whole new way, but so did the day. She didn't have to keep as close an eye on Grace. Skylar's friends just glared at Imperia for the rest of the day but didn't approach her, and Janie promised lunch again tomorrow.

None of that, though, cheered Imperia up because she doesn't want Dad to know about the punch heard 'round Beverly Hills.

Nor does she want Dad to know about her bruised hand or the confrontation in the cafeteria or the warning(s) she got from Principal Daley. The hand is the biggest problem, because either she wears the bandage which will guarantee that Daddy will ask, or she leaves the hand unbandaged, and then he can see the bruises on her knuckles.

Finally, just before the day ends, she borrows (well, steals, really) some fake tan stuff from one of the girls in the bathroom. She takes the tan stuff out of the girl's gigandous purse as she heads into a stall, and then replaces the tan stuff as the girl leaves. By then Imperia's hands are darker than the rest of her, but not that noticeable.

And if Daddy asks about it, she'll show him the tan spray on her left hand, not her evil right hook.

She decides not to ask Grace to keep quiet, because if she asks Grace, then Grace will concentrate real hard on not saying anything, and will eventually blow it because she's thinking about it rather than thinking about other stuff.

So after the last bell, they hurry out to the parking area, where Dad's waiting in his silver Mercedes. At first, Imperia loved it that Daddy came to get them from school, but now she hates it.

All the other kids get picked up by their parents' chauffeurs or their au pairs or someone who works in the house, not by the parents themselves. Because, Imperia has learned, if the parents show up that means the parents have nothing better to do, and if they have nothing better to do, then they're not important.

At least Daddy is on the phone as they leave school. Every real parent who shows up is always on the phone, because that shows how important they are too. Daddy has been talking on the phone a lot lately, and actually smiling again, which he didn't do when he learned that Mom just dumped Imperia and Grace with his parents.

Grace runs to the car. She's smiling, which is a first as she comes out of school, and Imperia has to hurry to catch up to her.

Daddy folds his phone closed, gets out of the car, and lets Grace hug him. He looks over her shoulder at Imperia, silently asking her what's changed.

She smiles too, and says, "Your idea worked. They won't pick on Grace any more."

Daddy opens his mouth to ask what happens, when Grace leans back and says, "Imperia impressed all the girls in my class, and they like me now, and we had lunch together and everything."

And then she starts to chatter about her new little friends. Daddy puts his hand on Grace's shoulder, leading her to the back seat where she's safer (at least, that's what all the experts say) and helping her adjust her little book bag.

He looks very suburban Dad-like, with his black and silver hair and his laugh lines and his glasses. He doesn't look like that Disney prince much—or maybe he looks like an older version, but not as old as Grandfather, who just looks scary even with the same square jaw and blue eyes.

"So it worked," Daddy says as Imperia gets into the front seat. Grace has taken a breath, but it's clear she's not done (thank heavens), so Imperia just nods, and lets Grace dictate the conversation.

Daddy gets behind the wheel and heads home, and he's smiling a little too, and that's when Imperia realizes that Daddy's relieved. This is the first time since school started that Grace has chattered. Up until now, Grace has been really, really quiet, even for Grace. Imperia just hadn't realized how quiet.

"What exactly did you do?" Daddy asks Imperia as they pull into the garage at the house. He hits the garage door remote, which brings the door down kinda like magic, although their housekeeper, Ruthie, explained it as something do with signals and technology and stuff, not that Imperia understands any of that either.

"I told Skylar to leave Grace alone," Imperia says, which is true. Imperia did tell her that first thing in the morning, and it didn't work.

"That was it?" Daddy asks as he shuts off the ignition.

"Actually," Grace says, "she—"

"I got some help from this girl named Janie," Imperia says. "She says that Skylar's mom is some famous actress, but Janie's grandfather runs the studio so Skylar has to listen to her."

"That's who Janie is?" Grace asks. "I knew she was somebody important."

Imperia sighs silently. Grace is already moving into Hollywood speak, which is probably better than not talking at all.

"So you've made a friend too," Daddy says.

Imperia shrugs, then opens the door. The garage is really clean and smells of exhaust. She heads to the house, hoping she doesn't get any more questions.

"Janie's really tough," Grace says behind her. Grace is clearly talking to Daddy. "But even she wouldn't take on Skylar without Imperia."

"That's good, right?" Daddy asks.

Imperia pulls the door open. The scent of chili wafts over her. Apparently, Ruthie has been cooking.

"That's really good," Grace says. "Together, they're like super tough chicks."

Imperia goes in the door. The garage door leads to an entry where she's supposed to hang up her coat, if she ever needed a coat, which she hasn't so far. The smell of chili makes her stomach growl.

"Super tough chicks," Daddy says slowly. He's suddenly right beside Imperia. "Is that hyperbole?"

"Of course it is, Dad," Imperia says before Grace can answer. "What do you think we're doing? Kicking butt like those girls in the urban fantasy novels from your store?"

Daddy frowns at her. "You've been reading those?"

"A few of them," Imperia says, working hard to suppress her smile of triumph. Topic of conversation successfully changed.

For the moment, anyway.

FIVE

I mperia counts the entire evening as a win. Daddy doesn't notice her darkened hands, which means he hasn't noticed her bruised knuckles, and he gives her The Lecture on reading books that are too old for her, which she can recite in her sleep (and which she's been ignoring for years) and Grace actually mentioned at dinner that she's looking forward to school the next day.

Can't get better than that.

Or so Imperia thinks. Then she goes to school.

Skylar's there. White tape makes an X across her nose, her eyes are black-and-blue and her face is puffy.

Best of all, she won't even look at Imperia. All Skylar's little minions just glare at Imperia whenever she walks by, but they keep their distance.

"I thought she's having some kind of Barbie surgery," Imperia says to Janie at lunch. They've hooked up for hamburgers again. Grace is sitting with her newfound friends and actually holding court.

"I guess she can't," Janie says. "Apparently you can't have plastic surgery before you stop growing."

"But she's all black-and-blue," Imperia says.

"Well, duh," Janie says. "You broke her nose. They had to reset it. She'll have a crooked nose for years. Good job."

But is it a good job? Imperia wonders that in class after class. She's a little appalled at the way Skylar looks. So appalled, in fact, that she actually thinks of apologizing, at least for a minute, until she remembers how mean Skylar was to Grace.

Imperia's keeping an eye on Grace, but mostly, she's keeping an eye on Skylar's friends. Because Imperia doesn't trust them. They're being too quiet.

Something bad is going to happen: she just knows it.

And of course, something bad does happen. Just not in the way she expects.

SIX

"Imperia!" Daddy says. He has a sound in his voice she's never heard before. In fact, if she had to guess who was talking, she might've said it was Grandfather, not Daddy. She never realized that they had similar voices before.

She's doing some math homework at the dining room table. She has a desk in her room, but she doesn't like being alone there. The dining room table is in one of the prettiest rooms in the house, with floor-to-ceiling windows that overlook the patio and an amazing garden.

Plus, the dining room always smells pretty good after dinner, and the best part of all is that she's not alone.

She doesn't really like being alone any more, not after all that weird stuff with Mom. Imperia just doesn't want to lose sight of Daddy or of Grace.

She likes to think she's protecting them, even though she kinda knows she's lying to herself. She's been lying to herself a lot, especially when it comes to how she feels about things.

"Imperia!" Daddy says again.

"Coming," she says, and stands up. She puts her pen in the middle of the textbook, and sets her tablet on top of it all. The pen isn't really a pen, but something that works on the tablet. She has the answer sheet there, and when she finishes, it uploads directly to her math teacher.

See, this stuff is like magic to Imperia, but she doesn't say that. She just acts like she's used to all this tech stuff, when really, it freaks her out.

She heads to Daddy's study, her stomach clenching. Daddy's study is off the dining room and has the same floor-to-ceiling windows overlooking the garden. The rest of the walls are covered with books, and the shelves go so high that Daddy can't even reach the books on the top. He has a ladder so he can climb up and get them.

Daddy is all about books, which Mom used to hate (probably still does, but Imperia tries not to think about what Mom likes and dislikes any more). Usually Imperia finds this room really comfortable but right now, she doesn't want to go in there.

It's like going into the principal's office, only scarier. She can't walk away from Daddy. (She doesn't want to.)

He's standing up behind his desk. She hasn't realized how powerful Daddy can look. He has Greater World power, like the men on TV, with his suit coat draped over the chair, his silk shirt a bit rumpled, and his tie loose around his neck. But he also has Grandfather's fierceness, which scares Imperia more than anything.

But she's learned through Grandmother that she should never show her emotions. So she doesn't. She just straightens up and pretends like there's nothing wrong.

"I just got off the phone with a man who claims he's the attorney for the Kennedy Campbell family. You'd know the woman as—"

"I know who they are," Imperia says. She's going to work as hard as she can to never know who Skylar's mother is.

"I suppose you do," Daddy says dryly. "I take it that his allegation is true then? You broke their daughter's nose?"

Imperia can't quite control her lips. They want to smile. She knows it's wrong, but dang, that moment still feels good. And so does that look Skylar keeps giving her, like Imperia's going to haul off and hit her all over again.

"She wouldn't listen to reason," Imperia says.

"So you hit her." Daddy's tone has a bit of wonder in it, like he can't imagine anyone doing such a thing.

"Actually, I punched her. I made a fist and everything."

Imperia raises her hand to show that fist. It makes her feel powerful all over again.

"Imperia," Daddy says in his most disapproving tone. "You know we don't condone violence."

She has two answers for that, both guaranteed to make Daddy mad. The first—Grandfather does—doesn't really put her on the side of good. And the second—You're the one who told me to defend Grace—won't stop the anti-violence lecture. It'll just raise the lecture's volume.

So Imperia raises her chin slightly and says nothing.

"Imperia," Daddy says, "this lawyer wants us to pay for the girl's surgery."

Imperia lets out a small sound despite her best intentions. "It's plastic surgery, Daddy, and she can't have it for years."

"I know," Daddy says. "The attorney also wants pain and suffering fees, whatever that means. I'm going to have hire an attorney of my own."

"What about Grace's pain and suffering?" Imperia asks in spite of her best intentions to keep quiet. Because—jeez—this just pisses her off (pardon her French, whatever that is. ["Pardon my French" is what Janie says whenever she swears]). "Grace was crying every day. Now she's happy. That's gotta count for something."

Daddy softens, just like Imperia knew he would. Mention Grace, mention Grace happy, and Daddy kinda melts. He sees Grace as a kindred spirit and maybe she is. Although Imperia doubts that Grace can ever get as fierce as Daddy is right now.

"This is one of those fights that can go on for years,"

Daddy says, but he's speaking quieter now, as if he's talking more to himself than to Imperia. Now she can see just how worried he is.

"No, it won't," Imperia says. "Just tell that lawyer guy that you have evidence of how mean Skylar really is and how it was only a matter of time before someone gave her a dose of her own medicine."

"She hits people?" Daddy says, with a little hope in his voice.

"No," Imperia says. "What she does is worse. She says really bad things about them, and that destroys them and then she makes everyone else act mean to them."

Daddy glances at the door, and Imperia can tell he's thinking about Grace and how sad she was. "I don't know how telling this attorney that Skylar is mean will help."

"You tell him you have proof that she's mean, and if they decided to do this legal thingie, you'll take the proof to the tabloids. Tell him it'll embarrass the whole family."

Daddy looks at her as if he's never seen her before. He frowns just a little. "Do we have this proof?"

"I think my friend Janie does," Imperia says, "but if she doesn't, I can get it no problem."

"How?" Daddy asks.

"I can video Skylar on my phone. It won't be hard."

"She's that mean that often?" Daddy asks.

"She's horrible," Imperia says.

Daddy sighs. "Poor thing."

Which throws Imperia completely. "Poor thing? How can you say that? She nearly destroyed Grace."

Daddy looks at Imperia. "She had to learn it somewhere,

Imp," he says. "Kids tend to learn that kind of stuff at home."

It takes Imperia a minute to understand him. "You mean somebody's doing this to her? At home?"

He nods and sits down. "Probably a parent."

Or a grandfather, Imperia thinks. But Grandfather never said any of that horrible anti-girl stuff to Imperia's face. He would just frown at her or command her to leave his presence. He would say that stuff to other people, who would then try not to let Imperia hear.

Imperia suddenly feels sorry for Skylar, and she doesn't want to. She really, really doesn't want to. So she thinks about the ways that Skylar picks on Grace, but she can only imagine someone picking on Skylar, so she tries to think about Grace crying, and even that isn't working right now.

So Imperia bunches up her fists, straightens her shoulders, and says, "So I solved it, right, Daddy?"

He looks up at her as if he's forgotten she's in the room.

"Actually, no, Imp," he says. "You probably deflected the court case—I keep forgetting how important this publicity stuff is here—but you haven't resolved the issue with Skylar at all. People who get hurt retaliate, as you well know."

"As I know?" Imperia asks.

"Skylar hurt Grace and you retaliated, right?"

Imperia let out a breath. Her cheeks are suddenly growing hot. "You told me to defend her," Imperia says, and doesn't like the fact that her voice sounds like a whine.

"But I wanted you to—ah, hell." Daddy runs a hand through his hair. "Yes, I told you to, and I didn't tell you how."

Uh-oh. He's starting into that he's-a-failure-as-a-parent crap. Imperia hates that.

"It's not your fault, Daddy," Imperia says. "I tried to talk to her. I'm just not charming like you are."

He looks up at her, his blue eyes suddenly as piercing as Grandfather's. "A lot of people aren't charming, Imp. They don't go around breaking people's noses. You have to make this right."

"What does that mean?" Imperia asks.

He shrugs. She doesn't want him to shrug, because that means he's not going to tell her. Then he surprises her by adding, "You need to defuse this, Imp. You need to stop this whole thing from escalating any further."

"How do I do that?" Imperia asks.

"I don't know," he says grimly. "But I trust you can figure it out."

SEVEN

I trust you can figure that out. Imperia hates it when Daddy says that. She hates it when anybody says that. The last time she had to figure something out, she ended up punching someone in the nose.

She bows her head and sighs as she heads back into the dining room. This thing with Skylar is harder to solve than all the math problems in her little book. She sits down, makes fists with both hands and props her chin on them. Her knuckles graze her cheeks. Her knuckles are sharp.

The thing that's bugging everybody about Skylar isn't

that Imperia defeated her. It's that she has a broken nose, and she'll be disfigured. The problem isn't the punch so much as the horrible medical treatment.

In the Kingdom, whenever Imperia injured something, she went to the palace wise woman, a healer who would then wave her magic wand over it or rub a potion on it or make some incantation.

And then the bruise would be gone.

Imperia leans back in her chair.

Of course. The solution is that simple—and that hard.

EIGHT

Imperia knows how to get to the Kingdom, even though she's not supposed to go without Daddy. She's not supposed to go anywhere without telling him either. She's going to break a lot of rules here, but she's going to do it so that she can make things right.

There are dozens, maybe hundreds of portals between the Greater World and the Kingdom. Imperia has traveled through some of them, always with Daddy, and always holding his hand. But she has done a lot of reading about them, and she knows that you don't have to have your magic to use them.

(This is how mortals—folks from the Greater World— end up in the Kingdoms. That's how the evil Brothers Grimm discovered the Kingdoms in the first place.)

There's a portal not too far from the house. Imperia slips out the back door at seven a.m., before everyone else gets up.

Ruthie doesn't even show up on Saturday, which is too bad, because if she did, Imperia would ask her to drive to the better portal in Sherman Oaks. That portal is bigger, but Imperia doesn't really need big on this day, because she's not traveling with Grace or Daddy.

It's hot outside even though it's early, and at most of the houses, the sprinklers have just ended their timed watering. Here, everything seems to run on technology, and everything has a time and a place. Even watering, because apparently, water is rationed, an idea that just plain scares her.

A lot scares her about the Greater World. Kids at school say they're not allowed to walk by themselves because they might be abducted. At first, Imperia thought they meant abducted by bad serial killer guys, like in the movies, but no, they actually mean by kidnappers, because their parents are so rich and so famous.

Abductions don't happen in the Kingdom, at least not for her or Grace, because if someone took them, that someone would be beheaded or worse. Grandfather has no problem with violence, and sometimes uses it to enforce his decrees. One unspoken decree is don't mess with his family.

Sometimes Imperia thinks that's a much better way than Daddy's insistence on talk, talk, talk.

A couple of people are outside, working in their lawns, trimming flowers and digging in the dirt. One woman actually says hi to Imperia, and Imperia gives her a startled hi in return.

She wants to run now, but she doesn't. She makes herself walk to the little park that only covers half a block.

According to the sign, the park was someone's property,

but that person donated it to the neighborhood so long as everyone takes care of it. There's an iron gate around the lovely trees, and a code on the gate so that only people who live here can get in. Imperia memorized the code the first time they came here, and now she taps it into the gate's keypad. She hears a click as the gate unlocks.

She pushes it open and steps in.

There are so many trees here that the place is actually cooler than the rest of the neighborhood. Flowers bloom everywhere. She has no idea what kind they are. There's a little shrine over what should've been a little pond with a fountain, but another sign says that the pond is empty because of the water shortage.

She steps behind the shrine to a gigantic palm tree that's so big it looks fake. She runs her hand on the tree's spiny bark and suddenly she's inside the portal.

She barely fits in it by herself. It smells of tree and a bit like fog. She knows how this works: she's supposed to think about where she wants to go in the Kingdom, but in case she doesn't have the think-power yet, she mutters, "Grandmama Lavinia's, please."

Then she worries that the portal won't know who Grandmama Lavinia is. At that moment, though, she stumbles forward into a familiar part of the Kingdom's forest, overlooking Grandmama Lavinia's house. The air is cool and filled with fog, and there's no sun at all.

Really, Grandmama Lavinia's house is a manor, and it originally belonged to Mom's dad. He inherited it from his dad. Mom's mom died when she was a little girl, and it took Mom's dad a long time to remarry. When he did, he remarried Grandmama Lavinia whom, the evil Brothers Grimm say, forced Mom to live like a slave, and sleep near the fireplace. That's why she was called Cinderella.

The truth is more complicated than that, and has to do with a big fight that Grandmama Lavinia and Mom had a few weeks before the ball where Mom met Daddy. Mom was living in the kitchen in protest when Mom's fairy godmother showed up—and that's where everything gets muddled.

Imperia doesn't really understand what happened, and neither does Dad. He just says that sometimes no one's right, and the entire situation can be hurtful, and he says that's what happened here.

But he loves Grandmama Lavinia, and so does Imperia. Imperia trusts Grandmama Lavinia more than she trusts most people. And Grandmama Lavinia won't report her to Grandfather, so she's safe for the time being.

The house is just around the corner, tucked up against the forest, at the end of a long road. Imperia smiles when she sees the square brown form, the stained glass windows on the second story, and the arch-shaped stone door. She loves this place more than any other place in the Kingdom.

She lets herself through the gate on the matching stone fence and takes a deep breath of the cool damp air. With luck, no one has seen her, and that means no one will report her to her grandfather.

She goes around the side and lets herself in the kitchen door. Cook is already bustling, making bread and cakes for the morning meal. When Cook sees her, she raises her eyebrows.

"N'one said you'd be coming here," Cook says.

"It's a surprise." Imperia knows Cook won't tell on her because here, Imperia has Authority. "Is Grandmama here?"

Her stomach clenches as she asks the question because she really didn't think ahead. What if Grandmama is visiting friends? Or on some prolonged trip?

"Upstairs," Cook says. She isn't showing the right amount of respect, but then she never has. The one thing that Imperia has gleaned from her mother's childhood stories is that Grandmama Lavinia has never been able to train her staff properly.

Imperia nods, then heads to the back staircase. She creeps up the side, like she used to do when she was really little and up too late. She reaches the top. Most of the doors are closed, including Grandmama's bedroom door.

Imperia knocks, then pushes the door open. She says, "It's me, Grandmama," just in case Grandmama thinks it's one of the servants.

"Imperia?" Grandmama sounds surprised. "Just one moment."

There's a flutter and a hint of perfume as Imperia steps inside. The bed curtains are stirring. With one bejeweled hand, Grandmama pushes the curtains back.

Imperia frowns. She would swear, with the curtains moving like that, that Grandmama has just gotten out of bed. But Grandmama is still in bed, and the bed is messier than usual. Grandmama has grabbed her black silk dressing gown and tugs it on as she sits up. She's tiny and blond, with slightly upturned eyes and an upturned nose. She almost looks younger than Mom.

There's rumors that Grandmama has mixed blood—part small fairy, part human. And while Imperia hasn't cared about that, her other grandparents do. They think Grandmama Lavinia is a bad influence because of it.

"What are you doing here, child?" Grandmama asks, smoothing her blond hair back with one hand. "Is there trouble?"

Imperia's eyes get wet but she blinks hard, bites her lower lip, and nods.

"Oh, my." Grandmama swings her thin legs over the bed and slips her feet into a pair of black feathery mules that she got in the Greater World recently, when she helped Daddy find the right house for the girls. "Did something else happen with your mother?"

"No." Imperia's voice is small.

"Is your father here?"

"No," Imperia says.

"Grace?"

"No," Imperia says.

Grandmama puts her hands on her hips. Her black silk dressing gown only comes to mid-thigh, and swings outward like a party dress. Her lips thin. "So your grandparents are here."

"No," Imperia says.

Grandmama straightens in surprise. Even with the heels on her mules, she's barely as tall as Imperia now. "You're here on your own?"

Imperia nods.

"From the Greater World?"

Imperia nods again. There's a lump in her throat. She missed Grandmama Lavinia more than she can say.

"What went wrong? Did something happen to your father and Grace?" She sounds panicked now.

"No," Imperia says. "They're fine. But Daddy's really mad at me, and I need your help."

Grandmama's eyes narrow. "You came here because your father is mad at you?"

Imperia nods. "He wants me to figure out how to fix something I did. And I don't know how."

"He wants you to figure this out on your own?" Grandmama asks.

"Yes," Imperia says.

"And you thought you could ask me to fix it?"

"No," Imperia says. "I thought you could help me fix it."

"Yeah," Grandmama says softly to herself. "That's figuring it out on your own."

She glances over her thin shoulder at the dressing screen near the back of the room. Then she comes to Imperia, puts her arms around her, and hugs her.

"Give me a minute, child," she says, "and I'll meet you for breakfast in the sun room."

Imperia glances at the screen too, but she doesn't know why. Then she nods, sighs, and heads out of the room. She hears voices behind her, and hopes that she's hearing servants.

She heads down the front steps to the sun room, which is really the let's-hope-there's-sun room. The sun doesn't come out a lot here, and when it does, it doesn't always reach this room.

Still the room is nice, and Grandmama Lavinia uses it as her dining area. There's a sideboard on the interior wall. The other walls are all glass, and Grandmama has flowering plants all around. An oak table dominates the middle of the room, and is already set up, with jams and cakes and plates in the middle.

Usually one of the servants actually sets the table. Maybe, because Imperia has hurried everyone along, the servants didn't have time for a real setup.

Grandmama sweeps into the room not five minutes later. Grandmama is the only person Imperia knows who can sweep. It's almost as if she can fly, which lends credence to that fairy blood rumor. (Imperia has never asked her about that. Imperia doesn't ask Grandmama much about her own life because, Imperia feels, if she asks too much she might suddenly be between Mom and Grandmama, and she doesn't want to be there.)

Grandmama takes a slice of cake and a pile of fresh fruit. Imperia already has three different slices of cake. Daddy doesn't allow sweets for breakfast so this is a real treat.

"All right," Grandmama says. "Tell me what this emergency is."

Imperia almost denies that it's an emergency, but then she realizes that it is. She has to deal with it and she has to deal with it before Monday.

So she tells Grandmama what happened, from the mean things that Skylar said about Grace, to Grace crying all the time, to the now-infamous punch, to the possible lawsuit, to what Daddy said.

Grandmama listens. Grandmama is a spectacular

listener. She doesn't say anything, but she frowns in the right places and nods when she's supposed to and just pays attention. Imperia likes that.

When Imperia finishes, Grandmama doesn't say anything judgmental at all. Instead, she says, "What do you think I can do? I don't know any of these people or how the Greater World works."

"I was wondering if you can help Skylar's nose heal right. Or if you can help me find someone who will." Imperia holds out her hand and shows off the bruises. "This is what Greater World medicine looks like."

"No wonder they think she'll be disfigured," Grandmama says, and in her voice, Imperia hears shock. Then Grandmama frowns. "Do you want to bring this Skylar here?"

"No!" The very idea startles Imperia. "I just thought maybe you know some spell or can give me some potion or something that will help her face heal."

"You want to recite a spell?" Grandmama says.

Imperia can tell just from her expression that reciting a spell is a no-go. "Or maybe you know somebody who can come with me and do the proper healing or something."

"Bring someone magical to the Greater World to help a mortal?" Grandmama says. "You know that violates all kinds of rules."

Imperia bites her lip. "Or a potion....?"

"Imperia," Grandmama says, "I thought you understood how dangerous magic is in the wrong hands."

"It'd be in my hands," Imperia says.

"And you would give it to someone nonmagical, who

might share it with her little friends who might share it with their friends, and suddenly something that should have stayed in the Kingdom is all over the Greater World."

"But—"

"No buts, Imperia," Grandmama says. "And no magic."

Imperia lets out a small sound. Grandmama broke rules all the time. Imperia was hoping Grandmama would break this rule for her.

"So what am I supposed to do?" Imperia asks.

Grandmama leans back in her chair and studies Imperia. Imperia hates it when Grandmama looks at her like that. It's always uncomfortable. It's like Grandmama can see to the tips of her very soul.

"Have you wondered why you punched Skylar?"

"She deserved it," Imperia says.

Grandmama nods, not like she agrees, but in a kind of dismissive way, like that's not the right answer. "You could have slapped her. You could have pushed her. Instead, you hit her so hard that you broke her nose. Have you wondered why?"

Imperia frowns. She hadn't thought of pushing Skylar until now. Come to think of it, the punch is not like her. No wonder Daddy looked shocked when he found out.

"She was being mean to Grace," Imperia says.

"By saying mean things," Grandmama says like that's not a big deal.

"And making Grace cry," Imperia says.

"But she's not the only person who has been mean to Grace lately, is she?" Grandmama says.

"Someone else has?" Imperia asks, feeling a surge of anger. "And nobody told me?"

"You know very well who has been mean to Grace," Grandmama says.

Imperia studies her, wishing she has the same ability to look inside Grandmama's soul. "No, I don't know."

"Oh, but you do, honey," Grandmama says. "Someone has been very mean to Grace, someone you can't hit."

Imperia crosses her arms. She's about to disagree when she hears Daddy's voice. Kids tend to learn that kind of stuff at home.

"Mommy," Imperia breathes. And then she mentally kicks herself. She vowed never to call that woman Mommy again.

Grandmama nods once, and this time, the nod is agreement. "Yes," Grandmama says. "Your mother has been very mean to Grace, and to you. Leaving you like that."

"I can handle it," Imperia says. "But it made Grace cry."

"And your friend Skylar made Grace cry," Grandmama says.

"She's not my friend," Imperia says.

"No, she's not," Grandmama says. "She sounds quite mean. But she didn't deserve a broken nose, did she?"

Imperia's cheeks heat. "I said that. I told you that. And I can't take it back."

And she can't just magically transfer that broken nose to Mom either. She wishes she could. Then Mom would be permanently disfigured and she wouldn't look like Imperia any more.

"That's right," Grandmama says. "You can't take it back.

And you can't use magic to change it, not in the Greater World."

"So what am I supposed to do?" Imperia says.

Grandmama looks at her. "Have you ever thought about what you and your little friend Skylar have in common?"

"She's not my friend," Imperia says again.

Grandmama smiles just a little. "Imagine what your mother would say if one day you showed up with a broken nose."

"My mom wouldn't care," Imperia says.

Grandmama winces. "Maybe not now, but what would she have said when you lived in the palace?"

"She would have been mad," Imperia says. "She wouldn't have let me out in public for weeks."

"Because...?"

"Because it would make her look bad," Imperia says.

"You told me that all along the problem is how Skylar would look. Not that her face hurts. Not that she has lost some status with her friends. How she looks. Even the family attorney is involved. Who called that attorney, do you think?"

Imperia closes her eyes. "I'm not like Skylar," she says.

"Maybe not," Grandmama says, and Imperia doesn't like that maybe. "But you understand her, don't you?"

Imperia opens her eyes. Grandmama is giving her that look.

"I don't want to understand her," Imperia says.

"You might not want to," Grandmama says, "but you do."

"What do I do with that?" Imperia asks.

Grandmama smiles. "Have a little compassion," she says.

NINE

Grandmama won't tell her anything else. They have a nice breakfast and then she sends Imperia back to the Greater World.

Imperia spends the whole weekend thinking about what Grandmama said and still can't come up with anything to do. She managed to get back home without Daddy knowing she went to the Kingdom, and she doesn't think she can manage another trip to maybe get a healer on her own.

Even if she does bring a healer back, she doesn't know how she could smuggle the healer to school. Nor does she think buying a potion is an option, not after what Grandmama says about the way loose magic could travel.

So Imperia doesn't have a plan at all when she goes to school on Monday. She even thought of staying out of school, making up some excuse or something. But, she figured, the more she lied to Daddy, the worse off she was going to be. Especially if he figured out that she had gone to the Kingdom during the weekend.

She kinda hopes she can go through the day without seeing Skylar, but of course, that doesn't happen. The first person she sees after Grace heads off with her little friends is Skylar, walking with her posse.

Skylar wears her uniform like a fashion statement. It's crisply ironed, and looks brand new. She's coated her shoes with some kind of glitter polish that makes them look like they're not the regulation shoe. Her purse is expensive, her phone is top of the line, and she has the latest tablet, one that hasn't even been officially released yet.

Imperia wonders if she can dodge Skylar, then Mikayla sees her and elbows Skylar while pointing Imperia out. Imperia takes a deep breath, squares her shoulders, and walks toward the group.

"What're you doing?"

She can hear Janie's voice behind her. Imperia didn't even know Janie was nearby. So Imperia pretends she can't hear her.

Imperia walks right up to the group.

Mikayla and Georgia stand in front of Skylar, arms crossed, like body guards.

"I want to talk to Skylar," Imperia says.

"No," Mikayla says.

Imperia tilts her head so she can see around Mikayla. Skylar is standing directly behind Mikayla, face still bandaged. Her eyes are less black now, more purple and green and yellow—and not in an attractive way. Imperia has never seen anything like it before.

"I want to talk to you," Imperia says to Skylar. "In private."

Skylar doesn't answer.

"Look," Imperia says to Mikayla, "if I lay a finger on her, I promise, I'll let you guys beat me up all year. You can break my nose too if you want, okay?"

"Don't say that." Janie has come up beside her. "They'll do it."

"I'm making a promise here," Imperia says to Janie and

to Mikayla. "I mean to keep it. I won't touch her. Not a finger. I just want to talk to her. Alone."

"No," Mikayla says.

"It's okay." Skylar's voice sounds funny. It almost sounds like she said Idsokey. It takes a minute for Imperia to realize Skylar's talking that way because of her nose. "I'll talk to her."

Mikayla turns as if she's going to protest. Skylar just raises her eyebrows—a very Grandfather move—and Mikayla walks over to the lockers.

The other girls follow and line up along either side, so they can rush in if Imperia hurts her.

"You too," Imperia says to Janie. "I want to talk to Skylar alone."

"It's not a good idea," Janie says.

"You're probably right, but I'm going to do it anyway." Imperia looks at Janie. Janie has a frown on her face. She holds her phone up.

"I'm recording it," Janie says.

Janie is actually worried about her. That touches Imperia. No one ever worries about Imperia.

"I'll be okay," Imperia says softly.

Skylar hasn't moved. She's watching warily. She really doesn't look pretty right now, even though she should. Her hair is perfect. She has make-up on that sort-of covers the bruising. But her face is a mess.

And Imperia did that to her.

"Go," Imperia says to Janie.

"I'm leaving in protest," Janie says, but backs off.

Imperia feels really exposed now, standing in the middle of the hallway, facing off with Skylar. "Let's go over there."

Imperia nods toward a wider area near the stairs where two corridors meet. The other girls can still see what's happening, but they can't hear.

"All right," Skylar says. She pivots and walks to the stairs, turning her back on Imperia.

In spite of herself, Imperia admires that. It shows a confidence that Imperia would never have.

Imperia follows her. Skylar stops a few feet away from the steps and waits, like Grandmother does on state occasions.

"What's so important?" Skylar asks as Imperia approaches. "I suppose you're going to tell me to drop the lawsuit."

Imperia starts. She thought Daddy had taken care of that. But she doesn't want to lose her focus. She's going to talk to Skylar, not let Skylar bully her.

"I don't want to talk about the lawsuit," Imperia says. "I want to tell you something about me and Grace."

Skylar's eyelids lower just a bit. It's a good move. It shows contempt. "Why should I care?"

She isn't going to make this easy.

"You know we just moved here," Imperia says as quickly as she can. If she doesn't get this out, she's not going to try again. "What you don't know is that we just moved in with our father too. Our mother ran off with some other guy and dumped us with our grandparents."

"So?" Skylar's voice drips with contempt, and it actually hurts. Imperia debated all weekend about telling Skylar the personal stuff because she was afraid it would give Skylar more ammunition, and now that looks like it might be true.

"So," Imperia says softly, "when you and I were fighting over Grace, I got really mad. So I hit you."

"Yeah, I got that," Skylar says.

"And I hit you hard."

"No kidding," Skylar says.

"And I shouldn't have. You didn't deserve that. I hit you really hard because I'm mad about all the other stuff too."

Skylar stares at her for a minute. Imperia has clearly surprised her, and for once, Skylar has nothing to say.

"So honestly, I'm sorry I broke your nose. I didn't mean to disfigure you for life. Really. I was mad about Grace—you shouldn't pick on Grace. She can't defend herself. Just pick on me from now on, okay? I deserve it. Grace doesn't."

Skylar frowns, but she still doesn't say anything.

Imperia shrugs. "That's all I wanted to say."

She turns, takes a deep breath, and hopes Skylar doesn't hit her.

"You didn't," Skylar says.

Imperia stops and looks over her shoulder. "I didn't what?"

"Disfigure me for life. You didn't hit me that hard. You're not as powerful as you think you are."

It sounds like an insult, but it's not. It's kinda sorta forgiveness. At least, Imperia thinks it is. But she has to ask. "What about the surgery?"

"I probably won't do it. My mom can't make me either. Got that?"

"Yeah," Imperia says.

"Good," Skylar says, and walks past her, back to her posse.

Imperia watches her go. That was kinda weird, but okay. Better than Imperia expected. She lets out a small breath and feels a little dizzy.

Janie hurries over to her. "What happened?"

"Nothing really," Imperia says. She wants to say more, but she thinks it's not about Janie, not really. It's not about Grace either.

It's about settling in, and the bleed from one world to the next. Magic isn't the only thing that can get loose. Anger can too.

Imperia sighs, then smiles at Janie. "Thanks for standing up for me," Imperia says.

"No big," Janie says.

But it is a big. It counts for a lot. But Imperia has already said that as best she can.

She and Janie walk the rest of the way to class. One person isn't a posse. But it's better than all the glitter and magic wands in both worlds.

Imperia was wrong. School isn't so bad. And the weird thing is she didn't have to talk about fairy tales or lies or anything like that to make it all better.

Nobody cares about fairy tales. Nobody cares about anybody else most of the time.

Except maybe your sister.

Or your posse.

Or your friends.

DESTINY
A WORLD OF THE FEY STORY
KRISTINE KATHRYN RUSCH

Solanda walked the cobblestone streets of Nir, the
capitol city of Nye, her tail up. She had a meeting
with Rugar, the son of the Black King. He had sent
a Wisp to find her, and it had taken the little creature nearly
a day to do so.

Solanda was in her cat form, as she had been since the
Fey captured this repressed country—and thus very difficult
to find. The Nyeians had many faults—they were prissy,
overdressed, and pasty faced, not to mention abominably
poor soldiers—but they did treat their animals well. She had
found a family who fed her to excess, allowed her to roam
outside, and pampered her as no cat should be pampered.

How appalled they would be if they ever discovered the
golden cat their daughter had adopted was really a Fey
Shapeshifter.

Solanda's tail twitched once in amusement. Every day
she imagined eating her lovely tuna dinner in the glass plate

that the family gave her, and then Shifting into her Fey form just to say thank you.

She didn't know what would appall the Nyeians the most: the fact that she was Fey, or the fact that she would be naked. She doubted any of them had seen a naked woman before: the wife managed to change her clothing one piece at a time, without ever taking it all off at once, and the husband didn't seem to think this unusual. He would probably be more shocked than his wife at the appearance of a naked Fey woman in his house. He would probably fall over in a dead faint.

Only the daughter, a girl of five, was redeemable. Esmerelda was a good child. She had to be. She was raised Nyeian. Her mother trussed her in layers upon frothy layers of clothing, making movement nearly impossible, and then yelled at the poor child whenever she did something natural, like running.

Sometimes Solanda thought she went back to that household at night because she felt sorry for the child. But in truth, she stayed there because they gave her fish properly deboned and they brushed her, and they put a warm cedar bed in Esmerelda's room. Esmerelda, good child that she was, never confessed to her parents that she often picked up the cat and carried her to bed, cuddling with her long into the night.

And Solanda would never tell anyone—Fey or Nyeian— that sometimes she purred when she slept, pressed against the little girl's back.

Shifters were supposed to be the coldest of the Fey, the most fickle members of a warrior people, incapable of real emotion, flighty, restless and completely self-absorbed. They also were supposed to take on the characteristics of the animal they had chosen to Shift into, so Solanda's fickleness —theoretically—was doubly compounded by the fact that she had chosen the cat as her alternate Shape.

Of course, it didn't matter how many times she had proven herself trustworthy. In the war against Nye, such as it was, she had done intelligence for the Black King. She had worn her cat form and slinked into Nyeian villages, soldiers' camps, and mess halls, keeping her ears open, and learning more than she should have.

Most countries that the Fey had fought had banned strange animals from military compounds. Solanda had heard that the Co had gone so far as to slaughter any strays, thinking they might be Fey reconnaissance. But the Nyeians had a fondness for cats, and while they kept stray dogs out of their camps, they fed cats on the side.

Solanda had spent most of the war the pampered resident of a Nyeian general's tent. He used to feed her bits of meat off his own plate while telling his staff his battle plans for the next day.

And then when he fell into his snoring sleep, she would go to the nearest Shadowlands and inform the Fey general of all she had heard. Toward the end of the war, she reported directly to the Black King, who shook his head at the stupidity of the Nyeians.

Conquering Nye was the first step toward world dominion. The Black King didn't say that, but Solanda knew that was his goal. The Fey were a great warrior people, but they only owned half the world right now. The Black King—and the Black Throne—wanted all of it.

Solanda entered the merchant sector of Nir, and silently cursed to herself. The merchants often shooed cats out of this area. Her presence here was suddenly noticeable, and she didn't dare Shift. She'd shock an entire community of Nyeians—which would probably be good for them.

Scents from the nearby vendor stalls caught her nose. Fried beef, more fish, some sort of vegetable something which turned her feline stomach. The fish was enticing. It almost made her forget that she was here because she had been summoned by the Black King's son.

Rugar had been her commander for part of the Nye campaign. He was an able warrior, frustrated under his father's tight leash. The problem with Rugar was that he believed himself to be the equal of his father, and he was not.

Solanda would rather work with the Black King, ruthless as he was, than with his less-talented son.

The tall stone buildings prevented the sun from getting to the cobblestone. The stone was wet beneath her paws from the morning rain. The air was thick and muggy, making the six layers of clothes the Nyeians wore look even more uncomfortable.

The handful of Fey who were on the street wore their traditional uniform—a leather jerkin and pants. The Fey were so much taller than the Nyeians that even if they didn't dress differently, they would be noticeable.

She ducked under some clothing stalls, past the buildings that housed the year-round indoor merchants, and turned on the street that led to the Bank of Nye. The Black

King had taken over the building. It was four stories of gray stone, towering over the buildings around it—as close to a palace as there was in Nye.

She sighed heavily and crossed the street, climbing up the stone steps and staring at the large stone door. She'd have to Shift just to get into the place.

Then she saw a nearby window ledge. The window was open. She leaped onto the ledge and jumped to the stone floor inside. She thought this building unusually cold for a Nyeian structure. The house where she was pampered was made of wood, and had thick rugs on its floors. Every surface was soft, and the air perfumed.

Here the air smelled like chalk and the stone was chilly despite the heat. There were no guards in this room, although there should have been. It looked like it was some-one's office—a desk in the center, chairs on the side for supplicants.

The door was open and led into a cavernous hallway. She heard voices and followed them. Several Fey guards huddled in an alcove. They were Infantry and young, tall even though they hadn't come into their magic yet. Their dark skin and black hair was a welcome sight. She'd gotten tired of looking at the pasty-faced Nyeians, and hadn't realized how much she missed her own kind.

"...fool's errand, don't you think?" One of the young men said.

"If it's so important, why doesn't the Black King go?" another asked.

"Blue Isle is important," said a young woman. "It's the only stop between here and Leut."

Leut was the continent on the other side of the Infrin Sea. The Black King wanted to go there more than anything. He wanted to conquer as much of the world as he could before he died.

"If we are going to conquer the world," the girl was saying, "we have to go through Blue Isle first."

"Then it doesn't make sense," the first man said. "Why send Rugar? He's not as good a commander as his father."

"Maybe," Solanda said in her most authoritative voice, "the best commander in the world has a plan that's too sophisticated for you to understand."

They all turned. They had similar upswept features, narrow faces, and pointed ears. Solanda had often thought that her people looked like foxes—most of them, anyway. Shifters, like her, often took some of the characteristics of their animals. Her hair and skin were more golden than dark, and she had the Shifter's mark on her chin—a birthmark that established who and what she was when she was in her Fey form.

But they couldn't tell now. All they could do was tell that a cat had spoken to them.

"Well," she said, sitting on her haunches and wrapping her tail around her paws. "Where do I start? Do I reprimand you for gossiping in the middle of the day? Do I tell you that I got into the building through a window that some careless fool left open and, if I had been some young Nyeian bent on assassination, I could have walked right past you and you wouldn't have noticed? Or do I ask that one of you poor, magickless fools get me a robe so that I can have my meeting with Rugar?"

They didn't answer her. She raised her chin slightly. Amazing how she could intimidate them, even though she was so very small.

"By the Powers," she snapped. "Get me a robe. And put a guard on the window."

She nodded over her head toward the room she had just come out of.

Two of the young men ran off toward the room. The third young man hurried off, presumably to get her a robe. That left the young woman.

"I really should report this," Solanda said. "Technically, you put the Black King's life in danger."

"From the Nyeians?" the young woman snorted. "You snarl at them and they run. They couldn't fight us in the war, and once they found out that they'd remain in charge of their businesses, they really didn't care that we took them over. Why would one of them try to get in here?"

"Revenge?" Solanda said. "We did, after all, slaughter half their army. Those young men were related to someone."

"Then that should take away half the threat, shouldn't it?" the young woman said. "After all, the Nyeians believe that only men are capable of fighting."

Solanda felt amused. "I have a hunch that belief has changed since they were defeated by us. What's your name?"

"Licia," the girl said.

"You haven't come into your magic yet, have you?"

The girl straightened her shoulder. Magic was always a touchy subject with Infantry. They were tall enough to show that they would get magic, but chances were if they neared adulthood and still hadn't come into their magic, their abilities would be slight.

"No," she said.

"You showed a tactician's mind. Why do you waste it gossiping with people who aren't worthy of you?"

The girl straightened her shoulders. "I don't normally guard. I am usually in the field."

"But there's no field at the moment, is there?" Solanda said. "What are you doing here?"

"Rugar asked me to come. He says his daughter needs more swordfighting training."

Solanda narrowed her eyes. Jewel, Rugar's middle child, was the most promising of all his raggedy offspring. She hadn't come into her magic yet either, but her height and her heritage suggested when her magic came it would be powerful. She was a good swordswoman now—Solanda had seen her fight in the last of the Nye campaign.

"Why would she need more training?"

Licia shrugged. "I suspect it has something to do with the fight Rugar had with his father this morning."

Solanda tilted her head to show her interest.

"They just left that room you came through. They were screaming at each other all morning long."

"About what?" Solanda asked, realizing that she was now gossiping. But she didn't want to go into a meeting with Rugar with less knowledge than he had.

"About going to Blue Isle. Rugar says he won't go without his daughter."

"Not his other children?"

"He didn't mention them." Then Licia smiled. "At least not at the top of his voice."

Solanda suppressed a sigh. The Black King favored Jewel. He felt that her brothers were idiots—and he was right. Their magic was slight, like their mother's had been. Rugar's entire life had been about defying his father. Rugar should have married a woman who had great magic. Instead, he had chosen someone he could control.

The young man returned with a flowing golden robe that was clearly of Nyeian origin. Solanda didn't ask where he had gotten it. She didn't thank him. Instead, she said, "Place it over me."

He did, blotting out the light. The robe smelled faintly of perfume and perspiration, but it clearly hadn't been worn in some time. The fabric was heavy satin—too heavy for a humid day like this—but she wasn't in the position to be choosy. If Rugar was planning something stupid, she wanted to meet him Fey to Fey. Psychologically, it gave her an advantage.

She Shifted, feeling her body slide into its familiar Fey form. Her body stretched and grew. Her tail and whiskers slid into her skin, her hair flowed down her back, her front paws became hands. She ended up in a sitting position, her knees drawn to her chest, the robe draped over her like a tent. Inwardly she sighed, and wished that there were a more dignified way of Shifting into clothes.

Then she slid her arms through the sleeves, and her head through the neck hole, letting the stiff fabric flow around her. It was a woman's garment, although she had no idea why someone would store one in a bank—or perhaps she did, and didn't want to think about illicit affairs among Nyeian bankers.

She lifted her long hair out of the garment's neck, and let it fall down her back. Licia bit her lower lip, and the other Fey looked down. They hadn't realized they were talking to the best Shifter in the Black King's army—at least, not until now.

Fools. Shifters were rare. How many of them would come into the Black King's dwelling and order Infantry around?

"Licia," she said, "announce me to Rugar."

The girl's skin colored slightly, but she moved in front of Solanda and led her down the hall. It got stuffier the farther in they went. Solanda was grateful that her feet were bare. The cool stone was going to keep her from melting in this robe.

Licia led her up a flight of stairs into a rabbit's warren of what had once been offices. Solanda smiled. Rugar was hidden here, in an obviously less desirable area of the building. The Black King had a thousand ways of showing his displeasure with everyone around him.

Licia knocked on a door at the end of the hall. Solanda stood far enough back that she wasn't visible from inside. She heard Rugar's gruff voice, and then Licia's response, announcing Solanda.

The door opened, and Licia stepped aside.

"I guess that means you're supposed to go in," she said.

Solanda stopped and put a hand on the girl's shoulder. She spoke softly so that Rugar couldn't hear. "If Rugar and his father are fighting," she said, "side with the old man.

Rugar is not the future of this race. You're better off remaining in Nye with the Black King than going to Blue Isle with Rugar."

Licia nodded, then glanced over her shoulder as if she were afraid of Rugar. Solanda walked past her and through the open door.

Rugar stood in the center of the small room. He was medium height for a Fey, and his features had a predatory, hawk-like look to them. His almond-shaped eyes were the deep black that Solanda associated with the Black Family. It was as if the Throne echoed in their very essence. He had thin, cruel lips, and an expression of permanent unhappiness.

For man in his fifties with grown children, he looked startlingly like a petulant child.

"You sent for me," she said, not disguising her lack of respect for him.

He clasped his hands behind his back, his father's favorite stance. "I'm taking an army to Blue Isle. You will be part of it."

She snorted. "I serve your father, not you."

Rugar glared at her. "He gave me permission to choose whomever I wanted from the standing armies in Nye."

"You have no need for a Shifter," she said. "Blue Isle is a tiny place, filled with religious fanatics who have never seen war. You'll sail in with your troops, wave a few swords, and be able to claim victory over an entire country in the space of a day. I'll be useless to you."

He shook his head. "I'm taking you, and a lot of Spies and Doppelgängers. I am to be military governor of Blue

Isle. My father will launch an attack from there onto Leut."

Solanda narrowed her eyes and was glad she wasn't in cat form. She probably would have found an excuse to scratch Rugar, and that wouldn't have been good for either of them.

"Spies, Doppelgängers, and a Shifter," she said. "It sounds like an intelligence force. You won't need it if you conquer the country as quickly as you believe you will."

His gaze went flat. "I will need it."

She stared at him for a moment. He knew something and he wasn't going to share it with her. Spies made sense, even in an easily conquered country. They would find the pockets of resistance. But Doppelgängers had no place there. They killed their hosts and then took over the body, including the memories. Except for the gold flecks in the eyes, no one could tell them from their victims. Doppelgängers had a sophisticated magic—one that the best commanders used sparingly. And certainly didn't waste them on an already conquered country.

"You have no need for me," she repeated. "I stay with the Black King."

"You'll come with me."

"Your father said so?"

"No, but he will."

"Because he already acquiesced on Jewel?"

Rugar started. He hadn't expected her to know that.

Solanda raised her eyebrows and allowed herself a small smile. "I am good at gathering intelligence."

"And," he said, "as you pointed out, there's no need for intelligence gathering in a conquered country."

She nodded. "I'll go to Leut with your father, when he's ready. Until then, I'll relax here."

"Solanda—"

"Rugar," she said, holding up a hand. "You and I have no great liking for each other. I have a hunch your father is sending you to Blue Isle to get you out of his sight. I'd rather not be associated with you in any way. Right now, I hold your father's respect. I'd rather not change that."

Rugar took a step toward her. She could feel the violence shimmering in him.

She grabbed the doorknob. "Touch me," she said, "and I'll scratch out your eyes."

"You can't touch me. I'm a member of the Black Family."

She smiled. "I'm a Shifter. Unpredictable, irresponsible, flighty—remember? I'm sure the Powers would let this slide."

"But my father would not," Rugar said.

"Oh," Solanda said softly, "but I think he would."

She tried to see the Black King before she left the building, but he was nowhere to be found. His personal guards were gone as well. She decided she would find him in the morning, and went back to her life as a pampered Nyeian cat.

The home that she had chosen was a large one on the outskirts of Nir. It had two stories filled with more clutter than any home she had ever seen. Books of poetry, musical instruments, incredibly ugly paintings, and furniture every-where. The only saving grace was that the furniture was comfortable and the kitchen had a cat door that she could escape through when the wife decided it was time for music.

Solanda slipped through the cat door, past the kitchen hearth. One of the three Nyeian servants was cleaning the pots from the evening meal. The air smelled faintly of roast beef, and Solanda's stomach rumbled.

Still, she didn't beg from the servant. She knew better. The idiot had kicked her "accidentally" once, and had the scars to prove it. But Solanda knew if she attacked anyone in the house too many times, she would be thrown out, and she wasn't willing to lose her rich dinners and soft bed just yet.

She blended into the hideous yellow wallpaper as she hurried up the stairs to Esmerelda's room.

Esmerelda sat on the edge of the bed, fingering a rip in her dress. She had a forlorn expression on her small face. Her brown hair hung limply around her cheeks, and a streak of dirt covered the pantaloons beneath the skirt.

Solanda had never seen Esmerelda look dirty before, nor had she seen the girl's hair loose at any time except bedtime.

"Oh, Goldie!" Esmerelda raised her voice in relief. She was speaking Nye, which was a language that Solanda hadn't known well when she moved into this house. Here her Nye had improved greatly, but she wanted to be fluent in it by the time she left.

The little girl launched herself off the bed and grabbed Solanda before Solanda could jump out of the way. Esmerelda wrapped her arms around Solanda and held tightly. Esmerelda had never done that before. If she had been a grabby little girl, Solanda would have been gone a long time ago.

So this meant, quite simply, that something was wrong.

Solanda let herself be held for a moment, then she turned her head toward the door and flattened her ears. Esmerelda, smart child that she was, understood both signals. She pushed the door closed, and then let Solanda go.

Solanda jumped on the windowsill. Esmerelda followed her, but didn't open the window like she usually did.

The room was hot and sticky. Solanda wouldn't be able to stay here too long if that window wasn't opened.

"I don't dare," Esmerelda said softly. "Mommy's really mad at me. She didn't even let me have dinner."

Now Solanda was interested, but she didn't want the story, not yet. She bumped her head against the window's bubbled glass.

Esmerelda bit her lower lip and shook her head.

Solanda placed a paw on the glass and meowed softly.

"Okay," Esmerelda whispered. "But if anyone comes, I'll have to close it."

Solanda almost nodded, then caught herself. When Esmerelda came close, Solanda bumped her affectionately with her head, and then watched as the little girl pulled the window open.

A cool breeze made its way inside. That was the other nice thing about this house. Esmerelda's room opened onto a large undeveloped area, so the smells of the outdoors came in strong. Breezes were unencumbered. Esmerelda's mother hated this, and often wished for close neighbors, but Solanda saw it for the blessing it was.

Esmerelda knelt down beside the window and put her elbows on the sill. She didn't touch Solanda, but she was still a bit too close. Her body heat was ruining the breeze.

"I been so bad," she said, "I won't get to go outside ever again."

Solanda watched her. The little girl had never been able to resist a cat's gaze. Solanda had never seen a child who was so very lonely. Esmerelda wasn't allowed to play—except with dolls whose clothing was frilly as the stuff she was trussed in—nor was she allowed to associate with the neighboring children who were, in her parents' mind, beneath her. She had lessons in poetry and music, art and dancing, but she liked none of it. What she really wanted to do was run as far as she could, and climb trees and learn how to swim.

She'd probably never get to achieve those goals.

"I was running this afternoon," Esmerelda said. Her face was wistful. She leaned her forehead against the glass. "Mommy was looking at fruit and I thought I could just go around the block, but she saw me. I guess she followed me."

Esmerelda had done this before, and it hadn't gotten her sent to bed with no supper. Solanda suspected the problem had something to do with the rip in the dress. Clothing was sacred, at least to this family. Solanda wanted to tear every piece so that this little girl could be free.

"She saw me fall." Esmerelda said, fingering her skirt. "She saw me hit a Fey."

Solanda stiffened. She almost asked who, and caught herself. Two near lapses in one conversation. She was getting much too relaxed with this child.

Esmerelda ran a soft hand over Solanda's head. Her touch was gentle again, as it had always been before.

"She said she was the Black King's granddaughter, and she yelled at Mommy for dressing me the way she did. And Mom yelled back. The lady said yelling at her was like yelling at all the Fey all at once."

Only one Fey woman could make that claim. Jewel. No wonder Esmerelda's mother was upset.

"And then Mommy told Daddy and he said that the Fey might hurt us. Because I ran." A tear coursed down Esmerelda's cheek.

And those fools were blaming the child for being a child. Solanda pushed against the girl's hand, and Esmerelda sniffled.

"I didn't mean to run. I just can't stay still sometimes."

Solanda understood that. She could never stay still. It was a curse of being a Shifter. It was the reason Fey wisdom said that Shifters were the most heartless of the Fey. Most Shifters did not have children, and most rarely stayed anywhere long enough to form a real relationship.

Esmerelda sighed. "I wish I was like you. I do what I want. Or like that Fey lady. She was nice to me. She didn't like Mommy though."

Neither did Solanda.

"She said children shouldn't be dressed like me. She said I ran into her because my clothing didn't let me run properly."

Probably true, Solanda thought.

"And that made Mommy really mad."

Esmerelda let her hand slide off Solanda's neck. She

bunched her hands into fists and rested her chin on them, looking fierce and strong. Solanda felt her whiskers twitch in amusement. One day, Esmerelda's parents would no longer be able to control this child. If she was this strong, articulate, and intelligent at five, she would be impossible to control at fifteen.

Especially with all of the Fey influence around her.

"I wish I had magic," the little girl said. "Just a little bit. Then I could run and no one would know. I'd make myself invisible and no one would see me."

Solanda looked out the window, knowing her expression was too sympathetic for a cat. There was a ring of oaks at the edge of the lawn. They were blowing in the breeze. Maybe there would be another storm. Maybe this storm would finally cool the place off, although she doubted it. Nye's hot season was the worst she had encountered in any country she had ever been in.

"Esmerelda!" her mother's voice echoed from the hallway. "Why is your door closed?"

Esmerelda gasped and pulled down the window so quickly she almost caught Solanda's tail in it. Then she leaped onto the bed, stretching out. Solanda jumped beside her and curled up at her feet just as Esmerelda's mother opened the door.

The woman's face was flushed. She looked like a tomato about to burst. She was so tightly corseted that her body looked flat, and Solanda wondered how the woman could even breathe. She wore an evening dress of white satin that accented the redness of her face. The sides were lined with sweat.

"What are you doing?" she asked. Then she frowned. "How did that mangy cat get in here?"

Solanda growled softly in the back of her throat. She was not mangy. And the woman had never called her that before.

"I told you that you were supposed to be in here by yourself to think about what you did today. Things could have been much worse. Fortunately, she was in good mood. You know what those people can do? Why it's said they can cut the skin off a person with the flick of—"

Solanda yowled, and the woman stepped back, a hand over her heart. Esmerelda sat up, worry on her small face.

"Are you okay, Goldie?"

Solanda licked her right paw as if she had twisted it. She was not going to let that woman tell this little girl about Fey atrocities—even if they were true.

"Come on, Goldie," Esmerelda's mother said. "There's some beef for you in the kitchen."

Usually that would have gotten Solanda off the bed. But she could sneak down after everyone was asleep and take what she needed. Right now, she wanted to stay beside Esmerelda.

"Goldie," the woman said.

Esmerelda, good child that she was, bit her lower lip and said nothing. She didn't beg for the company that she obviously wanted.

"Goldie!" her mother sounded exasperated now. Then she shook her head. "Why do we put up with this animal?"

Neither Solanda nor Esmerelda answered.

Finally, Esmerelda's mother sighed. "All right, she can stay. But I do expect you to sleep in that dress tonight and to think about how you could have hurt us all. That rip should be a reminder of the danger your misbehavior put us in. Nye isn't the place it used to be, child. Do something wrong, and those Fey will harm all of us."

Then she pulled the door closed, and Solanda heard the boards creak as she made her way down the stairs.

Esmerelda's fingers played with the rip. Solanda looked at it, then crossed the bed, took the skirt in her teeth and pulled. The rip grew. Esmerelda giggled, then covered her mouth. Solanda pulled harder. If the little girl had to sleep in these clothes, she might as well be comfortable.

Esmerelda ripped the pantaloons too, along the dirt line, giggling as she did so. "Mommy will think I did it when I was running," she said. "You're so smart, Goldie."

Of course she was. Solanda preened and allowed herself to be petted one more time.

Then Esmerelda looked at the door, her smile fading. "Sometimes I think Mommy doesn't want me. She wants somebody else. Somebody perfect."

Too bad she didn't realize that the child she had was better than perfect. Solanda sighed softly. Some people had more than they deserved.

The idea came to her in the middle of the night, in that hot and stuffy room. She could take Esmerelda away, and Esmerelda's parents wouldn't even know it had happened. But it would take the cooperation of the Fey Domestics.

Fey magic was divided into two parts: warrior and domestic. Warrior magic was designed for warfare. Some Fey magic turned its practitioner into a weapon, like the Foot Soldiers who had fingernails that could slice better than a blade. Domestic magic could not be used to fight any war. Domestics lost their magic if they killed. Their magics were healing magics or home-bound magics, such as spells that made chairs more inviting or fires warmer.

The next morning, after making certain that Esmerelda got breakfast, Solanda slipped out the cat door. She went to the Domicile that the Fey Domestics had set up just outside of town. The Domicile had been built especially for the Domestics, and covered with various protection and healing spells. It was a traditional U-shaped building—with hearth and home magics in one length of the U, the healing wards in the other, and the middle section as a meeting place in between.

Solanda usually didn't seek out the Domestics. They always wanted to experiment with her—have her try on a new cloak covered with some sort of rain protection or have her taste a new food to see if it had an effect on her Shifting. The last time she had been in a Domicile had been when she had broken a paw jumping from a tree in one of the last Nye battles. The Domestics had mended the bone, and had given her a smelly ointment she had to apply in cat form. She had thought the stench alone would kill her.

As she mounted the steps to the center part of the building, she shook off her paws. Here she would not Shift to Fey form. The Domestics weren't as obsessed with power as

Rugar was, so she didn't have to use her height as a reminder of the strength of her magic.

She pushed open the door and stepped inside.

The air was cool and welcoming. It smelled of a sea breeze. Bits of magic floated in the air. Spinner's magic. They were working on their looms. She could hear the hum just down the corridor.

A Baker entered, his fingers dusted with flour. They glowed. And she knew he had spelled the bread he'd been baking to remain fresh for as long as possible. It was a traveling spell, one most often used when troops were heading off to battle. She wondered if someone had requested it.

"I'm here to see Chadn."

The Baker nodded, then slipped through a door that led to the Healing part of the Domicile. Solanda hopped onto a chair. Her mood rose and she cursed, jumping down. She didn't need to be spelled, to wait, happy and contented, on a chair dusted with Domestic magic. Instead, she paced the cool floor and wondered why she couldn't smell the baking bread.

Finally, Chadn entered the room. She was a young Shaman, although the toll of her power had already turned her hair white. Her face was wizened, her mouth a small oval amid wrinkles. Only her eyes were bright—sparkling black circles of light in a ruined face.

She had been assigned to stay with Rugar during the war and she was happy to be free of him. Shaman were the most independent Fey: their Vision as strong as those of the Leaders, but their magic Domestic so they could not rule a warrior people. They were the wise ones, the advisors, supposedly the strength behind the Black Throne. The Black King required a Shaman of his son, but did not use one himself. He had dismissed his own, years ago, for disobeying him. It was one of many areas where the Black King broke with tradition.

"Solanda," Chadn said. "I had hoped to see you."

Solanda jumped on an end table and was relieved that her mood did not change. She sat on her haunches and looked into Chadn's face.

"I have a request," she said. "It's for a Nyeian child."

"A child?" Chadn sounded surprised. "Not a Fey child?"

Solanda shook her head.

"I had Seen you with a Fey child."

The Shaman's Visions—and the Vision that leaders like the Black King had—allowed them glimpses into the future. Some said that the glimpses allowed the Visionary to change the future. Others believed that the glimpses led the Visionary to that future.

Solanda's eyes narrowed. "I have not been with a Fey child."

Chadn nodded. "It was on Blue Isle. The child was a Shifter, and you kept her from death."

Solanda's whiskers twitched. "I told Rugar I would not go to Blue Isle with him."

"The future of our people lies with you, Solanda."

"And a child?" Solanda raised her chin. "Are you sure it was a Fey child?"

"Not entirely," Chadn said. "The child had blue eyes."

Solanda gave a soft grunt of surprise. She had heard of

blue-eyed people, but she had never seen one. "The child couldn't be Nyeian?"

"She was Fey, and newborn. She had a birthmark on her chin. Only her eyes were strange, and perhaps that was because of the Shifting. I Saw you put your hands on her lips, and swear to protect her, raise her, and make her strong. Then I Saw her full grown, saying you had been the closest thing she had to a mother."

Solanda laughed, although inside she felt cold. A Shifter only swore to protect a child who held the future of the Empire. A blue-eyed child that Shifted? The center of the Empire?

"Visions can be altered," Solanda said. "I am not leaving Nye."

"You may have no choice."

"I'll always have a choice," Solanda said.

Chadn inclined her head toward Solanda as if giving in on that point. "What does the Nyeian child need?"

Solanda took a deep breath. "She is different from any other Nyeian I've seen. Strong, independent. She met Jewel yesterday and is being punished for it. I would like to remove the child from her family and bring her here, to be raised among us. She will be useful when she's grown. She will be part of the second-generation, the Nyeians that rule Nye for the Fey."

Chadn stared at her for a moment. "So take her. Shifters steal children."

"This one's mother will raise a fuss if she's gone."

"What mother wouldn't?"

"She'll come to us."

"And you can't prove to the Black King that we must keep the child."

"Not yet, anyway," Solanda said.

Chadn folded her hands over her stomach. "You want a Changeling."

"Yes," Solanda said.

"How old is the child?"

"Five."

Chadn sighed. "Have you asked the child if she's willing to leave?"

"Not yet. I wanted to know if I have help first."

"You will keep the child at your side?"

Solanda frowned. That wasn't a normal request. Shifters rarely kept children. They usually brought them to Domestics to raise. "Must I?"

"At five, it will be you she trusts."

Solanda shrugged. "Then she shall stay with me."

"And you will stay away from Blue Isle." Chadn said that not as a question, but as a statement.

"Rugar will not let a Nyeian child in his war party."

"So the child serves two purposes." Chadn's eyes narrowed. "Has she magic?"

"Of course not." Solanda laughed. "There is not magic outside the Fey."

Chadn frowned. "I am no longer certain of that."

"Because you Saw a blue-eyed Shifter?"

"Because I Saw a great war, coming when we least expect it."

"War is part of Fey life." Solanda jumped off the table

and headed for the door. "I'll bring you news of the child tomorrow."

"I'll have Changeling stone ready," Chadn said. "But realize before you act, that this is for life."

"I already know that," Solanda said. "I have chosen well."

"I hope so," Chadn said.

S olanda went to the docks and sat on a fence. She loved it here. The Infrin Sea formed the most natural harbor on Galinas, and there was always some sort of activity. Toward the north end of the harbor, the Nyeian builders made the great ships. Those ships traveled all over the known world, and now Fey Domestics helped unload cargo that would go all over the Empire.

Ships from Blue Isle had stopped coming to Nye when news reached them of the Fey takeover. She would never see an Islander, never learn more about them than she already had.

And that would be all right.

For there were some things she couldn't discuss with Rugar's Shaman. Like the prophecies that had been made by another Shaman at Solanda's birth, prophecies that claimed her legacy would be in the children she saved.

Children—not child, like Chadn had seen. Solanda would influence the life of more than one.

The breeze was cooler here, carrying with it the smell of salt and a tinge of dead fish. That smell made her stomach rumble. She tried not to think of the things she ate in her cat form, things she would find disgusting when she was in Fey form. Right now, raw dead fish sounded extremely appetizing.

But she didn't go in search of the source of the smell. She had some thinking to do. Prophecies and Visions made her nervous. She had no idea what to do with the information Chadn had given her. Because, at various points in her life, Solanda had been told by Visionaries that her future held contradictory things.

One Shaman had told her she had to avoid the Black Family for she would kill a Black Heir. Another Shaman had told her she would raise a Black Heir. And now Chadn had Seen her swear to protect a blue-eyed Shifter, a newborn who couldn't survive on her own.

Solanda bowed her head. The prophecy she never mentioned, the one her parents had kept silent, had come the day of her birth and she had never forgotten it. The prophecy was a cold one: she would die before her time, far from home, for a crime she did not regret.

The Fey did not believe in crime. They were constantly at war, so the crimes that plagued other races—murder, theft —were absorbed into the wars themselves. The Fey only punished two crimes: treason and failure. Both of those crimes were considered crimes against the Empire. Failure was a large crime, encompassing the failure to follow an order, or the failure to defeat an enemy in a prolonged battle.

Treason was any crime against the Black Family and was such a heresy, that it wasn't even discussed among rational Fey.

Both crimes bore the penalty of death.

It seemed to her that she would never commit crimes like that, that the prophecies had come because she was a Shifter, not because of her character. She wasn't as flighty or as difficult as anyone said she was.

And besides, she had to take care of Esmerelda.

She wished she could be there the morning that Esmerelda's parents discovered the Changeling. It would look like Esmerelda, even act like her—if stone could act like a living breathing creature. But it would only last a few days, and then it would cease to exist. They would think Esmerelda dead, when, in actuality, she was only gone.

Then, perhaps, that wretch of a mother would regret how she treated her daughter.

Esmerelda would live a life she couldn't even imagine now. She wouldn't have to wear six layers of clothes on the hottest day of the year, and she would learn how to live life to its fullest instead of remaining indoors and studying all the time.

Esmerelda would be the closest thing to Fey that a Nyeian could be—and for the first time in her young life, she would be happy. Solanda would see to that.

They would both be very happy.

Solanda returned to the house after dinner. Ultimately, she found she couldn't resist the dead fish that were piled near one of the docks. She had eaten herself sick, and then had to clean every inch of her fur before she even attempted the walk home.

Not that the house was home. In some ways, Esmerelda was.

Solanda used the cat door. Esmerelda's parents were talking softly in the parlor.

"Perhaps boarding school," the mother was saying. "If she is this incorrigible now, imagine what she'll be like when she gets older."

"Give it time, darling," the husband said. "She's still a child. She will learn, as we all did."

"It's just I despair of ever teaching her manners. You didn't see her with that Fey..."

Solanda had heard enough. She hurried up the stairs. She would talk to Esmerelda tonight. Tomorrow the Wisps would come, carrying a bit of stone in their tiny fingers. They'd fly in the open window, leave the stone on the bed and it would mold itself into a replica of Esmerelda while Solanda was leading the real Esmerelda out of the house.

Quick, neat, and completely perfect. The parents wouldn't have to worry about manners or boarding school. Esmerelda would get her heart's desire. And Solanda would have her reason for staying in Nye.

The door to Esmerelda's room was open. Esmerelda sat beneath a lamp, a long skirt over her lap. The air was stuffier than usual, and Solanda saw that the window was closed.

It had probably been closed all day. Sunlight had poured in, and the poor child had had to sit in the heat, working on some task her mother assigned her.

When Solanda got close, she saw what it was. The child was attempting to mend her own ripped dress.

The stitches were uneven, and Esmerelda had stitched the bottom layer of fabric onto the top. That would make her mother even angrier. Esmerelda's eyelashes were stuck together, her nose was red, and there were tearstains along her cheeks.

"Goldie!" she said, and let the dress topple to the floor. She was wearing another dress, equally inappropriate to the hot weather. She reached for Solanda, but Solanda jumped onto the windowsill.

She was not going to be hugged by a hot sweaty child—not, at least, until the window was open and the fresh air came inside.

Esmerelda glanced toward the door. She put a finger to her lips, as if she thought Solanda were going to give her away, and then called, "Mommy! Can I go to sleep now?"

Solanda froze in her spot. She didn't want to be seen in here, not tonight. She wanted to have her conversation with Esmerelda in private.

"Are you done with your dress, darling?"

"Yes."

Solanda looked at it. The dress was ruined. The poor girl would have an even more difficult day than usual tomorrow.

"Then blow out the lamp. Good night."

"Good night." Esmerelda pushed the door closed. Then she went over to the window and opened it.

A strong breeze came in, and on it, Solanda smelled rain. Maybe, after she spoke to Esmerelda, she would go outside.

By then it would be raining, and she would be able to cool down.

Esmerelda put her hand over the lamp's chimney and blew. The flame inside the glass went out. Solanda blinked in the darkness, letting her eyes adjust. It only took a moment. There were clouds over the moon this night, and it was very dark.

Esmerelda went back to her chair. "I wish you knew how to sew, Goldie."

"I don't," Solanda said. "But I know someone who does."

Esmerelda let out a small yelp, and put her hands over her mouth. She peered around the room as if looking for the source of the voice.

Solanda had to go slowly with this. The child wasn't used to magic, not like Fey children were.

"I could take the dress to her tonight," Solanda said, "and by morning, you wouldn't even know there had been a rip in it."

Esmerelda's eyes were wide. She finally turned in Solanda's direction. "You can talk, Goldie?"

"As well as I can listen." Solanda jumped from the windowsill to the bed. The room had cooled down. The fresh air felt marvelous. "What would you think, Esmerelda, if I took you to a place where you could wear comfortable clothes, play with children your own age, run and jump and swim to your heart's content? What if I told you that you would never have to sew another stitch, have another music lesson, or sit in a corner when you've done something that your mother didn't like?"

Esmerelda looked for her, but clearly didn't see her. Cat's eyes were far superior in the dark. Solanda watched the child lick her lips, rub her hand over her knees, and then sigh.

"How long would I stay?" Esmerelda asked.

"Forever," Solanda said.

"Would I have to be a cat?"

Solanda laughed. For all her verbal sophistication, Esmerelda was still a child at heart. "No," Solanda said. "You'll stay just as you are."

"Would Mommy come?"

"No."

"Daddy?"

"No."

Esmerelda's shoulders stiffened. Her little body looked rigid. "Who would love me, then?"

Solanda started. She hadn't expected that question. "I would be with you," she said.

Esmerelda was silent, as if she were thinking this over. "Where would you take me?"

"To my people," Solanda said.

"I'd live with cats?"

"No," she said gently. "With the Fey."

Esmerelda gasped. She held onto her chair as if she expected to be dragged from it.

Solanda wondered if she should have said that, but she had never taken a child before. Certainly she knew of no one who had ever taken a child of this age.

But Chadn had said she had had to speak with the child,

and the choice to come had to be the child's. There was sense in that. Esmerelda, at age five, would always have a memory of living with her parents. She needed a memory of her choice to leave them.

"Esmerelda," Solanda said. "I—"

"No!" Esmerelda screamed. "No!"

She launched herself out of her chair as if her voice had given the ability to move again.

"Help! Mommy! Help!"

Solanda's ears went back. She hadn't expected this from Esmerelda, not her sane, different child.

"Esmerelda, I only want to give you a better life—"

"Mommy! Daddy! Help!"

Finally, Esmerelda pulled the door open and blundered into the hallway. Solanda followed, tail between her legs, ears still back. The little girl's screams echoed down the stairs. Her parents had reached her, and they both put their arms around her. Esmerelda was too terrified to be coherent.

Then the mother looked up the stairs. She saw Solanda, her gaze flat.

And Solanda realized she had no choice.

She Shifted, her body lengthening, her tail disappearing, her fur becoming skin.

Then she walked, naked, to the floor below.

Esmerelda's mother gathered her child in her arms and backed away. The father placed himself in front of his small family, arms out.

"You came from the Black King, didn't you?" the woman said. "To punish us by stealing our child."

"It's not about you," Solanda said.

Esmerelda peeked around her father, eyes wide. Solanda had never, in her entire life, been so conscious of her nakedness.

"Wh-what do you want?" the father asked. He was trying to sound brave. Like most Nyeians, he was failing.

"I had hoped to take your daughter, but it seems that she prefers this place, even though you treat her as less than house pet. It seems, for reasons I cannot understand, that she loves you."

"Of course she does," the woman said. "We're her parents."

"As if that's a divine right." Solanda stopped on the middle stair.

The family cringed below her as if they expected her to strike them with a lightning bolt. She didn't have that kind of magic. They had seen the extent of her powers, but apparently they didn't know that.

"She is a child," Solanda said. "She is to run and play. She is to have friends of her own age. She is to have comfortable clothing so that she can move without tripping. She is supposed to get dirty, to rip her skirts, and fall on her behind. She is to have some joy in her life. Do you understand?"

"I thought you Fey were supposed to leave us alone," the mother said. "I thought—"

"Be quiet," the father said.

Esmerelda clung to her father, her curiosity moving her closer.

"You will give her those things," Solanda said, "or I will take her from you. Do you understand?"

"Yes," the father said.

"You can't do this," the mother said. "You can't change our customs. The Black King promised you wouldn't."

"A promise made to a conquered people is worth nothing," Solanda snapped. "You will do what I say, or the child is mine."

"Mommy." Esmerelda reached for her mother. Solanda's eyes narrowed. Couldn't she see that her mother saw her only as a thing to be trained, to be forced into the right and proper life?

Probably not. It was too sophisticated a concept for her. The same innocence that allowed Esmerelda to accept a cat's speech, allowed her to believe that she was loved.

"Do I take her now?" Solanda asked.

"No," the father said. "We'll do as you say."

"But our friends—"

"Shut up," the father snapped. "Do you want to lose her?"

For a moment, the mother's gaze met Solanda's and in it, Solanda saw something she recognized, a coolness perhaps, a calculation. How would that woman have answered if she had been asked who would love me then? Would she have dodged the answer like Solanda had? Or would she have heard it at all?

"She will stay with us," the woman said. She sounded resigned.

Solanda felt a hope she hadn't even known she had die

inside her. "Then I'll watch. You will treat that child as if she is more precious than gold. And if you fail, even once, she's mine. Is that clear?"

"Yes," the father said.

But Solanda did not take her gaze from the mother.

"Yes," the woman said.

Esmerelda had stepped to her father's side. She was still holding his leg. "Are you Goldie?" she asked.

Solanda gave her a small, private smile. "Only for you."

The little girl slipped behind her father again. Her answer was clear, too. She would stay, no matter what. And Solanda had done all she could.

So she Shifted back to her cat form. For a moment, she watched them all, tail twitching, then she ran up the stairs and into Esmerelda's room. She stopped for only a moment, knowing she would never return.

She leapt onto the windowsill, and sighed. She had just lost her excuse for staying on Nye. She was bound to the Black Family. She had to do as they wished.

Rugar wanted her to go to Blue Isle.

Where a Shifter awaited her care. A newborn child, with blue eyes. A child who would think her the closest thing she'd ever had to a mother.

Solanda looked over her shoulder. She heard Esmerelda's voice, high, piping, excited; the soft answers of her parents. Solanda had lied to them. She would not be able to watch.

She hoped they would take good care of her little girl.

Then she jumped out the window, and climbed along a tree branch. Maybe her future had been preordained. Maybe she had no choice. She would raise a Black Heir, maybe kill one, and influence children.

How different would tonight have been if she had told the child that she would love her?

She would never know. Perhaps that was the moment in which everything could have changed. Maybe she had just missed her only chance to save herself.

KILLER ADVICE
AN ASSASSINS UNIVERSE STORY
KRISTINE KATHRYN RUSCH

Sixteen minutes. Sixteen minutes was simply not enough time to prepare for an onslaught. One would think with the recent breakthroughs in interstellar communication that a simple heads-up would be in order. Yet no one thought to contact Hunsaker.

Of course, the communications problem wasn't with the Presidio, who barely got off a single *we need help; we're docking soon* communiqué before their entire communications array went down. No, the problem was with Repair and Maintenance. Some idiot there forgot to inform Hunsaker that his resort would soon be full.

Not that the Vaadum Resort and Casino was much of a resort. It was more of a Hail Mary Pass. If you were passing through the Commons System (which was what most people did in the Commons System—pass through) and for some reason you needed to exit your luxurious spaceship for some downtime and you couldn't wait the extra day to go to

Commons Starship Resorts—which were real resorts, by the way, on full-size space stations—then you ended up at Vaadum Resort and Casino.

Hunsaker liked to think of Vaadum as a bit of a surprise. Vaadum was on the Vaadum Outpost, which predated the Commons Space Station by nearly two hundred years and looked it. Small, cramped quarters, a docking ring that couldn't accommodate most modern ships, a repair shop that was catch as catch can, a resupply warehouse that sometimes needed resupplying itself, and of course, the Resort.

Which, when Hunsaker bought it, was a seedy little rundown motel, operated by the repair crew, who learned (accidentally or so the histories said) that ships in distress often couldn't house their passengers. Better to place those passengers in a paying room than having them bunk on top of tables in the cafeteria.

Hunsaker was manning the front desk because sixteen minutes didn't make up for the six months during which he had neglected to upgrade the automatic check-in system. He hadn't cleaned the rooms in six months either—or at least, not all of them, nor had he checked the environmental systems.

He sent his entire staff—all two of them—off to dust, change linens, and ensure that each room had both oxygen and some sort of livable temperature while he scoured the entry, trying to make it somewhat presentable.

The Repair and Maintenance crew told him that the Presidio had twelve passengers and four crewmembers, so he would need a minimum of eight rooms, but it would be better to have sixteen.

It would be better to have all thirty rooms cleaned and livable, but really, where was the percentage in that? He had three functioning rooms at all times, and two of those were rarely full. The regulars that came through—and there were regulars, although not always the best of regulars—came for the casino, which had the only living breathing human dealer in the Commons System.

She was fifty percent fake. He didn't test the fifty percent theory or which part about her parts was rumor—although he did know that her breasts literally sparkled because she often dealt topless (hence the repeat audience).

She was a bit too vulgar for him. Vaadum Resort and Casinos was a bit vulgar for him, and quite low scale, and if someone asked him, he would have admitted that the entire enterprise had irritated him when he arrived, but didn't bother him so much now.

His standards had lowered, not because of the place, but because he didn't really deserve better.

He was just coming to terms with that.

The entry was the largest room in the Resort, not counting the restaurant or the casino. The entry had bench seats, no-die, regrow plants that he'd bought early in his tenure here and regretted ever since, and a large faux marble floor that, when he bothered to faux polish it, shined like a million bright stars.

He managed to clean the dust off the benches, prune the regrow plants so that their branches no longer took up most of the stairwell, and set up a make-shift computer system to handle the new guests, all in fifteen of his sixteen minutes. But he hadn't tried to clean the floor and he was grateful for that as the passengers of the Presidio pushed and shoved their way through the double doors.

All human (thank God for small blessings) and all sizes, the twelve passengers from the Presidio smelled—not so faintly—of burnt plastic. A few had smoke lines across their faces, and another few wore tattered clothing.

They also stank of sweat and fear and had that wild-eyed look of people Who Had Been Through It All And Weren't Yet Sure They Had Lived To Tell About It.

He had seen so many people like that over the years, and they were always distraught, always needy, and always demanding. He loathed demanding customers, even though his high-end education had prepared him for them. Once upon a time, he was the best at dealing with the most difficult of guests, back when he actually worked in a real resort that catered to the very wealthy, who, at least, were predictable in their very disagreeability.

He peered at the sea of humanity before him—well, all twelve of them anyway, which felt like a veritable sea to him, considering he probably hadn't seen twelve people all in one place since the last ship disaster nearly a year before. These people, with their untended hair and their air of complete panic, stared back at him as if he were their only savior.

He smiled unctuously—and he hadn't managed that expression in nearly a decade—and nodded his head to the first person in line.

She was a stout elderly woman, wearing a black business suit (now decorated with several rips to the right side) and matching sensible shoes. She even had a little hat perched on top of her graying curls. That hat looked like it was an afterthought—one of those things she had grabbed automatically as she fled the ship just to make herself presentable.

"Agatha Kantswinkle," she said with one of those operatic voices (complete with vibrato) that certain older persons cultivated. "I should like a single room."

She did not say please, nor did he expect her to. In fact, she raised her chin after she spoke to him.

She, at least, was a type he could handle.

"We only have a few rooms, madam," he said in his best toady voice. "You'd be more comfortable if you shared a double."

"I would not," she said. "I shall not ever room with any of these despicable people."

She leaned forward and whispered—as best an operatic voice could whisper, which was to say not at all—and confided, "There are murderers among them."

A middle-aged man in the middle, face covered with soot, rolled his eyes. A younger woman toward the back raised her gaze heavenward—if there were a heaven in space, which there was not. Still, Hunsaker didn't miss the gesture. Or the grimaces of dislike on the faces of the other passengers.

"Surely, it wasn't as bad as all that, madam," he said as he opened the file on the old-fashioned built-in screen on his desk. The comment was somewhat reflexive. He hated histrionics. But it was also geared toward the other passengers upon whom, he was becoming certain, he would have to rely to keep Agatha Kantswinkle under some kind of control.

"Not as bad as all that?" she repeated, slapping a palm on the desk, making his computer screen hiccup and nearly blip out. "Are you mad, man? When we left the Dyo System, we had fifteen. Do you think they stepped off the ship mid-flight? I think not."

Hunsaker raised his eyebrows and looked over her shoulder at the other passengers. The man with the soot-covered face shook his head slightly. The young woman had closed her eyes. A few others were looking away as if Agatha Kantswinkle's behavior embarrassed them.

He decided to ignore the woman, which meant getting her away from his desk as quickly as possible. "We have a single room, madam," he said, "but it's tiny. The entertainment system needs upgrading and the bed—"

"I'll take it," she said, handing him a card with her information coded into it, a method as old-fashioned as she was.

He charged her twice the room's usual rate and felt not a qualm about it. First (he reasoned to himself), the Presidio's parent company would probably pay for the extra stop. Secondly, the woman had already shown herself to be an annoyance, and he'd been a hotelier long enough (even at a disreputable place like this one) to know that customers often showed their true colors from the moment they walked in the door.

He was simply adding a surcharge for the difficulties ahead.

He finished adding her information to his file, resisted the urge to wipe his hands on the constantly sanitized towel he kept beneath the desk, and gave her his best fake smile.

"Your room, madam," he said with a nod, "is up those stairs to the left. It is the only room off the first landing."

Because it used to be a maid's room, back when the

resort had actual dreams of grandeur, in the days just after its first construction, long before he was born.

She did not thank him and mercifully did not ask him how she would unlock the door. He handed her the door's code, but it was a mere formality. The lock had broken long ago.

As she made her way toward the stairs, he processed four other passengers—real, sane, sensible people. They had all of their information coded into their fingertips like proper human beings, and they were solvent, which was good, since he debited their accounts immediately, although he didn't overcharge them (too badly) like he had Agatha Kantswinkle. People who were in a hurry to get to their rooms, relax and try to forget whatever it was that brought them to this godforsaken place.

Hunsaker was beginning to think that the rest of the check-ins would go well, when the soot-faced man approached the desk. He was taller than Hunsaker, but bent slightly, as if embarrassed by his height—which Hunsaker could well understand, since so many distance ships were not built for the egregiously tall.

"Sorry for the old lady," the man said as he extended his index finger, the only clean one on his hand. "We're really not that bad a bunch."

The finger, touching the screen, identified him as William F. Bunting, Bill for short, who began his journey in the Dyo system just like Agatha Kantswinkle. His occupation listed varied, which usually meant unemployed and searching for work, but he had nearly two dozen stellar (no pun intended) recommendations, so perhaps his occupation truly was varied and he had traveled from job to job as he traveled farther and farther from home.

"Sounds like you've had a difficult trip," Hunsaker said, offering the platitude the way another man would grunt with disinterest.

"You don't know the half of it," Bunting said. "If you had any other ship docked here, I'd request a transfer."

"Perhaps one will arrive while yours is being repaired," Hunsaker said, debiting Bunting's account, which looked full enough—especially for a man who had listed "varied" as his occupation.

"Please God," Bunting said, and sounded serious, which caught Hunsaker's attention.

For a moment, their gaze met. Then Bunting said, "I know you don't have a lot of single rooms, but you probably should give me one." He swept his hands toward his shirt. "These are the only clothes I have, and even I can smell the smoke on them. In a closed space, I'm not going to be someone people want to be around."

Even now, in a not-quite-so-closed space, Hunsaker could smell him. Hunsaker had figured the stench was the accumulated odor of all of the passengers, but maybe it wasn't. Maybe it was Bunting all by his egregiously tall self.

"We have a boutique," Hunsaker said, as if the little room stocked with clothes others had left behind really qualified as a fancy store. "I'll open it in two hours. I'm sure you'll find something to accommodate you there."

He made a note to go to that little room and run the clothing through the automatic cleaning equipment yet again. He had no idea when someone had last picked through the material. At least he'd figured out that he should display it all, and that no one would know that it had been previously worn.

"Thank you," Bunting said, and pulled forward a slightly pudgy balding man. "In that case, we'll share a room."

The slightly pudgy balding man didn't seem disconcerted by this. He looked grateful, in fact. Hunsaker took his information, also stored properly on his index finger—Rutherford J. Nasten—and sent both men to the best-ventilated room in the entire wing.

Hunsaker kept processing until he got to the young woman in the back, who, luck would have it, got a single room simply because Agatha Kantswinkle had demanded a single room and there were only twelve passengers.

"All I have is a room we call the Crow's Nest," Hunsaker said. "It's small, but it's at the top of this part of the station and it has portals on all four walls."

"That sounds good," the woman said tiredly.

"Sounds like the trip from hell so far," he said, actually interested for once, partly because she was so reticent and partly because she had been so expressive earlier.

"You don't know the half of it," the woman said, touching his screen with her left thumb. She was security conscious, then, not willing to follow the norms on how to behave.

It took a moment for the screen to display her information, almost as if it were tired of doing all the hard work, and for a moment everything blurred. Or maybe that was his eyes. He was unaccustomed to dealing with people anymore, and even less accustomed to the level of tension he had felt since the passengers had arrived.

"Breakdowns can be stressful," he said, as he monitored the information in front of him. The light above hit her face just right so that it reflected into the screen, making it seem like her information had come up superimposed over her image.

Susan G. Carmichael, daughter of Vice Admiral Willis Carmichael of the Dyo system. Hunsaker tried not to raise his eyebrows at her pedigree. A woman like this should have been upset at the meager nature of his resort, yet she didn't make a single complaint. Maybe she would make up for Agatha Kantswinkle.

"The breakdown was terrifying," Susan G. Carmichael said, her voice soft. "There was actually a fire."

That caught his attention. Ships had come here that had suffered melting in the systems, ships that had filled with smoke in an instant, ships that had lost power, but none had suffered from a fire. Fires were relatively easy to kill. All it would take was a momentary shutdown of the environmental system. No oxygen, no fuel; no fuel, no fire.

"A bad one?" he asked.

Her gaze met his. Her eyes were a shade of goldish brown that he hadn't seen before. He wasn't sure if it was natural.

"They didn't catch it right away," she said.

He stopped processing her information. "How could they miss that?"

"Apparently systems were already malfunctioning." She swallowed visibly. She was clearly still terrified and covering it up by pretending to be calm. "We were lucky that you were so close."

He hadn't realized—well, how could he have realized anyway, when he only had sixteen minutes to take a nearly empty (neglected) resort and turn it into a place where people could sleep somewhat comfortably.

"Do they know what caused the fire?" he asked.

"I'm not sure they know anything about anything," she said as she squared her shoulders. "What do I need to get into my room?"

Finally, someone asked the logical question. Perhaps the others had been too traumatized to think of it, or too overwhelmed to care.

"Just touch the door," he said. "I keyed it to your fingerprint."

Not that it mattered. He really did have to get the locks fixed first.

"Thank you." She slipped away from the desk, then stopped. "I heard you mention a boutique...?"

He shrugged, feeling honest for the first time that day (maybe the first time that year). "It's more of a whatnot shop. But we do have clothing."

"Anything is better than what I have," she said, and gifted him with a small smile before heading up to her room.

He stayed in the reception area for another few minutes, staring up the stairs. The hotel felt different with people in it. He'd often thought of the hotel as a chameleon, coloring itself with the attitude of its guests.

Which meant that the hotel was shaken, terrified, and a little bit relieved. He made himself take a deep breath. The air down here still smelled acrid. He set the environmental controls on scrub, not wanting to smell smoke and sweat for the next week.

Then he tallied up his single day's intake. More than he'd made in the last three months. If the repairs took another two days, which was the average time for repairs on this station, he would make most of his year's operating expenses. If the repairs took longer (and it sounded like they might), he might make a significant profit for the first time in nearly a decade.

But he would have to endure the mood, and he would have to stay one step ahead of these people. He had to get the clothes ready, open the boutique (such as it was), roust his one remaining chef to work the restaurant, and get the staff to clean a few more rooms just in case the living arrangements didn't quite work out.

Not to mention the fact that the ship's crew had yet to arrive and take their rooms.

He sighed. He had become even more cantankerous than he had been during the last big shipping disaster nearly three years before. It wasn't good for him to be so isolated.

Or maybe it was. Imagine how cantankerous he'd be if he had to deal with these types of personalities each and every day.

The thought made him smile. Then he continued planning his evening, realizing that to do things properly, he would get very little sleep.

The boutique wasn't a boutique, anymore than this resort was a resort. It was barely a hotel, although it did have private rooms, which was good enough.

Or so Susan Carmichael figured. She had hung back after Agatha Kantswinkle had shoved her way to the front of the line, after repeatedly announcing her intentions to have a room of her own as the group fled the ship for the safety of this little bitty place.

Susan hadn't been on an outpost this small in years, and certainly not one this old. She was relieved to hear that it had maintenance facilities, but worried that they wouldn't be up to the task. The Presidio was nearly ruined. It had suffered a catastrophic failure of most of its systems, and that fire had destroyed a section of the ship.

Destroyed was probably too grand a word. Made that section of the ship unusable, maybe for the rest of the trip.

Which she would not think about, at least for the next twenty-four hours.

She had waited the two hours the prissy little man at the front desk had told Bunting to wait for the boutique to open. She knew as well as anyone that the boutique wasn't a regular store, stocked with purchased merchandise, but a shop stocked with castoffs, leftovers and discards from hotel guests.

She didn't care. She had left her own wardrobe on board the ship, and she had instructed the crew to discard most items, even the most personal ones. Although "instructed" wasn't truly accurate. One of the crewmen—Richard Ilykova—had stopped her in the somewhat disorderly exit off the ship (hell, everyone was pushing, shoving, jostling, trying to get out), and told her that her cabin had been closest to the fire.

We won't be able to save your stuff, he said, clearly worried that she'd be angry. But you might find a way to clean it on the station. You want me to set it aside?

No, she'd said curtly and continued jostling her own way out of the ship.

She should probably have been more polite. Ilykova hadn't needed to say that to her. He hadn't needed to say anything. He'd kept a protective eye on her the entire time she'd been on the ship, and she wasn't sure if he was attracted or if he thought she was the one who had sabotaged the ship. She had found him attractive if a bit bland— one of those pale blue-eyed blonds who could vanish into the walls because he seemed so colorless. When she'd seen him watching her, she'd decided to keep an eye on him. Maybe he saw that as flirting, or maybe he had just been doing his job. She wasn't sure, and she wasn't sure she cared.

All she knew was that now, she needed new everything, from undergarments to blouses. She didn't like the idea of wearing someone's cast-off underclothes, but she didn't see much of a choice. She would have to ask about guest laundry facilities here, although she doubted there would be any.

The prissy little man from the front desk had done the best he could to make this small room seem like a store. Some of the clothes hung on racks, with others stacked on shelves along the walls. There were old entertainment pads, some with their contents listed on the back like a directory, and blankets, which surprised her. The blankets looked inviting, even though she was warm, which told her just how tired she was.

The prissy little man was hovering near the door, checking a portable pad as he kept an eye on her. He had already helped Bunting. Bunting had gone in and out in the time it had taken Susan to look for a single shirt.

At first, she'd thought the prissy little man a mere employee. He gave off that appearance, a man beaten down by his supervisors, afraid to make decisions on his own.

But once she got into her room, she'd accessed the resort's information logs and discovered that the prissy man actually owned the place. He had the kind of pedigree that upscale resorts usually paid excessive amounts to hire— degrees from prestigious business schools and exclusive resort management programs.

The fact that he was here, and he owned the place, suggested some kind of problem, probably personal. He seemed unimaginative enough to remain in the same business, and not quite bright enough to realize that a resort this far away from habitable planets wasn't really a resort at all.

Or maybe he did realize it and fled here on purpose.

She glanced at him. Dapper, small, furtive, the kind of man (like Ilykova) who could blend into the walls if necessary. Only the prissy little man had another trait—the ability to outsnob anyone in the room. That powerful ability to judge was as important to running a real resort as it was to governance. It made the weak cower.

It just didn't bother her.

She went to the rack holding women's clothes. She found black pants with no obvious problems, blue pants that needed just a bit of care, a fawn-colored skirt, and a very old white blouse that appeared to have real lace trim. She added four other tops and found undergarments on a back shelf.

She piled all the items on a nearby table, and beckoned the prissy little man.

"I know you have a corner on the market," she said in her most polite voice, "but this trip is turning out to be inadvertently expensive, and so I was wondering if I could get some kind of volume discount...?"

He didn't even look up. "The ship's parent company should reimburse you."

Meaning they'll deal with the much too-high prices. They might not even notice.

She thought of bargaining more, then decided against it. She wasn't going to charge the ship for the disaster, but she would take money if the parent company decided to offer it.

She clutched the clothing, which smelled strongly of some kind of cleaner, and headed toward the door. He said, almost as an afterthought, "The restaurant will be open shortly. Spread the word, would you?"

As if she wanted to see the other passengers. As if she were responsible for them.

But she was hungry, and she knew they were too, and all of their rooms were on her way back to the accurately named Crow's Nest.

"Sure," she said, "if you give me something to carry these clothes in."

He sighed and reached under a pile of men's shirts. As she walked back to him, he pulled out a cloth sack—something that looked like a cleaning bag, a low-rent version of a laundry bag that offered to do the cleaning all by itself.

She was long past caring what it actually was. She put the clothes in the sack, wrapped its drawstrings around her hand, and carried the entire thing to the stairs.

Dinner, restaurant, the damn passengers. Calling attention to herself all over again.

She wasn't entirely sure she cared. But one thing she did know.

She wasn't going to knock on Agatha Kantswinkle's door.

Agatha would want Susan to keep her company.

Susan wasn't ever going to do that, again.

The scream echoed through the stairwell. A woman's scream, sharp, high-pitched, startled. Cut off in the middle.

For a moment, Richard Ilykova bowed his head. The last thing he wanted to do was deal with another crisis. He stood in the lobby of the hotel, which was cleaner than some he'd seen on makeshift starbases. The owner, Grissan Hunsaker, looked up from the work he was doing behind the desk, his features contorted with fear.

No help from that quarter.

Richard sighed, then bounded up the stairs, feeling his exhaustion in every step.

The scream didn't sound again, but he heard footsteps

other than his own. Doors squealed open, slammed shut, and voices started.

He found a group of people clustered on one of the landings—the B Team, he privately called them. The people who had paid lower fares, filling out the ship's rooms, people who wouldn't even have gotten on the ship had the owners managed to sell all the tickets.

In the middle of them, a woman—Lysa Lamphere—lay prostrate on the floor.

He remembered her only because she was so pretty. Easily the prettiest woman on the ship this trip. But she didn't have the brains or the personality to match her beauty, which disappointed him.

Not that anyone who booked passage on the Presidio would look at him. They were all too important for that. Except Ms. Carmichael. She had smiled at him, which surprised him.

She had noticed him watching her, which had surprised him even more.

The group stepped back as he approached. Even though they weren't on a ship any longer, they seemed to think he was in charge.

Maybe he was.

"What happened?" he asked.

"Dunno," someone said.

One of the men—Bunting? Richard almost didn't recognize him in the new set of clothes he wore—added, "I was in my room when I heard the screaming. Sounded pretty awful, so I came directly here."

Richard had no reason to doubt it. Bunting had the

unfortunate ability to arrive first in any crisis. Unfortunate only because he didn't have the compatible ability to know the right thing to do once he had arrived.

Richard was of the private opinion that Bunting had made the fire on the ship worse by trying to fan it out rather than hit the controls for the room's environmental system. But Richard was number four man on the crew, the lowest of the low, and he didn't dare criticize anyone.

He crouched beside Lysa. She was sprawled on her back, her arms up as if they had been near her face when she had fallen. Her hands were clenched into tight fists, and her legs were twisted sideways.

He touched her face. The skin was soft, silky, the way that skin should be, the way that enhanced skin often wasn't. Her beauty was natural, then, and even more pronounced when that mousy personality wasn't front and center.

She had no fever, and she didn't look injured.

Richard glanced up, saw Hunsaker lurking near the stairs, said, "Do you have a doctor?"

"More or less," Hunsaker said.

"What is it?" Richard snapped. "More? Less?"

"More if she's sober," Hunsaker said.

Richard cursed. "I assume you have basic medical equipment."

"Yes," Hunsaker said.

"Then get it," Richard snapped.

Hunsaker fled.

The group remained, staring down. These were the

people who irritated him. The ones who had wanted the lighting in their room changed and didn't know how to do it themselves, the ones who woke him from a sound sleep to ask how to work the automatic cafeteria, the ones who thought he was at their beck and call even though, technically, he wasn't.

Right now, they were content to let him see if the woman was all right.

Hunsaker came back with a handheld medical scanner and a tray of medical pens, each with some kind of magical function. Magical because Richard didn't know much about medicine, at least this kind. He had some knowledge, but on the other end—how to turn the body against itself, not how to make it function again.

Hunsaker crouched near him and ran the scanner over her, clearly not trusting Richard with the device, which suited him just fine.

"I think she simply fainted," Hunsaker said with surprise.

"And hit her head?" Richard asked.

"Oh, she'll be bruised, but there doesn't appear to be much else wrong with her," Hunsaker said.

Then his gaze met Richard's, and Richard could tell what the other man was thinking. They both worked service in not-the-best conditions. They both knew that people rarely fainted without a reason.

"You think, perhaps, she's finally having a reaction to the trauma on the ship?" There was a hopeful note in Hunsaker's voice, a note that said, Please, don't make this my problem.

"I doubt it," Bunting said before Richard got a chance to reply. "I mean, she screamed first."

Richard closed his eyes for just a second. A brief indulgence, a moment to himself before it all started up again. He'd hoped for an interlude, a bit of quiet, a chance to rest, but it clearly wasn't going to happen.

He stood, eyes open now, and looked at the door.

It didn't look latched.

"Is this her room?" he asked, already suspecting the answer.

"Oh, no," Hunsaker said. "Miss Lamphere is rooming upstairs with—"

"Me," said one of the women behind Richard. He turned slightly. A slender woman with buckteeth stared back at him. He remembered her, because she had propositioned him late one night back on the ship. She'd been drunk, and in her drunkenness she assumed that the ship's promotion line, which said that the crew was there to serve her every need, apparently understood "every need" to mean every need.

Her dark eyes met his and a spot of color appeared on her cheeks. She remembered the encounter too.

"Miss Potsworth," he said, not using her first name—Janet—because he didn't want her to get the wrong impression, even now. "I take it Lysa was not in her room?"

"She'd just left a few minutes ago," Janet said. "We'd just been told there was going to be dinner and she was famished."

Famished. That was a word he hadn't heard in a very long time.

"So what was she doing here?" he asked, more to himself than to anyone else. The room was all by itself on this level, and it was a bit out of the way of the stairs.

"Oh, probably letting Miss Kantswinkle know about the meal," Janet Potsworth said. "Lysa was the only person—I think—"

And she looked around for confirmation. A few others nodded, as if she already knew what Janet was going to say.

"—who still liked Miss Kantswinkle. Although I would say that 'liked' is probably too strong a word. She felt that Miss Kantswinkle deserved our respect, given all her work with the children—"

"Right," Richard said, having heard Agatha Kantswinkle's long diatribe about her years of service with orphaned children a dozen too many times. "Miss Kantswinkle is in this room?"

"Yes." This from Hunsaker who was doing his best to revive Lysa.

"Then why isn't she out here?" Richard asked. After all, she was the nosiest women he had ever met.

He stepped over Lysa's arm, and rapped on the door with a half-closed fist. The sound echoed through the stairwell, rather like her scream had. No one answered, but the door swung open slowly.

Richard peered inside, but did not go in. A slightly metallic smell greeted him. The room was tiny, the bed pushed against one wall. There were no windows. A chair and a tiny desk pushed against the other wall.

And in the center of the room, on the floor, lay Agatha Kantswinkle, black shoes pointing toward the door, frumpy skirt slightly askew, meaty thighs pressed together.

She had not fallen decorously, like Lysa had. Agatha Kantswinkle had toppled like a tree. He half expected to see a dent in the floor. He wondered why no one had heard the fall from below, then wondered if there was a room below. He tried to remember the layout, and couldn't.

He could feel someone else peering over his shoulder, but he effectively blocked the door so no one else could see inside. Then he pulled the door closed and stood in front of it

"She's not there, huh?" Bunting asked.

"You could say that," Richard said, his gaze meeting Hunsaker's. Hunsaker was still crouched over Lysa. He didn't seem sure how to revive her.

Richard knew a few tricks—none of which used technology—but he didn't want to try them in front of the small group. Instead, he said to Hunsaker, "Let's take her back to her room."

Hunsaker looked relieved at the suggestion.

They enlisted the help of Bunting, who was one of the strongest men that Richard had ever met. Unfortunately, Richard knew this because he'd had Bunting's help carrying dead weight before. Only that weight had been really and truly dead, not unconscious like Lysa.

Richard helped Bunting get her upright, then Bunting scooped her in his arms as if she were no more than a pile of clothes.

"Which way?" he asked.

"I'll show you," Janet said, and Richard bit his tongue.

Better to remain silent than to warn the man she might show him more than her room.

Together they went up the stairs. Richard followed, mostly because he didn't want to be alone with the small group on the landing—and he really didn't want to talk to Hunsaker. At least not right away.

Instead, Richard would supervise the two in Janet's room and probably help Bunting make his escape.

Or Bunting would help him.

Richard frowned. This damn nightmare trip wasn't over yet.

Hunsaker looked at the medical equipment, then moved his gaze toward the closed door. The look that crewman, Richard Ilykova, had given him had sent a chill through him. As had his response when asked if Agatha Kantswinkle was inside her room.

Ilykova was one of those men Hunsaker had seen hundreds of times over the years on Vaadum. Working some kind of spaceship, going from one place to another because the previous place didn't suit.

After he'd checked in, on the company's money (unlike the passengers), he had moved away from the desk, so that he didn't see Hunsaker move all his information to the hand-held pad. Hunsaker usually did that with crew, because so many of them traveled under false names, with very thin personal identification documentation.

Ilykova's was better than most. In fact, that was what

caught Hunsaker's attention. Hunsaker had expected a tissue-thin biography, something that showed Ilykova wasn't who he seemed and seemed to ask the technological question *Really, this man is so unimportant. Who cares?*

But the identification looked real at first, so real that it nearly fooled Hunsaker. In fact, it would have fooled Hunsaker if it weren't for the fact that Hunsaker expected crew to be a bit dodgy.

So he'd looked a little deeper, saw a ripple in one bit of biography and followed it, finding another layer of biography under yet another name. Usually that meant someone was traveling on some government mission, and while he couldn't rule that out, he also couldn't rule out the fact that Ilykova was dodgier than most.

"Well," Hunsaker said to the people around him to get rid of them. "There's nothing we can do now. Did Miss Carmichael let you know that we're serving dinner?"

"She did," one of the women said.

"Then perhaps you'd best move along. My chef, while excellent, doesn't like an empty restaurant and will close if no one shows up."

"I'm not really hungry," the other woman said. "But I suppose I could eat."

"You never know when you'll get another chance," the first woman said to her.

Hunsaker watched through a slat in the railing as the women made their way to the bottom of the stairs. He waited until they were out of sight before he moved. Then he peered up the stairwell to make sure no one was coming down.

No one was. He was alone, for which he was quite relieved. Although that sense of relief didn't last long. His heart was pounding and his palms had grown damp.

He hated this part of the job. Back when he was training, they had called it "crisis management," but really, it was more like surprise roulette. Which bad thing would happen today?

He wiped his hands on his pants, then stepped toward the door. He pushed hard with his shoulder, knowing that the latch didn't work, knowing that he would regret that in the hours, days, maybe weeks to come.

The door creaked open. He made himself look down.

There she was, just as he expected, Agatha Kantswinkle, dead on the floor. In a room without a functioning lock or any kind of portal or any other way out.

She had placed her small bag of items on the bed—and he hoped it was that bag that gave off the slightly metallic smell that was now filtering out of the room. Because he could only think of two other things that could cause such an odor. One was a surplus of blood. The other—

He sighed.

He would check the other after he made certain the woman was dead.

He made himself walk into the room, hoping he wasn't stepping on anything important. He crouched beside her like he had done with Lysa, but with Agatha Kantswinkle, he didn't touch her.

There was no need. She was dead. He didn't need a doctor or any kind of expert to tell him that. Truth be told, he was probably the expert on the outpost, given how many dead bodies he'd dealt with in the past few decades. Really, it was one of his pet peeves—one of his major pet peeves—one of his major pet peeves that he could never admit to anyone—the habit that people had of dying away from home.

He'd known when that woman cut to the front of the line that she would be trouble, and here she was, being trouble.

He bit his lip so that he wouldn't curse her. He was just superstitious enough to think that might be bad luck. Instead, he sighed. Now he was going to have to call the base doctor and have her preside over this mess, even though he really didn't want to.

Not because he didn't want a doctor overseeing a corpse, but because he didn't want this doctor overseeing a corpse.

He left the room and pulled the door closed, hoping no one else would try to get in, since it was so damn easy. This time, he did curse, but he cursed himself. And shook his head.

And headed to the bar to fetch Anne Marie Devlin before she got too drunk to walk.

"A body," said Anne Marie Devlin with great relish. She hadn't had a body to deal with in at least six months, maybe even a year. She slapped her hands on the bar and slid out of the bar stool, hoping that Hunsaker didn't know how much she needed the leverage just to move.

She was drunk, but not as drunk as she got by the end of

the day. She would remember this, even if she didn't sober up, which she might have to, considering.

She grabbed her bar napkin—some lowly piece of cloth that Hunsaker believed necessary for cleanliness—and wiped the beer foam off her chin. She didn't know if she had beer foam on her chin, but she always thought it was better to wipe off the imaginary beer foam than leave the real stuff to cake.

Then she grinned to herself. Oh, sober, she probably wouldn't think that funny, but it was funny as hell at the moment.

"How much have you had to drink?" Hunsaker asked in that precise snotty tone of his, the one that showed all of his expensive education and his breeding and his superiority. Of course, her education had cost twice as much as his, and she probably came from a better family, and she should've felt superior, but she'd left that behind, along with her dignity.

She just wished Hunsaker would remember that. No, better. She wished he would honor it. He remembered it and snotted down to her each and every time he saw her.

"Natural causes?" she asked, blinking hard. The bar felt smoky, even though it wasn't. The fog was just in her eyes.

"Isn't it your job to figure that out?" he snapped, and that got her attention. Usually—if you could cite a usually, considering they'd only had three deaths together (and didn't that sound romantic? Only three deaths)—Hunsaker told her what the cause of death was, when it happened, and how she should fill out the death certificate. Usually, she got irritated that he told her how to do her job, and even more irritated when it turned out that he was right.

393

The fact that he was unwilling to say how the guest died was a revelation in and of itself.

"Excuse me," Anne Marie muttered and headed to the side of the bar. This place was ridiculously small, considering it was the outpost's only bar. People could drink in the restaurant and the casino, but they couldn't drink comfortably in either place.

She leaned against the bar and looked around. A few of the guests from that damaged spaceship had gone into the restaurant for dinner. She could smell roast pheasant or whatever the hell tonight's meal was called. It was always the same, some dish made of parts from unidentified meat or maybe synthetic meat or maybe even (oh, don't go there, but of course she did) corpses, mixed with some kind of gravy or sauce, and actual vegetables grown on the only really nice part of the station, the hydroponic garden.

She'd become a vegetarian a long time ago, mostly in self defense. She didn't want to think about the source of the meaty protein, so she didn't. Except when she dealt with corpses or illnesses or both.

Her stomach lurched. Served her right for drinking beer on an empty stomach. Beer made with real hops because she had insisted long ago. Sometimes she drank the whiskey brought in by ships or the wine imported from various faraway places, but at least she knew how the beer was made.

She had been hired to make it.

She had been the station's bartender, way back when. Before they realized that by the end of the evening she was too drunk to serve drinks. Before Hunsaker, even, because

394

he felt that an automatic drink mixer was better than a human one any day.

Hunsaker had ferreted out her secret, that she actually had a medical license and she kept it current. She had to. She didn't want to be sued by some passenger that she had to save because really, underneath the alcohol, she was the noble sort and felt that the Hippocratic oath had nothing to do with hypocrisy and everything to do with nobility.

Not that she could be hypocritical or noble with a corpse. She grabbed the breathalyzer and took a hit from it, feeling it clear her alcohol haze like a slap to the face. She hated this thing, not just because it cleared the buzz and made her sober in an instant, but because it would give her one motherfucker of a headache in 24 hours, and she wouldn't be able to do anything about that.

Except drink, of course.

She took a second hit for good measure, then turned to Hunsaker. He stood at attention, shoulders back, hands folded before him, mouth in a very thin line.

"Ready?" he asked in that damned tone.

She was thirsty, her eyes ached, and she could feel the depression that always lurked ready to crash down on her.

"As I'll ever be," she said, and let him lead her out of the bar.

Richard managed to escape Janet Potsworth's room just as Lysa woke up from what Janet was calling Lysa's faint. It wasn't a faint, because Lysa had enough time to scream before passing out, but she had slipped into unconsciousness very quickly, and he had a few ideas as to why.

But he wanted to think about them first, and that required him to get away from the conversation, and from Janet Potsworth who had grabbed his ass when he bent over to make sure Lysa was comfortable. Potsworth was a menace, and he would be glad to get rid of her—although he wasn't sure when that would happen, especially now that Agatha Kantswinkle was dead.

He hadn't expected her to die, probably because she had always been the first person on the scene of the other deaths aboard the Presidio. He'd come to see her as a stout little angel of death, and had found himself wondering more than once if she hadn't done something to cause them.

He still hadn't ruled that out even though she had clearly been murdered herself. Maybe her death was in retaliation for one of the others...?

He sighed. He had no idea. And he was going to need one, because it was clear—at least to him—that a murderer lurked on this station.

He trod lightly as he hurried down the stairs—he didn't want to call any more attention to himself than he already had. He'd shown a bit more expertise in these matters than he wanted to, and someone had noticed.

That someone was the hotelier, Hunsaker. Hunsaker was refined and organized, not the kind of man you'd normally find in this shabby place at the edge of nowhere. Usually the proprietors of places like this were down-on-their luck drunks who couldn't be bothered to wait on a customer even if the customer offered five times the normal room rate. Or the proprietors were well-meaning spouses of someone on staff in maintenance, some handy person with cooking skills and an ability to take the drabbest room and make it just a tad gaudy.

Hunsaker seemed like he had training in hotel management. He certainly took his time checking everyone in, which meant that he looked up their identification as well as debiting their accounts.

He'd noticed Richard and he'd understood what Richard had said when Richard had closed the door on Agatha Kantswinkle's corpse. Often Richard made those snide little comments for his own edification, knowing that no one else would catch his meaning. But Hunsaker had and Hunsaker had looked momentarily put out. Not panicked. Put out. Like any good hotelier.

Richard passed the landing where Lysa had passed out. The door to Agatha Kantswinkle's room was closed and no one stood outside of it. He wondered if anyone was inside, and if Hunsaker had dealt with the corpse yet.

He almost stopped—he had a few suspicions he wanted to confirm—but he didn't. He was afraid that if the old lady's body hadn't been removed, then he would make himself even more of a suspect than he already was.

And he knew he was a suspect. Everyone from the Presidio was.

The first death had occurred two days out, when they were in the deepest of deep space—an area the captain had called no man's land because there were no settlements within landing range and no outposts. The trip from the

Dyo System through the Commons System was dicey no matter what, but there was a section that was just plain empty. Humans weren't welcome at any of the stops for two full days of the trip. The captain had warned the crew—all three of them—that the first part of the run had nowhere safe to stop until Vaadum Station, and even then he liked to avoid the place because it was so small and so rundown. He preferred the extra day to Commons Space Station, where everyone could get off the ship and relax in style.

Richard braced himself for the extended run on a relatively small ship. He was particularly susceptible to cabin fever because he'd been the only survivor of a murderous rampage on a cruise ship as a boy. He'd been taking a trip with his father, who had died right in front of him. Everyone on that ship had died except Richard and the shooter, who had left in an escape pod before the ship docked at one of the many Starbase Alphas, this one nicknamed the NetherRealm.

And that had been just the beginning, of course. He'd seen a lot of death on small ships. Just never in quite such an odd manner as the three deaths on the Presidio.

He had argued that the Presidio shouldn't stop until it got to Commons Space Station, which had a security team and was in a sector with a real government, one that would actually look into the killings. There was no government here, even though technically, Vaadum was in the same sector as Commons. Vaadum was too far off the beaten path and too small to have so much as a leader, let alone some kind of official who would report back to the various governments presiding over the Commons System.

The captain had listened too, even though the three murders had terrified him—nothing like that had ever happened to the man, and of course Richard hadn't confessed his own history. Richard was only working the Presidio to gain passage across the sector. He was out of money and out of options, something that hadn't happened to him before. So he took one of his identities and used it to get work on the first ship that would take him.

Of course, that ship had to be the Presidio.

If the fire hadn't happened, if the ship hadn't had to stop here, Richard would've quit when they reached the Commons Station. He would have cited the killings as a hostile work environment and no one would have had second thoughts about his departure.

He couldn't leave here, now. There was no reason to stay on this station, since ships rarely stopped here, and he did need to keep moving. But he really didn't want to get back on that ship, provided the people in maintenance could actually fix the thing.

He let himself out of the "resort," through the double doors, past the restaurant. The smell of simmering beef—or was it lamb?—made his stomach growl. He wasn't sure when he last had a real meal.

Although he wasn't sure how anyone could serve real food here, either. He doubted supply ships made a huge profit coming in and out of Vaadum. But they probably got paid well to stop.

He hurried down the corridor toward the maintenance area. Clearly, the maintenance area had once been the entire station. The corridor proved it. The corridor was grafted on, little more than a tube with an environmental system, leading to the second part of the station, the resort, which someone had built on at least a century ago—and not from the best materials.

This part of the station felt very fragile. He could almost feel the corridor bounce with each of his footsteps, even though he knew that the thing wasn't built that way. It was his very active imagination, something he had failed to shut off for years now.

Finally, he got out of the corridor and into the maintenance area. It seemed huge, although it wasn't. He knew the sense of vastness was an optical illusion caused by the emptiness. The maintenance area was the oldest part of Vaadum, built two centuries ago to house at least six large ships in various states of disrepair.

Apparently, the station's owners throughout the years hadn't wanted to chop up the area, imagining, probably, that there might come a time when all seven repair bays were being used.

The Presidio had the center bay. It looked odd in here, since the ship wasn't built to be inside any kind of bay. Once it had been assembled, it remained outside buildings. But the station's tiny ring made it impossible to repair ships docked to it.

Richard was glad he hadn't been onboard when the captain had had to maneuver the Presidio in here. That must've taken some white-knuckle flying, particularly since the ship was so damaged.

Richard could see the damage from the entry. The fire had burned its way through one entire wing of the ship. The wing had remained intact, but here someone had knocked the exterior off. Through the hole—large enough to hold at least five men—he could see the scorch marked interior.

He shuddered.

He'd been afraid on ships before, starting with that cruise with his father, when the assassin had stood up, a laser rifle in his hands. He'd aimed it at Richard, and Richard hadn't cringed. He'd been twelve, too young to understand —too sheltered to understand—that the man who aimed the laser rifle at him meant to kill him.

Only the assassin hadn't meant to kill him. He'd left Richard—who was then known as Misha—alive, as a warning to Richard's mother, who had worked as some kind of double agent. Richard had never tried to understand the politics of it. All he ever knew was that his father and so many others had died because one government hired an assassin to warn his mother away from some job.

He wasn't even sure she had felt guilty about it, although she had been angry. And angrier at him when he had gotten his revenge on the assassin. She had wanted the assassin alive —for what reason, Richard never knew.

He never tried to understand his mother. But her life, her decisions, had caused him to be here now, decades later, on the run for half a dozen killings, all of them he could say —he would have once said—justified.

Especially that first one.

"Help you?"

One of the maintenance guys came over. He was holding some fancy tools that Richard had never seen before. The maintenance guy was the first person that Richard had seen on this station who looked like he belonged. Whip thin, angular, sharp dark eyes and hair cropped close to the skull. He had a smudge along one cheek.

"I work on the Presidio," Richard said. "I was wondering if you'd found a cause for the fire yet."

"Why?" the maintenance guy asked.

Richard studied him for a moment. The maintenance guy seemed solid enough, although Richard wasn't the kind of man who trusted easily. Hell, Richard wasn't the kind of man who trusted at all.

But the maintenance guy had been on this station for a long time, and he would have had no involvement in the fire or the deaths. Not even Agatha Kantswinkle's death.

"I want to know if it was deliberately set," Richard said.

"What's it to you?" the maintenance guy asked.

Richard blinked at him, and nearly snapped, What's it to me? If this outpost hadn't been nearby, I would have died on that ship. Murdered, if the fire was set. No one would have survived.

"Three passengers were murdered on that ship," Richard said, "and another just died here."

The maintenance guy started. He hadn't heard about Kantswinkle then.

"So I want to know if that fire was a coincidence or deliberately set. Because I'm not getting back on that ship with someone who sets fires in space."

"But you'd get back on the ship if it had design flaws that made it catch fire?" the maintenance guy asked.

Richard almost smiled. He hadn't thought of that.

Which showed that he was someone who didn't know much about ship mechanics, and knew too much about killers.

"Does it have design flaws?" Richard asked.

"All ships have design flaws," the maintenance guy said. "Some are deadlier than others."

"And this ship?" Richard asked, beginning to feel annoyed.

"This ship had some weaknesses that were easy to exploit," the maintenance guy said. "If you asked me to prove that someone deliberately set a fire, I can't. At least, not right now. If you asked me to guess how the fire started, I'd say that someone encouraged it. And I'd say you all were damn lucky to survive."

Richard felt a shiver run down his back. Two lucky survivals. If he were superstitious, he'd think that there was a third in his future.

"Can the ship be repaired?"

"It'll take us a few days," the maintenance guy said. "We have to rebuild a few things, replace even more, and then make sure that it's strong enough to handle space again. When we're done, it should be better than new."

He sounded confident. He actually sounded excited about the prospect of reviving the ship, of making it worthy to fly again. He probably didn't get challenges like this one often.

Or maybe he did. Maybe his job was all about cobbling ships together so that they would survive to the next port.

"Can you make it tamperproof?" Richard asked.

The maintenance guy gave him a sad look. "No ship is

tamperproof," he said. "Especially not a ship as old as this one."

Richard must've looked unsettled, because the maintenance guy added, "We'll make it better than it was. If you have a problem out there, it won't be because of the ship."

"Yeah," Richard said, "I'm beginning to figure that out."

Anne Marie Devlin still smelled of beer. Hunsaker wrinkled his nose as he stood inside Kantswinkle's room. Anne Marie had crouched over the body for only a moment, and then she started walking the perimeter of the room as if the room were big enough to have a perimeter. She inspected every little thing. The walls, the chair, the bed, the floor.

Everything except Kantswinkle.

Finally, Hunsaker couldn't take it any longer. "What are you doing?"

Anne Marie didn't answer him. She stood on her toes, and peered at the small control panel he'd installed for the guests. The control panel didn't give them much control over anything, just the illusion of control.

You let them operate the heating and cooling in their tiny space, and they thought they had charge of the universe.

"Anne Marie," he snapped. "I asked you a question."

"You did, didn't you," she said, her back to him. He had never met such an aggravating woman. She'd be a marvel if she didn't drink.

"What. Are. You. Doing." He enunciated each word so that she would know just how annoyed he was.

"I. Am. Investigating," she said, mimicking his tone exactly.

His cheeks heated. Did he really sound that obnoxious? Not to his own ears, certainly. "Investigating what?"

Anne Marie turned. She looked at the door first, and then at him. He pulled the door again to make sure it was pulled tight.

"Don't do that," she said.

"Why not?" he asked.

She walked to the door and cracked it open just a little. "It's better this way."

"Don't tell me you're getting claustrophobic now," he said. He'd heard about her other ailments. The alcoholism she refused to treat aggravated the depression she refused to acknowledge which was caused by something in her past she refused to talk about.

All in all, the most infuriating woman he had ever met. And one of the most brilliant.

"I have a hunch I'll always be claustrophobic in this room from now on." She peered through the crack in the door as she clearly checked the hallway, then pushed the door open just a bit wider. "We're alone."

He had to check on that himself. Not that he didn't trust her, but he really didn't trust her.

"What's going on?" he said when he was satisfied no one lurked in the hall or the stairwell.

"This poor dear woman," Anne Marie said, thereby

proving she had never met Agatha Kantswinkle, "suffocated."

He glanced at Agatha Kantswinkle's neck. No mottled marks, no sign of a struggle. If this woman had suffocated, she had done so without hands around her neck or something pressed against her nose and mouth.

He swallowed hard. "Even if the environmental system had shut down," he said, "she wouldn't have died this quickly."

"Yes, I know," Anne Marie said. "The problem is the environmental system hadn't shut down."

"Then how did she die?" he asked.

"I told you," Anne Marie said. "She suffocated."

"You can tell that from eyeballing her?" he asked.

Anne Marie smiled just a little. "I'll confirm with an autopsy," she said. "But I will confirm."

"No one touched her," he said. "And if it wasn't the environmental system, then what was it?"

"Oh, it was the environmental system," Anne Marie said. "That's why your other guest fainted. The door opened, she saw the body, she screamed, took in what she thought was a lungful of air to continue her scream, and passed out. Lucky girl. Had she been closer to the door inside the room, she would have died too."

Hunsaker was feeling dizzy. He realized he wasn't breathing either. He made himself take a breath, but it felt odd. He hadn't thought of breathing before. Maybe, like Anne Marie, he wouldn't want to be in this room alone with the door closed either.

"What did she breathe?" he asked.

"It wasn't pure carbon dioxide," Anne Marie said, "or her skin would be bright red. More likely a cocktail of gases, something that created the faint bitter odor that was in the room when we arrived."

He had been here earlier. The smell had been stronger. He didn't tell her that.

"How do you know?" he asked.

She held up one of her portable scanners. "I've been taking readings from various areas of the room. I'm getting a mixture of things that should never be in a residential area of a space station. I have the behavior of both women. I have the smell. And then there's the controls themselves."

She swept a hand toward them.

He walked past her and peered at them.

Someone had hit the override. The damn thing was blinking, asking for a manual code to confirm the oxygen mix, which was purer than it should have been.

Not only had someone tampered with the controls, but someone had tampered with them twice—once when Agatha Kantswinkle entered the room, and then again after she died.

"I would assume that these systems keep track of who touches them when?" Anne Marie asked.

He had no idea. The last time he'd used an override had been a decade ago. Since then, he'd replaced most of the guest room environmental controls, going to a simpler system—one that gave the guests two options—hotter or colder. Nothing as fancy as this little box, which even allowed the guests—with the override code—to mix their oxygen from thin to thick.

"I don't know," he said, feeling absolutely helpless.

"Well." Anne Marie smiled, clearly liking his discomfort. "I guess you'd better find out."

Pounding, pounding, pounding.

Susan sat up, filled with adrenaline. She'd been dreaming. Not dreaming so much as trapped in a memory.

The slight banging noise, rhythmic, feet against the thin wall.

Her mouth tasted of bile. She got off the bed, rubbed her hand over her face, and went to her door.

Janet Potsworth stood outside. She looked more disheveled than Susan had ever seen her.

"Oh, you're all right then," Janet said with obvious relief.

Susan frowned. "Of course I'm all right. Why wouldn't I be?"

"Because you didn't come for dinner," Janet said.

Susan rolled her eyes. She had asked the chef—if that man could be called a chef—to give her a meal for her room. He had obliged, serving her some kind of stew that wasn't on the menu.

The staff will eat this, he said. You will like it better.

She had carried it upstairs herself, and she had liked it. She ate alone for the first time in a week. No angst, no speculation, no fear.

Just a quiet meal in her quiet room. Then she let her exhaustion take her, and she had fallen into a blissful sleep.

Until she dreamed of Remy's death. The man had hanged himself in his room—which had taken some doing. The sheet wrapped around his neck, dangling off some fixture. She hadn't seen it, but she had heard his feet, banging, banging, banging, which she hadn't thought odd until later.

He wasn't bumping against the wall when they found him. She must have been hearing him die.

In fact, no one thought he had done anything except kill himself. He was the first, after all. They'd said some words over him, looked at his traveler's contract, saw that his body didn't have to be returned to anyone, and slipped him into the darkness of space, along with a few of his possessions.

An act they all regretted when the second body turned up. By then, it had become clear that Remy hadn't killed himself and that banging she had heard was his attempt to get her attention. Or to kick his way free. Or to find purchase for his feet. Or to get to his killer.

She hated thinking about it, but she did think about it. Often.

As did everyone else, it seemed. Including the killer. Who had to be laughing at them all.

She wasn't getting back on that ship. Not now, not ever. And she shouldn't have opened her door to Janet either. Janet was one of those obnoxious women who thought every man was a conquest and every woman was competition.

So there had to be another reason she was here.

"I'm fine," Susan said, and started to close the door.

"You can understand why we were concerned," Janet said, "considering what happened to poor Agatha."

Susan sighed. She was now supposed to ask, What happened to Agatha?... as if she cared. Agatha was the most obnoxious woman she had ever met. And that was saying something.

She didn't want to know what happened to Agatha. And if she took the verbal bait, she'd be regaled with some horrifying story of someone's rudeness to the most obnoxious woman she had ever met.

"Yes, I can understand," Susan lied. "Thank you for thinking of me."

And then she pushed the door closed.

"It started in this panel," said the maintenance guy. His name was Larry and he had been on the station for more than a decade. Larry loved his work. Out here, he said when Richard asked, my job is a real challenge. You gotta be creative, you know? And you gotta be right. We've never lost any ship that's left here, and we've never gotten any complaints about our work later on. It's the best job I've ever had.

Richard somehow found that enthusiasm reassuring. Reassuring enough to join Larry inside the burned-out section of the Presidio. It smelled of smoke and melted plastic. His nose itched with a constant urge to sneeze. He breathed shallowly through his mouth because he had a hunch if he started sneezing, he wouldn't stop.

"See right here," Larry said, pointing at a mass of blackened something-or-other, "there's one of those design flaws I mentioned. Nothing that would trigger on its own, but something that could be taken advantage of."

He explained it in rather technical language that Richard was surprised he understood. It sounded so simple, and yet he wouldn't have been able to do it.

"But this thing had been burning for hours when we found it," Richard said. "All the warning systems had been shut down."

"And the environmental system tampered with," Larry said. "The oxygen mix had to have been low here. There wasn't a lot of fuel for this fire, and there should have been. Also, this ship has a built-in system for putting out fires. It would have vented the atmosphere, and isolated the area. It did none of those things."

"Is that easy to tamper with?" Richard asked.

"For me, sure," Larry said. "For you, not so much."

"So someone who knew the ship's systems," Richard said.

"Most ships' systems," Larry said. "You have to know what's standard, what's unusual, what's expected, and what's normal."

"So someone who worked on the ship," Richard said.

Larry smiled. "Probably not. You guys were a week out, right?"

Richard nodded.

"That's plenty of time for someone to study the specs and figure out how this ship worked. Provided that he already had a base of knowledge on how ships in general worked."

"Could they time it?" Richard asked.

"Meaning what?"

"So that we were close to Vaadum when it happened?"

"Sure," Larry said. "That was the only smart way to do it. Unless your saboteur wanted to die along with everybody else. Or planned to take an escape pod. Of course, no one did. They're all here. I assume all your passengers are accounted for too."

"Yeah," Richard said. "They're all here. On the station. With us."

Nothing like murder to make a man stop procrastinating. After Hunsaker watched Anne Marie Devlin use one of the robotic carts to take Kantswinkle's body to the infirmary, he got his tools and finally fixed the lock on Kantswinkle's room. He couldn't shake the feeling that if he had done this before Kantswinkle had arrived, he would have prevented her death.

Then he would have had to deal with her the next two days while the Presidio was being prepared. That thought made him shudder—and made him feel guilty. It wasn't her fault that she was dead...

Except that no one seemed to like her, she was difficult to deal with, and if he had to pick someone to murder in this small group of stranded passengers, he would have chosen her.

Which made him shudder even more.

Had she died because of who she was?

Or because of how she acted?

Or because of the room he assigned her?

That last thought got him to find his staff (all two of them) and have them clean some of the other rooms, the ones with the limited environmental controls. Then he moved five of the passengers—Bunting and his roommate, Janet Potsworth and Lysa Lamphere, and Susan Carmichael.

The first four had left their rooms willingly. Then he had gone to see Carmichael.

He knocked, and she didn't answer. So he knocked again, harder. The door flew open, and Carmichael stood there, looking bleary.

She had struck him as the kind of woman whose hair was never out of place, and yet all the strands stood at odd angles with some kind of violent looking red mark on the side of her face. It took him a moment to realize that she had a pillow impression on her cheek, and her hair was mussed from the blankets. Clearly, Susan G. Carmichael was a messy sleeper, even if she never was messy awake.

She didn't want to be moved. She nearly slammed the door in his face, but he stopped her, and told her that if she stayed here, there was a good chance she'd end up like Agatha Kantswinkle.

Then Carmichael frowned.

"What happened to Agatha?" she asked.

He peered at her. She really and truly did not know.

"She's dead," he said.

Carmichael closed her eyes for a minute, sighed, and

leaned against the door jamb. "I suppose she was murdered," she said tiredly.

"Yes," he said.

Carmichael opened her eyes. They were a vivid blue. "I suppose it was too much to ask the murderer to stop killing once we got off that damn ship."

"I suppose," Hunsaker said, not knowing quite how to respond.

"He's going to run out of victims, and that will call attention to him," she said. She sounded angry, as if it personally affronted her that the murderer kept killing even though she didn't think it wise.

"I don't think he minds the attention," Hunsaker said. "Can I help you get your things?"

"There's not much," she said, indicating the purchases she had made earlier sitting on top of the chair. "I can get them."

Still, he took a pair of shoes and a blanket, just because he suddenly felt that he needed to be useful. Not that he hadn't been useful. He'd been more useful today than he had been in weeks, maybe months. He'd repaired locks on four doors, including Agatha Kantswinkle's (and then he sealed off that damn room, maybe forever), he'd gotten a whole bunch of rooms cleaned, he'd gotten the kitchen staff up and running again, and he actually had people in his hotel.

Until they murdered each other off, of course.

He left the door to her room open, since someone on his staff would be up here shortly to clean, fix this lock, and close off this room. No one was going to be in the older rooms, not while there were murderers on board.

"Did she suffer?" Carmichael asked as he led her down a flight of stairs, through a corridor, and into the newer—and, once upon a time, more hopeful—wing of his hotel.

He looked at her. She actually seemed concerned. No one had asked this question before. He hadn't even asked it when he'd been talking with Anne Marie, and he probably should have.

"I don't know," he said honestly—or as honestly as he dared. It took time to suffocate. If the death was merciful, she would have passed out like Lysa and then stopped breathing, but if it wasn't, she would have been gasping for air—

Although, he realized, had she had trouble breathing, all she had to do was step into the corridor and get far enough away from her door. She would have been able to clear her lungs, and maybe even get help.

"I suspect she didn't suffer at all," he added, now that he'd thought about it.

Carmichael grunted, which surprised him. He would have expected a "thank heavens" or some other kind of reassuring remark. Instead, she sounded almost displeased.

"Did you know her well?" he asked.

"No one knew her well," Carmichael said. "No one wanted to."

"Oh." He would have suspected as much. "What about the other people who died? Were they unpopular too?"

"What's it to you?" she asked.

He flushed. He usually wasn't that nosy.

"I'm sorry," he said. "I didn't mean to pry. I was just wondering."

"Murder really shouldn't be the subject of casual conversation, now should it?" Carmichael asked.

"I guess not," he said, refraining from pointing out that right now, the conversation wasn't as casual as she seemed to think. After all, three people had died on the ship, there was a fire, and now another person had died. Not that casual a conversation. Maybe even relevant.

They stopped at Carmichael's new room. He unlocked it for her and went in first, feeling a slight surge of adrenaline as he took his first breath. Would he always feel that now in his guest rooms? Would he always be afraid that a single breath could kill him?

"Well," Carmichael said following him in, "it's not quite as pretty as the other room, but it does look newer."

He hadn't thought of the other room as pretty, although it had personality which this one lacked. This one was like all the other rooms in this wing, big enough for a large bed, a table and two chairs, as well as an entire wall dedicated to in-room entertainment, if someone wanted to pay a premium price.

He didn't ask Carmichael what she wanted. He figured she could charge it to her bill if she decided she needed entertaining. He didn't want to be near her any longer.

He set her shoes and blanket on the floor, then backed out of the room. She didn't seem to notice. She was putting her clothing on top of the table as he left, as oblivious to his presence as a rich woman was to a robotic cleaner.

He hurried down the steps and back to the front desk,

feeling unsettled. This group of people was beginning to frighten him. He had no idea when he'd be rid of them either. The ship had to be repaired or some other ship had to come here and get them out of his hotel.

For the first time in a very long time, he missed having some kind of security on the station. Someone other than the burliest member of his staff threatening the guests with increased fees—which was usually enough to calm them down, since Hunsaker already had control of their accounts.

But he didn't want to threaten anyone here, because who knew how they would react?

He didn't want to think about it—any of it. Instead, he focused on a cleaning schedule for the vacated rooms. A cleaning schedule and a repair schedule. Time to make sure all the locks worked properly and all the equipment was tamper-proof.

Time he started doing his job.

Again.

Hideous man. Odious, actually. Who did he think he was to discuss other people's deaths as if they were entertainments?

Susan Carmichael sat on the bed in her new room, wide awake now, wondering if she would ever sleep again.

Agatha dead, here and not on the ship. That had shaken Susan as much as figuring out that Remy's death hadn't been suicide. Not that the thought of a suicide in the room next to her hadn't disturbed her too. Any death would have bothered her.

But the murders, the fire—somehow she had gotten it into her head as they fled onto Vaadum that they would be safe here, that their long nightmare was over.

She propped her pillows against the headboard and leaned her head back. She could feel the muscles in her back, so tight that any movement hurt.

She didn't like this room. The other one had the illusion of safety. She had gotten that room when she still believed that the outpost would be much better than the ship.

Now she knew it was no different. A limited group of people trapped in a limited amount of space.

There was nowhere to run, no way to escape. The ship was incapacitated, and—so far as she could tell—the Presidio was the only ship on the station.

Did the locals (what should she call them? Station rats?) —did they have a way to leave? She wasn't sure about that either, but she should probably find out.

She had been under the impression that Vaadum was one of the only safe stops between here and Commons Space Station.

But she didn't even know how far Commons Space Station was from here. Maybe she could convince someone to take her there. Or to hire a ship and have it arrive, getting her out of here.

Of course, some of the others would want to come, and that wouldn't work, because one of those others might be the killer.

She needed a way to defend herself. She didn't have one,

at least not yet. And now she wouldn't be able to sleep again. She needed to stay awake, stay vigilant, should anyone try anything.

Susan pulled her knees to her chest. She needed a plan. She just wasn't sure where to begin.

T he captain had found a spot in the bar, toward the back under the dim lights. Richard had to cross most of the room—which smelled of beer and sweat and spilled whiskey—to realize that the captain had five empty glasses in front of him.

Richard sighed.

The captain was a small man, former military—but with which army in what war, Richard had never asked (it was none of his business—and he'd learned, through his mother, politics was the most deadly business in the entire sector). The captain had run his ship on a tight schedule. He and the other two pilots had separate eight-hour shifts in the cockpit.

Richard had been hired on to do the menial work that had nothing to with flying the ship—keeping the passengers happy, making sure that the lower decks were spotless, maintaining the robotic cleaners and cooks. The food on the ship wasn't spectacular, but it hadn't been advertised that way. There were ships that made this run that were all about food, food every few hours, food from every culture in the sector, food as rich and varied as the passengers themselves.

But this ship hadn't been a cruise so much as a passenger

vehicle. It took people from here to there in a modicum of comfort, with as little fuss as necessary.

Until the first death, Richard had mostly dealt with trivial complaints—broken entertainment sectors, malfunctioning avatars in the gaming area, the occasional sudden (and he thought humorous) switch to zero-g in a toilet. Agatha Kantswinkle had tried his patience—her bed was too soft, the equipment near her room too loud, the cooking smell from the galley too strong—but he'd had the leeway to move her twice, and her final cabin seemed to suit her more than the others, which had cut the complaints to about half of what they had been.

He'd settled in for a flight filled with irritations and hard work, but he knew once he got to Ansary, he'd be done with real work and he'd have money for the first time in months.

He had vowed not to get that low on funds ever again.

Now, here he was, unpaid and trapped on a space station that had at least one killer on board.

He peered at the captain. The man was staring blearily into his glass, as if he could read information written on the bottom of it. The captain was the one man Richard knew wasn't behind any of this, for two reasons.

The first was circumstantial—the captain had been with Richard during the first two killings. If the captain had been involved, he would have had to have had a collaborator, and the captain never consulted with anyone.

The second reason was more practical—the captain owned his ship. It was part of a franchise operation, and he got paid per passenger for the entire trip. If the ship was full, he made a hefty profit. Half full, he made some money.

Empty, and he'd go bankrupt or have to get out of the business.

Richard could understand someone who wanted out so badly that he would destroy his own ship. But he couldn't understand doing it while paying customers were on board, nor could he imagine doing it with fire. There were so many other, much simpler ways.

Richard sat down across from the captain, jiggling the tabletop. The glasses clanked together, but it still took a moment for the captain to notice him.

Or at least to acknowledge him.

"Care to toast the end of my career?" the captain asked, lifting a glass.

"It's not as bad as all that," Richard lied.

"Ship's not reparable," the captain said.

"Yes, it is," Richard said. "I talked to them."

The captain shook his head. "Not flying that thing anywhere. Half the lower deck'd be unusable, it'd smell, and the environmental systems are whacked. Not safe. Least not by our standards."

By that, he meant the standards of the company he worked for.

"So are they sending a replacement ship?"

"Two weeks," the captain said. "Maybe. Or we can hire onto someone else's ship. Have to ask the passengers. What's left of them."

"Two weeks?" Richard asked.

"Coming from Ansary We'd go back to the Dyo System. We'd be back where we started. Not that it matters. I get to have a hearing. Like it's my fault they let some murderous nutcase onto my ship."

"You didn't check the manifest?" Richard asked.

The captain glared at him. Or tried to. It wasn't that effective a look, considering how wobbly his head was and how bloodshot his eyes were.

"What'm I supposed to? Turn away paying customers with spotless records? Of course, I checked. Not an idiot. Or didn't think I was."

The captain sighed.

"Someone's trying to destroy me," he muttered.

Which was a distinct possibility, one Richard hadn't thought of.

"Does someone hate you that much?" Richard asked.

"You mean besides me?" the captain asked. "Oh, hell, I don't know."

"You didn't do anything wrong," Richard said.

"Sent that first body into space," the captain said. "Didn't turn around then and there. Shoulda brought everyone back."

"We thought it was a suicide," Richard said. "And when the other two deaths happened, we were closer to Commons Space Station than to the Dyo System. It would've taken a week to go back to Ynchyn."

This nightmare trip started in Ynchyn.

"Seems logical, doesn't it? They don't train you for this kinda thing, you know. Maybe I shoulda confined everyone to quarters."

Richard nodded. After all, that had been his initial suggestion—or at least, his suggestion after the second murder. Ignatius Grove, a professor, heading to a new job at some prestigious university in the largest city on Ansary. The man taught mathematics of all things, and he had died when the skin in his throat had a growth spurt, shutting off both sides.

Everyone would've thought that a freak death as well, particularly since Ignatius Grove and Agatha Kantswinkle spent each meal complaining about their various food allergies, if Richard hadn't seen that particular form of murder before. He knew that there were little nanosomethings that could activate the growth mechanism in the skin. If swallowed, the nanosomethings invaded the throat. No one had ever done studies to see if any of them made it to the stomach or if that would've made a difference if the throat hadn't closed first.

Ignatius Grove had died a particularly hideous death. So had Remy Demaupin, the first victim. In fact, all three victims had died terribly. The third, Trista Jordan, had died when someone had sealed her mouth and nose with some kind of bonding adhesive. Richard wasn't sure what was used—some kind of liquid glue. She should've been able to use her call button to ask for help—and she probably would have, if she hadn't also been glued to the chair in her room.

The killer hadn't tried to hide that death, not that it would've mattered. There was no time to investigate it, because shortly after they found Trista, the fire had started.

Or at least had been discovered.

"Confining people to quarters," Richard said, "probably wouldn't have helped. We had a pretty determined killer on board. Still do, actually. Have any ideas who it is?"

"I'd've shot the bastard if I knew." The captain picked

up one of the other glasses and downed its contents. "Hell, maybe I should shoot everyone now. That'd take care of the problem. What do you think?"

"It's one solution," Richard said.

"It's as good as any," the captain said, and picked up the remaining full glass. "If I could just get my butt outta this chair. Which I'm not going to do. If someone wants to kill me, so be it. They might be doing me a favor. You want to kill me, Richard?"

The captain's gaze met Richard's. For the first time, the captain seemed sober. His expression was very serious. Richard had the sense that the captain knew more about him than Richard thought.

Richard had waited too long to pretend shock at the question. And he couldn't just wave it off, not considering the look the captain just gave him.

"If I kill you, what do I get out of it?" Richard asked.

The captain grinned and his head bobbled, that moment of clarity seemingly gone. "My eternal gratitude, my friend," he said, just before he finished the third drink. "My eternal gratitude."

Hunsaker sat behind the desk and dug through the files. He had his back to the wall and, out of the corner of his eye, he watched the entrances and the stairway. He didn't want anyone to surprise him for any reason.

He had a pad propped up on his thighs. His personal screen, not the one tied into the resort proper. He had upgraded the pad dozens of times, sometimes illegally. More than once, he'd stolen programs from his guests, and from one—a well connected gambler who liked the odds (and the breasts) in the casino—he had stolen an entire database of shady characters throughout the sector.

He didn't expect to see any familiar names in that database, but he found one.

Richard Ilykova, aka Yuri Flynn Doyle, Edward Michael Adams, and Misha Yurivich Orlinskaya, Mercenary and Assassin for Hire, believed to be responsible for more than two dozen deaths system wide.

Hunsaker shivered. He had known that Richard Ilykova hadn't been a common worker on a passenger ship. The man was too competent for that—not too mechanically competent, but too competent in the ways of death. He hadn't flinched when he had seen Kantswinkle's body, nor had he seemed too upset by this whole ordeal.

Yet all those deaths—the three on the ship and the fourth here—seemed awfully sloppy for a man who made his living killing people.

Hunsaker sighed softly and exited the illegal database. He felt dirty just thinking about Ilykova's job. About the man himself, actually. Ilykova hadn't seemed harmless—Hunsaker wasn't that naïve—but he had seemed...more efficient than deadly.

A movement caught his eye. Ilykova approached the desk. Hunsaker hadn't even seen him enter the room.

Hunsaker let out a little squeak. Ilykova raised an eyebrow in amusement. He'd clearly caught Hunsaker's moment of fear. Ilykova smiled—one of those knowing smiles—and then proceeded as if he had seen nothing out of the ordinary.

"Looking up the guests, are we?" he asked.

"So?" Hunsaker asked, then realized that probably wasn't the smartest response. Neither, he supposed, would be What's it to you? Or Get the hell away from me.

"So, does anyone have a history with lack of oxygen?"

"What?" Hunsaker asked, mostly because he hadn't been expecting that question.

"I realized when I was talking with the captain that all of our victims suffocated in one way or another. The fire would have caused the rest of us to suffocate as well. I was just wondering if we have some sort of revenge scenario going on here." Ilykova put his elbows on the desk.

"You tell me," Hunsaker said, his voice wobbling a little.

Ilykova frowned. "I don't have access to a deep database. You do."

Then his eyes widened just a little.

"Oh," he said. "You decided to research me first."

Hunsaker's heart was pounding. He had nothing to lose here—if Ilykova were going to kill him, it would happen here, now. So he called up the earlier screen, with Ilykova's history and pushed it across the desk at him.

"These things are so poorly done," Ilykova said. "It doesn't tell you much, does it?"

He looked up, his pale blue eyes twinkling. How could a man laugh about murder?

It made Hunsaker think of Carmichael: Murder really shouldn't be the subject of casual conversation, now should it?

Nor should it be something to smile about.

Apparently, Hunsaker's silence caught Ilykova's attention.

"We all have a past, Grissan," Ilykova said. "Yours involves embezzlement from every single resort you worked for. Quite creative embezzlement, I might add, the kind that would've made you very, very rich if you had kept to your original plan."

Hunsaker felt a warmth rise in his cheeks. No one knew about this. No one. How did Ilykova find it?

"The problem was, in your profession, that the younger, less experienced members moved from resort to resort, while the older ones got a well-deserved sinecure. That's the word, right? Sinecure?"

"Sinecure implies a job with little work. That's not true. To rise to the top of my profession, you must be willing to work at all times." Hunsaker's words were curt, showing his annoyance. He felt his face grow even warmer. He had let Ilykova irritate him.

Ilykova smiled slightly. "My mistake. I simply meant that you hit the top of your profession and remained in one place, a resort that became 'yours,' even if you didn't own it. You became the eyes and ears of the place, the face that everyone recognized. The person they associated with the resort. Which was why they bought you this place instead of prosecuting you. Did you know what a dive they got for you? It was the perfect revenge on their part, wasn't it? An effective banishment away from the populated areas of the sector. Did it embarrass you?"

Embarrassed, humiliated, angered. Hunsaker didn't say

anything, though, although he expected all of the emotions ran across his face.

"Still," Ilykova said, "you got to keep the money you stole from the other resorts. You could've vanished. You just chose not to."

Too ashamed to leave. Hunsaker simply couldn't face any of his old colleagues ever again. Ever, ever, ever again.

"We all have a bit of history," Ilykova said. "I'm sure you had a reason for your sticky fingers. I have a reason for my history as well. My mother was Halina Layla Orlinskaya. Look her up in your little database."

Hunsaker took the pad back, his fingers shaking, dammit all to hell. He wasn't as practiced at controlling his physical reactions to his emotions, not like he used to be.

He looked up Halina Layla Orlinskaya. She had half a dozen aliases as well. A high level spy, who defected with some devastating knowledge that changed the course of one of the border wars, she survived her last few years by hiring herself out as a mercenary to various governments.

"What it doesn't say there, I'm sure," Ilykova said, "is that she hired me out as well, as an assassin. She thought I had the personality for it."

"Did you?" Hunsaker wished he could take the words back.

But Ilykova didn't seem to notice. "Not really. I think one should feel passionate about his work. An assassin's job requires no passion at all. Don't you think that one should put his heart and soul into his job?"

"I used to," Hunsaker said.

"And I'll bet you miss that emotion," Ilykova said. "I

did. I wanted to do something with my life. Ah, to do something. Of course, now I'm broke and hiring onto ships as a lower-level employee just to get across the sector."

He leaned across the desk. Hunsaker couldn't lean away. His back was already pressed against the wall.

"So you see, I had no reason to kill those people," Ilykova said. "I didn't know them. And I'm certainly smart enough not to set a fire on a spaceship far from the nearest port."

"But," Hunsaker said, his voice smaller than he wanted it to be, "you knew Agatha Kantswinkle."

Ilykova smiled, a real smile, genuinely amused. "Didn't like her either, huh? No one did, so far as I can tell. But I didn't have to kill her. She would've gotten off the ship at Ansary. And here, on Vaadum, she was your problem, not mine."

Hunsaker swallowed. "So you're saying you didn't do it."

"That's right," Ilykova said. "Why would I?"

"Someone paid you?" Hunsaker asked.

Ilykova shook his head. "If someone paid me, I would've been a passenger. I wouldn't have signed on for work."

It sounded logical. It all sounded very logical. Hunsaker just didn't know if he should believe it.

"So what's this about suffocation?" he asked.

"Oh, just a theory," Ilykova said. "Everyone suffocated in one way or another. So if you think of these crimes as related, then maybe the manner of death came as a form of revenge for a death by suffocation...?"

"I wouldn't even know how to look for that," Hunsaker said.

"I would," Ilykova said, and took the pad away from Hunsaker.

R ichard was finding a whole lot of nothing as he dug through Hunsaker's database. The database wasn't that good. It was old, for one thing, and the updates hadn't been meshed into the system all that well. They had been grafted on and not efficiently, certainly not efficiently enough for a proper search.

He would have to get onto the Presidio. It had a good database and he might be able to find what he was looking for there.

Because, in this cursory exploration, he couldn't find anyone with any links to any suffocation deaths, murdered, accidental, or even natural.

He was about to hand the pad back to Hunsaker, when someone screamed.

"Oh, not again," Hunsaker muttered.

Richard tossed him the pad and ran up the steps, half expecting to hear a thump. He didn't though. But he did hear another scream and, he realized, these screams were male.

They weren't frightened screams or startled screams (except maybe the first one), more likely horrified screams, end-of-the-world screams, the kind you emit when everything was hopeless and all was lost.

Another scream, and then another. Doors slammed as people left their rooms. He was joining quite a crowd as he ran up the stairs.

The screams came from the top floor.

He arrived, along with three other passengers from the ship (Janet Powell, Lysa Lamphere, and William Bunting) to find a man he'd never seen before on his knees, hands over his face, screaming like a stuck alarm.

Another body lay on the floor, this one a woman, also someone he'd never seen before either. Her eyes were open and glassy, her tongue protruding slightly.

She was clearly dead.

Someone sighed behind him.

Richard turned slightly. Hunsaker stood near his shoulder, and stared at the woman on the floor.

"Now what the hell am I going to do?" Hunsaker said with great annoyance. "I mean, really."

J udging from the look on Ilykova's face, Hunsaker had spoken out loud. He felt that warmth returning to his cheeks. He kept his head down, so that he didn't have to look Ilykova in the eyes, and moved into the room.

He put his hand on Fergus's shoulders. Fergus had worked for Hunsaker since Hunsaker came to the resort. Fergus and his wife, Dillith, who now doubled as a corpse. Not that she was ever much livelier than a corpse. But for what Dillith lacked in energy, she made up for in precision.

She could find a speck of dust the robotic cleaners left

behind. She could turn bed sheet corners perfectly. She was slow, but she was anal.

And in Hunsaker's "resort," precision mattered more than speed.

Fergus stopped screaming when Hunsaker touched him. Fergus looked up, eyes sunken into his face, and said, "What am I going to do?"

His use of the sentence was plaintive. Hunsaker's had been self-involved. He had jumped from corpse/murder/crisis to who the hell was going to work for me in this godforsaken place? in less than a minute. He wasn't proud of that, but he really wasn't a man who developed much affection for his employees.

In fact, he believed affection got in the way of work. He didn't know much about Dillith and Fergus besides their names, their work methods, and the fact that they both preferred late hours rather than getting up early.

"Stand up," Hunsaker said with as much sympathy as he could muster, which probably wasn't enough. "We'll figure something out."

Fergus stood. He was a slight man, and he fell into Hunsaker's arms, much to Hunsaker's chagrin. He hadn't invited the man to hug him. He certainly didn't want the man to touch him. But Fergus was beyond noticing subtleties. He was sobbing. Hunsaker could already feel his shirt getting wet.

He patted Fergus on the back and maneuvered him out of the room. Then he looked at Ilykova who was watching him with that look of amusement again.

"Do me a favor," Hunsaker said to Ilykova. "Get Anne Marie Devlin, would you?"

"Who?" Ilykova said.

"The base doctor," Hunsaker said.

"I think this woman is beyond a doctor—"

"Just do it," Hunsaker said, resisting the urge to move Fergus toward Ilykova. That would show him passion, all right.

Ilykova nodded, then hurried down the stairs. Three passengers from the ship stood around as if this were a theatrical event.

"Go back to your rooms," Hunsaker said. "There's nothing to see."

As if a woman wasn't already dead on the floor. There was plenty to see. He just didn't want them gawking at it.

They, of course, didn't move. He glared at them and tried to look tough, which was hard to do when you had a member of the staff sobbing in your arms.

"Go," he said, and that seemed to work. Maybe it was his tone, his clear disgust at everyone around him.

The three left slowly. He watched them go down the stairs, patting Fergus on the back the entire time as if he were a baby who needed to be burped.

Then Hunsaker peered at the room. It didn't look that much different than it had two hours ago.

When he'd helped Susan Carmichael move out of it.

S he heard the screaming, of course. How could she have missed it? And she resisted her first instinct, which was to burrow deep under the covers of this new room, and pretend like she couldn't hear anything.

But Susan Carmichael wasn't a hider. She wasn't the kind of person who ran to the scene of a crime either, although she couldn't be entirely certain what she heard was a crime.

But someone didn't scream with that level of grief—and that was grief, wasn't it?—without a precipitating event, and considering Agatha's murder, the best assumption—the only assumption, really—was that a crime had occurred.

Again.

Which meant she had to get the hell off this station.

Somehow.

She changed clothes, slowly and deliberately, putting on the ivory blouse over the black pants. She slipped on her shoes, smoothed her hair, grabbed her personal information, and left this room as well.

The screaming had stopped, but she could hear faint voices in the distance. She glanced at the stairs, to ensure that no one was on them, and then she quietly made her way down.

It was time she stopped all of this. She gave up. She had been fleeing her family, but really, life out here was much, much worse than life with them could ever be.

Besides, her father had the capability of getting a ship here within twenty-four hours. He had ships all over the sector. One of them had to be nearby.

She just had to contact him.

She made her way down the stairs toward the main desk. Surely, there was some kind of interstellar communications node. Or maybe just a sector-wide node.

Or worse case—which was a case she'd put up with, after all—she would simply contact the nearest ship and have them contact her father.

And then she would wait.

Although she probably needed some kind of guard.

There wasn't a lot of choice. Everyone from the ship was a possible murderer, and there weren't a lot of people on the station.

But all of the murders she knew of took place while the victim was alone.

So the next key was to be with someone at all times.

Except right now.

Right now, she needed to contact Daddy.

After that, she would find a companion—and find a way to stay awake until help arrived.

Anne Marie Devlin was no longer drunk. She wasn't even under-the-surface drugged-sober drunk. She was so far past drunk that she felt giddy.

Actually, the excitement made her feel giddy. She felt useful for the first time in months.

If she didn't know herself better—and she knew herself quite well, thank you—she would say she had become a drunk because she was bored.

But she had been a drunk long before life ceased to be a

challenge. She knew that excitement was just a temporary high, while alcohol numbed the senses, which was usually what she preferred.

Right now, however, she needed all the senses that she had. She was inside yet another room—this one a favorite of hers—standing over yet another corpse that had been murdered by yet another tampered environmental system.

The question was, how had it been tampered with? And why?

She was peering at the system itself, noting something off, when she realized one of the ship's passengers was also in the room. A tallish white-blond man with pale blue eyes.

The man who had fetched her. Richard Something-Or-Other.

"I prefer to work alone," she said.

"So do I," he said.

They stared at each other for a moment. Hunsaker, who also preferred to work alone (she knew that because he had told her half a dozen times) stood near the doorway, his shirt soaked with Fergus's tears. She'd managed to get Fergus out of the room and down to the kitchen where the chef could watch him. Fergus was quite pliable most of the time. Right now, he was damn near catatonic.

Perhaps anyone would be after crying that much.

She turned toward Hunsaker. "What the hell were you thinking? Sending those two to work in these rooms with a murderer on the loose?"

"Who knew that the killer would come after one of us?" he said.

"I don't think the killer did," Richard Something-Or-Other said. "If you'll allow me."

He shoved—shoved!—Anne Marie out of the way, and peered at the control panel himself.

"You do realize if this man is the killer, he now has access to the evidence," she said to Hunsaker.

"You do realize if this man is the killer," Hunsaker said, mimicking her tone, "then you just gave him a reason to kill us."

They glared at each other again.

"I'm not the killer," Richard Something-Or-Other said, "but whoever is has some serious engineering skills."

She couldn't resist; she peered into the controls as well. These older models had digital readouts and mechanisms attached to mechanisms. She had just looked at the one in the room where Agatha Kantswinkle died—and that control did not have a secondary digital readout. This one did.

She looked at Richard Something-Or-Other. He raised his eyebrows at her, as if he were surprised as well. Then he touched the whole thing with a single fingernail. The second readout was loose, but had been attached into the control's mechanism. She peered at the mix. When Dillith had been in here, the atmosphere's mix had been the same as it had been when Agatha Kantswinkle died.

Anne Marie frowned. She glanced over her shoulder at the door. Hunsaker was still leaning on the jamb, glaring at her. He seemed to disapprove of what she was doing.

Or maybe he disapproved of Richard Something-Or-Other.

Or maybe he always disapproved of everything.

She sighed and walked to the door.

"Move," she said.

Hunsaker didn't.

"I mean it. Move. I need to see something."

"What?" he asked.

"It's easier to look than it is to explain," she said pushing him aside. Then she peered inside the locking mechanism. Another small digital readout had been attached.

"This door was closed when Fergus got here, wasn't it?" she asked.

"I don't know," Hunsaker said. "I didn't ask."

"You didn't bother to tell them to keep the doors open?"

Hunsaker's glare changed to something filled with a kind of fury. "Of course I did. It's part of the general instructions, anyway. The door should always be open when the staff is inside, even if no one else is."

"Hmm," she said.

"What?" Richard Something-Or-Other asked from his position near the environmental controls.

"This is a timer," she said. "It closes the door."

"And this timer," he said, "changes the environmental mix."

"It couldn't have been put in here when Dillith was here," Anne Marie said.

"Someone set it up earlier than that," Richard Something-Or-Other said.

"Which means that the killer wasn't after Dillith," Anne Marie said.

"He was after Susan Carmichael." Hunsaker said that

last, breathed it in fact. Anne Marie could hear the shock in his voice. "If I'd gotten here just a little too late, then—"

"You would've died too," Anne Marie said. "We have to brace this door open."

"I doubt the room will kill again," Richard Something-Or-Other said.

"But the other rooms might," Anne Marie said.

"I moved everyone out of the older rooms," Hunsaker said.

"Let's hope that's enough," Anne Marie said. She actually felt a little chill. She liked the chill. Excitement—she had missed it so much. "Maybe he'll start coming after the rest of us too."

"Oh, don't get your hopes up," Hunsaker snapped and left the room.

Richard Something-Or-Other raised his eyebrows again. "What was that all about?"

Anne Marie shrugged. "I guess he's upset by all of this."

Richard nodded. "I think it would be surprising if he were not."

Hunsaker stomped down the stairs. Now he didn't know what to do. Did he warn Carmichael? Did he put all the guests in the same room and let them duke it out until a ship arrived and got them out of his resort?

He stopped halfway down the stairs and leaned his head against the wall. All of his training, all of his long and fancy education, all of his experience good and bad did not train him for any of this. He could just imagine the lecture titled How to Handle a Murderer Loose in Your Resort.

Simple: Call the local authorities.

And if there were none?

He banged his head against the metal just once. If he rounded them up, where would he take them? The restaurant? The casino?

The casino at least covered a big area. It would be hard to tamper with the environmental system.

Maybe he should just force them all back to their ship, and if they killed each other, so be it. Hell, if they died from smoke inhalation, so be it. It wasn't his concern.

While they were here, they bothered him.

While they were on their ship, they had nothing to do with him.

That's what he'd do. He'd get the maintenance guys and make them act as security guards. Even the chef and the blackjack dealer could work security (so long as she put her shirt on). They'd round up these horrible people and put them back on their own ship and if they died, they died.

His stomach turned.

Maybe if they all died, he could just jettison the ship into deepest darkest space. He'd set it on autopilot and get it the hell out of here.

For a moment, his spirits rose.

Then he remembered he'd already charged their accounts. There was a record he couldn't tamper with of them being on his station.

Dammit.

He had no idea what to do.

Richard helped Anne Marie get the corpse down to the medical wing. He'd had enough of carrying bodies. By his count, this was the fifth this trip, and the only one he hadn't met while she was still alive.

The medical wing was in the farthest part of the station, and certainly didn't deserve the appellation "wing." It was a medical suite at best, a smallish group of rooms set up as an afterthought.

Agatha Kantswinkle lay on one table, naked—which was an image he'd never get out of his mind again—and, to his surprise, the other two bodies from the ship lay in clear refrigeration units, looking no worse for being dead the last few days.

He set Dillith on the closest table, and stretched his muscles with relief.

"Thank you," the doctor said in that tone all professionals used which actually meant you're done, now get the hell out.

Which he did.

And as he stepped into the corridor, he realized he'd been going about this investigation all wrong. He'd been looking for common ties, for suffocation deaths, for motive, and he, of all people, should know that motive mattered a lot less than the entertainments said it did.

His motive for most of his early killings had been because his mother had hired him out to do the job. The later killings had been because he could make money at it. Only the first killing had had a real motive:

the man had murdered his father and ruined Richard's life.

Richard didn't need to look at motive.

He needed to look for experience. Technical experience.

With environmental systems.

He scurried back to the hotel's main entrance, and hoped that Hunsaker's horrible aging database had at least enough information to solve all of this.

S he wasn't hysterical. Hunsaker could've dealt with her if she had been hysterical. He had training in hysterical. High-end hotel guests often got hysterical about nothing. And here, which was decidedly not high-end, people got hysterical because...well, because they were here.

Susan G. Carmichael had every reason to be hysterical. She could've died in her room had he not taken her out of it. But she had already figured out that she might die and she was calmer than he was.

She had even found a way to contact her father, who was such a famous Vice Admiral that Hunsaker had even heard of him, and he was sending a ship that would be here in 18 hours sharp, along with some kind of back-up that would take care of the problem.

Whatever that meant.

But she wasn't returning to her room.

To any room, really.

She wanted to remain with Hunsaker, thinking that somehow, Hunsaker would be safe.

He sat on his chair with his back against the wall, no longer sure what safe was. She was sitting on the edge of his desk, surveying the area as if she ran it instead of him.

He was still debating whether to get everyone else out of their rooms when Ilykova burst through the doors.

"I need your database," he said.

"Whatever happened to please and thank you?" Hunsaker muttered, knowing he was being a complete ass, as he handed over the pad.

Ilykova ignored that, although he did glance at Carmichael. He didn't seem that surprised to see her. Then he leaned against the desk and started trolling the database, his fingers moving faster than Hunsaker's ever could.

The three of them didn't say a word as Ilykova worked. Carmichael watched him. Hunsaker kept an eye on the doors and the stairs, not that it had made any difference in the past.

Then Ilykova looked over at Carmichael. "Were you and Agatha Kantswinkle ever alone?"

"Here?" she asked.

"On the ship," he said.

She looked down. "I talked to her once. After that incident—you know. I felt so sorry for her that—"

"What incident?" Hunsaker interrupted. It wouldn't have been his business had everything happened on the ship, but the ship's problems had spilled into his little resort, and he felt he had a right to know.

She looked at him. "We had a dinner hour on the ship. We all got fed at the same time, and the room wasn't that big. We got to know each other better than you usually got to know people on passenger ships, which wasn't necessarily a good thing."

Ilykova nodded, although he kept his head down, still searching the database as he listened.

"Anyway, just after Professor Grove died, we were all on edge, and Agatha started into how we needed someone to take charge, to make sure things wouldn't get worse, and Mr. Bunting had enough. He told her she was a nosy snobbish old woman who wouldn't know how to treat other human beings even if she had special training, and she certainly couldn't be in charge of anything, and he didn't believe anything she said about herself and—." Carmichael shook her head. "I was agreeing with him at first, she was an unpleasant woman, and I would've given anything to avoid her as much as possible, but he didn't stop, and by the end, she looked just devastated."

Ilykova was looking up now. Hunsaker was surprised as well. He couldn't quite imagine Kantswinkle looking devastated.

"I waited until everyone left," Carmichael said, "and told her that we were all on edge and that he had no right to lay into her like that, and she started to cry, which made me very uncomfortable. I walked her to her room, and told her to get some rest, that it would all seem better in the morning, and then I left."

"Then what?" Hunsaker asked, expecting more to the story.

"Then we found Trista's body and the fire and we barely made it here," Carmichael said.

"I got the distinct impression you wanted nothing to do with Ms. Kantswinkle," Hunsaker said.

Carmichael looked at him in surprise. "I thought I hid that."

"You avoided her in the lobby, checking in," Hunsaker said.

Carmichael looked down, sighed. "She was clingy. Halfway through our discussion, I realized she was bombastic because she was lonely and needy and I'd made a huge mistake trying to comfort her. If this had been some kind of normal flight, I wouldn't have been able to shake her for the rest of the trip."

"If it had been a normal flight," Ilykova said, "you wouldn't have spoken to her in the first place."

"True enough," Carmichael said. Then she frowned at him. "Why did you ask about us?"

"I have a theory," he said.

But he didn't say any more. And he continued to tap on the pad, which annoyed Hunsaker.

"Are you going to share the theory?" Hunsaker asked.

"I think someone thinks you saw something," Ilykova said. "Did you?"

Carmichael shrugged and shook her head.

"It would've been when you two were alone together."

She shook her head again. "Nothing."

He grunted as if he didn't believe her. He continued to work.

After a long moment, he said softly, "Well, I think I found something."

"What did you find?" Hunsaker asked. Carmichael crowded close. Richard didn't answer right away. First he made certain no one else could hear. He checked the doors, and looked up the stairwell.

When he came back to the desk, he spoke as softly as he could. He explained his idea—that he search for expertise, not motive. He didn't discuss how he feared the database would be limited (it was, but it didn't matter, he'd found enough).

"When I searched for expertise in environmental systems, I got two names. I expected at least one from the crew, but that was wrong."

"Which names?" Carmichael sounded panicked for the first time since he saw her down here.

"William Bunting and Lysa Lamphere."

"Bunting," Hunsaker said. "He was the one who yelled at Agatha Kantswinkle, you said."

Carmichael nodded.

"But," Richard said, "whoever killed Agatha and went after you, Susan, had a short window to do so. You had your room assignments already. Did you let anyone in your room?"

"Janet Powell," Carmichael said. "But I never left her alone and she never went near the controls."

"Anyone else?"

She shook her head.

"Where were you after we found Agatha's body?"

"I didn't leave the room," Carmichael said.

"Except to buy clothing," Hunsaker said.

"Yes," Carmichael said. "I bought clothing. But Bunting couldn't've done it then. He was in the boutique with me."

She used the word boutique with a touch of sarcasm. Richard frowned for a moment. Bunting had yelled at Agatha Kantswinkle, and made her cry. She wouldn't have let him near her. But another woman...?

"Did she have any troubles with Lysa?" Richard asked.

Carmichael shrugged. "I have no idea. I'm not even sure they spoke."

He didn't want to push her too hard. "Did you see either William Bunting or Lysa Lamphere that night you were alone with Agatha?"

"Lysa," Carmichael said. "But it was no big deal. She had forgotten something in the dining area. She went past us, looking a bit concerned. It wasn't important."

"Past you from where?" he asked.

"I assume she came from her room," Carmichael said.

"But you were walking Agatha to her room."

"Yes," Carmichael said.

"From the dining area."

"Yes."

"Which was nowhere near Lysa's room."

Carmichael looked at him.

"Her room was in a whole different area of the ship."

"And the fire started not too far from Agatha's room," Carmichael said.

Richard nodded. He felt certain they knew who the

killer was now. Lysa Lamphere had killed Agatha and gone after Carmichael because they could tie her to the entire event.

"It all sounds so nice and pretty," Hunsaker said, "until you remember that Lysa nearly died from inhaling the same toxic air that Agatha died from."

"Did she?" Richard asked. "She went into the room, made the switch with the environmental controls, maybe even watched Agatha die, and then switched them back. She waited until everything cleared a bit, and then went through her charade. I have a hunch if we search her room, we'll find some small breathing equipment, something she hid before going back to 'discover' Agatha."

"Why would she do that?" Carmichael asked.

They were all so naïve. Or maybe he wasn't naïve enough. It seemed obvious to him. Once he had Lysa's name, he understood how everything happened. And a little bit of why.

"So that no one would ever suspect her. You ruled her out even after I discovered her expertise because she had suffered as well."

He almost added, any good professional would've done that. But he didn't. Still, he saw the way Hunsaker looked at him. Hunsaker knew that.

"May I have the pad?" Hunsaker asked.

Richard handed him the pad, bracing for the next question, which came with predictable swiftness.

"I don't suppose you have expertise in environmental systems?" Hunsaker asked.

Richard resisted the urge to smile. "No, I don't."

"I will check," Hunsaker said.

"Do," Richard said. "But remember what I told you before. I wouldn't have started the fire. If you want to scuttle a ship, there are better and quicker ways to do it. She didn't want us all to die. She knew we were close."

"But why kill five people?" Carmichael asked.

"That's what I mean to find out," Richard said.

I t took a bit of work. Buried deep in all the information was one single tie. To the mathematician. His new job was a promotion, one she didn't feel he deserved. She had studied under him, and he had refused to grant her a degree, saying she was sloppy. She moved to engineering, and graduated, although not with honors, and not in a way that gave her any currency in any job. She would've needed more education for that.

She had boarded that ship with a plan to follow him to Ansary, maybe destroy his career there. Or maybe kill him. But she didn't.

Trista died because she had seen the murder, and she planned to do something about it. Lysa had never planned for Trista's body to be discovered. She probably thought the fire would've been found sooner. By the time someone had found it, the entire ship went into a panic. Which, if Richard thought about it, meant that her calculations had been off.

Professor Grove, the mathematician, had been right about her after all. Her math skills hadn't been up to the task.

Then Agatha Kantswinkle and Susan Carmichael had seen Lysa in that area, and if there were an investigation, they might've mentioned her. She didn't want to risk it. So she planned the last two murders, and might've gotten away with all of it, if Hunsaker hadn't moved Carmichael out of her room.

What Richard couldn't figure out was why she killed Remy Demaupin.

"I didn't," Lysa snarled. They had tied her up and moved her to the bar, along with all the other passengers. No one wanted to be alone any longer. They all worried that Richard and Hunsaker and Carmichael had caught the wrong person, even though Lysa had made it pretty clear from the moment she got tied up that they hadn't.

"What do you mean you didn't kill Remy," Carmichael said. "We know you did."

Lysa shook her head. "He killed himself," she said. "In fact, he inspired me. I figured everyone would look for a connection between him and Professor Grove. Then we would have the emergency and everyone would forget and..."

She lowered her head. Richard watched her, realized he'd met her type before. The type that imagined what they'd do, then did it, and wondered why nothing quite worked the way they'd planned.

"You should've just shoved him out of an airlock," Richard said.

Everyone looked at him. He realized he'd said too much.

He shrugged, pretending a nonchalance he didn't entirely feel.

"What I mean is that had you done something simple, no one would've thought twice about it. All this elaborate stuff was your downfall."

That still sounded bad. He sounded like one killer giving advice to another. Which, in fact, he was.

Hunsaker crossed his arms, watching Richard, a slight frown on his face. Anne Marie stood in the back of the room, listening. The captain was still at his table, drowning himself in drink. Carmichael kept checking the time, hoping that her father's ship would get here soon.

Everyone else sat very far away from Lysa, as if her particular brand of insanity was catching.

Richard didn't stay that far away though. For all her brand of insanity, her elaborate kills, and her mistakes, she was what a murderer should be.

Someone who had a reason to do what she did—not a bloodless reason. A personal reason. An important reason. Something that was, to her, life and death. So she acted in a life-or-death manner.

And he found that both inspirational and appropriate.

He didn't ask her any more. Carmichael's father could take them all in his various ships. Somewhere Lysa would get prosecuted for what she had done. Not that this was a happy ending for anyone.

The captain would probably lose his job. Carmichael was going back to a situation that she clearly didn't want to be in.

And Richard would have no way to get to Ansary.

Not to mention all the people who had died. Their families would never be the same.

He walked back to Anne Marie Devlin. Pretty woman. Or she would've been if she weren't a depressive and a drunk. She was sober right now, but he could see the tendencies. She was the kind who didn't want to change because she saw no point in it.

Besides, change was hard. That was becoming clearer to him, each and every day.

The ships arrived in fifteen hours, not eighteen, and they took everyone away. Once Hunsaker realized who Carmichael's father was—he truly was a mucky-muck of high muck who had a lot of mucking money—he made noises about the damage to his resort and how embarrassing it would be if it ever came out that his daughter had been a target.

When that hadn't moved her father, Hunsaker added that it would also be embarrassing for people to know that his daughter had been fleeing from him when all of this occurred.

Hunsaker got a tidy payout, enough to renovate the entire resort if he felt like it. And he felt like it. He wanted this place as tamper proof as possible. He didn't ever want to be in this situation again.

Ilykova hadn't left with the rest. He wasn't going to testify either, no matter how much everyone pleaded with him. He sat in the bar these days and watched Anne Marie drink, which was a sight to behold. He didn't seem miserable, but he didn't seem happy either.

He was waiting for the next ship, for a way out. Although he clearly didn't know where he was going.

And Hunsaker had been thinking about it. The station was a world unto itself. Technically, anything that happened here was prosecuted in the Commons System, but no prosecution had ever happened.

Hunsaker wasn't sure what he would've done if Ilykova hadn't been here. Ilykova wasn't big or burly and he didn't seem tough. But he had experience.

And he had no qualms about doing what it took to keep the peace.

You should've just shoved him out of an airlock.

Hunsaker couldn't've done that to anyone. Ever. But he could pay someone to do it while he looked the other way.

That wouldn't've worked in this circumstance, of course. But it might in future circumstances.

And if Hunsaker had learned anything from this experience, he had learned it was better to be prepared.

If he had been prepared, none of this would've happened.

The doors would've locked properly, the environmental controls would've been up-to-date, and all the rooms would've been cleaned.

Woulda coulda shoulda

He wasn't going to have any regrets. He was going to move forward.

He squared his shoulders and walked to the bar. He paused for a brief jealous moment when he saw how close

Ilykova was sitting to Anne Marie. Then he saw the look of disgust on Ilykova's face, and realized that the man would never be interested in her.

So Hunsaker sat down at their table, and offered Ilykova a job.

No one was surprised when Ilykova said yes.

STOMPING MAD
A SPADE CONUNDRUM
KRISTINE KATHRYN RUSCH

She called herself the Martha Stewart of Science Fiction, and she looked the part: Homecoming-queen pretty with a touch of maliciousness behind the eyes, a fakely tolerant acceptance of everyone fannish, and an ability to throw the best room party at any given Worldcon in any given year.

So when a body was found in her party suite, the case came to me. Folks in fandom call me the Sam Spade of Science Fiction, but I'm actually more like the Nero Wolfe: a man who prefers good food and good conversation, a man who is huge, both in his appetite and in his education. I don't go out much, except to science fiction conventions (a world in and of themselves) and to dinner with the rare comrade. I surround myself with books, computers, and televisions. I do not have orchids or an Archie Goodwin, but I do possess a sharp eye for detail and a critical understanding of the dark side of human nature.

I have, in the past, solved over a dozen cases, ranging from finding the source of a doomsday virus that threatened to shut down the world's largest fan database to discovering who had stolen the Best Artist Hugo two hours before the award ceremony. My reputation had grown during the last British Fantasy Convention when I—an American—worked with Scotland Yard to recover a diamond worth £1,000,000 that a Big Name Fan had forgotten to put in the hotel's safe.

But I had never faced a more convoluted criminal mind until that Friday afternoon at the First Annual Jurassic Parkathon, a media convention held in Anaheim.

The convention was officially called Dinocon because Crichton's people, or Spielberg's people, or some studio's people, wouldn't give permission to use the Jurassic Park name with a non-sanctioned project. I normally don't get involved with a media con, especially one held in Anaheim, but this one had a million dollar budget and a state-of-the-art computer system, and I simply couldn't resist the challenge.

So I was in Ops with most of the folks running the con when the call came through. Ops, for those of you who've never seen one, is a hotel function room with most of the furniture removed, replaced with tables covered with computer equipment, too many chairs, and tons of print out paper. Most of the people working Ops look haggard and stressed by the time the convention starts, and many of them are ready to collapse by the time it's over. So we really didn't need to hear some security person, young by the sound of him, on the two-way radio:

"Hey, ah, we got a, um, Situation X, here."

Everyone in Ops snapped to attention. The actual term was a File X—always a pun, everything a pun—and it was only supposed to be used for an extreme emergency.

"Copy that," Doris, a muscular woman the size of Stallone, said. She headed security, and had at every major con I'd ever worked on. Security is important at sf conventions, perhaps *the* most important thing, because these cons, as most of you know, aren't your simple suit-tie-and-briefcase affairs. The big conventions have three levels: the fans, most of whom dress in costume (some medieval barbarians, some Captain Kirk, some space aliens); the pros, most of whom write, act, or somehow work in the science fiction field; and the dealers, most of whom sell sf paraphernalia—books, videos, posters, and the ubiquitous Bajoran earrings. Media cons had more earrings, videos, and actors; fewer books, writers, and intellectual discussions. Behind it all is the concom, the army of people who run the entire shebang, and put out any and all fires along the way. Security deals with most of those: from regular hotel guests who are scared by the werewolf in the elevator to the teenagers who've stayed up all night playing the card game *Magic*, and who suddenly think it fun to pull the fire alarm on the second floor.

Never, in my twenty years of fandom, have we gotten a call for this kind emergency, and never have I heard a security person sound so scared.

"It's in room 4708. Can someone come here?" The security kid's voice cracked, confirming my suspicion: he was a volunteer, and he was eighteen at most.

"What's the nature of the emergency?" Doris asked.

"I don't think you want me to describe it on an open channel," the kid said.

"All right, be right there," Doris said, and left.

We mused about the "Situation" X for a moment. "Maybe," Ruth, the con chair, said, "he saw a fur bikini for the first time."

"It's the masquerade tonight," John said behind her, and we all laughed. He probably saw a costume, got scared, and decided to call it in. We'd all had that happen before.

"Or maybe it's pea soup," said Ben, and I, being most senior on the staff, groaned. I remembered that one, which had now eased into fannish legend. Just after *The Exorcist* came out, some fans in Baltimore held a room party and served pea soup along with the usual potato chips, cheese, and beer. After midnight, when the crowd got really drunk, someone had the brilliant idea of imitating Linda Blair in the famous vomit sequence. Of course, everyone had to do it, and by the time security arrived, a sea of pea soup was running down the corridor like the Blob without the assistance of the special effects people.

"Please, ghod, anything but that," I said.

At that moment, the phone rang. Ruth answered, and handed it to me, her tired face filled with confusion and surprise. "It's Doris," she said. "For you."

I slid my chair back and grabbed the phone, feeling as confused as Ruth looked. Doris could have radioed me. That would have been procedure. Maybe something was really up in 4708.

"Yeah?" I said.

"Spade," she said—my fannish friends had called me Spade since I solved the first case almost twelve years before —"you've gotta come up here. Now."

"What's going on?" I asked.

"An absolute disaster," she said, and hung up.

"Why didn't she use the radio?" Ruth asked.

I shrugged. "I guess she didn't want anyone else wandering up to the room." I eased myself out of my special chair, the one that I insist a con-com bring to every convention if they want my services, and with a push of a button, shut down the financial files on Dinocon's main computer. Then I made my way slowly—because I never hurry—to the fourth floor of the main convention hotel.

Dinocon had 8,000 registered attendees, and it was only Friday afternoon. The convention was scheduled to go through Sunday, and another 2,000 people were expected at the door on Saturday. Most of these folks were already crowding the halls, having conversations with friends they hadn't seen for a while and trying to discover where that night's parties would be held. I squeezed my way through—negotiating packed hallways was never easy for a man of my bulk—and made it to the elevator in time to nab the last spot. No one complained, though, as I squooshed people toward the back. Part of that was my con-com badge—regular con attendees knew better than to harass a person in a con-com badge—and part of it was my reputation.

"Hey, Spade!" someone yelled from the back. "You get a piece of that diamond?"

"I don't charge for my services," I said, in a gently chiding voice. I made my money years ago as an early employee of Microsoft. I took all my bonuses in stock, and then retired at the age of 31, not as rich as Bill Gates, but rich enough.

"He's a gentleman detective," someone else said from the back, and the entire elevator chuckled.

"Imagine," I said as the doors opened on four, "a gentleman—and a scholar."

I got off, but not before I heard more giggling as the doors closed. Fannish humor was not the stuff of stand-up routines, but it was usually full of sweet, if not always socially adept, affection.

The room 4708 was on what had been designated by the hotel as a party floor. On these floors, it was okay to have loud conversation all night, to serve beer in rooms, and to talk in the hallways. Other floors, the non-party floors, were for people who actually wanted to sleep during the con, something I hadn't done in the last thirteen conventions I had attended.

Photocopied 8"x11" signs were taped onto the wallpaper, most of them announcing bid parties for other conventions. The signs on 4708 looked professionally done on slick glossy paper. They announced the first annual Literature Con to be held in an ancient Hilton an hour outside of Manhattan. I stared at the signs for a moment, frowning. Anyone with half a brain knew that most of Dinocon's attendees weren't likely to attend a literature con, especially one held all the way across the country. But the posters had another draw besides their slick appearance.

Food.

Come to our bid party, the sign read, *and dine at your heart's content. Award-winning chocolates, Lucinda's World Famous Chili, and gourmet dishes from the farthest reaches of the Solar System. Come to* the *party of the convention. You'll talk about it for the next three lifetimes.*

Curiouser and curiouser. Lucinda was Lucinda Danielle Stanhope, also known as the Martha Stewart of Science Fiction. Lucinda hated media cons, thinking that they ruined "pure" science fiction. Pure science fiction, to her, was anything beautifully written with long treatises on science. She thought plot-driven fiction an abomination, and sf on movies and television beneath her notice.

Although she might have changed that opinion, since her current boyfriend, who had started as Science Fiction's answer to James Joyce, had gotten a job as a story consultant for a major studio. ("A guy has to make a buck," he said to me at the last Worldcon. "Besides, since *Independence Day,* everyone is hot for sf properties.")

She might have changed her opinion, but I doubted it.

I had known Lucinda for a long time. She and I had had a run-in at Con Diego (called Con Digeo by its attendees because of all the typos in the program book) several years back and I had tried, unsuccessfully, to avoid her ever since. Our conversations from that day on had consisted of only two words, uttered in passing.

Asshole, she'd say.

Bitch, I'd respond.

I sighed, squared my shoulders, and braced myself for the verbal onslaught as I knocked on the door.

Doris answered. She looked grim and shaky. She motioned me inside and closed the door.

The suite smelled of fresh bread, chili, and something foul, something I had never smelled before and wasn't sure I wanted to smell again. We stood in an entry that led to the bathroom on the left, a main room just before me, and a bedroom on the right. The security kid so skinny he was skeletal and a shade of green I'd never seen outside of a black-light poster, leaned against a faux Louis the Fourteenth table. He had a hand over his mouth and was taking deep breaths, as if to calm his stomach.

"What is it?" I asked.

Doris pointed toward the main room. I lumbered in, cautiously, not sure what to expect. A chocolate pterodactyl hung from the ceiling and flower arrangements that looked vaguely prehistoric stood on every end-table, along with cute little origami triceratops heads. A human-sized tyrannosaurus rex made entirely out of cheese stood on a circular mirror stand in the center of the room. Crock pots filled with chili bubbled on a table leaning against the wall dividing the main room from the bathroom.

"What —?" I started to ask again, and then I saw her.

She was sprawled on the floor, her left hand resting on the glass double doors leading out to the patio. The doors were closed. I cautiously made my way around the cheese dinosaur and the main table, still in the middle of preparations for the night's party, and stopped near her apron-clad torso.

There was no doubt it was Lucinda. She wore a linen pantsuit beneath that apron, and in her right hand she held an apple partially julienned into a stegosaurus. It was her head that was the problem.

It had been stomped flat, crushed into unrecognizability. More gray matter than I would have expected spattered the teal carpet, mixed with more blood than I had ever seen in my life. I swallowed twice, hard, not wanting to repeat the pea soup episode and contaminate the crime scene. Then I cautiously made my way back into the foyer.

"You call the cops?" I asked.

"No!" Doris said. "They'd shut us down."

"Damn straight they'd shut us down," I said. "We have a murderer on the loose here."

The kid moaned and headed toward the bathroom.

I grabbed his arm. "Uh-uh," I said. "Puke in the public restroom. You don't want to contaminate a crime scene."

"Too late," he mumbled, yanked free, and stumbled into the bathroom, kicking the door closed behind him.

"Poor kid," Doris said. "I'm amazed he has any stomach left."

"Listen, Doris, we gotta call the cops." I covered my hand with my sleeve and reached for the black rotary dial on the faux Louis the Fourteenth.

Doris put her hand on mine, forcing the receiver down. "It's Friday afternoon," she said. "Think about what that means."

Eight thousand attendees, all of whom would demand refunds. The hotel, which would sue for breach of contract. The reputation, which would shut down all Los Angeles area conventions for the foreseeable future, not to mention all media cons, not to mention all conventions held in this hotel chain forever.

Millions of dollars, all because Lucinda made someone stomping mad.

"Can't we at least wait until tomorrow?" Doris asked.

Retching sounds echoed from the bathroom. My stomach rolled in sympathy.

"Tomorrow?" I asked. "Don't you remember the party signs that are up all over this convention. For tonight? In this room?"

"Can't we change them to tomorrow night?" she asked. "Then we won't have to refund, and we won't be in breach of contract."

But we would still have the reputation problem, along with another one. "Tampering with a crime scene is illegal, Doris," I said softly.

"Can't you solve this?" she asked. "Can't you solve this before the cops get here?"

"I've never done a murder investigation before, Doris," I said.

"*Please*," she asked. "If we can give them a suspect, they won't shut us down, and Ruth and I can handle the PR problem, at least long enough to save the con."

"You don't care that a woman has been trampled in her own hotel room?"

Doris crossed her muscular arms. "You really need to ask me that, Spade? I wouldn't be so rude as to ask you."

She could have, though. Because I was upset. Lucinda had

her points. She made a mean chocolate soufflé, and she knew more about fannish foods than anyone I had ever met. She also had her moments: the charity auction she ran for literacy at Orycon in the early '90s brought in $5,000 more than usual because she browbeat the attendees into spending more money. And she got them to do it by having them buy signed books.

Sometimes I found myself in complete agreement with Lucinda's arguments.

And that terrified me.

I stared at Doris.

"Will you help us?" she asked.

I sighed. "I won't tamper with the crime scene, and I will meet with the police when they arrive. You will call them from this room and you will make sure that no one else enters here. You'll also keep the kid from talking to anyone but me. If I happen to solve this thing before the police arrive, fine. But I won't go any farther than that. I'm not going to let some murderer run loose because you want to hold a media con honoring one of the lamest movies of all time."

"The special effects were cool." The kid had opened the door to the bathroom. He was now a chalk white.

"But the plot sucked," I said. Then I nodded at Doris. "Call. I'm going to snoop a bit. And don't leave until I tell you to. Got that?"

She nodded and reached for the phone. I stopped her. "Cover your hands with your sleeves. And don't touch anything besides that receiver."

She glared at me, but followed my instructions. I

prowled into the bedroom, deciding to talk to the kid after his breath cleared up.

Lucinda, not surprisingly, was a neat freak. She had arrived and unpacked, her clothing hanging on her hangers in the walk-in closet. Each item was separated by tissue paper, and her hats were in boxes on the shelf above. Her shoes were lined up below in neat little rows beneath the matching clothes. She had two wigs on the dressing table, one studded with little plastic dinosaurs—the clear, brightly colored kind that bartenders used to put in drinks in the mid-sixties. A silver lamé dress hung from the plant hook in the ceiling. Lucinda had planned to go all out on this party, and it surprised me. She had to be doing a favor for someone. Media cons were beneath her—and while she enjoyed fannish cooking, she hated fannish clothing.

I got back into the foyer as Doris hung up the phone. "I didn't tell them it was a murder," she said.

I mentally shook my head. That would be her problem when the cops arrived. It would be better for all of us if I had some idea what had happened.

"Okay, kid," I said to the security boy, "come into my office and talk to me. And don't touch anything."

The kid's color still hadn't returned. He followed me into Lucinda's bedroom and started to close the door.

"Don't touch," I said. We went deep into the bowels of the room, and stopped near the bed. I knew that Doris would have trouble hearing us from this spot because I had had trouble hearing her on the phone.

"What's your name?" I asked.

"Chad," he said. I raised a single eyebrow, Spocklike. I

had never met a kid who worked con security named Chad. Or at least, a kid who worked con security who would admit to being named Chad.

"Okay," I said, "I need to know: what made you come to this room in the first place?"

He wiped his mouth with the back of his hand. That stomach of his was amazingly weak. "I was by the flyer table —that was my post—when these fans came down the stairs and told me they'd heard a huge pounding on the fourth floor. They took me to their room on three and I heard it too, like something really heavy was going to crash through the floor. Then I came up here. The door was open, and I let myself in. It was really quiet. I called out to see if anyone was here, and then I saw the food. I went in to grab a snack and —"

He burped, then covered his mouth, swallowing hard. "Sorry," he said.

"It's all right," I said. "Do you know who these fans were?"

"Not by name," he said. "But they have the room below this one."

And were probably preparing for another party since the room below also had to be a suite. I rubbed my chin in proper detective fashion. I had a conundrum. I needed to talk to those fans, but I didn't want to leave Doris alone in the room. Nor did I want anyone else to know what had happened to Lucinda.

Then I realized it didn't matter. Doris had been in the room without me already. I had investigated, and I knew how things looked. I had seen everything but the bathroom, and that could be remedied.

I took the kid back to the foyer. "Wait here," I said, and peered into the bathroom. The kid had already contaminated the crime scene—several times—but there didn't seem to be much to see. The bathtub was still maid-spotless and the counter had Lucinda's make-up and nothing else. The toilet seat was up, one of the towels was askew, and otherwise everything looked fine. It didn't even smell as bad as I thought it would.

"Okay," I said as I emerged. "Let's find those fans. You wait here, Doris, and don't touch anything."

"Don't worry," she said, looking faintly annoyed at the suggestion.

The kid and I slipped into the hallway. The con was filling up. Two women wearing belly dancer skirts and midriff tops conversed about the proper navel jewel. Five teenage boys compared tattoos. Three grown men, in Klingon boots and armor, adjusted each other's forehead ridges.

The kid and I took the stairs.

The third floor was filled with people in dinosaur costumes. Some were cheap Halloween masks, while others were full-bore papier-mâché or plastic. The costumes looked heavy, they looked hot, and they smelled of glue. I stared at them, mostly at the feet, wondering what kind of pressure a person would need to drive those hard plastic soles through a skull and crush it.

Then we were in front of 3708. The kid knocked on the door. His hand was shaking.

It was opened by a slender woman whose black hair formed perfect Louisa May Alcott ringlets around her face. She wore a lavender satin shirt with purple satin pants, and the outfit somehow looked perfect on her. Her convention badge was clipped to a tiny piece of cardboard inside her shirt's high pocket, so as not to ruin the satin.

"Hi," she said, looking a bit confused.

"Security," the kid said, glancing at me. "Remember? You asked about the big stomping?"

"Oh, yeah." She was staring at me. Her eyes were lavender, like the shirt. I'd never seen eyes like that in person before. Only in photographs of Elizabeth Taylor. "Who're you?"

"I'm from Ops," I said. "Mind if we come in?"

"Why?" She was asking the kid.

"Because when I went upstairs," he said, "I found —"

I kicked him. He shut up.

"He found that he had a few more questions to ask you," I said. "Mind if we come in?"

"No," she said. "I guess not."

She got out of our way, and we stepped into the foyer. It exactly matched the suite above, only here the carpet was brown. Two men sat in the suite's living room. They looked vaguely familiar. They stood as they saw us come in.

"Something wrong?" the first one asked.

He was tall and muscular—those fakey kind of muscles that come from too much health club, and too much low-fat food. His shirt was unbuttoned below the navel, revealing a washboard stomach, and his bare feet looked manicured. His companion wore ripped jeans and a *Star*

Trek t-shirt, but unless I missed my guess, his hair had been permed.

Interesting look, for fans. It looked a little too Hollywood, a little too put together, for my tastes. Maybe these folks were slumming.

"You guys with the convention?" I asked.

"What's this all about?" T-Shirt asked. He had his hands on his hips. Same fakey muscles, and he didn't look as if he had ever cracked a book. But, I reminded myself, this was a media con. Folks here didn't have to crack books, even though most of them did.

"Of course we're with the convention," the woman said, and tugged gently on her badge as if to prove it.

"What's your interest?" I asked. "Filking?"

"Excuse me," Manicured asked. His face flamed and he looked insulted.

"Fill-king," the kid said, "not fucking."

Interesting comment, I thought, but I didn't look at him. "Pipe down, Chad," I said. "What are you guys doing at the con?"

"Anyone can come," the woman said, apparently realizing that my questions had more importance than the guys were giving them credit for. "Right?"

"Of course," I said, "but usually people have special reasons for attending. What are yours?"

"We like dinosaurs," T-Shirt said.

"Fascinating," I said in my best Spock voice. No one laughed, even though most fans usually did. My best Spock voice was pretty damn good. "So what's your favorite dinosaur? A plugosaurus or a brontodacdyl?"

"All of 'em," T-Shirt said.

"Hmmm," I said. "Hear you had some noise problems."

"Yeah, man, sounded like weird pounding upstairs," Manicured said. "Like someone was trying to punch a hole in the floor."

"Sounds serious," I said. "Will someone move that chair over here?" I pointed to a square wooden chair that seemed to be the sturdiest thing in the room. T-Shirt moved the chair to the place I pointed to, right next to the balcony doors.

"Spot me, Chad, will you?" I asked as I climbed up.

"Ah, um, ah, you might want me to do that," he said.

"No need," I said, even though the chair was groaning under my weight. I reached up and removed the ceiling panel. Gobs of dust and dirt rained on me, and I had to clear a spider web, but after that I had a pretty good glimpse of the space between the ceiling and the floor above.

"Looks normal," I said, and to my surprise, it did. I put the tile back. "You guys are safe."

"That's it?" the woman asked. "That's all? It sounded wretched up there."

"It was," Chad said. I braced myself on his shoulder and squeezed as I got down. It shut him up again.

"That's it," I said cheerfully. "I hope you have a good con."

"Ah, thanks," T-Shirt said. He was frowning at me.

The kid and I left. The dino costumes flooded the hall. The newer ones looked even more realistic than the earlier ones. Especially the Spielbergian velociraptors. All terrifyingly icky except for the guy wearing blue jeans and a tie-dye brontosaurus head. And the inevitable tot dressed as Barney.

One glance at the elevator told me we weren't going back to the fourth floor that way. Too crowded. It also meant the cops wouldn't come up very quickly when they arrived.

"Where to now?" the kid asked.

I didn't answer. I was feeling pretty annoyed with him. Pretty annoyed with the whole thing, really. I wanted to get back to my Ops computer with its lovely numbers and forget I had ever gotten involved with this detecting business.

Even if I was good at it.

We took the stairs and I was puffing by the time we reached the fourth floor. I hadn't had this much exercise in weeks. And I was moving faster than I liked.

Most of the dino costumes were on the third floor. Regular con-goers littered the fourth. None of them looked like the three ringers downstairs.

I shave-and-a-haircut knocked on 4708. Doris answered immediately. "What took you so long?"

I didn't answer. As I came in, I asked, "Did Lucinda know I was coming to Dinocon?"

"How should I know?" Doris asked.

I glared at her.

She sighed, exasperated. "Probably. If she was looking. You would have been hard to miss since your name was in the con-com listing in all the progress reports. Why?"

I had my suspicions. I made my way back into the suite's main room.

"Hey!" the kid said. "What're you doing?"

His voice had gotten increasingly shrill. I ignored him. I

made my way to the body, and, just as I remembered, the floor didn't sag under my considerable weight.

I knelt beside the body. The gray matter and blood were drying in a perfect arch.

"Hey!" the kid yelled. "You said no tampering."

"Grab him, Doris," I said through my teeth. He was getting on my nerves. This whole thing was.

I grabbed the right wrist, dislodging the julienned stegosaurus, and felt—plastic. Soft, lifelike, fake plastic.

"Bitch," I mumbled. I half expected the crushed dummy to mumble "asshole" in return. Then, louder, I said, "Doris, did you call 911?"

She didn't answer. I turned. She was frowning at me.

"Doris?"

She flushed. "No," she said. "I called the regular line. I wanted to give you as much time as possible."

Her caution had worked to our advantage. "Call and cancel," I said. "Then break that kid's arm if he doesn't tell you where Lucinda is."

"Lucinda —!"

"Just do it." First time I'd ever understood the sense of a Nike ad.

She twisted the kid's arm up behind his back. Within seconds, he was screaming, "Executive Suite! Executive Suite!"

I got up and walked over to him. "Key," I said.

He handed me a specially marked executive floor key. "Come on, Doris," I said. "Keep a good grip on this kid and commandeer us an elevator."

She did exactly as she was told.

On the way up, I explained the whole thing, and the kid wisely said nothing, confirming all my suspicions. I was trying to contain my anger, because this thing had just become personal.

And to think I would have mourned the bitch if that had truly been her on the floor below.

You see, the plan was simple: the execution was hard. Lucky for Lucinda that her boyfriend had his new job in Hollywood and even luckier for her that most special effects guys are also sf nerds. Ironic that she needed media people to tamper with a media con. But Lucinda had always been a bit dim when it came to irony.

And, apparently, detail, at least non-food related detail.

First there was the fannish clothing. No matter what kind of theme party Lucinda gave, she never, ever dressed in fannish clothes. No wigs decorated with little plastic dinosaurs, no silver lamé dress. She might have consented to work a media con, but she would never have given up her stylishly proper clothing. She planned the perfect media party, all right, down to the clothes, forgetting that she would never, ever wear those clothes because, of course, she didn't plan to.

But that wasn't the only detail that bothered me. The three "fans" on the floor below had been extras in a straight-to-video sf release that I'd been watching at home a few nights before the con. I would have made them as non-skiffy folk anyway. All science fiction fans—media and lit alike—

know the difference between a real dinosaur and a made-up one.

And then there was Chad, clearly another actor for hire. Except he overdid the vomit bit, and the bathroom smelled as if the maid had just left. Lucinda probably hadn't counted on the strength of my sniffer.

But she had counted on me. In fact, I had been the center of her plan. Without me, it wouldn't have worked. She knew that I knew better than to tamper with a crime scene, no matter how great the temptation. She knew that I had a healthy respect for the authorities and that I would insist on cops being present.

And she knew that the cops would see this for the hoax it was. She would appear at the right moment, blame the convention for overreacting to her little party, piss off the cops just enough to get the whole con shut down. The hotel chain would have been angry, the attendees would have demanded refunds, and the whole cascade effect that Doris had foreseen when she first saw that body would have occurred. Media cons, not just in LA, but all over the country would have suffered, and possibly died.

Lucinda's little stunt would have caused more damage than the murder. It was sabotage, served cold.

When we reached the executive suite, Doris made the kid open the door. Lucinda saw him, stood up, and cooed. She was dressed for her act in a white sheath that accented her lightly tanned skin and golden hair.

When she saw us, her eyes widened.

"You bitch," Doris said, blowing my line and letting go of the kid. He started to back away, but I shoved him forward and closed the door behind us.

"Back off, Doris," I said. "She's mine. There won't be any cops, Lucinda. You won't ruin this convention."

"I'm going to see that you're banned from cons forever. I'm going to make sure that your name is taken out of the Fannish Directory. I'm going to—"

"For what? For a little party I planned to throw for some friends?" Lucinda asked. "Don't you think it rather cute? I do."

"You—"

Doris lunged for her, and I caught her, staggering a bit under her power. The kid bee-lined for the bathroom, fear making his intentions real this time.

"Go to Ops," I said to Doris. "Tell them everything is fine. I can take it from here."

"I'm going to get you," Doris said, but she listened to me. She knew as well as I did that strange things happened at sf conventions, and that there was no proving malicious intent here.

Knowing about it was something else.

"Misunderstandings are so tragic, Doris," Lucinda said, blinking her blue eyes guilelessly.

Doris growled and disappeared out the door. I stood in front of Lucinda. "Media cons aren't your style."

She smiled. It was sweet as rhubarb pie. "They're not yours either."

"I don't see anything wrong with people having fun. I'm

a bit more open-minded than you, Lucinda. I believe people can enjoy reading and watching movies. I believe there's room in fandom for both."

"You're so naive," she said. "These cons are so anti-literature. They appeal only to the ignorant. People who don't understand real science, or real science fiction."

"I think people who think they guard pure science fiction may not understand real science or real science fiction either," I said pointedly.

"Good god," she said, "a philosophical discussion when I have a party to finish."

"It seems strange to me that you'd put on a party here, Lucinda."

She shrugged. "I thought I'd give these people the opportunity to come to a lit-con and see what they were missing."

"So kind of you," I said.

She smoothed her dress. "We all do what we can in the circumstances provided."

At that moment, I almost told her what tripped her up. I almost told her that it was her lack of scientific knowledge, her lack of understanding of forensic science that had destroyed her. First, the splatter had been too pretty, too uniform. Second, and more importantly, the type of force it took to stomp out someone's brains would have caused damage to the plywood floor. Damage someone of my weight would have felt in loose boards or groaning wood.

But I didn't. Why give her the ammunition? She might try again someday.

"Am I excused?" she asked brightly.

"There is no excuse for you, Lucinda," I said in my best fannish manner, and moved out of her way.

T he bane of the non-licensed investigator is that we have no real authority. We can't arrest. Worse yet, people with authority often look down their noses at us.

So we are forced to take some matters into our own hands.

Lucinda, misguided as she was, was clever. Who could prove that the panic the kid, Doris, and I felt was anything more than a product of our own imaginations? She would say that she had planned a perfect party, and we had nearly ruined it.

In fact, that night, she did carry off the party with full aplomb. She did change the victim from her clone to that of a lawyer, in keeping with *Jurassic Park* (the movie) tradition, and she did pour ice in the bathtub, but those were the only changes she made. The party was the hit of the convention, and became the talk of sf—both media- and literature-oriented—for years to come. It was, in its own way, the Woodstock of science fiction. Eventually everyone who was anyone claimed they had been there, even if they had been clear across the country at the time.

Everyone who was anyone except me.

You see, I was in Ops, checking the computer records. We had an unexplained power failure just as I was transferring Lucinda's credit card information from her con file into an active file so that we could bill her account. Unfortunately, the accident caused blips in her credit record that cascaded down the system and destroyed her credit rating for the next year. She had to defend and deny and repair, all of which took time away from cons and con parties, and fandom.

And somehow she got it in her pretty little head that this would happen again if she ever attempted to sabotage—even accidentally—a major convention again.

Misunderstandings are so tragic.

But we all do what we can in the circumstances provided.

THE CASE OF THE STOLEN MEMORIES
A SPADE/PALADIN CONUNDRUM
KRISTINE KATHRYN RUSCH

H e brought them with him, his old friends. Every convention, Ira Hartmann carted his Kodak Carousel slide projector and hundreds of slides into the suite he had sweet-talked the con com into providing for him. Ira was a member of First Fandom, an organization founded in 1959 to bring together science fiction fans of the "golden era"—the pre-1938 era.

Why 1938? Because of the Great Worldcon War of 1939. At least, that was what Ira called it, and I had adopted the terminology, because I'd first learned about the 1939 Worldcon first from him.

My name is Spade. I've been around fandom long enough that most people believe I know everything about everything fannish, but I don't. I am just old enough to have spanned a couple of eras. I knew a lot of members of First Fandom, and I also knew people who should've been in First

Fandom, and I knew writers from the Golden Age, and I knew writers from just a few years ago.

Most folks would not say I'm a sensitive soul, but I kinda sorta am. I knew that there were topics the First Fandom folks did not like discussing. Ask Ira about the Exclusion Act at NY Con 1 (as its detractors called that first Worldcon), and he'd give you a sad look. Then he'd change the subject and happily tell you about how he was standing outside the "pavilion" when he spied "this kid from California," who just a few years later would "become" Ray Bradbury.

To hear Ira tell it—all of it—those early years, the 1930s, were glorious. Yeah, they were kids, and no, they didn't have money, but they all loved each other and they all loved science fiction, and *Hey, Spade, look at what we built, kid. Look at what we built.*

What they built. A network of conventions that had been going around the country ever since that very first Worldcon in 1939, a gathering place for people who loved science fiction, people who loved reading and books and movies and games and all kinds of things that were shunned back in Ira's day.

Ira's day. I was never really certain what Ira's day was. The man was impressive as hell. He was an ambitious talker —probably an annoying one in 1939. He'd been fifteen that year when he met some of the most important people in his life. He became an agent for some of them—I like to imagine this punk kid, talking to big-time editors all of whom I imagine looked like Perry White in the oldest of the old Superman comics—square-jawed, loud-talking, salt-and-pepper hair and a take-no-guff persona.

Yeah, kid, yeah. But tell me, kid, why ya think we should waste ink on that *story, huh?*

Come to discover, years later, that the editors Ira was selling stories to weren't much older than Ira himself. In fact, some of them ran that first Worldcon, and a couple of them might've caused the split heard 'round fandom.

I don't know all the details because I don't *want* to know all the details. Most of the folks involved were friends of mine—elderly friends of mine who would stiffen up whenever anyone mentioned that first Worldcon.

All those years later, it was still a source of great pain. Hell, during one of the First Fandom Hall of Fame Award presentations at a Hugo ceremony in the '90s, the two factions almost came to blows—and we're not talking young people. We're talking people in their sixties and seventies screeching at each other about something that happened *decades* ago.

I'd been working security that night. I had to pull two men apart before they broke bones in their hands trying to punch each other. Still, they both ended up with black eyes and one might've lost a tooth or two.

There's a lot of dirt back there, stuff I don't want to know about my heroes. I watched too many of them grow clay feet over the years. Some because of their boorish behavior and some because of stories about them that I simply can't get out of my head.

Modern SF has epic wars, but most of them are online now. I try to avoid them. Back in the day, though, the stuff got hashed out in person. Or in APAzines (amateur press association mimeographed fan magazines). Or in rumor and innuendo.

It was as bad then as it is now. It just didn't happen quite as fast. It didn't go from incident to kerfuffle to picking sides to hatred in the space of a few hours. Usually it took weeks, sometimes months.

Yeah, fandom stuff can get serious. And it lasts. The friendships last, and the enemies last.

Ira knew that. He did his best to avoid the controversies. I can imagine scrawny little Ira, talking his way past all the "older" members of what would become First Fandom, ducking punches and deciding to placate the feelings of others, probably doing it with an overflow of words.

Ira was always overflowing with words—except that morning.

That morning, I saw an Ira hardly anyone saw. Maybe his wife, back when she'd been alive. Maybe a couple of his friends. Maybe.

He had been sitting on the bed in his suite, hands on both sides of his head, body hunched. He wouldn't answer when anyone talked to him, and finally Doris Xavier, who'd been running con security, sent for me, thinking maybe I knew who his family was.

When someone hits their eighties, which Ira was that day, folks suspect severe illness before they think of anything else, which I think of as not all that fair, really, particularly as I age.

That morning—that case. I don't talk about it.

Or I didn't.

But Ira's gone now. SF isn't quite the same as it was.

Half the eras that I spanned are no longer there. I'm inching into the older generation and I gotta tell you, it's weird.

In those years, Eschercon took place in April. They moved it when a larger convention—with comics and movie stars and some really good cosplay—kept eating away at their membership.

But April—not really the best month to hold a convention in Upstate New York. Either we'd have snow or slush or ice or some damn storm that would delay arrivals. Except the locals who knew which train to take, and who didn't mind getting picked up at the train station by a fan who couldn't drive worth a damn.

I always flew in, because at the time I lived in Seattle proper. I'd made my millions from Microsoft (I'm one of the original Microsoft millionaires), the Victorian I'd bought near the university had quadrupled in value, and I had only just started thinking of selling it.

I'd actually considered going to NY, because so many of my fannish friends lived there. So I was working as many NY conventions as I could, getting to see the back parts of towns that no one normally saw.

The hotel where Eschercon was in those years was the strangest hotel I'd encountered—at least to that point. The local fen (the fannish plural for fans) called it the Escher Hotel, and it was how the con got its name.

The Escher Hotel was really three hotels mashed together. You'd walk down a hallway on the fourth floor and suddenly the carpet would change color and according to the signage you'd be on the eighth floor. Stairways led nowhere, and the third floor rooms in one part of the hotel would dead-end into a blank concrete wall which had once been the outside wall of one of the mashed-up hotels.

To make things even weirder, the hotels stood on a definitive corner, where three (former) villages met. That intersection was the place where street names and zip codes changed. Each hotel was in a different village, and to this day, I have no idea what village the intersecting parts of the hotel(s) stood in.

That year, Ira's suite was on the top floor of the newest hotel, where the guests of honor were staying. I had a suite on that floor too, not because I was special, but because I had money to burn, so I burned it—at least at conventions. I believed in comfort more than anything else. Still do.

So it didn't take me long to get to Ira's room. Doris was hovering at the door, looking nervous, and some sweet young fan, a pretty girl of a type that Ira always seemed to attract, hovered with her.

The sweet young fans, as Doris and I called them, were arm candy for Ira. He was still stubbornly faithful to the wife he'd married at nineteen, and who had died of some awful cancer twenty years before. But he liked to pretend he was a ladies' man, and maybe, by his gentlemanly standards, he was.

"What's going on?" I asked as I barreled through the door.

Forgot to tell you that I'm more Nero Wolfe than Sam Spade. I'm not fond of orchids and I do leave my house and I don't have an assistant named Archie who runs into danger, but I am large and imposing and I like my creature comforts more than I like dishing out a punch.

I don't usually barrel either, but someone had said there was a problem with Ira, and for Ira, I barreled.

Doris stepped to one side and the sweet young fan looked at me like she'd never seen a fat man run before.

"I can't get Ira to tell me what's wrong," Doris said, sounding worried. Doris never sounded worried. That's why I liked working with her.

I glanced at the sweet young fan, about to tell her to go somewhere else, when I realized she was rubbing her hands together. Apparently, that gesture is called wringing, although for the life of me, I've never understood it.

"I came to get him for brunch," she said. "The door was open."

Her voice got a little louder, a little more insistent. Someone had probably already questioned whether or not she had spent the night in the room.

Ira never fought the perceptions of his manliness, unless it got the sweet young fen in trouble. Then he was Sir Galahad, ready to ride in on a metaphorical horse.

"I called his name, and he didn't say anything." She bit her lower lip. "I went in farther, and there he was."

She waved a hand at the bedroom, and my heart clenched. At that moment, I hadn't seen Ira yet, didn't know that he was hunched, didn't know that he was even alive, although I figured Doris would've told me if he wasn't.

I pushed past the sweet young fan and barreled toward the bedroom. I know CPR. I've had to use it, but I was afraid to use it on Ira. He was still a small man, and in his eighties, he had become frail.

I wasn't sure I'd be able to do the compressions without shattering a bone.

But I didn't need to. Ira sat on the edge of his bed, his head bowed, his shoulders shaking, clearly alive.

I let out a gusty sigh of relief and walked over to him. I put my meaty hand on his shaking shoulder and said, "Ira, it's Spade."

He didn't acknowledge me.

That was when I realized he was crying. And, as I looked around the room, I noted that the bed was made, and the old fashioned he'd brought with him for a nightcap the night before was still sitting, untouched, on the nightstand. The ice had melted long ago, the bitters had settled on the bottom, and the whiskey wasn't that golden anymore, given the amount of water now in the glass.

Ira used drinks like that to help him sleep—or so he said —and I'd watched him down plenty before turning in. Ira was from that generation: he was a drinker, and proud of it.

I crouched. My knees cracked so hard I thought they probably heard the snap in New Jersey. I peered up at him. His hair, usually manicured away from his face with some sickly sweet gel, had fallen across his cheeks. His hands looked glued to his skin.

"Ira," I said again. "Ira, look at me."

He didn't. He wouldn't. I wasn't even sure he saw me.

I turned, straining my back. I would never get out of this position again, I was sure of it.

"Doris," I said none too loudly, because she was hovering near the door, the sweet young fan behind her, "call 911."

"No." The word was barely audible. A croak, really.

I looked back at Ira. He still hadn't pulled his hands away from his face, but he was sitting up a bit straighter.

"I'm okay," he said, even though it was clearly a lie.

He finally let his hands drop. His large nose was red, his eyes were puffy, and his cheeks were chapped.

His lower lip trembled, and that's when I realized he'd been crying. Crying for hours. The kind of crying that people did when someone died.

"Spade, you stay." Then Ira attempted a smile, maybe even one of his charming smiles, and said to the sweet young fan, "Honey, I'm skipping brunch, okay?"

"You sure?" she asked. "I mean, food would probably help—"

His smile had a bit of an edge now. I saw the Ira who had become a big Manhattan lawyer, who had given up fandom to negotiate deals in TV and theater when New York City was the center of the entertainment universe.

He had only come back to us after he retired and his wife died. And then he never mentioned all the things he had done in the name of entertainment. Just what he had been doing in SF before he had Become Somebody.

"Honey," he said in a way that made it clear that right now, he couldn't remember her name, "don't you worry about me."

She didn't notice. She was still hovering. It didn't matter how pretty or seemingly normal fen were, they were still fen. And there were reasons she was in the SF crowd. Apparently her inability to read a room was one of them.

I turned even farther so I could give her hand signals that

I hoped she could understand. *He's okay* and *Go away*. I didn't quite make a shooing motion, but I almost did.

Doris took pity on her. Or on me. Doris took the sweet young fan by the arm and helped her out of the room as if she was the one in trouble, not Ira.

Then Doris pulled the door closed, and I collapsed onto the floor. My knees were not meant to hold all four hundred pounds of me in a crouch for that long.

Ira frowned at me.

"You okay?" he asked with a bit of an edge. On the one hand, it was typical Ira. He was concerned for someone else, always, wanting the best for people, always, but on the other hand, it was Ira the Lawyer. *You okay, because I gotta situation here.*

"Just needed to plant my butt on the floor," I said as if I did that every day.

It actually got a small smile from him.

"Tell me what's going on," I said, and the small smile faded as if it had never been.

His lower lip started trembling again. "My slideshow. It's gone."

My turn to frown. "Did you leave it somewhere?"

"Yeah," he said. "Here. In this room. I already did the show, Spade. You didn't come."

"I'm sorry," I said automatically. That tone—slightly blaming, slightly accusing—reached into a part of me that had once been smaller and less sure of himself. My mother used to use a tone like that when she had been disappointed in me, and that's what it felt like now, with Ira.

He waved a hand as if my lack of attendance didn't matter, even though it clearly did.

I wasn't going to tell him the truth, not about that. I only caught every third show that Ira did at conventions, because mostly, they were the same—Ira walking down memory lane, telling stories that were fascinating the first three or four times. The show was best when we were in a place like New York, which had First Fandom members heavy on the ground, and they could fight or argue or challenge Ira's memories. Or add to them.

I learned a lot about the early days of SF from those verbal tussles. He was right: I should have been at this one. I had forgotten all about it.

"It wasn't good," he said. "It got heated."

He always thought the contentious "shows" were the worst ones, primarily because they made him uncomfortable.

I had met the Hartmann clan on more than one occasion and when they got together, Ira's word was law. They all loved him—from the middle-aged adult kids down to the littlest of grandchildren—but no one disagreed with him.

I was pretty sure that the only place that anyone disagreed with Ira was in the tight little hotel rooms at various conventions, when his Kodak Carousel took center stage.

"And you're positive that you brought the entire show back to the room," I said, because I had to clarify.

"Spade, do I look like a *schlemiel* to you?" he snapped.

Since my only encounter at that moment in my life with

the word *schlemiel* had been in the opening credits to *Laverne and Shirley*, and I never knew what it referred to, I figured this was not the time to guess. So I did not respond to the question exactly.

"Ira," I said. "I would ask the same thing of anyone. Sometimes we get distracted, especially if your panel was heated."

"It wasn't a panel," he said sullenly. "It was a presentation, and I got interrupted. *A lot.*"

He hated getting interrupted. He took the interruptions personally sometimes, as if people were discounting his memories. Longtime friends knew how to ask questions or volunteer their memories in a way that wouldn't anger him and derail the presentation.

"Who interrupted you?" I asked.

He waved a hand. "It's not important. What's important is that I got here, I put my equipment on that table over there—"

He continued to wave his hand, this time indicating the round table that most hotel rooms had as a "dining" table. This suite had an actual dining table in the very large living/dining/kitchen area, so this table was just an extra.

"—and then I went to dinner." He peered at me. "You remember dinner, right?"

It was a passive-aggressive jab, the kind I'd heard Ira use with his kids and some of his longtime friends, but never with me.

"It was a lovely dinner," I said. "Of course I remember it."

And if I didn't, my black American Express card would have reminded me at the end of the month in the form of a charge of $750 for the five of us who had been there.

"The soup could've been better," Ira muttered.

"It could have been," I said, mostly to get him back onto what actually happened.

"I had a drink with..." And he waved his hand again, this time to refer to the sweet young fan, whose name I couldn't remember either. "...and then I came back up here. *Alone*."

He eyed me as if to reinforce the point. I knew he never brought the sweet young fen back for after-hours romping. I'd actually checked on Ira's activities with younger women. There weren't any. When I ran security at various conventions—something I hadn't done in a long time now—I made sure that whatever looked suspicious wasn't suspicious or criminal or had happened without consent.

With Ira, there was no need for consent, because he always walked the ladies to their doors—and left them there, in the hallway, before he toddled off to his own suite.

"You walked her home first, right?" I asked.

"Not last night," he said. "She retired early. I was talking to Ava Walters."

When Ira "talked" with Ava Walters, it was never really talking. It was shouting and fist-pounding and disagreements that could never be settled.

I'd seen photos of Ava back in the day, and she looked like Ava Gardner's not-quite-photo-ready sister. Same curvy figure, same big eyes. But Ava Walter's hair was always clumped or falling out of its pins, and she never did manage the art of makeup.

She had grown into a round woman who looked like someone's really nice mother (or grandmother these days) until you looked at her eyes. A glance from those eyes was enough to bring anyone to their knees.

She and Ira fought like cats and dogs all the time. But, from the things Ira said sideways when she wasn't in attendance, I got the sense that she was the one who got away.

"Did you settle anything?" I asked.

He glared at me. The look wasn't as powerful as usual, given his red tear-stained eyes.

"I had some new slides," he said. "She claims I mislabeled them."

"New slides?" I asked, unable to keep the surprise out of my voice. He hadn't had new slides in all the years I'd gone to the presentation. He had *different* slides, ones that would go in and out of the rotation, but never anything new.

"If you had come, you would've seen," he said.

"I'm sorry I missed it," I said, finally able to apologize with sincerity. Because I was sorry I missed the new slides. "What were they?"

"My son was cleaning out our basement," Ira said, "and he found an entire box I'd put there and forgotten about. I have *lots* of new slides."

I processed all of that information. Cleaning out the basement of old items in the house an eighty-five-year-old man had shared with his long-dead wife sounded more like cleaning out the house itself.

"And before you ask," he said, "yes, I'm moving. My son found me a place in his building."

His son lived in one of the newer condo complexes in

Midtown. Very upscale and posh. I knew that Ira could afford it, but I was surprised. He had said he never wanted to leave the memories.

A shiver ran down my back. Maybe there was more to the tears than the lost Kodak Carousel.

"He insisted that I have a housekeeper come in every day." Ira's lips formed a thin line. "I guess he didn't like how the house was looking."

I gave him a sympathetic smile. "He wouldn't like how my house looks either, Ira."

Ira smiled at me, but it was perfunctory.

"So he's moving things, and found the slides," I said.

"And I've been labeling them," Ira said. "I'm going to donate everything when I go."

I knew that. He was having trouble finding a place for his memories, though. He'd thought of going to the newly established Science Fiction Hall of Fame, but it was too pro-focused for him. Even though the Hall of Fame was founded by a subset of fandom, they really didn't seem to respect the fannish community. And there were other problems as well.

I'd backed the project initially, but was seeing the night-marish handwriting on a very political wall. So I stepped back. Ira had asked me a few times to help him find a univer-sity to take his things. I'd suggested the Eastern New Mexico University in Portales, but Ira made a face every time.

Which baffled me, because that collection was anchored by Portales resident Jack Williamson, who was also First Fandom-eligible (whether or not he'd joined, I had no idea) and who was a decorated, important science fiction writer, who'd been published in every decade since the 1920s.

I never asked, although it seemed impossible to me that anyone would dislike Jack. I guessed, though, it was Portales or New Mexico. So far from the coasts and what Ira believed to be the Real World that I had a hunch he saw it all as also-ran.

"I brought out some of the new ones for the first time yesterday," Ira said. "I passed the word. You didn't get the word?"

I hadn't, but that didn't mean much. My attendance at cons was always more about running them in those days (heck, and in these days too) than it was about attending panels.

"I've been spending most of my time in Con Ops this convention," I said.

"You," Ira said, wagging a finger at me, "need a life."

I nodded, because I didn't want to disagree with him. I considered convention going and SF fandom my life. But Ira still believed in the 1950s American Dream. He thought I needed a wife to take care of my household and at least 2.5 kids.

I once made the mistake of telling him no woman would have me, and he spent the next con-year trying to fix me up with his sweet young fen.

"The slides," I said, trying to focus him on the problem. Trying to control a conversation with Ira was like trying to wrestle an aging but canny tiger.

He slid to the edge of the bed, so he could lean closer to me. His eyes actually lit up.

"They are of the 1939 Worldcon," he said. "They're

valuable. My father gave me a Canon Rangefinder, and spent a small fortune, let me tell you."

Ira's father was one of the few who made money during the Depression. Ira would never tell me what his father did, but I looked it up. His father had a hand in the illegal alcohol industry and, like Joseph Kennedy, had entire boatloads (literal boatloads) of European booze ready to sell the night Prohibition ended.

"I spent another fortune in film," Ira was saying, "and developed it all after the convention."

He grinned. The grin relieved me more than I could say.

"People called me obnoxious because I was always sticking a camera in their face. That whole weekend. They kept calling me a pesky kid. One of them threatened to take the camera and smash it over my head."

I raised an eyebrow, Spock-like. "Do you remember who that was?"

"I wanna say it was Fred Pohl, because Fred had a lot of secrets, you know?" Ira said. "I'm not sure he was faithful to Leslie, even then. And he was a communist. You knew that, right?"

Fred Pohl was another of SF's most famous early writers. Fred's personal history was colorful to say the least. He had been married five times, and there were a lot of rumors about other women, particularly in the 1940s (when three of his marriages occurred). He had been a member of the Communist Party in the 1930s, when he was a teenager, and renounced the party about the time of the first Worldcon. He went on to serve in an elite air unit in World War II, something I never heard him talk about.

Nor did he say much about his controversial years as a literary agent, although a lot of people hated him because of it. And his years as an editor.

Fred never showed up at any of Ira's talks, and I often wondered about their relationship. They never sat near each other, even when they were both in the greenroom at a con before a panel, and I didn't recall them ever exchanging words about anything.

It would make sense if their relationship was contentious. I sometimes saw the questionnaires that went to author guests, where they could ask to avoid other writers or fans, and Fred's had some really well-known names on them.

Ira never filled out one of the questionnaires because he only did his slideshow. He refused to sit on fannish panels, but that was something that only the Secret Masters of Fandom who ran conventions knew. Ira tried not to say anything bad about anyone at a convention, which made his comments about Fred—sideways as they were— unusual.

"You say you wanted to say it was Fred, but you're not saying it was Fred," I said. "Was it Fred?"

Ira shook his head. "I thought it was, the day it happened. But turns out it, it was Mervin DeGrastene."

That was a name I had never heard before.

"Who?" I asked.

"Nowadays you'd call him a Big-Name Fan," Ira said. "He was at every East Coast gathering before the war. And he looked a lot like Fred. Everyone said so. It really made Fred mad, too, because Fred got blamed for some of the things that Mervin did. When I think about it now, I wonder if Mervin encouraged the confusion."

I felt a little off-kilter. I had thought I knew everyone who had been part of science fiction in those early years. Or at least knew of them.

"What happened to him?" I asked.

"Mervin?" Ira frowned. "I don't know. I just stopped seeing him around."

"When?" I asked. "Before the war?"

"We all served, Spade. There was no during the war, and after..." Ira shook his head. "A lot of us became grown-ups after. Put away our childish things."

He gave me a sad smile. I knew part of this history, but I let him say it.

"Unfortunately, many of us saw SF as a childish thing," he said.

"Did you?" I'd never really asked him that before. I'd heard a number of reasons why he left fandom. Most people said it was because of his wife. She didn't approve at all.

He looked down at his hands. I looked at them too, twisted and swollen with arthritis. He saw my gaze and put them on his knees as if he was trying to stretch the fingers out.

"You don't know what it was like after," he said. "We built a peaceful world for you kids."

I waited. I'd heard that before. The world wasn't peaceful. I grew up in the Cold War, and it was scary. Small skirmishes and border wars always felt like they could spill into something much bigger and much more sinister.

But I was also aware that our generation had been spared the worldwide terror that had been the Second World War.

He shook his head, as if he was testing sentences and rejecting them.

Finally, he said, "Look, Spade. After the war, we, none of us, were the same. We'd seen things..."

I waited. His gaze still wasn't meeting mine.

"...and then there was the bomb. We did that. *Science* did that. Science wasn't this joyful benign thing anymore. I mean, even Jack Williamson came out of that war wondering how any of us could glorify science anymore."

I never thought of the early writers as glorifying science, although that was an element of SF from the beginning. Ira was right, though; 1950s' SF was decidedly darker than any we'd seen before, but that was true of every literary aspect of the 1950s. And movies too.

"So," Ira said, "a lot of us, we went on to other things."

So there it was, why Ira really left SF. It was easier to say that his wife forced him to do so. Pieces of Ira and parts of the stories he told fell into place now.

"The new slides," I said, changing the subject back. "They're all of the nineteen thirty-nine Worldcon?"

"No," he said. "But the ones I brought here are. They're from the local meetings and from the Worldcon and from just some of the get-togethers."

"And Ava was at those?" I asked.

He shook his head. "Not all of them."

"She angered you, though."

He gave me a sad smile. "She always angers me. I worry about you as a detective, Spade, if you haven't noticed that."

"Enough to be bothered by the interruptions at your presentation," I said.

"She approached me after the presentation," he said.

"So who interrupted you there?" I asked.

"Well, Sam," he said. "But Sam always interrupts me. He has to remain the authority on the history of SF, you know."

Again, with the bitterness. Which didn't surprise me with Ira's relationship to Sam Moskowitz. Sam was considered *the* authority on the early history of science fiction. He was the guy who barred several Futurians from entering the 1939 Worldcon. Sam. The authority.

The Futurians were a group of SF fans, many of whom ended up being truly influential in SF. People like Fred Pohl and Don Wolheim (who founded DAW books). Sam was a member of the Futurians until real-world politics got in the way. Most of the Futurians at that point were members of the Communist Party, which Sam did not like...or something like that.

As I said, I never did learn all the details. I liked all of these people, even the most contentious ones, and I'm educated enough to know that folks who flirted with Communism in the 1930s didn't really understand what the party was.

Especially teenage folks, which almost all of them were.

I never asked Ira which side of the great divide he fell on, but he probably wouldn't have told me anyway. But given the way he and Sam fought, I often wondered if Ira identified with the Futurians in that argument.

Although, in the 1950s, when Ira became a highfalutin lawyer, being affiliated with the Communist Party in any way was dangerous. And Ira had fingers in Hollywood, which meant he could have been called before the House Un-American Activities Committee if he so much as sneezed wrong.

I understood the caution then. Not so much now. Although I knew that the habits of a lifetime often became ingrained.

"Who else interrupted you?" I asked Ira.

He shrugged and looked down. I had never seen that kind of response from him before. He usually deflected a topic he didn't want to discuss by changing the subject.

"If you want me to find the carousel," I said, "then you need to tell me everything."

He raised his head, his eyes still lined with tears. "There is no everything, Spade. Some of us just disagree, is all. We've disagreed for sixty years. The fen were fighting when I left SF to go to war, and they were still fighting when I came back ten years ago."

"But it bothers you," I said.

"Yeah," he said quietly. "But not so much as Ava."

My legs were cramping up. I needed to get off this floor, but we had finally gotten to the meat of this discussion. I didn't dare move yet.

I waited. I wasn't sure if he was responding to "bother" in the literal sense or in the sense that she bothered a part of him that he didn't like to acknowledge after his wife's death.

"She says..." His voice trailed off and he looked down again.

When it became clear he wasn't going to say any more, I

spoke for him. "She said that you didn't label everything properly on the new slides. Do you believe her?"

"*NO!*" He startled himself when he shouted, and actually scooted back a bit on the bed. "Sorry, Spade. Sorry."

It was clear from that kind of outburst that we were actually getting somewhere.

"What did she think you mislabeled?" I asked.

"If we had the slides, I could show you," he said.

"Do you still have the photos themselves?" I asked.

"Yes," he said. "Where'd you think I got the slides?"

"Are the photos here?" I asked.

His bushy eyebrows came together in a frown. "I had the slides. Why would I need the photos?"

I was groping at something. "Do other people know that you still have the photos?"

"I didn't say it, exactly," he said. "Not that it would've mattered to anyone. Sam thought the pictures were unimportant."

"But Ava didn't," I said.

"Oh, she didn't talk about importance," Ira said. "She pointed out—repeatedly, I might add—that I once again confused Fred with Mervin."

I tilted my head a little. "You'd done it before?"

"*No*," Ira said. "She always thought I did, though."

"Why is that important to her?" I asked, mused, really. Then I saw the stricken look on Ira's face.

"Why? I thought you were a detective, Spade. All the little details in everything, they're the most important." Ira leaned back just a little. He had forgotten about the theft, at least for the moment, and that made him calmer.

"Fred doesn't come to your presentations," I said. "What about Mervin?"

Ira barked out a laugh. It wasn't a laugh at my expense or anything else. Instead, it was a laugh of surprise.

"I thought you knew fannish history, Spade," he said.

"I do," I said.

"Then you know that Mervin DeGrastene never made it to the war. He died in Queens about a month after that Worldcon." Ira lowered his voice. "Everyone thinks he was murdered."

There was a lot to unpack in those three sentences. I started with the most obvious one.

"Was he murdered?" I asked.

"He was nineteen, and he died because he hit his head. The police thought he tripped and kiboshed himself on a table."

"But you don't," I said.

"None of fandom did," Ira said. "But most of us didn't know nothing. I didn't even hear he was dead for two weeks after."

I nodded. I felt a little chilled. I had no idea that anyone had been murdered in fandom. I didn't think of us as a particularly violent bunch. Even the Great Worldcon War never really came to blows. Ira and Sam agreed on that at least.

Murder. It happened in our community like every other community, although not at cons. Like Barbara, who ran a comic book store in Michigan. She was murdered just a few years before this conversation, and later (much later) her husband was convicted, and it all became fodder for a *Date-*

503

line episode a few years back, because of the SF/comic connection.

The mention of an old homicide, though, got me thinking like the detective I'm supposed to be.

I asked, "When you introduced the new slides, did you mention that they were part of a group of slides you just found or did you not mention that at all?"

"I didn't say I found them," Ira said stiffly. "I said my son happened upon them. An entire box. A big box."

I shifted slightly, wishing I could stand without being rude.

"And you said there'd be more in future presentations?" I asked.

"Yes, Spade. That's just good marketing. You know that."

"Are the photos protected now?" I asked.

"Protected?" Ira's voice went up. "Protected? What do you mean, Spade?"

I didn't mean to upset him further, that was for certain. But I was. Still, I needed answers to these questions.

"Where are they?" I asked with trepidation. "At your house?"

"No," he said, and shook his head for emphasis. "I gave them to my son. He's having them all converted to slides at my request."

"This is David, right?" I asked. Ira had three sons and a daughter. I had just been assuming that the son who had the pictures was the son who lived in Manhattan.

"Yes, David. Everyone else left New York." Ira said that as if he couldn't believe anyone would make that choice ever.

I let out a small breath.

"Why?" Ira asked.

"Noodling," I said. "The other slides, they have photographic backup too, right?"

Ira's lower lip started trembling again. "No. I thought you knew that. My wife made me keep them in a storage unit and it got flooded in the 1970s. Negatives, everything. Gone."

By the end of that speech, his voice was trembling too. That was what disturbed him about the loss of the slides.

He couldn't replace them.

He leaned forward and grabbed my hands, startling me.

"They're all I have of those years," he said. "All I have of those friends. It's how I..."

He shook his head, and that movement shook a tear loose.

"I understand," I said, and I thought I did. I do understand more now, as I'm writing this, even though I'm still not even close to eighty-five. But Ira is gone now, as are so many others of my friends, and all I have of them are memories that no one else shares.

I couldn't—and can't—imagine the weight that a gregarious eighty-five-year-old felt when faced with continual losses spread over decades.

"I'll find them," I promised. Stupidly. Real-life detectives, police officers, and others—they never make promises like that.

But I did.

Ira squeezed my hands again.

"It's okay, Spade," he said. "My son, David, he tells me I

505

gotta let the memories go. I can't keep everything that reminds me of something."

He choked on the last few words. Then he swallowed and continued.

"I'm trying, Spade. I really am." He gave me a watery smile. "Getting old. It ain't no picnic."

"I know," I said. I was sincere, even though, in hindsight, I didn't know at all.

Okay, I'm ashamed of this next part, but I'm going to tell it anyway.

After I managed to get Ira to head downstairs to join the sweet young fan for a belated brunch, I went to Con Ops. That was where my Tower of Terror lived.

I brought some of my computers with me everywhere. They were large towers that held disks and data and had hard drives and all kinds of what were then more powerful than any locomotive that other desktops had. I always have state-of-the-art computer systems because of my Microsoft days, and back then, I ran everything in Con Ops from those Towers of Terror.

On a Sunday morning, Con Ops had an eerie resemblance to the *Marie Celeste*—the ghost ship that was discovered that looked like everyone had vanished midmeal. There were candy wrappers everywhere, open cans of Coke, Dr Pepper, and every other soft drink you could think of except the zero-calorie kind, as well as coffee cups scattered across every surface, except the one holding my computer.

The folks who ran conventions learned long ago that the only time I ever showed anything like wrath was if someone brought food or drink near the Towers of Terror. In that, I was the 1970s Lou Ferrigno Hulk, only without the body builder's muscles. Just the Bill Bixby catch phrase:

Don't make me angry. You wouldn't like me when I'm angry.

I was one of the first people ever to move my paper Rolodex onto my computer. And because I had a lot of confidential information from my days as a forensic accountant, I had the thing password protected at the NSA level.

But I also kept every phone number and piece of contact information I ever gathered, and that included the contact information for Ira's son David, acquired when we were planning a non-con dinner in Manhattan a dozen years before.

After I found the number, I wrote it on a piece of paper and took it up to my room. I didn't want anyone to overhear the conversation and have it get back to Ira. Even though Con Ops was empty that Sunday morning, I knew it probably wouldn't remain empty for long.

My suite was smaller than Ira's and not as tidy. After five days of almost no sleep (I generally arrive at cons I'm working at on Tuesday), I can't be expected to clean up past picking my underwear and dirty T-shirts off the floor.

Housekeeping hadn't arrived yet, so I sat on one of the flimsy chairs in front of the so-called desk that this room had and punched David's number into the hotel phone.

To my surprise, David answered on the second ring.

"Pops?" he asked.

"Um...no," I said. "It's Spade."

After I got the name out, I wasn't sure if he would remember who that even was.

"Oh, Dad's detective friend. It's been a long time." David's voice was wary. "I expected a call from Dad from this number."

Apparently, David had put the hotel's number into his Caller ID.

"He okay?" David asked, and that was when I twigged to the worry. David was afraid that something would happen to his father, alone at an SF convention.

"He's a little emotional," I said, "but otherwise all right."

David let out a sigh of relief. "So this is about...?"

I told him about the missing carousel. I also asked him not to tell his father that I had called.

"I'm looking into what happened," I said. "But before I conduct an actual investigation, I need to know something."

"What?" David sounded wary all over again.

"Your father," I said. "How's his memory?"

"*My* father?" David asked, sounding incredulous. "You're asking about *my* father?"

"Yes," I said. "He mentioned his moving out of his house and I was wondering if it was because, you know, of health issues?"

"You're asking if he has dementia." David laughed. "Seriously. My father. No, Mr. Spade. He doesn't have dementia. He's the guy who remembers every time I farted at the dinner table from 1972 through the present."

I chuckled because I was supposed to.

"His memory is fine. The move is his idea. The house is

too big for him, and I think something spooked him. He tripped or he dropped something or maybe he just realized that a house like that is a landmine for the unwary." The laughter had left David's voice. "He's moving into my building, but still will have his own place. With fewer traps for the unwary. The tough part is getting rid of all the family heirlooms. I made my siblings promise to take their fair share, even if they put the crap into storage. Otherwise Dad wouldn't have moved."

I understood that. I had no idea what would happen to my possessions after I no longer had use for them, but I wasn't willing to part with them—not yet, anyway.

"Thanks," I said. "I was concerned. Your father calls these memories, and I wasn't sure if his memories were stolen by a person or by time itself."

"Naw," David said. "My father's memory is as sharp as ever, maybe sharper. I wouldn't argue with him about anything, Mr. Spade. He has more room in that brain than anyone I've ever met."

I nodded, feeling embarrassed. I hadn't trusted my own instincts with Ira. I always thought he was a man who forgot nothing, but I let his age and one small detail about his life shake that perception.

But I did need to know whether or not he had gotten absent-minded. Or worse.

And now I did.

"Listen," David said before I could end the conversation, "don't tell my dad but someone broke into the house this morning. That's why I don't want him to live there."

Now, he had my attention. "Did they take anything?"

"Naw," David said. "My dad has the nosiest neighbors this side of a *Bewitched* episode. Their version of Gladys Kravitz called the cops and they arrived within five minutes. Dad's not going to have that kind of service in Manhattan, let me tell you."

"Was someone arrested?" I asked.

"Stupid small borough cops," David said. "Arrived with sirens blaring and lights flashing. No, of course they didn't catch anyone. Not sure they wanted to."

I thanked him, frowning. Old detectives in books always said there were no coincidences, but you live long enough and you realize that there are a lot of coincidences.

Just not here. I was pretty sure that break-in and the loss of the carousel were tied together. I needed to find that carousel before whoever took it had a chance to destroy it and all the memories contained in those little 2" x 2" slides.

To start, I needed Doris's help. I hadn't worked much with the Escher Hotel on that year's Eschercon, so I had no contacts there. I needed to know something that I wasn't sure they could tell me.

I found her in the greenroom, settling an early morning fight between two Big Name panelists. Each wanted to moderate the ten a.m. panel and use it to force an agenda that the other disagreed with.

I didn't have time to wait for the eons' old fight to find some kind of momentary truce. Instead, I beckoned her, told her I thought that Ira's slides had been stolen, and asked her to go with me to the front desk.

She looked shocked and asked the $64,000 question: *Who would want to steal those slides?*

I told her I didn't know, even though that was half a lie. I had a small idea as to who might have stolen them, although that plus the break-in at Ira's house did take the theft to a level I hadn't expected.

Doris grabbed Carole B, who was making sure that the greenroom snacks were being replaced (particularly the coffee) and assigned her the task of getting the Big Names to their panel.

Then Doris led me to the front desk, and asked for the manager. When she arrived, she looked all official in her suit jacket, except for a tiny Superman pin that she must have gotten from Julius Schwartz, one of the most influential editors from the Silver Age of comics, who handed the pins out to anyone he liked or who had done him a favor. The pin endeared her to me. She could have just thanked him and put it in her desk.

"We had a theft in one of the rooms," Doris said quietly, even though no one was near the front desk at the moment.

Most of the fen had Monday checkout, so they could stick around for the Dead Dog Party. Those who didn't had late checkout, and hadn't even gotten up yet.

The manager looked disturbed and was about to ask a question, when Doris continued, "It was a targeted theft. Only one very precious item was taken."

I could see dollar signs flashing over the manager's head.

How much liability did the hotel have? What would this do to their reputation? What if the culprit was someone on staff?

So I stepped in. "The item had value only to the person in the room. And obviously to the person who stole it. We're not talking about the Hope Diamond or anything."

To her credit, the manager's expression didn't change, although her shoulders visibly relaxed.

"What do you need from me?" she asked.

Doris looked at me. I'd thought for a while how to phrase this question.

I gave the manager Ira's room number and said, "I need to know who had a key to that room."

The manager immediately jumped on the computer and dug up the information. "It looks like the couple staying there have the only two keys."

She was referring to actual keys, not key cards. Back then, only the high-end hotels in the biggest of cities had them.

"Couple?" Doris said. "Do you have the right room?"

The manager repeated the number to her. "That's the room, right?"

I put a hand on Doris's arm, stopping her. "When did the wife pick up her key?"

The manager clacked a few keys. "Yesterday at five thirty."

Not long after Ira's presentation finished. And a half an hour after the group of us met for dinner. We'd been loud and laughing as we headed over to the most expensive restaurant in the Escher complex.

A lot of people would have noticed us.

"Did she leave her name, by chance?" I asked, knowing it was a long shot.

She thinned her lips. "Your questions are making me wonder what's awry here."

"Ira's a widower," Doris said.

"And he's not prone to taking other women into his room or to giving out his key," I said.

"Someone's going to get in trouble for this," the manager said.

"Don't," I said. "It's not your desk's fault."

"They should have checked identification," the manager said.

"And probably did," I said. "Many people in our community don't share last names. I'll wager the woman who got the key was of an age with Ira, so your employee thought nothing of the request."

"You're being charitable," the manager said. "I think we should call the police."

"Not yet," I said. "What's been stolen has no physical value. So the police won't really pay attention."

The manager frowned at me.

"I would like to talk with the person on the desk last night, if I could," I said.

"He won't be in until two," the manager said.

I hoped to have everything wrapped up by then, but I didn't mention that. "Do you have a security system? Maybe a camera pointing at the desk?"

"We don't record," the manager said. "Privacy concerns."

I resisted the urge to look at Doris. I'd been telling her

that the Escher Hotel was getting rough around the edges, but that comment confirmed it. Hotels usually didn't care about that kind of privacy unless they knew their hotel was being used for illegal hook-ups or other shady businesses.

We thanked the manager and left the desk. If my assumption was correct, my suspect pool was small.

"What do you want to do?" Doris asked me.

"I'm going to talk to a few people," I said, "and then I'll let you know."

The first person on my list was standing, bleary-eyed, at the coffee and pastry spread that this convention was famous for. So many fen didn't want much more than that for breakfast. They wanted to grab something quick and head to their panel.

I excused myself and walked over to the table. I grabbed a paper plate and covered it with a cherry Danish.

"Ava," I said to the woman next to me. "Can I have a minute?"

She blinked at me. "Oh, the pretend detective man," she said.

I made myself smile. "That's me."

"For the record," she said. "I didn't do it. I claim credit for all of my crimes and I haven't committed one since I got here."

"Good to know," I said. "But I don't want to talk to you about crimes."

"Oh?" she asked.

I could see Doris out of the corner of my eye. She looked surprised too.

"Let's just grab a seat," I said, waving a hand at one of the seating groups at the far side of the lobby.

"You got fifteen minutes, Big Boy," Ava said, and picked up a coffee to go with her plate full of croissants. I took a water. I'd get something caffeinated later.

We walked across the lobby to the pleather chairs. No one was sitting there, although a few more fen were emerging from the nearby elevators, looking as bleary as Ava had.

"I wanted to talk to you about Ira's presentation," I said.

"You don't get to yell at me, kid," she said. "Ira's been passing off his memories as the truth for years now."

"I'm not going to yell," I said. "I want to know about the new slides. You said he got a few things wrong."

I didn't add that it bothered Ira, because she already knew that. Besides, I wanted the focus to be on the slides, not on Ira.

"Oh," she said, "he's been doing it for years."

"What's that?" I asked.

"Confusing Fred Pohl with Mervin DeGrastene." She took a bite from a croissant and immediately pastry flakes covered her gray *I'm old, not stupid* sweatshirt.

"Why does that bother you?" I asked.

She frowned at me, then leaned back. Those eyes were sharp. "Does this have anything to do with Ira's sad face this morning?"

"Very good deflection," I said, hoping I could deflect as well. "Please, just answer the question."

She looked down, saw the pastry flakes, and wiped them

off the front of her sweatshirt. I got the sense that she didn't want me to see her reaction.

"Look, kid," she said, "details matter. It matters that he confuses them."

"Why?" I asked. I almost said, *They're his memories, after all*, but that would make this about Ira. I had a sense it was something more.

She sighed. "You're not gonna let this go, are you?"

"No," I said.

She looked up, and all pretense was gone from her face. I saw a tired woman who, in her own way, looked as sad as Ira did.

"No one remembers Mervin, not really, and I'm not sure they should."

"Then why did you bring it up?" I asked.

"Because his pictures need to be excised from all writings about fandom," she said with such viciousness that I almost leaned back.

"Why?" I asked.

"Oh, just ask any other woman who was around then," she said and started to stand.

I reached out and almost grabbed her arm, then decided that was a bad idea. "Please," I said. "I'll work with Ira, if you just tell me what's going on."

"You know Mervin was killed, right?" Ava said as she sank back into the chair.

"I just found out this morning. I heard it was an accident."

"Accident schmaccident," Ava said. "In my day, some-one'd call that justifiable homicide."

I stiffened. "What happened?"

"I honestly don't know for sure," Ava said. "But I do know cops investigated and talked to half of the women in fandom at the time. Which was probably three of us."

She let out a bitter laugh.

I waited, because what else could I do?

"He did the same with all of us," she said. "We don't talk about it. I didn't go near men for a long time after that, not that anyone noticed or cared. And then the war, and there were other things..."

Her voice trailed off. But her eyes remained defiant.

"You know, Ira always thought I pushed him away because of him. In those days, Mr. Pretend Detective, women didn't talk to anyone but other women about men like Mervin. We warned each other to stay away."

She still wasn't saying exactly what happened, although I could guess.

"He hurt you," I said, deciding to be as elliptical as I could.

"Oh, hell, no," she said. "Hurt is not the word you young people use. He took what he wanted and I couldn't fight hard enough. Clear enough for you?"

My cheeks were flushed. I wasn't going to use the word *rape* if she wasn't. I didn't want to shut her down.

"Clear," I said.

"And there was one of us," Ava said. "I know she went to Mervin's apartment that day, voluntarily, because I couldn't talk her out of it. I also know she was a mess for years, and I know that she once asked my husband—a career prosecutor in the City—if you shoved someone and they died, was that a homicide?"

"What was his response?" I asked.

She glared at me. "I loved my husband, but he wasn't the most sensitive man in the history of the universe. He said, depends on the circumstances, but unless you called the police and reported it right away, it would probably be considered manslaughter at best."

I let out a small breath. Manslaughter. "Do I know this person?" I asked.

"Yeah," she said. "And it isn't me, if you were wondering. But that's all you'll get out of me."

I nodded as if that was okay, which, on some level, it was.

"The photos, what did they show?" I asked.

"Have Ira show you," she said.

"I can't," I said. "Someone stole the carousel."

I didn't tell her that the same someone had a friend or friends break into his house to find other pictures.

"Oh, for Pete's sake," she said, then let out a sigh. "The photos weren't of Fred and his latest patootie, which is what Ira said. I pulled him aside later, said he was disrespecting Leslie—"

Leslie Perri, Fred's first wife, whom he met in fandom around that time, and who had died long before I entered fandom.

"—and he needed to cut it out. Fred always had women, but he was faithful when he was married." Ava sighed. "Ira's just jealous. Fred could attract women by doing nothing. Ira had to work at it. And before you ask, I was not one of

Fred's 'patooties.' God, I hate that word. But Fred and me, we still don't get along much."

"Yet you're defending him," I said.

"I'm not," she said. "He just shouldn't be confused with that piece of filth Mervin."

"So who was the woman he was with?" I asked.

"C'mon, Mr. Pretend Detective," she said. "Two plus two shouldn't be that hard for someone like you, especially since she got scared and actually stole the evidence."

"Evidence of what?" I asked.

"Unless I miss my guess," Ava said, "that photo was the last one taken of Mervin alive."

In all my years investigating small crimes at SF conventions, I'd never had a fictional detective moment before—y'know, where the pieces fell into place so quickly that a chill ran down my back. I'd also never dealt with an actual death before, even if it happened years before I was born.

Ava was right. Two plus two wasn't hard. And she was wrong about one thing. There were more than six women in those early years of SF, although not all were members of First Fandom or even came back to fandom after the war.

But Evelyn Chastain had. In Ira's photos, she looked like a tiny bird with great taste in clothes, always wearing a dress with a flare skirt and low heels that made her look like a 1930s movie star, until the camera caught her face and couldn't get past the thick glasses to reveal her eyes.

Evelyn still wore thick glasses, but on a birdlike elderly woman they looked appropriate.

I found her in the hallway outside a panel on the roots of modern science fiction.

"May we talk?" I asked.

She hobbled toward me, her walker barely keeping her upright. At least it was the proper height. She was maybe five feet tall these days and so thin it looked like she could disappear if she turned sideways.

"You haven't destroyed Ira's carousel yet, have you?" I asked.

She looked at me sharply, and nearly lost her balance. "How'd you know?"

I could've told her about the things I'd discovered, but I didn't. I also knew she had the means and the wherewithal to hire someone to break into Ira's house and take that box.

"I talked to the front desk," I said. "They believed that Ira's wife asked for an extra key. The young man at the desk would've believed that only a few people here were married to Ira."

She let out a sad laugh. "Age wins again," she said.

"Did you destroy it?" I asked.

"No," she said. "Not that it matters."

"It matters to Ira," I said. "His memories are in there."

She leaned one arm on the walker and tapped her forehead with the other. "His memories are in there."

I shook my head. "Ira's a little different than most people. He likes to see his memories in black and white."

Her mouth thinned, but she didn't say anything.

"If I get Ira to promise not to show any pictures of Mervin DeGrastene," I said, "will you return the carousel?"

"Ira confuses Mervin and Fred," she said quietly.

"I know," I said. "You have no problems with the old slides. Just the new ones, right?"

She raised her tiny chin. "You know why," she said with a touch of incredulity.

"I know nothing," I said. "Except that as far as the police are concerned, Mervin's death was labeled an accident, and there's no open case file."

"And that matters how?" she asked.

I wasn't a lawyer. I'm still not. But I do think about justice sometimes.

"As I see it," I said, "there's four potential crimes here. One attempted but thwarted, one that would've been charged the way a prosecutor told you years ago and a modern jury would've considered self-defense. Then there's a minor theft of a valueless Kodak Carousel, and a more serious break-in at an elderly man's abode."

Her eyes narrowed. The movement seemed larger than it was, thanks to her thick lenses.

"It seems to me," I said, "that the only one today's police would care about is the break-in. Then they'd want to know why, and they'd start digging in places that don't need any investigation at all."

"Is that a threat?" she asked, her voice wobbling just a little.

I hunched, trying to make myself less threatening.

"No." I made my voice as gentle as possible. "I suspect whatever happened—"

"It was self-defense!" she said so loudly that all five people in the corridor (two Klingons, a hotel employee, and two not-yet-famous writers) looked at us.

"I know," I said, and let the words hang.

She stepped closer to her walker, as if she felt wobbly, but I knew better than to touch her.

"I'm not going to say anything," I said. "And other people, who've suspected for years, haven't said anything either."

"Then how do you know?" she asked.

"I pulled it out of the wife of that prosecutor who scared the crap out of you," I said.

Evelyn smiled at me. "You think you can get me to confess."

"To the carousel, yes," I said. "The rest of it, there's nothing to confess."

She looked down at her walker, then said, "You know, Ira and I don't agree about much. He thinks the history is so danged good. He thinks we were all so happy. None of us were happy. That's why we banded together. We needed something else to talk about besides having no money and what was going on in Europe."

I waited.

Then she looked up at me and shrugged. "I should never have gone to his presentation."

I nodded.

She squared her thin shoulders. "If I give him back the carousel, can you make sure he doesn't use the slides of Mervin? That bastard doesn't deserve to be mentioned as part of fandom."

"I think I can do that," I said.

"*Without* telling Ira what happened," she said.

That would be harder, but I had a hunch I could do it.

"Yes," I said.

"I don't want to talk to Ira," she said.

"You don't have to," I said. "You still have his key, right?"

"Yes," she said.

"Let's just put the carousel back in his room."

Which was what we did. I had to tell Ira that I dealt with the culprit, so that he wouldn't worry that he had somehow missed seeing the carousel. I didn't want him to suddenly be concerned about his own mental health.

Then I lied to him. I told him that Fred still didn't like being confused with Mervin and it would be better for all if any Fred or Mervin pictures weren't in the presentation.

"I can do that," Ira said so quickly that I realized that the history between him and Fred was as touchy as I thought it might have been.

At future cons, Ira used new slides, but kept his promise. And he also kept his carousel locked up in the hotel safe at night.

He never asked me who took the carousel. He was just happy to get it back. I'm not sure if Ava told him. I know Evelyn didn't. Until the end of her days, she remained true to her word. She never showed up at one of his presentations again.

They changed, those presentations, particularly after

more and more of the original members of First Fandom passed. Ira removed the slides that used to anger Sam after Sam died. Ira added a few gorgeous slides of Ava after her death—loving shots that I think he never ever showed her.

A few weeks ago, Ira died. His son David called me and offered me the entire slide show.

"I thought your dad was giving it to the Science Fiction Museum," I said.

"They want someone to go through it," David said. "I don't have the heart or the knowledge."

So Ira's slides—Ira's memories—are spread out over my kitchen table. I'm going to digitize them to preserve all of them.

But I keep staring at one of a birdlike woman who was no one's patootie next to a man who bore a slight resemblance to the young Fred Pohl. Only that man had ice-cold eyes, and hands the size of meat hammers.

I like to think I would have seen Mervin DeGrastene for what he was if I ever met him, but I'm not sure any of us ever see others for who they are.

The histories that Ira knew and conveniently forgot, the undercurrents among a group of young adults who had no idea what kind of hell their generation was about to face, are lost now. Some of the faces in these shots I don't recognize, and the people who could've identified them are gone too.

There are candid shots that aren't going to the museum and some photographs that'll never see the light of day because of my conversations with Evelyn and Ava.

Ira left me his memories so that I could sort them, and make sure they didn't hurt anyone. Ira had cleansed them, made them harmless, made his friends harmless, and took all the complexities out of their young lives. The good, the bad, and some of the ugly.

Stories. That's what he trafficked in. That's what he turned his memories into. Stories that comforted him and pretended that everything was right for a brief shining moment in the world before it spiraled into a nightmare.

Because for him, that's what the moment was. Even with the Great Worldcon War, that he ignored. The Exclusion Act, the split in his beloved fandom, the fact that most of these kids continued their fight long after it ceased to matter.

It was small. It was easy to focus on. It allowed them to ignore the pain of life midcentury.

I get that now, and I want to talk to him about it.
But of course, I can't.

Hear From Kris & Dean

Want More From Kris and Dean?

For Kristine Kathryn Rusch's newsletter
go to kriswrites.com.

For Dean Wesley Smith's newsletter
go to deanwesleysmith.com.

Get the latest news and releases from all of WMG's authors
and lines, including Kristine Grayson, Kris Nelscott,
Pulphouse Magazine, and so much more...

To sign up, **go to wmgbooks.com.**

ABOUT THE AUTHOR
DEAN WESLEY SMITH

Considered one of the most prolific writers working in modern fiction, *New York Times* and *USA Today* bestselling writer, Dean Wesley Smith published over two hundred novels and over seven hundred books in forty years, and hundreds and hundreds of short stories. He has over thirty million copies of his books in print.

At the moment he produces novels in four major series, including the time travel **Thunder Mountain** novels set in the old west, the galaxy-spanning **Seeders Universe** series, the cold case mystery series, **Cold Poker Gang** series, and the superhero series staring **Poker Boy.**

During his career, Dean also wrote a couple dozen *Star Trek* novels, the only two original *Men in Black* novels, Spider-Man and X-Men novels, plus novels set in gaming and television worlds. Writing with his wife Kristine Kathryn Rusch under the name Kathryn Wesley, they wrote the novel for the NBC miniseries **The Tenth Kingdom** and other books for *Hallmark Hall of Fame* movies.

He wrote novels under dozens of pen names in the worlds of comic books and movies, including novelizations of almost a dozen films, from *X-Men* to *The Final Fantasy* to *Steel* to *Rundown.*

Dean also worked as a fiction editor off and on, starting at Pulphouse Publishing, then at *VB Tech Journal*, then Pocket Books, and now at WMG Publishing where he and Kristine Kathryn Rusch serve as executive editors for the acclaimed *Fiction River* anthology series. He took over the editorship of the acclaimed *Pulphouse Magazine* in 2018.

For more information about Dean's books and ongoing projects, please visit his website at www.deanwesley smith.com

f facebook.com/deanwsmith3

P patreon.com/deanwesleysmith

BB bookbub.com/authors/dean-wesley-smith

About the Author
Kristine Kathryn Rusch

Kristine Kathryn Rusch has sold more than 35 million books. Generally, she uses her real name (Rusch) for most of her writing. Under that name, she publishes bestselling science fiction and fantasy, award-winning mysteries, acclaimed mainstream fiction, controversial nonfiction, and the occasional romance. Her novels have made bestseller lists around the world and her short fiction has appeared in eighteen best of the year collections. She has won more than twenty-five awards for her fiction, including the Hugo, *Le Prix Imaginales*, the *Asimov's* Readers Choice award, and the *Ellery Queen Mystery Magazine* Readers Choice Award.

Publications from *The Chicago Tribune* to *Booklist* have included her Kris Nelscott mystery novels in their top-ten-best mystery novels of the year. The Nelscott books have received nominations for almost every award in the mystery field, including the best novel Edgar Award, and the Shamus Award.

She writes goofy romance novels as award-winner Kristine Grayson.

She also edits. Beginning with work at the innovative publishing company, Pulphouse, followed by her award-winning tenure at *The Magazine of Fantasy & Science Fiction*, she took fifteen years off before returning to editing with the original anthology series *Fiction River*, published by WMG Publishing. She acts as series editor with her husband, writer Dean Wesley Smith, and edits at least two anthologies in the series per year on her own.

To find out more about her work, go to her website, kriswrites.com

f facebook.com/kristinekathrynruschwriter

P patreon.com/kristinekathrynrusch

BB bookbub.com/authors/kristine-kathryn-rusch

THE MAKE 100 KICKSTARTER SERIES

Dean Wesley Smith's Make 100 Challenge

The First Thirty-Three

The Second Thirty-Three

The Final Thirty-Four

Colliding Worlds

A Science Fiction Short Story Series

by Kristine Kathryn Rusch and Dean Wesley Smith

Volumes 1-6

Crimes Collide

A Mystery Short Story Series

by Kristine Kathryn Rusch and Dean Wesley Smith

Volumes 1-5

Fantasies Collide

A Fantasy Short Story Series

by Kristine Kathryn Rusch and Dean Wesley Smith

Volumes 1-5

Hearts Collide

A Strange Romance Short Story Series

by Kristine Kathryn Rusch and Dean Wesley Smith

Volumes 1-5

ALSO BY DEAN WESLEY SMITH

THE POKER BOY UNIVERSE

POKER BOY

The Slots of Saturn: A Poker Boy Novel

They're Back: A Poker Boy Short Novel

Luck Be Ladies: A Poker Boy Collection

Playing a Hunch: A Poker Boy Collection

A Poker Boy Christmas: A Poker Boy Collection

GHOST OF A CHANCE

The Poker Chip: A Ghost of a Chance Novel

The Christmas Gift: A Ghost of a Chance Novel

The Free Meal: A Ghost of a Chance Novel

The Cop Car: A Ghost of a Chance Novella

The Deep Sunset: A Ghost of a Chance Novel

MARBLE GRANT

The First Year: A Marble Grant Novel

Time for Cool Madness: Six Crazy Marble Grant Stories

ALSO BY KRISTINE KATHRYN RUSCH

THE FEY SERIES

THE ORIGINAL BOOKS OF THE FEY

The Sacrifice: Book One of the Fey

The Changeling: Book Two of the Fey

The Rival: Book Three of the Fey

The Resistance: Book Four of the Fey

Victory: Book Five of the Fey

THE BLACK THRONE

The Black Queen: Book One of the Black Throne

The Black King: Book Two of the Black Throne

THE QAVNERIAN PROTECTORATE

The Reflection on Mount Vitaki: Prequel to the Qavnerian Protectorate

The Kirilli Matter: The First Book of the Qavnerian Protectorate

Barkson's Journey: The Second Book of the Qavnerian Protectorate

Incident at Serebro Academy: The Third Book of the Qavnerian Protectorate

MORE FROM THE FEY

Destiny: A Story of The Fey

Lessons From The Writing of The Fey

THE RETRIEVAL ARTIST SERIES

The Disappeared

Extremes

Consequences

Buried Deep

Paloma

Recovery Man

The Recovery Man's Bargain

Duplicate Effort

The Possession of Paavo Deshin

Anniversary Day

Blowback

A Murder of Clones

Search & Recovery

The Peyti Crisis

Vigilantes

Starbase Human

Masterminds

The Impossibles

The Retrieval Artist

THE DIVING SERIES

Diving into the Wreck: A Diving Novel

City of Ruins: A Diving Novel

Becalmed: A Diving Universe Novella

The Application of Hope: A Diving Universe Novella

Boneyards: A Diving Novel

Skirmishes: A Diving Novel

The Runabout: A Diving Novel

The Falls: A Diving Universe Novel

Searching for the Fleet: A Diving Novel

The Spires of Denon: A Diving Universe Novella

The Renegat: A Diving Universe Novel

Escaping Amnthra: A Diving Universe Novella

The Court-Martial of the Renegat Renegades

Thieves: A Diving Novel

Squishy's Teams: A Diving Universe Novel

The Chase: A Diving Novel

Maelstrom: A Diving Universe Novella

Writing as Kris Nelscott

THE SMOKEY DALTON SERIES

A Dangerous Road

Smoke-Filled Rooms

Thin Walls

Stone Cribs

War at Home

Days of Rage

Street Justice

And

Protectors

Writing as Kristine Grayson

The Charming Trilogy, Vol. 1

The Charming Trilogy, Vol. 2

The Fates Trilogy

The Daughters of Zeus Trilogy

www.ingramcontent.com/pod-product-compliance
Lightning Source LLC
Chambersburg PA
CBHW010725100726
47899CB00009B/2927